THE SURGEON'S TALE

To
Roger and Annabel
With my very best wishes.

[signature]

30/1/2021

akq
James Avery

First published in 2020
by Avery Publications Ltd

ISBN 978-1-5272-7308-5

Copyright © James Avery 2020

The right of James Avery to be identified as the author of
this work has been asserted by him in accordance with
the Copyright, Designs and Patents Act 1988.

This is a work of fiction. Any resemblance to actual
persons, living or dead, or actual events, is purely
coincidental.

Typesetting by Hawk Editorial Ltd, Hull

Cover design by Vanessa James

THE SURGEON'S TALE

A deliberate disaster and the attempts to cover it up

JAMES AVERY

To my wife, my children and grandchildren, on the understanding that nothing written here happened to me.

PROLOGUE

'Your life in their hands' is the usual optimistic attitude of a patient undergoing a surgical operation, and that is usually the case, but in this story the hatred between a consultant surgeon and a junior doctor results in a deliberate display of arrogance that ends in tragedy.

Are surgeons particularly arrogant? Not all of them, certainly, but they probably have a higher proportion of arrogance compared with other medical specialities. It is a fearful sight to see some of them barking orders at the nursing and technical staff, brandishing and throwing heavy stainless-steel instruments around the room, the operating theatre, which for a few glorious hours each week is their fiefdom where they can behave like medieval warlords terrifying anyone who crosses swords with them or deviates from the strict set of rules they have imposed.

After a long career in hospital medicine I have noticed that surgeons who behave particularly badly are those with the least technical ability and their shouting and belligerent behaviour is often a way of covering up for a lack of confidence and skill. I have also noticed that when analysing the causes of surgical accidents it is unusual that a single mistake results in injury to a patient but is more likely to be due to a train of unrelated errors. Although all the individual mistakes undoubtedly contributed to the accident described here, nevertheless, the sheer malice of a surgeon deliberately removing a clamp sealing off a large blood vessel in order to humiliate one of his junior doctors was a display of arrogance beyond belief.

I have to reassure the reader that after a lifetime in surgical practice I have never seen or heard of this happening and it is purely a figment of my own unrestrained imagination.

This is a novel set in the latter years of the Swinging Sixties, an age when a new generation became alive, released from the privations and rationing following the Second World War, fuelled by the introduction of rock'n'roll music played by Fats Domino, Chuck Berry, Elvis Presley, Jerry Lee Lewis, Little Richard and many others in the USA and translated into the uniquely British sound of the Beatles, the Rolling Stones, Pink Floyd, the Searchers and other bands in this country.

Rebelling against the restraints of traditional parental authority, their clothing marked them out as a different generation, with the fashion industry headed by Mary Quant designing the miniskirt, hot pants and flowery frocks for the girls while the men sported drainpipe trousers, Cuban heels and greasy duck's arse hairstyles.

The pharmaceutical industry introduced reliable birth control in the form of the contraceptive pill, which allowed greater sexual freedom without the fear of an unwanted pregnancy. Even that could be resolved by suitably qualified doctors under aseptic conditions when the Abortion Act was passed by Parliament in 1967, rendering at a stroke the end of backstreet abortions and the appalling disease and deaths they caused. Even this merciful, benevolent and civilised Act caused rifts among gynaecological surgeons, most of whom welcomed the legal freedom to help girls in distress, yet there were others in the speciality who were bitterly opposed to it and regarded it as an encouragement to promiscuity among young girls.

This is a story about hospital life in those times and the modern reader will surely be horrified by the change in attitude and behaviour among doctors over the past sixty years. Political correctness had not yet arrived on the scene and doctors on duty drank alcohol and smoked without any fear of criticism and nurses were not averse to a little sexual flirtation with junior hospital doctors living away from home when on call.

The title of 'junior' when applied to doctors conjures up an image of a young doctor in training in his or her mid-twenties, but in reality it applies to all grades beneath consultant and, although it varies between the different specialities, in obstetrics and gynaecology one did not usually achieve the title of consultant until the age of thirty-eight. Until then one had to endure many years of exhausting hours of work which created difficulties with family and social life for a relatively low income compared with friends from university days who were making a lucrative living in other occupations.

The life of a junior hospital doctor who had to live in a monk-like cell to be on call every other night away from home was very different from that of today, and sexual freedom, abuse of alcohol, bullying and racism were not constrained by the political correctness that exists nowadays.

To put this into context, I clearly recall when I was a junior doctor at a university teaching hospital in London some benefactor had donated a sum of money to ensure that each junior doctor had a pint of beer to accompany his lunch, and it was well known that one of the senior surgeons would share a tipple of Speyside single-malt whisky with his Scottish ward sister in a loft above the male surgical ward before starting his operating list. In modern times such behaviour would not be tolerated and alcohol is universally banned in hospitals and no longer appears even at retirement parties.

In the late 1960s, verbal bullying by consultants was the norm, and a friend of mine who is now an eminent orthopaedic surgeon at a hospital in Wales told me that as a junior doctor he was regularly referred to by his consultant in Liverpool as a 'Welsh sheep-shagger'. He accepted this abuse with equanimity and a sense of humour, yet in 2018, two years before this book was written, almost a third of the cases reported for disciplinary hearings before the General Medical Council were for bullying or harassment of junior doctors by consultants, and in the first half of 2019 the British Medical Association has supported more than 590 cases of alleged bullying of medical staff.

During the past ten years of my long surgical career I was often called upon to act as an expert witness to examine hospital accidents in minute detail, in order to give a report to the court for them to decide if there had been negligence on the part of the medical or nursing staff and for them to suffer disciplinary action if required or pay large sums in compensation to the injured party.

It would be unthinkable for an act of wanton and deliberate malice to take place during a surgical procedure as described here so readers should not fear if they are on a waiting list for a surgical operation.

There are now compulsory checks before an operation is allowed to commence, and the World Health Organisation has issued a list of obligatory steps that have to be verified by all the staff in the operating room to ensure that all the equipment is in working order and that blood is instantly available if required. The site of the incision is often marked with a felt pen and checked with the patient still conscious in the anaesthetic room to avoid operating on the wrong limb or the wrong organ. Few medical mishaps are due to deliberate harm or malice, and the vast majority are caused by a train of errors that in themselves could easily be corrected but when linked together often result in tragedy and serious harm. Giving an expert opinion often involves a certain amount of detective work and I have occasionally discovered efforts on the part of the claimant or the medical staff to alter the evidence or the clinical records in an attempt to cover up the events leading to the injury, but never to the extent described in this book. Nevertheless I have observed animosity between individuals, sometimes between senior consultants and sometimes between senior and junior doctors and nurses and midwives, which has impinged on good patient care and resulted in tragedy, but I have never seen or heard of an act of deliberate malice such as occurred during the operation described in this book.

The doctors and nurses depicted here are entirely fictitious and bear no relationship to people I have met in my professional career.

THE CANTERBURY TALES

The Physician's Tale – but no Surgeon's Tale

T he *Canterbury Tales* is a collection of twenty-four stories written in Middle English by Geoffrey Chaucer between 1387 and 1400. The tales, which are mostly written in verse, are presented as part of a story-telling contest by a group of medieval pilgrims as they travel together from London to Canterbury to visit the shrine of St Thomas Becket at Canterbury Cathedral. The prize for this contest is a free meal at the Tabard Inn at Southwark on their return to London.

The group of twenty-nine travellers come from a wide range of classes and types of people including religious, military and civilian. Among the most well known is 'The Miller's Tale', told by the drunken miller Robyn, a stout and evil churl fond of wrestling who relates the infidelity of the carpenter's wife and ends with bawdy and obscene acts and language.

'The Wife of Bath's Tale' is told by Alisoun, a five-time widow who has travelled throughout the world, and 'The Physician's Tale', told by an academic doctor of physic, is based on a story by the Roman historian Titus Livius that tells a horrific tale about the beautiful, virtuous Virginius who is claimed by the cruel judge, Appius. When the girl relates the events to her father she is offered the choice of being shamed by the judge or death by her father's hand and, since she chooses the latter, she is beheaded. This horrific story gets worse when the judge sees her severed head in court and orders the father to be hanged immediately.

The barbarity divulged in this tale makes one almost relieved that there is no 'Surgeon's Tale', which may even have been worse save for the fact that there were no surgeons in the time of Chaucer. Their predecessors were barbers and one was employed by their guild in every monastery to be on hand to cut the monks' hair regularly, as they needed to be tonsured. This was the religious practice of shaving the top of the head in order to create the effect of a halo. In the Middle Ages the barber surgeon was generally charged with caring for soldiers during and after battle. In this era, surgery was seldom performed by physicians but instead by barbers, who, possessing sharp razors and the slick coordination indispensable to their trade, were called upon for numerous tasks ranging from removing bladder stones (lithotomy), blood letting and, with increasing military conflict, to amputating limbs. Admiral of the Fleet, Horatio Nelson, employed many barber surgeons on his ships and before the Battle of Trafalgar issued an order that their surgical implements should be heated, since he had unpleasant memories of the feeling of the cold steel saw used to amputate his own right arm following the injury caused by a musket ball shortly after stepping ashore during a doomed night assault on the Spanish island of Tenerife in July 1797.

Formal recognition of their skills in England goes back to 1540, when the Fellowship of Surgeons, who were trained by apprenticeship rather than the academic training of the physicians, merged with the Company of Barbers, a London livery guild, to form the Company of Barber Surgeons.

Another link is the British use of the title 'Mr' rather than 'Dr' by surgeons. This dates back to the days when surgeons did not have a university education. This link with the past is retained despite the fact that all surgeons now have to gain a medical degree and doctorate from a recognised university as well as undergoing several more years of training in surgery. The union of the barbers and surgeons was never easy to manage and the relationship continued uneasily for 200 years. In 1745, at the request of the surgeons, a Bill was finally passed and the surgeons left the company, forming what eventually became the Royal College of Surgeons of England.

Another anomaly in the British medical system is the fact that senior nurses in charge of wards, departments or operating rooms are referred to as sisters. They have no religious affiliation and they are not nuns and, as parts of this book describe, they certainly do not behave like them.

PART ONE

THE HOSPITAL

S t Giles' Hospital was one of many London teaching hospitals built in the mid-nineteenth century when there was a need for modern healthcare to provide for the rapidly expanding population of the capital city of the United Kingdom. It was situated on the west side of Edgware Road about a mile north of Marble Arch, with the main building in Paddington catering for the needs of NHS patients connected by a tunnel under the Edgware Road to a much more luxurious establishment catering for the whims and foibles of private patients who paid handsomely for individual care by part-time consultants who saw them in the opulent surroundings of their private consulting rooms about a mile to the east in Harley Street.

The medical school was affiliated to the University of London and being close to Marylebone Station tended to take medical students from the home counties, although some came from Birmingham and even further afield from the Potteries in Staffordshire.

Although most specialists at this university hospital spent most of their working week looking after the ailments of NHS patients, they were allowed three sessions to look after the rich and famous, thereby tripling their income. About a third of the specialists, usually those with a socialist bent, refused to involve themselves with private patients and cynically referred to Harley Strasse as the Street of Shame. There were other imposing buildings along the Marylebone Road reaching as far as Marylebone Station – one used exclusively for gynaecological surgery and the other for ophthalmic surgery.

Like St Mary's Hospital, which is situated in Praed Street about a mile to the west next to Paddington railway station (which services the West Country and Wales), the medical student intake of St Giles came from those regions. St Mary's in particular had a large intake from South Wales and since Lord Moran, physician to Winston Churchill, was the dean, selection was based more on personality than intellectual ability and, more importantly, sporting ability, which accounted for their excellence on the rugby field.

Alas, St Giles no longer exists in the form described in this book and was demolished to make way for the extension of the M40 and the glass and concrete buildings either side of the Edgware Road flyover.

At one time there was a plan to rebuild it, but the powers that be in the corridors of the Ministry of Health decided that there were too many hospitals in central London, and therefore it was moved to a new site near Harrow on the northern outskirts of the capital and renamed the University Hospital of North London, while St Mary's Hospital was enlarged and many new wings added over the Paddington basin of the Grand Union Canal.

Chapter One
The resident doctor's quarters, St Giles' Hospital, Paddington, London

'Burnt buttocks.'

Patrick Stanley repeated the words slowly, deliberately, almost like an oath. 'Burnt buttocks.'

He fumbled in his jacket pocket for his lighter and, almost subconsciously, went through the lazy ritual of lighting a cigarette.

A clatter of noise echoed up the main hospital stairway. Automatically he checked his watch, seven o'clock, visiting time, another half an hour before supper would be served in the doctors' dining room.

Patrick inhaled deeply, picked up the solicitor's letter and blew out a worried cloud of smoke as he settled back in his armchair to read the unpleasant contents for the fifth time that day.

'Our client has suffered extensive injuries to her private region, including full thickness burns to both buttocks, as a result of an operation negligently performed by you at St Giles' Hospital on February 14th, 1968. In view of the obvious disturbance to her marital life, it would appear that our client may have a claim against you for damages and we would be most grateful to receive a photocopy of the hospital notes.'

Patrick Stanley was facing legal action for arson, for wilfully setting fire to an innocent fanny. Not just the vagina with its protective entrance gates, the labia majora, but the entire pubic region, North, South, East and West – the whole caboodle. The pubic hairs, in particular, had gone up like a Corsican pine forest on a dry day.

In spite of the enormity of the offence, Patrick had been surprised to receive the solicitor's letter. His first reaction was to be hurt, then to be indignant and finally to be angry. He fingered the letter impatiently and frowned at the nasty legalese and its implications, feeling, more than anything, a distinct sense of betrayal.

He rose from the chair and paced uneasily up and down the linoleum floor of the small bedsit that served as his quarters when he was on duty at the hospital.

Patrick went to the window and, using it as a repository for his bottled-up

4

venom, hurled it wide open with a loud crash despite the protestations of the resisting sash that was designed to shield the fragile glass from such violence. He leaned out, and breathed the cool air of the London night, listened to the proximate sounds of the hospital, the grating of leather against stone as an army of visitors' feet surged up the main staircase, the unanswered ring of a telephone in an empty office, the distant clang of stainless-steel sterilisers and then, beyond the roof, through the orange glow of the sodium lamps, the noise of the big city with the constant rumble of traffic and the distant roar of the jet-liners on the descent path to Heathrow. He gazed across the tangled roofscape of the hospital, watched a stray cat as it prowled around the gutters, fleetingly illuminated by the harsh glare from a skylight.

The chill of the night brought him slowly back to reality, to the incident that had happened some months previously and to the reproving finger of the law that was pointing uneasily at him. Patrick had made no attempt to cover up the accident, almost the reverse; he had sat on the side of her bed and carefully explained the reasons for the disaster and had done his best to apologise to her for the pain and discomfort she was undoubtedly suffering.

He had personally seen to it that the burnt tissue was dressed twice daily with sofra-tulle to prevent secondary infection, and when he had viewed the result in the outpatient department six weeks later the whole area looked perfectly satisfactory apart from the absence of pubic hair. It reminded Patrick of an aerial view of the Vietnam jungle after a defoliation attack with Agent Orange. Above all, it was still perfectly serviceable and, apart from the depilation, he was not displeased with the result. He had written in the outpatient notes, 'the functional integrity of the genital tract has been preserved'.

He had managed the aftercare of the patient so well that by the time she was finally discharged from the hospital they were on quite friendly terms. They even addressed each other by their first names and Patrick was sure that he could bury the whole unpleasant experience somewhere in the darker recesses of his memory. Now this letter, three months after the event, brought all the emotions and worry back to the surface. He was badly in need of some fatherly advice so he returned to the heat of the room and telephoned his senior registrar.

'Switch, is Mr Hampson still in the hospital?'

''Ang on pet, I'll just enquire.'

Patrick listened to the strong Liverpudlian accent of one of the evening switch-board operators asking her colleague, 'Any idea where Mr Hampson is, Viv?'

And then her voice on the mouthpiece, 'E's on forty-four or would you rather I bleeped him?'

'Not to worry, I'll ring him direct.'

Humphrey Hampson was sitting in the deserted typing pool in the hospital basement, dictating discharge summaries so that the general practitioners could discover what, if anything, the hospital had done to their charges. He had taken off his tie and was dictating 'American style' with his feet up on the desk, waving the microphone in the air with all the zest of an enthusiastic orchestra conductor. He had about twenty folders to get through which, he judged, would take him about an hour and a half, and then he could go home. He was a very methodical and conscientious individual and did his best to complete them within a few days of the patient being discharged from the hospital.

He cursed as he heard the telephone ring and was even more disgruntled to find that the interruption was due to Patrick Stanley requiring some convivial company in the public house across the road from the hospital. He tried to excuse himself, but when the Irishman mentioned the legal letter and the need for some personal advice he relented and agreed to meet him in half an hour, by which time he would have finished a third of the dictation.

Patrick locked his room in the residents' quarters and went down the gloomy corridor that led from the dark sequestered domain of the junior medical staff residence to the outside world. The walls were a murky yellow and devoid of any decoration – not even the occasional portraits of long-dead physicians and surgeons did anything to relieve the monotony. The floor was late-Victorian grey stone slabs worn by the tread of many generations of medical feet. The whole aspect of the junior staff quarters reminded him of the interior of a prison; unwelcoming, institutional and drab.

He went down to the porter's lodge at the main entrance, depositing his white coat behind the door and handing his staff location bleep to Mr Hare, the tall ex-policeman who guarded the hospital entrance during the trouble-some evening hours when the effects of alcohol were superimposed on the usual truculence of the local residents of Paddington. In spite of his age of sixty-four and a bad chest, Old Hairy-Arse, as he was affectionately called by the students and the junior doctors, still presented an impressive figure of a man and was the key to the hospital in the evening.

No disrespect was implied by this nickname and, as he once pointed out philosophically, 'the lads 'ave got to call an old bleeder like me something'. For many years he had been a policeman in the local force and had eventually risen to the rank of sergeant. He knew everything there was to know about the local area around Paddington Station and after a lifetime spent in its seediness, squalor and sin, this information was invaluable in the evening hours after the pubs had discharged their human rabble on to the local streets. He could sniff a troublemaker as soon as he put foot inside the hospital entrance and seemed to have a hotline to the local police station so that in the event of violence, a Black Maria and some hefty coppers were on the scene within minutes of the first fists a-flying.

Although in his middle sixties, Mr Hare was still a well-built man and could probably hold his own in the event of trouble. Unfortunately, after a lifetime of inhaling London smog and Will's Woodbine cigarettes, he had the cockney diseases of bronchitis and emphysema and his exercise tolerance was not good. Indeed, his coughing and breathing difficulty sometimes combined to make it hard for him to relay an audible message over the telephone – it would just come out as a succession of coughs and wheezes, and the doctors would have to go to the porter's lodge where he wrote the intended message on the side of the *London Evening Standard*.

Nevertheless, he had established a reputation in the police force that brooked no nonsense. Many a meths or whisky drinker aimed unsteadily towards the hospital casualty department for a free night and clean sheets after the pubs had closed, and it only required the massive six-foot presence of old Hare with his dusky red face and flared nostrils to avert trouble.

'Cor blimey, Sarge,' as they looked up the steps from the main entrance. 'Oi didn't know you was still around.' And they would scarper off and create trouble at St Mary's which was in Praed Street next to Paddington Station. Hare had worked the evening shift at the porter's lodge overlooking the main hospital entrance for the past fifteen years after retiring early from the Met on the grounds of ill health and had acquired something of a reputation as a diagnostician.

'I wouldn't go to bed just yet, Doc,' he would say. 'We've just had one brought

in by the blood-wagon boys. Looks like acute pancreatitis to me.' Or, 'Any customers, H-A?' 'Couple just arrived in a coma. One looked diabetic so he'll go
to the medical unit. The other was one of our regulars. I think they'll keep him
in Casualty to sober him up, and then boot him out. I told the casualty officer
to spray a little ethyl chloride on his balls to freeze 'em up a bit. Make him less
anxious to return 'ere, sir. That's what I reckon anyway. I think you're all right
for a few hours over the road.'

And he was rarely wrong. In fact, many a new houseman, when perplexed by
a difficult clinical problem, would usually plump for H-A's diagnosis. Sometimes it was a little awkward the following day when the consultant would ask
for the rationale or logic behind the diagnosis and they were loath to confess to
following the advice of the local policeman after having supposedly attended
medical school for almost six years.

He was reputed to possess a sixth sense that could sniff out trouble long
before it had arrived. Patrick therefore considered it essential to have a brief
chat with Mr Hare before leaving the building for the pub across the road.

'All quiet on the Western Front, H-A?'

Mr Hare put down his copy of the *Evening Standard* and rose to his full
height despite the effort on his poor lungs. His nostrils flared and he bent his
head, steadying himself on the desk with his hands and pausing until he could
get enough wind to speak. His cheeks had that dusky cyanosed look of the
chronic respiratory invalid and his nose was large and red and surmounted by
dark horn-rimmed glasses that added a headmasterly touch to his large frame.
He was indeed an impressive figure. He always rose, despite the respiratory
effort, to address one of the doctors. It was a mark of respect.

'All quiet on your side, Mr Patrick, but Dr Brackenbridge has been called up
to maternity and I suppose that means anything could happen.'

Patrick grinned. It was uncanny how the old man could get such an accurate
analysis of the characters of the housemen who had only been with them for
a few weeks. Brackenbridge had been nicknamed 'Bodger' by the nursing staff
because of his inherent clumsiness and it seemed that his reputation had now
spread beyond the confines of the delivery suite.

'I'm just going over the road for a snifter, H-A. Try to keep the wolves at bay
for me.'

'I'll do that, Mr Patrick. Make sure you don't have more than half a dozen of your snifters. Remember you have to keep your eagle eye on Dr B.'

Patrick laughed. His capacity for alcohol was similar to that of most of his compatriots from the Emerald Isle and it always seemed to surprise the staff at each hospital that he could remain passably sober after so many pints of ale or Guinness. He went out into the cool night air and shuddered involuntarily since he was now without his white coat and only in a thin shirt; poor protection against the cold and damp of the London night. He walked down the side of the hospital past a line of waiting ambulances and under the bridge that connected the hospital with the pathology laboratories and the Medical School. He crossed the busy main street to the pub – Patrick's favourite retreat from the rigours of hospital life.

The Sun in Splendour was a fine upstanding public house just opposite the front entrance of St Giles' Hospital. Students and doctors retired to its welcoming bars to quench their thirst, loosen their tongues and enjoy each other's company. Some students spent as much time in the pub as they did on the hospital wards and it was lovingly considered as a sort of spiritual extension of the hospital building. It was a spit and sawdust pub of the finest kind and did a booming trade with the medical men and some of the local population. To generations of St Giles medics it was affectionately known as the 'Lust in the Dust'.

Patrick elbowed his way to the crowded bar, murmuring greetings to various other groups of housemen and medical students. He ordered two pints, and holding them above his head, pushed his way back to a corner table, spilling the odd foamy drop on the heads of people who impeded his progress.

Normally he would be drinking with one of these rowdy groups standing around the bar, but tonight he wanted to discuss his problem with Humphrey Hampson, so he sat awkwardly at the corner table staring morosely into his beer mug. He loathed drinking alone and wished Humphrey would hurry up. He looked around self-consciously, half hoping he was invisible. He was obsessed by the absurd notion that others in the bar would think of him as a social outcast, ostracised from bar society because of body odour or halitosis.

Patrick was a tall, gaunt Irishman in his early thirties who, despite his professional status, generated a look of mild depravity. Beneath an unruly mop of gypsy black hair, deep furrows ravaged his forehead. His heavily hooded eyes were either twinkling with humour or gave the impression they were leering at you. His bushy eyebrows and slightly hooked nose made him look like an old caricature of Punch and his appearance was made more piratical by the scar on the end of his hooter caused by the recent explosion in the operating theatre. He had full-bodied lips that retained something of a cupid's bow, and women of a certain type found the upper one in particular especially sensuous.

The final effect of all this genetic and environmental chiselling was a face that was attractive, not in a pretty way but with the lascivious manner of a character who had lived a rather debauched and wild existence. His right cheek bore the marks of two scars inflicted in street brawls when he was a medical student in Dublin. He had the rugged appearance displayed by the old generation of Hollywood's beloved uglies like Charles Bronson and Lee Marvin.

The man he was waiting for was altogether different. Humphrey Hampson was the very model of the English gentleman: reserved, dapper and balding, but always impeccably dressed. He was some years older than Patrick and bore a superficial resemblance to the American vice-president at the time, Hubert Humphrey, and many people called him Hubert rather than Humphrey. It was all rather confusing and, to add to the difficulty, Humphrey possessed an embarrassing stutter that was particularly pronounced when he was in the company of members of the opposite sex – a strange affliction for a gynaecologist who spent most of his working life in their presence. It was particularly bad when he started on a conversation; once he was under way it tended to disappear.

Humphrey breezed in, his cheeks reddened by the cold night, and plunked his briefcase on the table in an unnecessary display of heartiness.

'H-h-hello, old f-f-fellow,' he stuttered. 'How's the p-p-p-pubic p-p-pyro-maniac?'

'Oh, fuck off, Hubert.' Patrick had suffered enough from jokes like this since the accident. 'I asked you down here for some fatherly advice and assistance.'

'S-s-s-sorry, old man. Let's have a l-l-look at the letter.'

He adjusted his waistcoat, took a sip of his beer and studied the verbose legal jargon of the lawyer's letter.

'I shouldn't worry too much about it, old man, these things always sound worse on paper. Whatever you do, make sure you don't reply to them directly and for God's sake don't let them take a gander at the hospital notes without your own solicitor's consent. Just send a detailed report to the Medical Defence Union and they'll look after your interests. Don't worry about it.'

'Oh, I'm not worried about the cost, I just…'

'Won't cost a p-p-p-penny, old man.' Humphrey smacked his lips as he quaffed his pint of warm ale. 'The Medical Defence Union will have to cough up. That's what we pay those hefty annual subscriptions for.'

'Oh, it's not the money I'm…'

'Worth it, mind you, when you go setting fire to people's privates.' Humphrey grinned contentedly; he was enjoying himself.

'For Christ's sake, Humphrey, let me get a bloody word in. You're worse than a goddamn wife. You're meant to be here as a sympathetic listener but I can't even get started.' Patrick's Irish brogue was always much thicker when he was angry.

'Go ahead, old m-m-man, tell your problems to Uncle Humphrey. I'm all ears. What's on your mind?'

'I've forgotten. Your prattling along like an old mother hen has made me lose my train of thought.'

'At least you're covered,' Humphrey reminded him.

'That's not the point. What gets my goat is the deception. She took it all so well when I explained it was an accident. She seemed such a nice person; so understanding. I can't believe she would double-cross me like this.'

'Oh, don't be such a sentimental t-t-t-twit. You gave her that beautiful sincere look of yours, sat on her bed and held her hands. You could have done anything you wanted with her.'

'Hardly, Humphrey,' Patrick sneered. 'She couldn't even sit on her twat without wincing, never mind doing anything else with it.'

'Exactly. She no sooner gets home and tells the neighbours that some maniac set her fanny alight than one of them suggests she might make a few quid out of it. So she forgets the doctor's lovely bedside manner and visits one of those ambulance-chasing lawyers. When he sees that she can't even sit down, never mind a bit of the other, he knows he's on to a winner. Most judges sit on their arses all day and they're bound to be sympathetic to someone with a burnt behind. I should imagine the MDU would settle out of court. You weren't the only one to blame; the hospital authority will have to share half the costs for the part the nursing staff played in handing you such an explosive mixture. You could always plead that you asked for a different solution.'

'But I didn't. I just asked her to give me the usual stuff.' Patrick idly stirred the foam of his beer with the small finger of his left hand as he remembered the events leading up to the incident. 'It was my first day here – you know what it's like arriving in a new hospital, each consultant has a different routine and it takes a few days before you learn the ropes. Well, that bitch of a staff nurse saw that I was uneasy and decided to cash in on it. Every move I made she tried to put me on the spot; you know the way some of them like to put up a show of strength with a newcomer.'

'But surely she must have known the correct prep solution for a cervical cautery. I mean, it's a completely routine procedure.'

'She just repeated my demand for the "usual stuff" to that dago wop Pedro who was leaning against the wall painting his fucking fingernails as usual.'

'You don't seem to like him.'

'Fucking poof. The whole thing was his sodding fault.' There was no mistaking the hatred in Patrick's voice. 'Instead of handing over the correct solution the idle sod merely lifted a gallipot off one of the trolleys that was waiting for the next case, which was an abdominal procedure.'

'And it was inflammable.'

'You can say that again. I pressed the foot pedal of the electrocautery and a great whoosh of flame leapt out of the vagina and burnt me on the hooter.'

Humphrey could not suppress his laughter. He started a series of deep-throated guffaws like a sow in labour and ended up obscenely spluttering in his beer.

'Oh my God!' he gasped, as he surfaced for a breath of air, 'I'd love to have seen your face. I'd give the little toe on my left foot to have seen your face.'

'Oh, big deal.'

Patrick smirked, his humour returning. 'One moment I'm gazing fondly at a friendly looking fanny and the next, bejaysus, it was like a dragon on heat. Flames everywhere, the towels caught fire, the crackles of the pubic hair. My Christ, 'twas a terrible shambles. The whole theatre smelt like a Chinese chip shop.'

Humphrey had calmed down by now and his face became more serious. 'What about Reith? He was none too pleased from what I heard.'

'That's the understatement of the year. He went stark raving bananas. Of course, in his book the whole bloody thing was my fault. You know what he's like; he threw a major epileptiform tantrum and well…' Patrick's voice trailed away as he remembered the first major confrontation with his new consultant.

'What did he say?'

'Oh, forget it.' Patrick shrugged his shoulders, and then he relented. Humphrey had to know everything, especially where Reith was concerned. 'I had a bit of an argy-bargy with him over the phone just before lunch. He questioned my competence to manage the cases and when I told him I'd done hundreds before he accused me of being arrogant. It seemed that nothing I could say would satisfy the old bugger so I just let him rabbit on and get his sooth said.'

'But he'd never seen you operate before, it was your first day in the job.'

'Exactly, that's why I couldn't understand his attitude especially when he announced that he was taking the afternoon off to collect his mother from some old folks' home at Woburn halfway up the M1.'

'So, effectively, you had no one covering you.' Humphrey was wearing a puzzled frown across the large expanse of his forehead. 'What did he say when he discovered what had happened?'

'He went berserk with rage. He started bellowing like a wounded bull.' Patrick mimicked the consultant's lowland Scottish accent. 'Remember the words of Sir William Osler, laddie, 'First do no harm. First do no harm.' Then he stalked off down the corridor banging his clenched fist against the walls shouting, 'First do no harm: primum non nocere.' Passers-by must have thought that he was an escaped lunatic.'

'It's one of his favourite quotations. He bases his life on it. He holds Sir William in great esteem. The longer you stay here the more you'll get to know the quotations of that illustrious physician. Osler was an almost endless provider of quotations; Reith knows them all.'

Patrick's attention was diverted by one of the students yelling his name from the corner of the bar where the telephone was situated. He was wanted in the hospital. He excused himself and elbowed his way through the crowd to find out who needed him. After a brief conversation on the phone he came back to Humphrey's table, cursing like a trooper. Humphrey looked up at him.

'P-p-p-problems?'

'Old Bodger's up to his elbows in meconium trying to put the Kielland's forceps on a case of foetal distress. I'd better go and see that he doesn't do too much damage.'

'How do you find him?'

'Oh, he's not too bad. A bit holier-than-thou. He's only been with us a month or so but he talks as if he's the Professor. I've never come across such a pompous and overbearing houseman. At least he's dedicated and he doesn't drink, so he makes up for my sins. Cheers!' Patrick downed his fresh pint in one draught.

'You can say that again. You must be the most alcoholic heathen we've had in years. Anyway, I must take the crushing machine hell-bent for suburbia. Don't worry about the case, Patrick, just leave it to the medical defence lawyers, they'll sort it out for you.'

'Thanks, Humphrey, I'll contact them tomorrow.'

Patrick crossed the road to the hospital and bounded up the steps to the labour ward to find Dr Brackenbridge sweating away over a forceps delivery. Certainly he did not look very pompous now and great drops of sweat were pouring off the young man's forehead and some had gathered on the end of his nose. His proboscis was so enormous and wet that the mask had slipped off it and now droplets of perspiration were dripping down from the end of his nose into the stainless-steel bucket at his feet. In addition his horn-rimmed glasses were halfway down his nose and looked as if they might be next in line for the bucket. It was hardly a sign to encourage confidence in the poor hapless patient who was yelling and straining to expel her baby.

Patrick immediately took over. He donned a mask mainly to contain his beery breath and stood behind the patient, holding her hand tightly and looking down at Bodger who was stationed between her spread-eagled legs.

'Now, love, next contraction, I want you to put your chin on your chest and give a really big heave right down into your bottom. Wait until the contraction comes.' He was feeling her swollen abdomen with his other hand.

'Right. One coming now. Chin forward. A really big push.' Then he looked at his junior doctor. 'Pull more towards the floor, a steady pull as she pushes down. Further down. Here, I'll show you. Gloves. Sister, get some 7½ gloves for me. Keep pushing, sweetheart, don't waste the contraction. Gone now. Rest a bit in between. That's right. Mop her brow, someone.'

He put the gloves on, pushed Bodger aside and took over the grip on the forceps.

'Now, next push and we're going to have this baby. Sister, tell me when she gets a contraction and get her pushing properly.'

'One coming now.'

'Right. Push away, sweetheart.' Then to his houseman, 'Now gently pull down like this. OK down here in the axis of the birth canal until it crowns. Here, put your hand on mine to get the feel. Now slowly up. All right, dear, start panting. Sister, get her to pant. No pushing now. Slowly deliver the head. Suck, someone. Nurse, shove that sucker down its throat. Fine, gently off with the blades and deliver the shoulders. Another little push, dear. Syntometrine. Someone, give her some syntometrine. There we go.' He held the baby aloft. 'A little girl, dear. A lovely little girl. Two clamps, Bodger, cut the cord, will you? Give it to the paediatrician. It might need a tube down. Looks a bit flat to me. Come on, you little bugger, breathe.'

The paediatrician took the baby like a precious jewel and carried the bluish blood-covered bundle over to the resuscitation table in the corner and aspirated some thick greenish mucus from the pharynx and slid a plastic endotracheal tube down the tiny windpipe to supply life-giving oxygen to the lungs. The mother gave a grunt that signified that she was exhausted and glad it was all over. But she had forgotten about the third stage. As the oxytocic drug took effect, Patrick stared vacantly at the vagina for the tell-tale gush of blood that warned of placental separation. He pulled gently down on the cord with one hand and pushed the uterus up with the other to stop it turning inside out. He felt the cord give as the afterbirth sheared away from its bed inside the uterus.

'OK, sweetheart, a small push and then we're finished. This is just the luggage.'

The big glistening placenta slid out of the vagina, followed by the remains of the membranes and umbilical cord like a lethargic eel, and Patrick deposited it in a stainless-steel kidney dish with a sacrificial gesture. He rose from the stool and peeled off his gloves while one of the nurses undid the strings securing his green sterile gown at the back.

'Well done, love. That wasn't too bad, was it?' He patted her affectionately on her deflated belly. 'You'll be able to see your feet again. Just a few stitches to be inserted by my colleague here and then the girls will give you a cup of tea. The baby doctor will give you your baby to cuddle in just a minute.'

He turned to his houseman and spoke to him in a more businesslike tone. 'Cobble her up, Bodger. Just the edges of the episiotomy. Don't close off the entire orifice or anything daft like that. I'll be over in the pub if you need me.'

And with that he was gone, straight back to the 'Lust in the Dust' where he stayed for the rest of the evening quaffing pint after pint until he was laughing and singing like a bawdy trooper with a noisy group of medical students. They long overstayed the legal limit for drinking up time and were finally jettisoned like human garbage on to the grey flagstones of the pavement by the persuasively brawny arms of Old Fred, the publican.

It was to become a familiar pattern for Patrick Stanley, and although inebriation on his part could in no way be implicated in the disaster that followed, his reputation for bacchanalian bawdiness destroyed his credibility and would ultimately bring him to ruin.

CHAPTER TWO
The gynaecology operating theatre, St Giles' Hospital, Paddington, London

'Give me some sharp curved scissors, Sister. These wouldn't even cut water. Look, woman, the points don't even meet.'

The consultant gynaecologist hurled them on the operating theatre floor in anger and Sister Brewer felt the familiar panic symptoms rise up in her throat as they did every Thursday morning. She took a few deep breaths and clenched her fists in an effort to control her tone of voice. She was determined to stand up to this Scottish tyrant for once in her life.

'You can't behave like that nowadays, Mr Reith. Everything's packed in the Central Sterile Supply Department and now I have to open a completely new hysterectomy pack just to get out a pair of scissors.'

'I'll behave any way I want in my own theatre,' he bellowed, transfixing her uncomfortably with angry brown eyes that rested uneasily beneath a pair of bushy eyebrows, which were all that was visible of his authoritarian features between the top of his surgical mask and the green cloth cap that covered his head. 'I just want a pair of scissors that cut. We're not here to satisfy the bloody administrators, Sister. We're here to get this old buzzard's box out.'

He tapped the anaesthetised torso on the thorax with a long pair of toothed dissecting forceps to give his speech added significance.

The senior theatre sister started to cluck like a distressed duck and, to mollify her slightly, Reith lowered the pitch of his voice and decided to be less aggressive in his tactics.

'All right, Sister, just give me a pair of Metzenbaums.'

Her heart sank. She had prayed all week that he would not ask for his special scissors again.

'They still haven't arrived. I've been telephoning the suppliers but they say they're waiting for a shipment from America.'

'Good God, woman, I've been asking for those damned scissors for the past six months. Can't you get some ruddy British scissors? I just want to get on with the operation. I could do it a damn sight better with my wife's kitchen utensils.'

They waited for another pack to be undone to retrieve a satisfactory pair of scissors. A tense atmosphere was building up in the theatre. Angus Reith was a notoriously difficult consultant to work with and most of the junior sisters had been thrown out of his operating theatre for insolence, indolence, inefficiency or a mixture of all three. Miss Brewer alone seemed only just able to contain him and the strain was plainly telling on her. The Thursday morning operating session was preceded by a night of restless insomnia and, of late, she had to take a couple of valium capsules before retiring to her little room in the nurses' hostel.

Silence. Uncomfortable silence.

Angus turned to his old friend and colleague, Harry Squires, who was sitting beside the patient's head puffing a bladder-like bag with one hand, concentrating mainly on the *Times* crossword puzzle, which appeared more difficult than usual. Harry and Angus had gone through medical school together and had worked together ever since.

They formed one of St Giles' most famous mutual admiration societies.

'The old place is going down the drain, Harry. All this burble about modern technology. In the old days at least they made scissors that cut, eh, Harry?'

'There's no loyalty left, Angus. They're all nine-to-fivers. They don't give a damn about the quality of the work any more.'

Sister Brewer flashed an angry look at Harry Squires and he looked down uncomfortably at his anaesthetic cylinders. It was enough that she had to take all this from 'Lord' Reith but she would not be insulted by that silly old buffer of an anaesthetist. She would speak her mind to him afterwards. Reith only came to the operating theatres for one day in the week but Harry spent all his working life there and his influence was diminished accordingly. He was part of the furniture.

Angus turned to the medical student who was assisting at the operation. He prodded down in the pelvis with his dissecting forceps. His thick Scottish accent boomed a question at him.

'What is the name of that structure, laddie?'

Silence.

Andrew Jennings was totally confused. He felt completely ill at ease in these unfamiliar surroundings. He had been sent up to the theatre suite as part of his introductory course to the clinical side of the hospital. It was like an entirely foreign environment. He was terrified to touch anything and had tried to tuck himself in the corner and remain unobtrusive. With Angus Reith as the consultant in charge this was virtually impossible since he demanded total subjugation of any living thing in the room, with the possible exception of old Harry Squires.

Normally the student who admitted the patient was expected to be present to assist during the operation. The patient who was first on the list this morning had been admitted by an Old Etonian, Miles Jamieson, who regarded Angus Reith as an 'insufferable troglodyte' and further added that he had no intention of going up to the operating theatre to be insulted. He sent word that he intended to be ill in his bed and since no one had volunteered to take his place, Andrew found himself summoned by the surgeon to get scrubbed and assist. His terror had mounted with each clumsy attempt to get into all the green sterile clothing. He did not even know what size of gloves to ask for and one of the more vindictive theatre staff nurses had watched him with an eagle eye and insisted that he start from square one every time he made a mistake. After the third attempt he had waddled clumsily into the theatre and had hung back behind the consultant. Then he had been hauled into the inner circle beneath the spotlights and been given a Deaver retractor to hold and, although he was unable to see into the operating field without getting in the way of the surgeon, he was expected to keep the retractor in exactly the required position. Every time it had strayed a centimetre or so, Reith would rap him painfully on the knuckles with a heavy stainless-steel instrument, in this case a pair of cholecystectomy clamps and rebuke him. Now he was expected to identify something he could hardly see. Everything was covered in blood. It was not like the corpses preserved in formalin that they had dissected in the basement of the anatomy school in Cambridge. Sweat began to trickle down from his forehead. He could not even think properly.

'Come on, laddie. What is it? A piece of string, maybe?'

Andrew was so terrified that he came out with a totally inane remark in an effort to play for time.

'No, sir,' he said. 'I don't think it's string.'

Angus exploded again. He had found a new target for the bottled up frustration of the afternoon.

'Of course it's bloody well not a piece of string. This is a human body we're looking at. God's finest creation. Adam's rib. It's not a blithering model aircraft.'

Reith looked despairingly first at the student and then at Harry.

'God help us all, Harry. I should think the average garage mechanic is more acquainted with his subject that this lot nowadays.'

'They seem to get worse every year, Angus. They've all heard of the Laurence-Moon-Biedl syndrome but they don't know which side of the body the liver is on.'

Patrick Stanley was standing across the table from Reith acting as first assistant and felt morally bound to spring to the poor student's defence.

'He's only just started, sir. He's one of the new introductory course – the Oxbridge students who join us in the middle of the year.'

The consultant's bushy eyebrows twitched and the cold eyes appearing over the mask bore into the registrar. He had already detected a sniff of alcohol on the young man's breath and lunchtime drinking was a habit that he would not tolerate.

'Thank you for your unsolicited testimony, Mr Stanley. I hardly think a question on basic anatomy should be beyond the ken of anyone who has passed the second MB. It's the urachus, man. Have you never heard of it? Now perhaps you'll tell me what it represents.'

A flash of inspiration. Maybe he could even redeem himself.

'The obliterated umbilical artery, sir.'

'Good lad. At least we now know that you're not here under false pretences. Not like that Arab. Did you hear about that Arab, a Sudanese wallah, Harry? Never been near a ruddy medical school yet he waltzes into the dear old National Health Service and without a by-your-leave, secures three posts in the casualty departments of London teaching hospitals. Never even been qualified, Harry. Not even graced the portals of the Khartoum Medical School; not that that would have made much difference, anyway. Can't even speak the Queen's English, yet we welcome him with open arms and let him loose on the poor unsuspecting British public. As far as I recollect Sudan is not even part of the great British Commonwealth of Nations. In fact, I seem to remember we were at war with the blighters not so very long ago.'

'The worst thing about that story, Angus, was that no one even suspected him. The sister at St George's even said he was better than most casualty officers they had been having over the past few years.'

'Course anything can happen at a place like St George's. Never did think much of that place. Damned glad they've pulled it down and expelled it from central London to Tooting. Always found something odd about the fellers from that place, eh, Harry?'

'I don't think that's really the point, sir,' Stanley interjected in a solemn tone. 'The point is that the sisters have become so used to total incompetence from most of these foreign casualty officers that they just stand over them and tell them exactly what to do with all the trivial rubbish that occupies most of their time. If anyone really ill arrives they immediately call the registrar of the speciality concerned. That's why they go undetected. The nurses do all the work and cover up their ignorance.'

Angus grunted. He didn't approve of the junior staff chipping in on the consultant's conversation. He certainly never did in his day. It would have been unthinkable impertinence to interrupt Sir Hector in the middle of one of his amusing operation yarns. Times had changed; for the worse, in his opinion. He reiterated his demand for sharp scissors, grunted with dissatisfaction when they were produced from the new sterile pack and reapplied himself to the inside of the pelvis.

He was a brusque and thorough operator. He had no time for those surgeons who would clamp and tie off every bleeding artery. He liked to bash on, get the uterus out and then tidy up afterwards. He hated to see a great array of clamps in the field of the operation.

'Too much damned ironmongery,' as he rapped Patrick Stanley's knuckle for innocently trying to clamp off one of the branches of the uterine artery that was furiously pumping out spurts of bright red blood.

Patrick was quite an experienced gynaecological surgeon but he had been told, in no uncertain terms by Reith, that he could forget all he had learned in the past. He was here to do things Reith's way so he could begin by learning to be a proper assistant. He had to anticipate Reith's every move and act accordingly without any command from the surgeon. Any mistake and he received a painful crack on the knuckles from whatever stainless-steel instrument Reith happened to be brandishing at the time. Patrick had to meekly take this kind of treatment despite the fact that he yearned to be actually doing a hysterectomy again by himself. Reith insisted that all new members of staff, regardless of previous experience, must spend six months learning his way of operating and then they would be allowed to perform the operation under the eagle eye of the great man himself. The politics of megalomania. Reith considered himself to be one of the country's leading gynaecological surgeons. Unfortunately he must have spread the word around since his fame was far in excess of his ability.

The uterus was out, together with a large cervical fibroid that contributed to the increased vasculature in the region of the vaginal vault. The pelvis was filling up with blood and Andrew was handed a long plastic suction tube to keep the surgeon's field of view clear of the red stuff. Despite all the sewing and tying, one artery to the left of the vaginal angle was proving particularly elusive.

Old Harry looked up from his crossword and peered over the green sterile drapes that partitioned his field of activity from that of the surgeon.

'Is she losing too much?'

'Nothing to speak of, Harry. Lovely anaesthetic, Harry. Blood pressure just right.'

'Looks a nice operation, Angus. Doesn't seem to be losing too much.'

Patrick grinned over his mask at Sister Brewer, who returned his smile. This circus of mutual admiration whatever the circumstances had become a part of the folklore of the hospital. These two old buffers would be coming out with this congratulatory mumbo-jumbo even if the poor patient was at death's door. A rap on the knuckle brought Patrick's wandering attention back into the operation field. The artery was resisting all efforts to stem its flow.

'Damned bleeder,' fumed Angus. 'Give me a long Roberts.'

Sister Brewer fumbled in a tray of spare instruments that were not usually asked for but were ready at every operation to suit the whim of the surgeon. With the packing now done by unqualified women in the Central Sterile Supply Department, one could never tell what would be missing from each pack.

'I can't find any Roberts, sir.'

'Oh, damn it all, woman', Reith shrieked. 'I'm not asking for the Eiffel Tower.'

'I'll send out for some Roberts. Nurse Richardson, could you...'

'For God's sake, Sister, give me any old long curved clamp. I can't wait for your dumb nurses to ferret all round the hospital. Tell CSSD that if they forget my Roberts again I'll boot their bloody supervisor's arse all the way down the Bayswater Road. Light. Someone adjust the light. Stanley, can you see where that blighter is? Where's all the red stuff coming from? Swab on a stick. Sister, give me a swab on a stick. Wipe down there, Stanley, so I can see. Suck. Stop waving that blithering thing about, boy. Sister, take that sucker from that im-becile or we'll never get it stopped.'

This time Andrew received a rap on the knuckles with a heavy pair of curved Kocher's forceps and the sucker was wrenched from his grasp. He felt suddenly redundant and uncomfortable and, realising that this was his first operation and that one was meant to feel faint, he wondered if in fact he wasn't feeling a little woozy. He pumped his calf muscles furiously to try to direct blood up to his brain.

Angus was still going after the infidel artery like a crusader at the gates of Jerusalem.

'Light, for God's sake. It's like a bloody coal mine down here.'

Nobody moved.

Angus continued to bellow at no one in particular. 'Adjust the damned light, someone.'

No one took any notice at all.

Andrew looked around blankly. Surely someone must obey the 'Royal Command'. Since he had been robbed of his sucker he was the only one with a free hand. He looked from face to face but no one returned his look.

'Light. How many times do I have to ask?'

Andrew stretched up a gloved hand and started to adjust the position of the overhead spotlight.

Suddenly an enormous bellow came from his right. Like a wounded animal, Reith was puce in the face with anger.

'Not you, you bloody fool. You're supposed to be sterile. Get out. Get out. You're dirty. Contaminated. Get out of my theatre.'

Andrew was completely overcome by the ferocity and injustice of this attack and left the room in a turmoil of anguish. He was only trying to help. How was he supposed to know? Christ, he thought, ejected from the operating theatre on his first visit. It certainly didn't augur well for his future career.

'My Godfathers, Harry. What will they do next? Lord Lister died in vain, Harry. I don't think these young fellows have the least notion of the meaning of asepsis.'

'It's the post-antibiotic generation, Angus. They don't know what we went through before that mad Scot Fleming invented penicillin down the road at St Mary's. Biggest mistake ever made, in my view.'

Patrick Stanley's sense of fair play once again prompted him to intervene.

'He's new here, sir. I think he was only doing his best to help.'

Angus Reith fixed his registrar with a venomous look.

'I don't give a damn how long he's been here. I didn't ask the young fool to start swinging from the chandeliers.'

At the sound of the word 'chandelier', the old anaesthetist's memory was suddenly jarred out of its halothane haze and he burst into song with one of the drinking refrains of his youth.

Head flung back, his silver grey hair moved in time to the tune of 'The Ball at Kirriemuir' as his eyes twinkled behind his rimless spectacles.

Four and twenty virgins came down from Inverness
And when the ball was over there were four and twenty less
Singing...
Balls to your partners
Arse against the wall
If you've never been shagged on a Saturday night
You've never been shagged at all
Ohh...
The village vicar he was there
Up to his favourite trick
Swinging from the chandelier
And landing on his...

Harry blushed and held his hand to his masked face. Had he gone too far? Sister Brewer was fixing him with a look of Dominican piety. Since he'd had his prostate removed, the old buzzard behaved worse than the students.

'I'm terribly sorry, Sister.'

Everyone laughed, including Sister Brewer, who was a notorious virgin. The tension eased and they finished the operation in good spirit.

'Splendid operation, Angus.'

'Splendid anaesthetic, Harry.'

CHAPTER THREE
The delivery suite in the maternity unit, St Giles' Hospital, Paddington, London

The Delivery Suite was quiet now. The one patient in early labour had been well sedated and was sleeping soundly. Most of the nurses were away at first supper on Sister Taylor's instructions. The two remaining girls were relieving on the antenatal ward during supper break. Actually the girls referred to it as lunch but it seemed impossible for Patrick to think of any meal served in the dead of night as lunch. To this was added the confusion caused by Sister Taylor who, coming from the North of England, talked of lunch as dinner and dinner as tea.

They had just performed an emergency caesarean section and Patrick was writing the operation notes at the desk of the nursing station with Sister Taylor next to him entering the details of the birth in the labour ward register. Patrick finished first, rose from his chair and stretched his arms, emitting a yawn. He looked down at her partially exposed back. Without doubt this woman did something to him, he could already feel the blood coursing around his crotch. The brown tan of her naked back looked especially enticing as it was displayed between the parted blue material of her operating theatre pyjama top. The top five buttons were undone in the usual provocative fashion that was one of the hallmarks of this particular night sister.

Patrick was always a little shy at making the first move in any sexual encounter. He held his breath slightly and slowly bent forward to undo the next button. He was uncertain of the reaction this would provoke.

There was no resistance. Neither was there any response.

He undid another button. She did not move. The last button yielded to his fingers.

Sister Taylor merely uttered a mild reproach.

'Doctor!'

Was it a warning or an invitation to proceed? The back was now completely bare and his hungry eyes followed the protrusions of the spine all the way down to where it disappeared to give way to her delicate little bottom. Sister Taylor was still writing her report, seemingly unconcerned with her increasing nudity. Patrick wasn't quite sure what to do next. It was either forward or back and his half-filled penis told him that a retreat at this stage would be tinged with subsequent regrets. His emotions ordered the bugles of his super-ego to sound the advance and with one deft movement he slipped his hands around either side of her chest and grabbed her breasts firmly in both hands. They were superbly shaped, with protruding nipples that could be compressed between the sides of his fingers. This was a heavenly feeling steeped in the anticipation of final possession.

The triumph was short-lived. She emitted a soft shriek and sprung to her feet, pushing the chair hard with her backside so that it crashed into his bollocks. He groaned with pain and reluctantly let go of his prize.

'Doctor!'

This time she admonished him with a voice that sounded sincere and offended, but the soft grin that accompanied the rebuke suggested some pleasure from the encounter.

'Really, Mr Stanley. What a way for a professional man to behave.'

She buttoned her top back up and this seemed to signify Patrick's dismissal from the court of pleasure. Anyway, he was too shy to start again.

'I'll have the rest of you next time,' he laughed.

'Like hell you will. You've already had more than your fair share. Sleep well, Doctor, sweet dreams. Good night.'

Patrick stalked off down the corridor to the changing room, chuckling softly to himself. He must lay plans to seduce that girl. What he had seen and felt had fired his imagination. She always called him 'doctor', in that taunting voice. Most of the other girls called him by his first name, but not this one. And it wasn't out of respect for rank or anything like that. She was just trying to take the proverbial piss out of him. She really excited him. A real North country prick-teaser.

He pushed open the door of the changing room and took off his green operating pyjama trousers. The red blood from the operation had soaked through, causing dark patches on the material. He threw them on to a huge pile of operating theatre garb that had been used the previous day. Despite several notices on the wall pleading with the surgeons to put the used pyjamas in the laundry bag, they invariably flung them all over the floor. The domestic supervisor had attempted to gain the co-operation of the surgeons with a humorous notice on the wall. It read: 'When the floor is full, please use the laundry baskets provided.' To no avail. The place looked like a battlefield.

He cursed softly when he noticed that his underpants were also covered in blood. Most of the obstetricians wore a rubber apron to protect them from the blood and liquor that was invariably spilled in large quantities during a caesarean section but Patrick hated the amount of sweat they caused. Sweaty genitals were OK at the right time and in the right place, but during an operation he preferred the air to circulate freely around his undercarriage. He took off the underpants and soaked them in the washbasin, using them as a flannel to clean the blood from his genitals and the front of his thighs. He dried himself with a towel and looked at himself in the full-length mirror on the wall. His mind was miles away. He was still half thinking of Sister Taylor and was projecting his naked reflection from the mirror into some pleasantly erotic fantasies. He studied himself critically and cast away the towel. He turned to look at himself in profile. He had quite a good body; well tanned on the upper half with strong biceps and powerful shoulders. His bottom was small, white and masculine with no trace of fat. Gallons of beer consumed over the past decade or so had deposited some of their calories in his abdominal wall but if he breathed in he could still recapture his youthful shape. Not bad for a man past thirty and over the hill. His penis was faintly aggressive and now pulsing with more blood than usual because of the thoughts inspired by the nubile nurse. Not an erection by any means but a pleasant pre-sexual glow.

Suddenly the door burst open, shattering his bout of narcissism. Sister Taylor shrieked with the victory of her surprise attack and the added bonus of finding her victim unclothed. Like a two-titted Amazon on the war path she let rip with two half-litre plastic infusion containers filled with five per cent dextrose. Firing from both hips like Mexican Pete she directed the jets of intravenous fluid at the surprised registrar aiming with extraordinary accuracy first at his torso and then the exposed genitals with a great war-cry of mirth.

'Whoopeee – we are a lovely boy, aren't we?'

And suddenly she had disappeared as fast as she had come. Patrick was dripping wet and the surprise water bath had considerably dampened his ardour. It was absolutely unheard of for a woman to enter the male surgeon's changing room. It was like entering the inner sanctum. Patrick dried himself off hurriedly. He was burning for revenge. He had been taken completely by surprise. He couldn't have been caught in a more embarrassing position. Not only was he nude with a semi-erection but also he had been quite plainly admiring himself in the mirror, something that men were not supposed to do. He shuddered to think how this story would be circulated around the nurses' hostel. He couldn't very well pursue the woman down the hospital corridors in the nude.

He didn't like to be on the receiving end of practical jokes. So he'd groped a little with her titties, but she had seen him completely harry starkers. He gulped. She couldn't be allowed to get away with it. He heard the slam of the door of the girls' changing room next door. Both rooms were connected by inner doors to the surgeon's scrub room adjacent to the operating theatre. Patrick went to the inside door. He opened it quietly. The scrub room and the theatres were in complete darkness. He went in, keeping as quiet as possible. His heart was beating hard. It felt quite strange and terrifying to be in the operating theatre with no clothes on. My God, what if someone saw him like this? His career would be ruined. Nevertheless, he was too excited to turn back now. His heart was pounding like an express train. He tried to hold his breath. He listened to the sounds from inside the female changing room. The clanking of a locker door signified that someone was changing their clothes. Was it more than one person? No, it sounded like only one. What if it wasn't Sister Taylor, what if it was old Chopper Mallett, the night matron? How could he explain himself? They would lock him up. They would send the men with nets for him just like the way they did back in Ireland in the old days. Imagine the scandal. He listened again. He had to choose exactly the right moment – preferably when she was half undressed. He knew she never wore a bra. He quivered with excitement.

Now.

He burst into the room like a jungle savage. Lizzie swung round in complete amazement. She only had a pair of tights on. She screamed lightly, more a catching of breath, as she instinctively tried to cover her breasts with her hands. Patrick grinned with the sex lust of a rapist. All his emotions were suddenly discharged and he scooped the petite figure up in his arms and bundled her over his shoulder in a fireman's lift. A Viking raider dragging his struggling captive off to the woods. He carried her kicking and struggling back to his camp and deposited her in front of the mirror.

His intention was only for revenge. To put the struggling female under the cold shower. But suddenly she stopped struggling. She came forward close to him and nestled her head under his chin, pushed her breast against his chest and eased her hand slowly down towards his penis. She felt it grow in her hands and Patrick felt his warlike emotions replaced by a much stronger desire. His powerful arms held her tight as he kissed her neck, and as she raised her lips to meet him he kissed her deep and strong. She was his prize and now all his manhood reared up to claim her.

He kissed her breast and let his tongue glide down to her navel and follow on downwards to her pelvis. She shivered slightly and he looked at their reflection in the mirror. She was watching in a state of detached fascination. It was like a scene from a film. She saw him slowly and gently pull down her tights, sliding them over her feet and discarding them on the floor. Her heart was racing. She was mesmerised by the image. She was unable to resist. The eroticism was overwhelming as he eased her panties over her bottom and down her thighs, guiding them firmly to the floor. Then he pressed his head into her silken black triangle and kissed firmly taking in the scent of her sexual arousal. She grasped his hair and kept him there for what seemed like ages.

He stood up slowly and moved beside her. They were both facing the mirror now.

It seemed so unreal; as if they were intruding on the privacy of another couple. Mr and Mrs Naked Ape. He slipped his hand down to her groin and she made a similar gesture towards him. Her hand closed around his solid penis and she slowly moved the skin up and down. Suddenly they felt embarrassed and insecure. What if someone came in? One of the maids. 'Lord' Reith to deliver a private patient? But they were too far gone to turn back, they both needed it now.

'We can't do it here. Someone might come in.'

'The theatre. No one would go in there at night. Only us and we're on call.'

'We can't do it there, for God's sake, not there. It's been disinfected.'

'Then let us infect it. Why not?'

He led her urgently through the scrub room. Two naked figures moving stealthily in the night.

She had a brief moment of doubt. It was cold and dark and horribly aseptic.

This was the temple of sterility and they were about to defile it. And then she thought just how they would defile it and the urgency cried louder than anything else in her ears. She climbed up on to the operating table. It was lined with a special corrugated rubber to stop the patients sliding off. Electrostatic, to repel dust, it was almost designed with this in mind. It was certainly more comfortable than the floor. She let her legs fall apart and splay on either side of the table and then pulled Patrick to her, but he needed no second bidding. This was no place for aficionados of foreplay. He skilfully parted her labia, already moistened by her desire, and thrust himself deep inside her. He kissed her deeply again with his tongue searing deep into her mouth while his pelvis thrust hard at her. She clasped her thighs around his waist so that she could feel him deeper still and together they briefly took flight from reality and their bodies were locked in pure animal pleasure. It was over in minutes. The prelude had been so erotic and the surroundings so dangerous that the loving demanded excitement and vigour.

They both lay there panting rapidly, their hearts pounding and a film of sweat suddenly cold between their bodies. The scent of sex.

Then the reality returned, the orgasm had dispelled the dream. They were suddenly aware of the immense danger of their situation. A senior member of the nursing staff and a young specialist screwing on the operating theatre table while on duty. They were both suddenly terrified of discovery.

'Christ!' she said. 'What if someone comes in – one of the theatre porters or even Night Matron, Old Chopper? Jesus God. What the hell would she say?'

'Shhh!'

He put a finger over her mouth and eased himself out of her. They slid off the table naked and cold in the empty silence of the operating room and slunk off to their separate changing rooms. Now unaware of each other they hastily put some clothing back on and assumed a veneer of respectability once again. No one had seen them. A sigh of relief. Patrick's heart almost sang with delight and wonder.

He waited in the dark empty corridor for her to come out of her changing room. He suddenly felt shy. He held her hand gently and slowly passed his fingers through her hair. She looked up at him, met his eyes and smiled in a timid fashion. How would they react to each other in the unforgiving light of the day? Would it seem like some kind of dream? They kissed gently.

'I have to go now.'

He squeezed her hand and grinned mischievously. Like a spy in the night he discreetly returned her tights and panties.

'I know you don't wear a bra but you'd better put these back on or someone might take advantage of you. You can never be too careful in this hospital.'

She laughed and bit her lower lip like a naughty girl.

'Thank you, doctor.'

'Be good. Don't call me unless you have to.' And then, as he looked into her soft brown eyes, 'Thanks, Lizzie.'

Another squeeze and she was gone.

CHAPTER FOUR

Accident and Emergency department, St Giles' Hospital, London, summer 1968

The job of an Accident and Emergency doctor in any hospital is essentially a halfway house between a well qualified signpost and a nightclub bouncer. He is called upon to eject the abusive drunks and malingerers from the premises but he also has to point the serious customers in the right direction. This is a crucial stage in the life of a hospital inmate. A mistake may mean that he or she eventually leaves the hospital after selected parts of their anatomy have been whittled away by overenthusiastic surgeons or, alternatively, the poor patient is given an esoteric diagnosis by the more academic physicians and finally discharged clutching armfuls of tablets that could make him sicker than the original disease. It all depended on the doctor who saw him or her first in the A&E department.

Unfortunately the atmosphere at St Giles' Hospital during the evening hours was more akin to a medieval jousting tournament than a serious dedication to the healing arts. Most of the doctors who were on duty in this shabby Victorian building felt imprisoned and persecuted by the society they were meant to serve, so they took their revenge on the system by avoiding work at all costs.

For the A&E doctors it was often a nightmare to persuade the duty registrars to accept a sick person into one of their beds. The surgeons and the physicians would battle like feuding barons over patients with haematemesis, arguing coherently why the patient could not possibly be accepted into their speciality. Meanwhile the poor hapless patient was vomiting his blood and his life away on an uncomfortable trolley in the A&E corridor blissfully unaware that he was such an unwanted guest.

With even more aggression the gynaecologists and the surgeons would fight over women with lower abdominal pain, the surgeons maintaining that it was acute salpingitis (gynaecological) while the gynaecologist swore that it was acute appendicitis (surgical). Patrick Stanley, of course, revelled in these skirmishes and it was a point of honour for him to present the next duty registrar with a clean sheet of 'no admissions' after a night on call.

Patrick was in a particularly grisly mood when the telephone rang. In order to pacify the turbulent passions raging beneath his cranium, he was shampooing his unruly mop of Irish hair in the cracked porcelain washbasin in his room. He swore and let it ring a few times while he deliberated on this new hair shampoo he was using. It was flavoured with wild red apple (of all the unlikely things), and at first he found the smell interesting but with the second application it was definitely nauseating. Once he had satisfied himself that he disliked the shampoo he cursed the telephone for its insistence and with the white foam of the shampoo all over his hair and his hands, he picked up the receiver. Thank God they didn't live in an age of video-phones; the sight of a wild eyed Irishman with soapy suds all over his head would put off all but the most dedicated of callers. Once he realised it was the A&E registrar speaking he changed his mind.

'Patrick, Mike Varley here in A&E. I've got an interesting case that…'

'Man or woman?' interrupted Patrick incisively, being particularly careful not to sound friendly.

'That's the interesting point, Patrick, it's a man and…'

'Then it can't be gynaecological, and anyway,' he added, 'Men don't interest me at all.'

He was about to replace the receiver and get back to his shampooing but Mike Varley became even more insistent.

'Look, Patrick, it's a young fellow who says he sat on a plastic cup by accident and now it's jammed halfway up his rectum.'

'Accident, my arse,' groaned Patrick, momentarily unaware that the pun was rather inappropriate. 'I bet he's a bloody poof and he's got another fairy down there with him fretting about the place like a mother hen.'

'Well, so what if he is. Surely that's his business.' Mike Varley sounded like a politically correct sandal-wearing liberal.

'Well, if he is, you can bloody well tell him from me that I've had enough of queers to last me a lifetime. You probably heard on the hospital grapevine how that poof Pedro in the theatre has landed me in the shit with the law as well as burning the end of my hooter.'

Varley let out an exasperated sigh and then continued. 'I haven't time to listen to your prejudices right now, Patrick, but the fact is that the surgeons can't manage to disimpact it and Simon Bailey wants to do a laparotomy to get it out.'

'Is Simon over there?'

'No, but Nathan Goldberg, the houseman on surgery tonight, has talked to him on the phone and he's coming in to open him up.'

'Open who up? Goldberg or the poof?'

'Oh, for Christ's sake, Patrick, this isn't the time for your Irish wit. The point is that Goldberg could just feel it with the tip of his index finger and came up with the notion that it might just be possible to get it out with obstetric forceps.'

Patrick groaned and then spoke in a tone of voice that suggested he was communicating with an idiot. 'Listen, Michael, I don't know whether you've ever done any obstetrics, but you don't go putting obstetric forceps up people's arseholes. Just in case they never told you, they were designed for delivering babies through a completely different channel.'

'Patrick!' Mike Varley was shouting with despair. 'This fellow has sat on a plastic cup.'

'Michael,' Patrick replied, equally firmly, his Irish accent even thicker than usual. 'I don't care if he's sat on a bust of Queen Victoria. If he's a fellow he can't be gynaecological.'

Patrick replaced the receiver and resumed his hair washing, aware that he had been even more unreasonable than usual.

A few minutes later the telephone rang again but now his hair was dry, he was in a better frame of mind and, anyway, it was Joe Gibson, one of his drinking cronies.

'Now, Paddy, don't be so bog-Irish stubborn and listen to me. I've been called over here to put this character to sleep and normally I don't give a frig what goes on at the other end.'

'Good for you, Joseph. A particularly apt point of view in this case.' Patrick chuckled.

'But.'

'But what?'

'But Bodger Brackenbridge has somehow got in on the act and I can see him now, through the scrub room window, greasing up an enormous pair of forceps and brandishing them about like Attila the Hun.'

'Oh, dear Lord.' Patrick groaned.

'And although this character's arsehole has probably become accustomed to a certain amount of abuse, I've seen young Bodger in action over in the obstetric unit and…'

'All right, all right.'

'And lastly, Paddy.' Joe was warming to his conclusion now. 'I bet you a pint of draught Guinness that you can't get that egg cup out with a pair of forceps.'

That did it. 'Tell Bodger he's needed for an emergency on the fifth floor of the private wing, then put the poof to sleep and I'll be there in a flash. If you're willing to put your money where your mouth is, you'd better phone old Fred over in the Lust in the Dust and tell him to set the stout up.'

The following morning, Patrick was drinking coffee in the surgeon's changing room. He had been doing a list of minor cases with Joe Gibson administering the anaesthetic. They were waiting for Humphrey Hampson who had promised to perform a vaginal repair operation on one of the staff patients and Patrick had agreed to assist.

While they were having their second cup of coffee, Humphrey breezed in looking bright and eager. His stammer was particularly bad before lunch.

'M-m-m-m-m-morning all.'

He clapped his hands together and rubbed them briskly, indicating he was cold, and helped himself to the horrible chicory mixture that the hospital kitchens tried to pass off as coffee.

'H-h-heard you p-p-performed something rather st-st-staggering last night, P-Paddy old m-m-man.'

'Oh, twas nothing.' Patrick rather enjoyed basking in the reflected glory.

'He was brilliant,' said Joe Gibson. 'It came out a treat. He did it with such finesse that you'd have thought he'd been crawling up people's arseholes half his life.'

'Bollocks to you, Joseph Gibson, just because you lost your bet.'

'Best ch-ch-china, was it?' said Humphrey, delicately sipping his beverage as if he was at a vicar's tea party.

'Tupperware,' Patrick replied. 'Meant to be unbreakable.'

'M-m-m-meant to be?'

'Until Bodger came rushing in and was understandably rather agitated because he had missed the fun. He picked it up to examine it as if it was a precious Meissen porcelain vase then dropped it and smashed it on the theatre floor in dozens of pieces.'

CHAPTER FIVE
The Private Wing, St Giles' Hospital, London, August 1967

Angus Reith was a creature of habit and one of his habits was to take the last week in July, just after Matron's Ball, as a holiday to recuperate. Most of the senior staff who had been forced to dance with Matron or one of her high priestesses felt much the same way, but most of them only succeeded in floating around the wards of St Giles' looking haggard.

During Reith's absence Stanley was expected to assume consultant responsibility although, of course, he did not receive an increased salary appropriate to his elevated status. During that week the firm ran particularly smoothly; there were no temper tantrums, no tears and none of the patients was upset by medical brusqueness or rudeness. At the end of the week Patrick had been chatting socially with Sister Taylor and between them they had seriously concluded that the consultant rank was a definite obstacle to the smooth running of the National Health Service.

Well pleased with his week as top tit he had spent a quiet weekend with his parents-in-law, who owned an old pub in Midhurst, West Sussex. He had once thought that it was an astute Irish move to marry into the brewing trade but he had second thoughts after his in-laws had criticised him non-stop for the poverty that the salary of a junior hospital doctor brought to their daughter, when he could be driving a Rover 2000 and living in style like the rest of the well-off general practitioners in the neighbourhood.

On Monday he was in charge of the labour ward and was happily isolated from the rest of the hospital. On Tuesday he had spent the first half of the morning on a business round with Bodger Brackenbridge to make sure that all the patients were adequately clerked with all the requisite blood tests and radiological examinations performed in readiness for Reith's Grand Round the following day.

After morning tea he usually had an hour and a half to devote to a research project but invariably he found that some well-meaning soul had thought up another use for his only spare time during the week, although, in fairness, Patrick had no interest whatever in research. Predictably he received a phone

37

call from Humphrey Hampson, the senior registrar, informing him that Reith wanted him at eleven o'clock to assist with a total vulvectomy in the private wing of the hospital.

Patrick walked through the tunnel under the Edgware Road to the opulent private wing where the consultants ministered to the ills of the rich and famous. It always amused Patrick that the National Health side of the hospital was situated in the deprived district of Paddington, whereas the private wing had an address, much more exclusively, in Marylebone.

He changed into his theatre garb in the rather plusher surroundings of the private operating suite. Up here one wore white and the pyjama tops and bottoms tended to match, so one looked rather more like a television surgeon than was possible with the odds and sods apparel provided by the health service. He put on some white half-length rubber wellington boots and a smart white hat and went into the surgeon's coffee room to find Reith sitting in a corner chair reading some official correspondence while old Harry Squires was still tackling *The Daily Telegraph* general knowledge crossword from the previous weekend.

'Good morning, sir. Morning, Dr Squires.'

Neither of them moved or acknowledged him so Patrick went to help himself to some coffee. Real coffee in the private wing. He settled himself down in a chair, aware of the uncomfortable silence. The very act of stirring his coffee seemed to be making an outrageously loud noise. After an interminable time, old Harry announced that he was going off to anaesthetise the next case.

'Anyone important, Angus? I like to be able to give the appropriate chit-chat if they're out of the pages of *Burke's Peerage*.'

'Nothing to get excited about, Harry. She's the wife of the publican of the Rose and Crown down at Richmond. Been pulling pints with one hand and scratching her fanny with the other for the past twenty years. Fearful case of pruritus vulvae and leukoplakia; one of the worst I've ever clapped eyes upon. We took several biopsies and one area showed a low-grade vulval carcinoma so we might as well honk the lot out.'

Harry grunted and went out, leaving a stony silence in the room interrupted only by Reith turning the pages of his memorandum and Patrick slurping his coffee. When the consultant finished reading the document he carefully tucked it away in the breast pocket of his operating pyjamas and folded his arms over the rubber apron that covered his front.

'I've been wanting to have words with ye, laddie, about your conduct while I've been away.'

'Did you have a good holiday, sir?' said Patrick innocently, trying to take the sting out of the older man's words.

'Aye. Well, not really. The wife's been clamouring for a walking holiday in Scotland for years but, as it happened, it rarely stopped raining and when it did she refused to step foot out of the hotel because she could never see the tops of the mountains.'

'Often the way up there, sir. Quite similar to Irish weather, so they tell me.'

Reith frowned, rather disconcerted by this attempt to waylay him from the scent, but like a true Scottish terrier he continued to sniff the trail when he smelt blood at the end of it.

'Be that as it may, laddie, I'm concerned to see the large number of terminations done in my absence and even more concerned to see that five are booked on tomorrow's list.'

'I'll be quite happy to do them, sir,' said Patrick. He almost added 'as usual' but thought better of it.

'Not the point, laddie. When I leave you holding the fort I expect you to do things my way. You are surely aware of my opinion with regards to promiscuous young women. You know very well that if I'd been in command most of them would have been turned away.'

Patrick cringed. Ever since the Abortion Act had been passed in 1967 the gynaecological establishment had been split down the middle. There were those like Reith with conservative attitudes and those like Patrick who were more liberal. Patrick considered that his function as a doctor was to advise and inform the patients but never to impose moral judgments on them, while Reith abused his position to vent all his wrath and malice on these poor hapless young women carrying the fruits of their often illicit liaisons.

'I'm sorry, sir.' Patrick was clutching the handle of his cup. 'I find it very difficult to turn these girls away. I've a very compassionate nature and I've always tried to practise medicine according to my conscience.'

Reith looked blankly at him. 'Are ye a Catholic, laddie?'

39

'A lapsed Catholic, I'm afraid. I don't hold with the dogma as far as repro-
duction is concerned.'

Reith sighed. 'I thought so. Well, that's between you and your priest but
when I'm on leave, things will be done my way. When you're a consultant.' He
paused. 'I suppose I mean if you're ever a consultant, then you can do things
your way. In the meantime, in my absence there will be no more terminations
of pregnancy. And now, if you'll be so kind, you'll scrub up and help me take
this barmaid's vulva out.'

During the course of the long operation Patrick fumed inwardly from this
rebuke and settled into a protracted Irish sulk, but Reith was in fine voice
with a continued flow of banter, and vituperative criticism of the administration, the system and even the government flowed back and forth between the
surgeon and the anaesthetist.

A radical vulvectomy was a vile mutilating operation that involved hacking
out a huge segment of the lower abdomen and thighs and depriving the woman
of the clitoris and the labia majora, the cushion-like lips of tissue guarding
the entrance to the vagina, as well as removing all the lymphatic vessels that
drained the vulva and could act as channels for the spread of cancer.

Patrick reluctantly had to concede that Reith was good at this kind of surgery.
This operation required a coarse, aggressive approach with little need for per-
nickety dissection. The entire room stank of burning flesh as Reith divided the
yellowish fat tissue with the hot diathermy spatula in an attempt to cauterise the
ends of the numerous arteries as they were divided. For the really large arteries
this was insufficient to stem the flow and every now and then an enormous
spurt of bright red arterial blood would fountain into the air and Patrick would
be expected to dive into the wound to clamp off the severed vessel. Reith finished the dissection with the scalpel, hacking away at a huge area of skin and
yellow fat, brandishing his surgical knife with all the ferocity of a Visigoth from
the distant past.

The operation was completed by a futile attempt to bring the skin edges
together to close off the defect, but the stitches were under tension and Patrick
knew that over the next few days they would cut out and break down, leaving a
large gaping wound that would gradually granulate and heal over in the course
of the next six to eight weeks. Reith beamed with satisfaction after his hour

and a half of surgical assault, but the real work lay ahead for the ward sister and her team of nurses. They would have to dress the wound several times each day to prevent infection, de-sloughing and anointing it with honey or fresh papaya brought in at their own expense from the local street market to promote healing, turning the patient every few hours to prevent bed sores and, above all, cheering and cajoling her spirit and morale to prevent her from the inevitable feeling that the stinking ugly wound was a sign that she was rotting away.

After it was all over Patrick took his leave of the consultant and went down to the restaurant in the Medical School basement for lunch.

Even as he started to descend the stairs he could hear the combined noise and chatter of several hundred students and doctors interspersed with the clatter and clashing of crockery and cutlery.

Patrick took his place in the self-service queue and looked uneasily behind him to find a friendly face. He always dreaded the idea of having to eat alone or, even worse, having to deposit himself among a table of strangers. He was relieved to see Humphrey Hampson reading the *Times* in a far corner of the room as he collected a plateful of the chef's special, and went over to join him.

'Hello, old f-f-f-fellow.' Humphrey looked up over the top of the *Times*. 'What's that p-p-poison you're eating?'

'Chef's Special. Old Rose has decided to go continental and today's special is risotto of rice, of all things. Chef's knowledge of Italian is almost as fucking useless as his attempt at their cooking.'

'That's why I stick to cheese salad. Not much that can go wrong with that. Was His Lordship in good form this morning?'

Patrick nodded. 'He was in his element; radical vulvectomy on the landlord's wife of the Rose and Crown down by the river at Richmond.'

'That should see you clear for a few pints on the house.'

'Oh, I don't know. I'm not that desperate.'

Humphrey frowned. 'That's unlike you. Are you sick or something?'

'No, I'm just bloody well pissed off with the old sod.'

'Have you two had another fight?'

Patrick gave his sticky rice a disinterested stir.

'He just hauled me over the coals for agreeing to a load of terminations when he was away. I mean, Christ, what the hell am I supposed to do? I can't just turn these girls away and anyway, if he expects me to look after the shop when he's away he can surely let me do things my way.'

'That's probably why he overreacted in the clinic yesterday; caused quite a commotion. Did you hear about it?'

Patrick shook his head.

'Some poor Irish girl was asking for her third abortion and he went completely berserk. He called her a 'filthy whore' and accused her of coming over on the 'banana boat' to secure a free abortion at the expense of the British taxpayer.' Humphrey chuckled as he imagined the scene. 'He even accused the poor girl of having a 'potato picker' for a father.'

'The bastard,' said Patrick, slightly annoyed that Humphrey should find the situation even remotely funny. 'He's an arrogant bigot. It's so easy to take advantage of a pathetic Irish girl who's got herself in trouble. Personally I find that the most reprehensible abuse of our special position in society.'

'He went through the usual ritual, congratulated her on being pregnant, told her all about his infertility patients and how lucky she was compared with them. Even produced his celebrated pathology specimen of a fully formed foetus in utero just to show her what was being killed.'

'Reduced her to tears, I suppose.'

Humphrey nodded. 'The usual thing. Then after he examined her he announced that she was too big for a suction termination and told her that he would need to open up the uterus to remove it and would only do a hysterotomy if she agreed to be sterilised at the same time.'

'How many kids has she got?'

'None. Just three abortions by the age of twenty-three. Reith called her a 'filthy trollop' and said she wasn't fit for parenthood.'

'Jesus Christ.' Patrick almost choked on his food in disgust.

'She didn't agree, did she?'

'Apparently she did. She was as thick as a post and couldn't see beyond the problem of getting rid of her unwanted pregnancy.'

'I can't believe it.' Patrick pushed his plate away from him; the story had taken away all his appetite.

'A young girl deprived of motherhood at a stroke. Someone somehow has got to put an end to that bastard.'

On the other side of the Edgware Road, in the more opulent surroundings of the consultants' common room, the story aroused similar disgust. Angus had narrated the episode to his colleagues as he leaned back in a deep leather armchair puffing on an expensive cigar.

'Cheap little liar, abusing the facilities of the health service. I made damn sure she wouldn't be knocking at my door again.'

Maurice Hellman was in the room and although every cell in his body was incensed and disgusted by this action, he couldn't bring himself to voice any form of protest. Everything he had achieved in medical society had been by way of Angus Reith and though he was theoretically now on an equal footing, he still felt very much like the senior registrar of many years ago. He remembered only too clearly the times when Reith would level those bushy eyebrows at him requiring only a nod of assent at his every command. A nod of approval was required now, even though he could have happily vomited in disgust. A young girl of twenty-three was being sterilised, just because of the neo-Nazi viewpoints of her medical adviser. Adviser, he felt, was hardly the word to describe 'Lord' Reith, as he condemned the poor girl to a life deprived of the happy clatter of children's voices. Maurice Hellman have would given anything to stand up and tell Reith, in front of all the other consultants, that his action was as bad as anything that had taken place in the Nazi sterilisation camps, but his courage totally failed him; his legs turned to jelly, a small rivulet of perspiration trickled down from his forehead. He was spineless. He loathed himself at times like this. He left the room and avoided lunch for a long angry walk around the Serpentine in Hyde Park.

The Swinging Sixties had catapulted the youth of London into a permissive and promiscuous age. The evidence of venereal disease and drug abuse by teenagers was rising to epidemic proportions and the prevailing social atmosphere was one that condoned anything and everything. It was against this background that the Abortion Act became law, and the poor patients finding themselves with an unwanted pregnancy would drag themselves unwillingly to the hospital outpatient clinic to be met by consultants with differing opinions. If they were seen by Hellman, they would invariably get an abortion. If they were seen by Felicity Bundle, they would never get one because she campaigned actively on religious and humanitarian grounds for the rights of the unborn child. If they saw Reith, they might get one if they were married and overburdened with kids, but were unlikely to get one if they were single. Reith loathed promiscuous young girls, but his prejudices could be overcome by the hefty fee of a private consultation and he would be more inclined to perform an abortion in a West End nursing home if the patient was first seen privately in Harley Street. Somehow he acquired a different set of moral principles for the more elite clientele of Harley Street.

Reith's outpatient sessions were gaining a reputation as a kind of Gestapo interrogation session, and the students in his clinic would return to an eager audience in the junior doctors' common room to tell of the latest victim of his anger. Some of the phrases he used to describe these poor girls had become almost legendary, and many a tear was spilt during these sessions. Instead of pacifying him, they seemed to move him to greater depths of tyranny. He almost appeared to enjoy these interviews. They seemed to give him an opportunity to vent his revenge on the promiscuous society that he loathed so much. In reality, he detested them and was often heard to complain that since the invidious Act had been passed, he hated the outpatient clinic. Before, he used to look forward to Thursday afternoon but now, the end of the week was anticipated with dread.

It used to amaze some of his junior staff how little insight he had into his own behaviour, but in fact the Abortion Act had thrust itself like a dagger into his personal life. It had deprived him of a daughter, virtually lost him a wife and made an enemy of Maurice Hellman, the man whom he had guided through the career grades to consultant status in much the same way that Sir Hector McIntyre had nurtured him.

Maurice Hellman ruminated on these things as he walked around the Serpentine. He was a tall, gaunt man with childish features and golden-brown curly hair. His nose was upturned in an impish manner and from the nostrils sprouted some long bristly hairs that seemed so out of place on such a juvenile face. His features had held on to youth to an almost embarrassing degree and even as a consultant in a large teaching hospital, he was always being taken for a student by the patients. His appearance was always made more collegiate by his habit of wearing a Trinity College Field Club scarf and a pair of kid gloves even in summer. Added to this, he often sported a pair of granny spectacles, similar to those worn by John Lennon, which was his sole outward concession to the trendiness of the age he lived in. Inwardly, however, he seethed with ideas of women's liberation and equality of the sexes, which often made people remark that his sex chromosome karyotype and that of Felicity Bundle had somewhere suffered a translocation phenomenon.

He sat on a bench and watched some children feeding bread to the ducks as the Norland Nannies looked on and formed a huddle, exchanging gossip about their rich and famous employers in Knightsbridge, on the other side of the park. He gazed at the surrounding serenity as the beautiful park displayed its greenery in the sunshine and became an oasis of peace and tranquillity with rowing boats on the placid lake, and he saw grandfathers taking their children's offspring for a walk, their misty eyes displaying all the hidden secrets of rejuvenation. He saw all these things, and instead of inhaling the friendliness of it all, his eyes showed the anxiety and troubles that were at the source of his neurasthenia. That's what the psychiatrist had called it. The old-fashioned term that had been largely abandoned since the Great War had been recalled by a well-known London psychiatrist to explain his problem. His recurrent migraines, tension headaches and insomnia, which took him away from work for several days each month, and owing to the cyclical nature of his complaint, were always referred to by staff and students alike as 'Hellman's dysmenorrhoea'. He knew they looked upon him as a woman with all the associated monthly frailties, but to him, they were utterly real and his monthly migraine was an ordeal that he could scarcely endure and no medication that he had tried could prevent it. He was regarded as a feeble member of the department who was unable to take any strain and who was repeatedly pleading sick to excuse himself from emergency calls. Yet, underneath all these psychosomatics was a mind that had championed abortion law reform and had adhered resolutely to the ideas that he believed in. Therein, of course, lay the basis of his altercation with Reith, for in his own way, Maurice Hellman was equally stubborn. Unfortunately, his feeble frame and delicate emotions lacked the charisma to win in any outright battle and he shuddered as he recalled his head-on conflict with the pillar of the establishment who had been his consultant for so many of his formative years.

Fate had played an interesting role as impresario in the drama, and the devil himself must have watched happily as the plot unfolded and the inevitable debris and wreckage was left in its wake, in much the same way as a hurricane marches over a tropical island destroying everything in its path. It was fate that arranged for Reith's lovely daughter Louisa to lose her virginity to one of the local rogues while Reith was away on a conference-cum-world tour with his wife in Australia. He had taken an extended leave of three months and by the time he had returned he should have been unaware that his daughter's pregnancy had been signed, sealed and delivered into a black plastic bag and burnt in a hospital incinerator.

Poor Louisa. She was the product of two struggling parents. Her father had risen from the coalfields of Lanark to the upper echelons of London medical society, and, for all of his youth, he had made medicine his mistress, eschewing female company until he was safe and secure in a top consultant post. Instead of marrying a nurse and living in relative poverty during those early lean years, he had waited until wealth and possession were his, and then had married someone who was far removed from his milieu. His wife, Helena, was a model; highly successful with a wispy figure that was guaranteed to make clothes look good. She had been on the cover of *Vogue* and *Elle*, but despite the aristocratic peal of her assumed name, she came from some slum tenements in Stepney, and although the accent had been removed at Lucy Clayton's School of Modelling, the abysmal ignorance of her thought processes were all too apparent by the howlers she often dropped when they were in intelligent company. Angus had married her for her body and her fame and her refreshing candour about sex. She had invited him to bed on the first evening they met, and after the wildest night that his dour Scottish fantasies could imagine, she had from then on withheld her favours until a promise of marriage was forthcoming. She held him foaming at the mouth and there was scarcely time for an engagement, although the wedding, being a society function, took a while to organise.

Many a model is a failed actress, but Helena Reith took the stage in her stride and, for the next few years, she played mother and socialite and even aspired to helping on the Wellbeing of Women charity committee at the Royal College of Obstetricians and Gynaecologists and manning the Ladies' Association flower stall on two evenings a week outside the hospital during visiting hours; for this was expected of consultants' wives.

If she had affairs, they were always discreet. Just as she had been the model of a model, she was now the model of a wife, but as a mother she always remained a little distant. She felt, somewhat unreasonably, that the arrival of Louisa had ruined her career. In fact, she had regained her figure admirably and could compete with many a teenage model, but her husband, reacting like a Scottish autocrat, had strictly forbidden any further commercialisation of his wife's image. In a sense, he was insanely jealous of her, and although he pretended it was unseemly for a consultant's wife to work, he was merely protecting himself from her involvement in the obvious fleshy temptations of the world of the fashion industry.

Angus was many years older than Helena, but despite the disparity in years the family functioned as a viable unit and affection was lavished on the only daughter by a doting father and a beautiful mother. To Angus, his daughter was perfection incarnate and could do no wrong. She went to the best schools, had the best clothes and was only introduced, socially, to the best of friends. It would have come as a great shock to him to find that, instead of staying with school friends during his absence in Australia, his seventeen-year-old daughter was having a liaison with the long-haired son of the local Italian restaurant owner. Louisa was remarkably uninformed about the possible consequences of her pleasure, since she had always been treated by her parents like a china doll and, in their eyes, she was still a child. The Italian boy obviously thought differently and in an age when nearly all his lays were on the pill, he was unable to revert to coitus interruptus in the face of so much visual excitement, for young Louisa was indeed lovely.

Like a forest on a dry day, she ignited immediately and after her first missed period, she consulted with her knowing friends and sent off a little bottle of urine to a discreet pregnancy testing service that advertised in most women's magazines. When the result was a sickening positive, she turned to the only medical friend she knew, her father's young colleague, Maurice Hellman.

Maurice had often been invited for tea when he was Reith's registrar and later on when he was promoted to consultant, he was allowed to come to dinner. On several of these occasions Helena would be in one of her moods and Reith would be occupied with piles of paperwork. Maurice had become part of the family and he spent much of his time talking and joking with Louisa. It was only natural that she should turn to him in time of trouble and she was secretly grateful that this particular dilemma was during her father's long absence in Australia since the two doctors shared adjoining consulting rooms in Harley Street.

Hellman was pitched into a nightmare situation. Here he was, a staunch believer in abortion, especially for young unmarried teenagers, suddenly confronted with the beguiling eyes and beseeching expression of the daughter of his mentor. Ethically and morally, he was at a crossroads and there were huge warning signs in all directions. He knew the feelings of Reith on the subject of illegitimate pregnancy and he shuddered to think of the wrath if he found his beloved Louisa in this condition. The fact that the putative father was an Italian Catholic would more than treble the decibels of his rage. Not only was Reith anti-Catholic but he regarded all foreigners as less than adequate.

On the other hand, he could not bring himself to abandon his own principles and he also had a genuine desire to help the poor girl since she was so utterly distraught and tearful and hopelessly out of her depth. He thought for a while and decided that he would have to take a risk and see if the whole procedure could be completed before Reith returned. Luckily, Hellman worked only part-time at St Giles. He spent several sessions each week at a hospital in north London and he arranged to have Louisa admitted there. He asked her to be discreet and not to tell the junior doctors or nurses who her father was. He then spoke to his registrar at the West Hampstead Hospital and told him to make sure that absolute discretion was maintained throughout.

The operation went smoothly and Hellman himself performed the honours. He took care that only his trusted theatre sister was present in the operating theatre and that everyone involved should be utterly secretive, and when she was discharged he was certain that the secret would be well guarded. There was no possible way that Reith could discover what happened, unless, of course, Louisa told him, and that was unlikely. Everyone involved started to relax and although they felt like conspirators, it was generally agreed that the chance of discovery was remote indeed.

Unfortunately, fate had stepped in and ensured that there were two loopholes in all this knavery that had not been closed. In the first place, Louisa had been so nervous when she had registered at the hospital that she had made a stupid error. The registration desk was manned by a horsey-looking female in a tweed jacket and horn-rimmed glasses secured by a chain. She looked at Louisa with obvious disdain as she took her particulars.

'Name?'

'Age?'

'Address?'

'Married, single or widowed?'

'What are you in for? Let's see – what are you in for?'

A glance at the admissions card and a look of thinly disguised hostility.

'Religion? If you're an atheist, we just put C of E.'

'Next of kin? So that we can contact them in the event of emergency or death' – very reassuring, these clerks, and this is only the first impression of the hospital.

'Have you been admitted here before?'

'Name of consultant?'

'Name of GP?'

'Oh,' said Louisa. 'We don't have a GP. Daddy looks after all our aches and pains.'

The receptionist looked up, scarcely bothering to disguise her disapproval.

'Oh, he does, does he? How nice for you. And what do we call 'Daddy' just for the records?'

'Well, it's Reith, of course. Dr Angus Reith. We look upon him as our GP.'

The receptionist reached behind her and removed a copy of the medical directory to check on the validity of this person. She gave the impression that she trusted no one. Finally, after thumbing the pages, she grunted and wrote down: GP Dr A Reith, 157 Harley Street, London W1.

The interrogation was over and Louisa was directed to her ward.

Hellman had covered every possibility. He had directed the registrar not to send a GP's summary on the case, and had explained the reasons for this. Unfortunately, fate put its ugly foot in things yet again.

The compilation of summaries was one of the most tedious chores in the registrar's working week. After a hard day in the operating theatre or the out-patients' department, he was expected to look through the notes of the patients who have been discharged from the ward and dictate a concise summary of their hospital stay. The GP received a tentative diagnosis about one of his flock and usually accepted the suggested line of treatment.

In point of fact, these summaries were not done on a daily basis and they tended to pile up in the medical secretary's office. Usually, they were done on the Saturday afternoon of a weekend on duty with the registrar sitting alone and forlorn surrounded by silent typewriters under their protective dust covers. He spoke intermittently into a dictaphone, pausing frequently to decipher the appalling writing of some of the housemen. The summaries tended to become more clipped as the afternoon wore on and he occasionally inserted the odd joke for the typists when they returned on Monday morning, especially if some of them were flirtatious, and some of them usually were.

Hellman's registrar at the West Hampstead was valiantly trying to finish all his outstanding summaries before he went on his annual holiday. It was usually considered uncharitable to land a pile of notes on the poor unsuspecting locum when he arrived to take your post for two weeks. He was also more mindful on this occasion, because Hellman had created such an aura of secrecy around the abortion of Louisa Reith. He was careful therefore not to send any summary on her particular case.

The dictaphone was connected to a central recording bank next door to the secretarial supervisor's office. On Monday the supervisor listened briefly to the records dictated over the weekend and distributed them to the individual secretaries of each department. She grunted with disapproval as she listened. Someone had found the machine to have finished recording and had gone down to the recording bank and had fiddled with central control, despite her regular warnings to all medical staff not to do this. Doctors never took a blind bit of notice of the clerical staff and now one of them would have to suffer as a consequence. After the gynaecology registrar had completed twelve summaries, he had been interrupted in mid-sentence by one of the cardiothoracic team. She looked at the pile of gynaecology folders and saw about sixty that were supposed to have been completed. She sighed again. It was hard enough to get the doctors to do these things at all, and it was even harder for her to make them understand they would have to do them again. She returned the folders to the gynaecology secretary's office again with an explanatory note and they were left for the locum to finish them during his fortnight as a substitute. The man in question was an Egyptian, rather lonely in London, and for want of something better to do, he applied himself with vigour to the uncompleted summaries, and, quite unaware of the conspiracy surrounding Louisa, he sent a concise reconstruction of her termination of pregnancy to the GP listed on her admission sheet – Dr Angus Reith of 157 Harley Street, London W1.

CHAPTER SIX

Ladbroke Grove, west London, summer 1968

One of the most perverse peculiarities of the National Health Service as far as the patients are concerned is the fact that it is difficult to get uniformity of opinion or care during the time that they are being processed through the socialised sausage machine. The girl whom Patrick was going to operate on through the laparoscope the following day was a case in point. Her name was Joanna Spinetti, a trendy, intelligent girl who spoke English with a Cheltenham Ladies' College accent despite her Italian name, and who gave her occupation as 'in television'. This was about as far as most media people were prepared to commit themselves to the hospital records clerks. They were either 'in television' or 'in newspapers' regardless of whether they owned the thing, wrote its scripts or merely scrubbed its floors. They were almost universally hostile to doctors and hospitals because many of them were trying to get copy from their illnesses or misfortunes and they usually found more to write or talk about if they provoked the staff.

In return, the doctors usually loathed journalists, and other media folk only slightly less so, because they seemed to be unable or unwilling to report even the simplest facts correctly. When St Giles had successfully performed more than a hundred renal transplants, some bright spark from Fleet Street had proudly proclaimed in headlines that they had just operated on their first. Transplants were all the rage at the time because of the media frenzy surrounding the first heart transplant in South Africa by Chris Barnard, and some reporter, his brain doubtless addled by alcohol after a boozy lunch at El Vino in Fleet Street (where they served Montrachet by the glass), had decided to mark up a first for a London teaching hospital – five years too late. It was this total incompetence and ineptitude at medical reporting that annoyed the doctors and it was the physicians' arrogance and pomposity that upset the media people. Both sides were squaring for a fight from the time of admission to the day of discharge and unless the reporters went out in the tin box they usually had the last say.

Admittedly, Joanna Spinetti had something to complain about. She had been to see her local general practitioner for the first time since moving into her new flat in Little Venice. He had a practice on the dubious frontier between St John's Wood, inhabited mainly by the trendy and wealthy, and Kilburn, with its ghetto of West Indian immigrants and poor London Irish. Little did she know that her GP operated a crafty scheme whereby he paid junior doctors from St Giles the princely sum of three guineas to take his evening surgery while he made fifty times that amount in a private practice in Notting Hill Gate, an area famously populated by affluent bankers, trendy hedge fund managers and the rising stars of the silver screen.

For Patrick, this was his first experience of general practice and, as it turned out, it strengthened his resolve to stay in hospital medicine. He had arrived slightly early at a dilapidated building in Ladbroke Grove and had been horrified by the squalor of the surroundings. The waiting room was not only filthy but was seething with humanity of all ages, shapes and sizes. A middle-aged and rather testy receptionist had guided him through the crowd into the consulting room, which was drab and dreary and furnished only with a cheap desk and a bare examination couch.

'Is that where I examine the patients?' Patrick asked anxiously, for there were no sheets or pillows on the worn leather surface.

'Oh, I hope you're not one of them that goes in for that kind of thing. I've had enough trouble with folks like that from the hospital playing all high and mighty. There's not much wrong with most of this lot, you either write them up for some pills or a sick sheet and any that have a real problem you refer to the outpatient department up at the hospital otherwise we'll be here all night. Suit yourself but I shut up shop at seven prompt and I'm on the bus for home ten minutes later. Anyway,' she added, to banish the finer clinical thoughts from his mind, 'we don't have no gloves and at the moment we don't have no running water so there's nowhere to wash your hands.'

With that she dumped a wad of blank prescriptions on the desk and told him to sign fifty of them, 'for the regulars'. Patrick was concerned by the dubious legality of this but she soon silenced his protests by describing the alternative situation of a clinic that might go on forever.

After the first few patients he soon settled into the routine. He found that they usually told him exactly what they wanted: sick leave, a prescription for contraceptive pills or just some tonic to pick them up. They were coming in every minute or so and he soon found that his pen was poised on the prescription pad after merely glancing at them. They were a motley crowd of snivelling kids, sore throats, raving neurotics and malingerers and anything that looked as if it might require more than fifteen seconds of thought was sent up to the hospital. Joanna Spinetti fell into the latter category.

Joanna was having a prolonged and heavy period that had lasted for just over three weeks and after trying a number of home cures found herself sitting opposite Patrick Stanley in this rather grubby consulting room. This was her first visit and as far as she was concerned this was her new general practitioner. For Patrick this was a problem belonging to his own speciality that required a diagnosis to be made before the appropriate treatment could be instituted. He looked forlornly at the bare examination couch with its rickety legs, and then the thought of his hands smelling of vaginal secretions on the tube all the way back home to Acton had soon abolished any altruistic notions from his head. He merely told her that this was a job for a specialist and wrote a short referral letter addressed simply to 'The Consultant Gynaecologist, St Giles' Hospital', and sent her on her way to arrange an appointment.

One can only imagine her surprise when three weeks later she found herself in the hospital outpatient clinic confronted by Patrick Stanley, the very person who had referred her in the first place. It was the week after Matron's Ball, Reith was on leave and Patrick was acting as consultant in his absence. Stanley looked at the letter written in his own handwriting and, as if it was the most normal thing in the world, proceeded to take an accurate history of her complaint and then examined her under the watchful eye of a nurse chaperone in the adjoining room. At no time did he indicate that they had met before and it was no wonder that she started to think that members of the healing arts were slightly bent.

Patrick had found a cyst on the right ovary about the size of a plum. It was only just palpable when he performed a deep bimanual examination, but he could just distinguish it as a soft cystic structure between the finger of his right hand deep in the vagina and those of his left hand that were kneading her abdominal wall as if he was making bread.

'Sorry to be so rough, but there's just a chance that I can burst it by pressing it between my fingers.' This was acutely painful for Joanna, and she was relieved when he desisted. 'Listen, dear, you've got a wee cyst on one of your ovaries and it's secreting rather a lot of oestrogen, which is causing this long period. Usually they go away on their own accord but we'd like to check you again in six weeks to see if it's grown any bigger. If it has then we usually do a small operation to remove it.'

'Operation', she gulped, her eyes opening wide with alarm.

'Only a small one and we usually do it through a special telescope so that it leaves no scar.' He gave her one of his most reassuring Irish smiles and patted her gently on the shoulder. 'These things are very common in young women. It's not cancer or anything nasty like that so don't you go and worry your pretty little head about it.'

Six weeks later she found herself in the imposing presence of Angus Reith, who was so delighted to find some palpable pathology that he had about six students examine her with varying degrees of delicacy until she felt like a well-used whore.

Reith was very excited and put her down to come in the following day for laparotomy.

'But the other doctor said it was nothing to worry about.'

'Oh, I wouldn't take any notice of him,' said Reith with an air of amused dismissal. 'He's only a beginner. I'm the consultant in charge of this firm.'

Joanna's eyes shot up as her man of so many parts was so tritely dismissed. 'But he said that it could probably be dealt with using the telescope so that there would hardly be any scar. That's important to me, you see, because I'm in television.'

'Madam, I don't care if you're the Royal Ballet and the Dagenham Girl Pipers all rolled into one; when I say operation I mean operation and there's an end to it. Before this silly trend for parading around beaches in bits of string, women were prepared to suffer a surgical scar and indeed many of my older patients point to it with a certain amount of pride.'

Joanna was bristling with anger and alarm but in the six-week interval between her visits, she had read a good deal about her condition and taken advice from several of her trendy friends and the glamorous lady doctor at London Weekend Television where she worked. It appeared to be rather fashionable to have a laparoscopy and Joanna was prepared to stand up for her rights.

'I'm sorry but I refuse to put up with any unnecessary disfiguration. A friend of mine had a similar thing done at University College Hospital where they used the laparoscope and the scar is almost impossible to see, so I will just have to go along there.'

She could not have hit on a more tender spot for Reith. There were two consultants that he loathed with all his venom and both of them worked at University College Hospital, and he could not abide the thought of their condescending comments about such a referral. He reluctantly agreed to let her have a laparoscopy on condition that they could proceed to a formal laparotomy if they were unable to deal with the cyst through the laparoscope.

Her admission to St Giles was no less confusing as she passed from one white-coated figure to another. She found it difficult to distinguish between doctors, medical students and porters. When she finally reached the ward an untidy youth in a short white coat took her story yet again and she began to wish she had brought a tape recording of her condition. She surmised that he must be a student because although he was very talkative and affable, he was rather nervous and gave advice on her complaint that was both vague and nebulous.

Later still, another white-coated figure appeared and listened to her chest again and put off all her questions by announcing that although he was an anaesthetist he would not be giving her anaesthetic and she would have to address her questions to a different person in the morning.

Around nine in the evening another doctor appeared. This one was rather serious with heavy horn-rimmed glasses on a prominent nose and he, like the others, made her take off her nightdress yet again. Unknown to her, this was Bodger Brackenbridge who was rather late clerking the new admissions because he had been attending a prayer meeting. Joanna stripped off her clothing and idly wondered if word had got around that she had a spectacular pair of tits and any of the hospital staff who felt so inclined were coming along to take a surreptitious peep.

After Bodger had performed the same ritual examination he handed her a piece of paper to sign which said, in long-winded legalese, that she had absolutely no choice whatever when it came to the surgeon who performed the operation or even the operation he performed.

'But I absolutely refuse to sign this document. It's monstrous. I'm virtually signing my life away.'

'Now listen, dear, please don't get hysterical with me because I didn't invent the form. It's an absolutely standard document that is used in all hospitals throughout the country and I'm told on good authority that legally it's not worth the paper it's written on. So be a good girl and sign on the dotted line or they won't put you to sleep.'

'But I insist the consultant does the operation – after all, he's the one that arranged to have me admitted.'

'Oh, you media people can be an awful pain. You take up twice as much time as anyone else.' Bodger rubbed his eyes wearily and replaced his glasses on his nose.

Joanna decided that the time had come to put her foot down. She was virtually screaming at Bodger. 'I absolutely insist that Mr Reith does the operation.'

'I hate to tell you this but Mr Reith doesn't even know how to do the operation. Doesn't know one end of a laparoscope from the other. Mr Stanley's the best we have when it comes to laparoscopy – absolute star, crackerjack – in fact, I would say that he is the current whizz kid in keyhole surgery.'

'But he's my family doctor!' cried Joanna.

'Must be a different Dr Stanley.' Bodger was yawning now. 'Listen, dear, I'm awfully tired and I've still got three patients to see. Just sign on the dotted line and we can all start thinking about a bit of shut-eye.'

Joanna was so confused by now that she signed the form like a zombie. Her mind was racing with conflict and worry but the only person to talk to was the night cleaner who was gently sweeping under her bed.

'As ah sees it, luv,' the old girl said in a broad cockney accent, 'it's a case of them wot can does. Don'chew worry yerself, ducks. They all worry like you the night before but most of 'em pull through. Of course we 'ave 'ad the odd nasty but it's generally all over wiv'em before they're under starter's orders. You'll be all right, luv, you mark my words.'

Joanna wearily took the sleeping tablets that were offered her by the night staff nurse and sank into a dreamless sleep.

CHAPTER SEVEN
Gynaecology operating theatre, St Giles' Hospital, London

Although Reith made such a song and dance about abortions, he was delighted to be able to perform sterilisations. The simple ritual of tying tubes and combating the population explosion was one of the small pleasures gynaecology still offered him. Even in this sphere he was being forced into a defensive position by recent developments.

This was due to the invention of the laparoscope, a stainless-steel tube about eighteen inches long which carried an optical rod lens system and was illuminated by a fibre-optic cable coming from a halogen light source set beside the patient. Once inserted, the operator was able to get a splendid view of all the pelvic organs and could also see the appendix and even as high up in the abdominal cavity as the liver and gall bladder.

Reith had stood against the rising flood of popularity for this instrument like King Canute before the incoming tide. As a bastion of the old establishment he had resented the intrusion of a technique that he could not master, or at least would not master, for he had made no serious attempt to learn how to use it. Instead he had decried, derided, criticised and scorned it, and for a long time had forbidden it to be used on his patients.

Somewhere in the back of his mind, he wanted to be remembered as one of the great masters of pelvic surgery and to have a portrait to this effect in the hall of the Royal College of Obstetricians and Gynaecologists in Regent's Park. He wanted his name to be revered alongside those of Fothergill and Hawkins, Bonney and Fletcher Shaw. It was simply not dignified for a man such as him to have to learn a new technique at the age of fifty-eight. He made a few half-hearted efforts but they had always ended dismally and he had cast aside the expensive pieces of stainless-steel optics and asked for a scalpel so that he could do the operation the 'proper way'.

Unfortunately, the era of the consultant dictators was on the wane. In modern times the patients themselves increasingly requested their treatment of preference after studying their condition or symptoms in general medical textbooks which were increasingly available in the local library. Did he do sterilisations through the laparoscope? Certainly not. And they would go away to another unit where they could be de-fertilised in a cosmetic manner leaving virtually no scar. Then there was the increasing awareness of cost-effectiveness and medical auditing that would have made Sir Hector shudder in his grave. Little men from the Department of Health, armed with clipboards, were always demanding to know why the bed occupancy per operation was abnormally high in his unit.

So he gave in slowly and reluctantly trying, whenever possible, to castigate this 'instrument of the devil' as he called it. But more than the instrument itself, he resented the new breed of doctor who used it with such consummate skill. Patrick Stanley was one of these; he virtually never missed and he did it with such grace and finesse. Ice-cool. Never a wasted movement and always that look of haunting confidence that Reith was beginning to hate. He had even published papers on the use of the laparoscope in certain gynaecological conditions and, worse, the Professor of Medicine was referring cases directly to him so that he could do laparoscopic liver biopsies. The ignominy of it. When Reith was a registrar, referrals from other units always went as a matter of courtesy to the consultant but, as the Professor of Medicine had pointed out with his familiar brand of logic, this was quite pointless since the consultant gynaecologist was unable to perform the procedure.

So the laparoscope had come to stay, but Reith had refused to adjust to the presence of the newcomer. He never made anything more than the feeblest attempts to learn how to use it and had poured scorn on every problem that arose in association with its use. He insisted that he be present when Stanley used the laparoscope 'just in case he gets into any trouble'. He had to be shown the view of the pelvis although he always insisted that he couldn't see a blind thing through the laparoscope. He always told the patients how much pain they would feel the following day and would be deliriously happy whenever any minor complications arose. Against this background it was a tribute to Patrick's tenacity that he could survive and even succeed under such a barrage of hostility.

Reith was teaching the students in one corner of the theatre but he was watching for any mistake so that he could pounce. Stanley knew this but never let it erode his confidence for he had done many hundreds of laparoscopies and was aware of his special talent with this instrument. Modesty and humility were not prominent among his attributes; he knew he was bloody good at his job and that helped him through these ordeals when less positive characters might have wilted.

Joanna Spinetti was asleep. The assistant had emptied the bladder with a thin plastic catheter and had put a toothed pair of vulsellum forceps on the cervix. He had introduced a special stainless-steel dilator to open the cervical canal to about five millimetres and then gently inserted it into the cavity of the uterus and clamped it into place so that he could move the womb in any direction that the operator required. Patrick turned around with a flourish and painted the abdomen with iodine and then covered the patient with sterile towels. He looked like the magician at a children's party, his every gesture deliberate and almost theatrical. Reith was watching him with ill-concealed malice.

Joanna had an athletic figure with a prominent pubis that made her look rather bony when she was anaesthetised. Patrick regarded a woman's body like a treasured work of art and he took immense care making a small vertical incision about one centimetre long just inside the navel so that it could never be detected.

'Get on, laddie, it's not the Mayo clinic.' This was Reith's standard remark when any of his juniors tried to disguise the ugly scars of surgery.

Patrick paid no attention to these ringside comments that flowed freely during his laparoscopies. He connected the Veress needle to the carbon dioxide insufflator to check that it was patent. This needle was invented by Janos Veress, a Hungarian chest physician, in the early part of the twentieth century, in order to collapse the lungs of his tuberculosis patients before the invention of the anti-tuberculosis antibiotic streptomycin. It was a thin hollow needle with a sharp tip about eight inches long with a clever mechanism to lessen the chance of the bowel being perforated during insertion. As soon as the peritoneum, the thin membrane that enclosed the abdominal cavity, had been pierced there was a sudden loss of resistance, causing a spring-loaded mechanism to function and push a blunt end over the sharp edge of the needle. This was the most delicate part of the procedure. In the next few minutes, the operation could fail or succeed. There were several structures that could be pierced and it was vital to get the needle point just beneath the peritoneum without damaging the bowel or bladder or, even more seriously, the great vessels running in front of the vertebral column that were perilously close, especially in a thin girl like Joanna Spinetti.

Patrick picked up a fold of skin midway between the navel and the shaven pubic hair. He poised the needle like a pen and, with delicate artistry, he traversed the layers of the abdominal wall using the sensations transmitted to his fingers to tell him the exact anatomical position of the needle tip. He felt the distinctive double click as he pierced first the dense fascial layer, then the elastic peritoneum, and he knew he was just right. A few more centimetres and he would be into the guts with the danger of a faecal peritonitis or into the covering omentum that, if distended with gas, would ruin the whole procedure. A few centimetres less and the gas would be on the wrong side of the peritoneum, producing emphysema of the abdominal wall as it filled with carbon dioxide gas, forcing him to abandon the procedure and submit to Reith's mockery.

He fitted the plastic gas pipe to the carbon dioxide insufflator machine and by looking at the flow and pressure recorders, he could be happy that the gas flow was not obstructed. It was flowing freely and the pressure was less than ten millimetres of mercury, which was satisfactory and indicated that the needle was in the correct place.

In a girl of this size, he would put about four to five litres of gas into her until the pressure reached twenty-five millimetres of mercury, so he busied himself checking his instruments and wiring up the diathermy connections and putting the laparoscope itself in a long container of warm water to prevent it from misting up and obscuring the view. He made a few inconsequential remarks to Joe Gibson, the anaesthetist, who was watching the electrocardiogram oscilloscope in order to detect any cardiac arrhythmias caused by hypercapnoea, due to the large amount of carbon dioxide introduced, and to the splinting of the diaphragm caused by the distension of the abdominal cavity with this large volume of gas. In addition, the operating table was adjusted to give a steep seventy-five degree head-down tilt to get the wormlike coils of intestine out of the pelvis so the reproductive organs could be clearly seen.

Because of these problems, old Harry Squires, the consultant anaesthetist, had much the same fear and trepidation about laparoscopy as did his surgical colleague. He preferred to leave the electronic monitoring and the difficulties of the anaesthesia to a younger colleague.

So the two old buffers stood in the wings making disparaging remarks while the younger generation demonstrated their skill. Patrick percussed the stretched drumskin of the patient's abdominal wall to satisfy himself that it had a uniform tympanitic sound and that the gas was evenly dispersed. Then he picked up the heavy sharp trocar that was going to enlarge the tunnel into the patient's abdominal cavity. This part of the procedure called for strength of the wrist and a certain knack in getting the wide-calibre hollow tube into the abdominal wall. This was where most would-be laparoscopists failed and, in particular, some of the more delicate female gynaecologists were unable to gather the requisite strength for this manoeuvre.

Angus grimaced.

'Easy with that thing, Stanley. I don't want any deaths on my operating table. Looks damned dangerous to me, Harry.'

'The whole procedure's damned dangerous, Angus. Did ya hear they had a mishap in Edinburgh a few months ago? Lost a young mother of four during a simple sterilisation. Perforated the aorta and she was dead by the time the vascular surgeons arrived. I wonder we don't a lose a lot more than we do.'

Patrick looked knowingly at Joe Gibson.

Both of them were now well used to this mumbo-jumbo diatribe from their respective consultants. Patrick picked up the long, pointed trocar and with the head nestling firmly in his cupped palm, he exerted sufficient force and a gentle screwing action to get this wider tube with its sharp point into the now distended abdomen. The danger here was to push the trocar too far, which was why he had inserted so much carbon dioxide that the abdominal wall was as far as possible from the great vessels. He had heard of the case Harry Squires was referring to when a registrar had inserted the trocar at the wrong angle and had pierced the abdominal aorta, the largest blood vessel in the body. As he released the pressure valve, a great spurt of blood had leapt out of the body like a fountain rising several feet above the patient. In fact, they didn't lose the patient. As chance would have it, the consultant gynaecologist supervising him had, amazingly, completed six months in vascular surgery and was able to slit the patient open in seconds, stop the flow of blood by applying pressure to the large artery and then repair the damage with the help of another vascular surgeon and reinforce it by a synthetic fibre graft.

Once he had pierced the peritoneum, the shiny membrane lining the abdominal cavity, Patrick carefully altered the angle of insertion by forty-five degrees and aimed the sharp point into the pelvis but even so, he knew he was only an inch or so away from the aorta as it coursed over the sacral promontory, the lowest part of the vertebral column. Once he was safely in, he immediately stopped pushing and withdrew the sharp trocar, leaving the hollow tube running through the abdominal wall. He pressed the valve plunger and the reassuring hiss of gas under pressure told him that he was in the correct place.

With a flourish, he reached for the long telescope, and at the same time, lifted his nose upwards as if to register an expression of disdain or contempt, but in reality to dislodge his mask from his nose so that the eyepiece of the laparoscope would not get fogged by condensation from his breath. He released the valve briefly, introduced the laparoscope and connected the fibre-optic cable from the light source. Now the scene was entirely his. His own world of 'What the Butler Saw', but this time he was seeing the sexual diorama from the inside. He nosed around, asking the assistant to move the uterus this way and that so he could take in the whole field of view.

Reith resented this moment more than any other. This protracted silence robbed him of his consultant superiority. He would dearly love to wrench the instrument out of the hands of his precocious junior, but the laws of asepsis and sterility were sufficiently ingrained in him to prevent such a barbaric intrusion.

'See anything, Stanley, or are you in the bladder? Don't keep us in suspense, laddie.'

Then he would hover behind Patrick's shoulder like a child trying to get at his Christmas parcels. Patrick could feel his breath on his shoulder but he deliberately prolonged this moment of glory, much to the consultant's chagrin.

'Mmmm.'

Silence.

'What can you see, laddie?'

'Uh, huh… Mmmmm.'

'Come on, Stanley, have you been struck dumb or something?'

God, he'd like to kick his registrar up the arse for keeping him hanging around in anticipation like this.

'Does she have a mass on the left?'

'Mmmmmm. Interesting.'

'Well come on, laddie, does she or doesn't she? We can't wait around all day.'

Patrick stood up abruptly, causing Reith to take a smart step backwards to avoid contaminating the surgeon.

'She has an ovarian cyst. It looks like a corpus luteum haematoma or a follicular cyst that has had a bleed into it. That would account for her pain, of course. At the very outside a haemorrhage into a cystadenoma. Would you like to have a look, sir? Incidentally, the cyst is on the right.'

Reith crouched over the telescope after Stanley had checked the field of view. He was forbidden to touch the instrument because he was technically unsterile. In a sense, it was humiliating having to accept whatever scene his junior chose for him. He would love to have seized the laparoscopes and conducted his own personal tour of the pelvis, but regrettably this machine was forbidden fruit. He had heard that one or two hospitals had connected a small television camera to the laparoscope so that everyone in the operating theatre could view the operation on a television monitor, but such technology had not yet arrived at St Giles.

'I can't see a bloody thing. It looks like the fiery furnace in there.' Patrick looked a little concerned and checked the telescope again. A drop of blood had covered the end so he withdrew the laparoscope and cleaned it on a gauze swab and applied some siliconised solution to prevent further misting of the lens. He reinserted the instrument and presented Reith with a good view of the pelvis. 'Oh, yes. Good heavens. Jolly good view, Harry, come and have a peep. I can't actually see the corpus luteum, Stanley, but I'll take your word for it. After all, I felt the cyst with my own hands, so I know damned well it's there.' He was excited now, like a schoolboy. Gone was his contempt for the instrument; he was discovering new vistas and, above all, he was seeing some pathology and the confirmation of his diagnosis. The feel of satisfaction at having been right. The fact that the swelling was on the wrong side was only a minor embarrassment.

'Come and have a look, Harry.'

Old Harry peered into the eyepiece but the woman's pelvis had never been his forte, so he merely mumbled incomprehensibly, hoping to signify that he was aware of the object of Reith's excitement, whereas in fact he could only see a blur of miscellaneous human tissues.

Angus now decided that it was his time to enter the limelight. He clapped his hands to signify enthusiasm and to gain attention.

'Right, Sister, get the laparotomy pack out, we're going to have to open her up. Would have saved a great deal of precious time if we'd done that in the first place. An experienced pair of fingers can usually arrive at the diagnosis in a fraction of the time this takes if you ask me.'

His beam of satisfaction was soon erased by the cool protest from his junior.

'That won't be necessary, sir. I can use the biopsy forceps to puncture the cyst and evacuate the contents with a suction catheter all under laparoscopic vision.'

Reith was halted in his tracks. 'You sure you know what you're about, laddie? Doesn't sound very safe to me. What about the bleeders?'

'I'll cauterise them with the diathermy electrode. Obviously,' Patrick shrugged his big shoulders like a mountain bear, 'if I can't, we'll have to perform a laparotomy.'

Reith looked anxiously at him.

'Well, I don't know.' He was fumbling for an excuse to be seen to win. 'What if it's a tumour? A carcinoma even?'

'She's a bit young for that. The history isn't really suggestive, no weight loss or anorexia.'

Reith was doing his best to humiliate him. He could always draw on his great depth of clinical experience to twist an argument.

'Biology doesn't obey mathematical rules, laddie. If it did we might as well shift aside and let the computers and robots take over. Remember that dentist's wife from Epping, Harry, just after the end of the war. She presented with a similar history and she was dead six weeks later.'

Patrick was determined to continue the procedure. He knew Reith was being deliberately difficult to win points in front of the medical students.

'It certainly doesn't look like a carcinoma macroscopically. It's uniform and smooth and there are no adhesions of signs of metastatic spread.'

'They can be very small sometimes. Even a localised area. I've seen a Brenner tumour of the ovary that could only be seen when the ovary was sectioned serially.'

'We can send the aspirated fluid for exfoliative cytology and I'll take a biopsy with the Palmer forceps. If they find any malignant cells in the path lab we can always go back in later.'

Reith grudgingly conceded defeat and rejoined the students near the window to give them a concise resumé of the historical aspects of surgery of the ovary while Patrick set about the difficult task of dealing with the ovarian cyst.

He made another tiny nick above the pubic bone. This time he introduced a much smaller trocar after trans-illuminating the body wall with the light from the laparoscope inside the abdomen to make sure that he would not puncture any large blood vessels coursing just under the skin. He inserted the long biopsy forceps, a slender tube about a foot long with a small pair of toothed claws that could be opened and closed by moving the handles at the top end. Raoul Palmer, from Paris, was generally regarded as the father of laparoscopic surgery since the French were way ahead of the British in the development of what the media referred to as 'keyhole surgery'. A diathermy cable was connected from the machine to a switch by Patrick's right foot.

He could feel the sweat running down his neck. It was phenomenally difficult to catch the cyst in the forceps because the surface of the ovary was glistening and slippery and the ovary itself is a fairly mobile structure. He gave more directions to the assistant to move the uterus far to the left and push forward by putting his hand deep into the vagina. Even so, it kept slipping out of the grasp of the forceps and he was aware of an ache in his back from the uncomfortable position and a sudden hush in the theatre as all eyes were on him. He felt like Spartacus trying to grapple with an elusive opponent with a javelin and the damned ovary kept falling away each time he lunged at it.

Reith could see the sweat gathering on his forehead, and like the vindictive old bastard he was, he couldn't resist another chance to take a jibe at his junior.

'Could have done a radical hysterectomy and pelvic clearance in the time all this is taking. Sometimes, Harry, I think we all get carried away with these newfangled gadgets.'

Patrick could feel his Irish temper beginning to rise, but he desperately tried to keep it under control. He needed every ounce of nerve just now and his back was in agony.

He was working the open jaws of the forceps along the stalk of the ovary where all the large blood vessels entered. If he could just manage to pin it against the sidewall of the pelvis for a second, he could buzz the diathermy. He held his breath and shifted the forceps along a few more centimetres away from the artery into the cyst wall and then stabbed his foot on to the switch on the floor. He watched a sizzle of burning tissue and to his relief a thin jet of thinly bloodstained fluid came rushing out of the small hole he had made.

He stood up to ease his back and whipped out the long rod of the forceps like a successful matador.

'Suction catheter, Sister.'

And then he turned to the students and, deliberately ignoring Reith, he spoke to them in a triumphant voice.

'It's not as easy as it looks, of course, but the advantage to the patient is tremendous. She can go home tomorrow with relatively little discomfort and no scar, whereas a formal ovarian cystectomy would keep her in hospital for seven to ten days. We'll be out in a minute, Sister, have they sent for the next case?'

Reith looked at Harry with a mixture of resignation and distaste. One day, as sure as hell, he'd get his own back on that arrogant bastard of a registrar.

Reith's bedside manner was amazingly ambivalent. If he had performed the operation himself he would offer encouragement and sympathy, but if the knife had been wielded by one of the junior staff he would positively look for complications. With some of the old biddies he would sit on the bed and hold their hands and indulge in the most extraordinary small talk, but if the patient was young and attractive he would automatically assume that she was promiscuous and he would be offensive or deliberately callous and, if she was wearing a sexy negligee, would bypass the bed completely and turn his attention to another patient. This attitude gave him the reputation of being a misogynist, a not uncommon finding among male gynaecologists. To try to avert any unpleasantness Patrick Stanley used to go around the post-operative cases before the consultant's business ward round on Friday morning. This gave him an opportunity to explain the problem and prepare some of the patients in advance.

Joanna Spinetti was reacting to the pain of her operation in a predictably hysterical fashion. She had already had three injections of pethidine with apparently no pain relief and was rolling around the bed in a theatrical display of agony. The dramatics tended to stop completely whenever she spoke and this made Patrick feel there was a large psychological component to her suffering.

'You said it wouldn't hurt,' she told Patrick accusingly.

'I said it would hurt less than a proper operation. Sometimes a little blood gets trapped under the diaphragm and this can cause discomfort for twenty-four hours or so but most people are ready to march home the following morning.'

'Well, I can tell you for free that I'm not one of them. Anyway, what did you find?'

'Just as we predicted, a benign retention cyst about the size of a golf ball.'

'You bloody doctors and your sporting metaphors.' She groaned to impress Patrick and lay back on the pillow like a wounded animal. When Reith came round with his staff an hour later he was fairly bristling with unpleasantness.

'Well, Miss Spinetti, and how are you feeling on this happy morn?'

'Absolutely awful,' she moaned. 'I'd no idea pain of this intensity could exist.'

'Oh, indeed it can and I must sympathise with you. These newfangled techniques are all very well but they can be fearfully unpleasant the following day. Give me a good old-fashioned laparotomy any day.'

Patrick winced at the end of the bed. He could see an ugly scene brewing and from what he had seen of this girl so far it appeared that the Spinetti blood had rather a bad temper in it. Reith, on the other hand, seemed to be enjoying himself.

'Well, why the hell didn't someone tell me?' Joanna whined.

'I certainly tried my best, lassie, but you remember you threatened to remove your carcass to UCH.'

'Anyway, Mr Stanley told me it was a large cyst so I suppose it had to be done.'

Reith chuckled. 'They're famous for their sense of exaggeration where Mr Stanley comes from. It was nothing but a tiny wee thing, barely visible through the laparoscope. I dare say it would have gone away on its own in a few days.' He turned to Stanley. 'Since she's making such heavy weather over your handiwork I think you had better keep her in for a few more days. We can't have the telly people accusing us of inhospitality.'

At the end of the round Patrick was unfortunate enough to be the last in the white-coated procession to leave the ward. He suddenly found himself accosted physically by Joanna Spinetti clawing at his arm like an angry cat.

'You're a bastard, Mr Stanley, lying to me like that.'

Patrick was surprised and hurt by the viciousness of her attack, particularly since her long fingernails had dug into his skin. She had made a surprising recovery for someone who had seemed to be at death's door only a few minutes previously.

Patrick had been furious that Reith had chosen to humiliate him in front of a rather difficult patient who, in fact, had good cause to be thankful for his technical skill. Now his anger burst into an explosion at being physically attacked in public.

'Listen, woman, I did the bloody operation while Reith stood in the corner talking to students. I saw the cyst down the laparoscope, not him, so you can believe who you bloody well like. Now let go of my arm, you silly little bitch, and get back to bed.'

Joanna's mouth fell open. In her media-orientated mind her medical heroes like Dr Kildare and Dr Finlay never shouted at patients like that.

'That bloody Irishman,' grunted Reith to Humphrey Hampson as they walked fast along the corridor to the secretaries' office. 'Been cooking the bloody figures for puerperal pyrexia to get himself a bit of pocket money. Damned man from the Ministry wanted to know what the hell was going on round here. What do you make of the fellow, Humphrey?'

'The m-m-m-man from the M-m-m-ministry, sir?'

'No, dammit, man, that young puppy, Stanley. What d'you make of the fellow?'

Reith looked resignedly at his senior registrar. Sometimes he harboured the uncharitable thought that poor Humphrey had lapsed into premature senility. They would have to try to secure a consultant post for him before he started drawing his pension.

'He's not a b-b-b-bad chap, sir. The students seem to like him a lot. They reckon he's a darned good teacher.'

Reith grunted. 'Teaches them to drink Irish stout, I'll be bound.'

'And he's pretty good with his hands. Something of a technical wizard with the obstetric forceps.'

Reith scowled. To suggest that one of the juniors was particularly dexterous was tantamount to poaching on his own reputation. He considered himself the only master craftsman in the department.

'Probably thinks they're some kind of agricultural implement for planting potatoes in the Irish bog where he comes from.'

Humphrey was surprised at the venom coming from his chief. He felt Patrick was being unjustly harangued, although he knew there was no love lost between them.

'The other night in Casualty he…'

'I heard about that,' Reith interrupted huffily. 'Just because he can yank a cup and saucer out of someone's arsehole doesn't make him a good obstetrician.'

They were approaching the door of his office. Humphrey held the door open for his consultant, as courtesy demanded.

'It-it-it-it wasn't the saucer as well, sir, just the cup. And only an egg cup at that.'

'He's far too damned sure of himself. Not healthy, Humphrey, for a fellow to be so cock-a-hoop sure of himself at that stage of his training.'

Reith sat down heavily in the high-backed chair on the far side of his large mahogany desk. His face was heavily jowled, like a bull mastiff, and his words took on a vehemence that worried the senior registrar. 'One day, Humphrey, I'm going to teach that young Irish puppy a lesson he'll never forget. He's going to have to learn the hard way that it doesn't pay to cross swords with the likes of Angus Reith.'

Unfortunately he was not to know the price he would have to exact in terms of human suffering in order to fulfil this fateful promise.

PART TWO
THE WATSON FAMILY

Jeremy and Jennifer Watson are a fairly typical English middle-class married couple living in Knutsford, which is a lovely village just south of Manchester in Cheshire, an area often described by the inhabitants of southern England as 'Posh North'. There are many black-and-white houses dating from the days of the Tudors and its chief claim to fame was that the Victorian novelist Elizabeth Gaskell lived there and it was the setting for two of her best-loved novels, *Cranford* and *Wives and Daughters*.

Jeremy is the manager of the local branch of Lloyds Bank and as such enjoys a privileged position in the community and earns a respectable living, but far less than many of his friends who commute daily into the financial hub of the prosperous Victorian City of Manchester.

He met Jennifer, a teacher at the local primary school, at the annual ball of the Knutsford Tennis Club, where they were both active members. Following a relatively short courtship they were married in the local church and after a respectable interval Jennifer gave birth to Sarah, who is now 18, and Hilary three years later. Both pregnancies were free of complications and the births were straightforward without the need for any medications to relieve pain. Two years later Jennifer was pregnant again, but this time she underwent an incredibly painful miscarriage at the relatively late stage of fourteen weeks accompanied by the loss of a frightening amount of blood.

The consultant told them that it was likely to have been a genetic abnormality and suggested they both undergo genetic screening, but both Jeremy and Jennifer felt that their two daughters were so fit and healthy that they would call it a day and Jennifer had an intra-uterine coil inserted to prevent further pregnancies. One can only imagine their surprise when some eight years later Jennifer started to feel sick and felt a familiar tenderness in her breasts and, when the pregnancy test proved positive, she had a ultrasound scan at six weeks' gestation and they detected a foetal heart. A further scan at eighteen weeks showed a male foetus amazingly clutching the intra-uterine device in his right hand. The surprise result was John, who arrived by an uncomplicated delivery still clutching the IUD that was intended to prevent his existence. His unexpected appearance after such a long gap meant that all the love of this happy family was lavished on him and he grew up spoilt rotten.

Jeremy was a passably good golfer with a handicap of twelve and was a member of the exclusive Tatton Park golf club, which occupies a small corner of the vast Tatton Park estate. This was his only concession to luxury living, and apart from that all his energy, warmth and love were directed to his wife and children, whom he worshipped. The high point of their year was the annual three-week holiday in their camper van in France which he planned meticulously, although this year it transpired that they were in for more surprises than he had anticipated.

CHAPTER EIGHT
Over from Dover – Port of Calais, northern France, summer 1968

Like most bankers, there was a streak of meanness in Jeremy Watson, and when he discovered that the green card for car insurance on the continent had increased in price yet again, he determined that he would take one for exactly three weeks and not a penny more would he pay. Accordingly he took one from August 1-21 and did not allow himself the latitude of a few days at either end as he had done in the past. He had long forgotten about this when, finding himself entitled to an extra day's holiday on some bonus scheme, on July 29, a Thursday, he motored down to London with his wife and three children in their Volkswagen camper van, planning to take a hovercraft from Dover the following day. He had big plans for getting across northern France in the afternoon, then indulge in an expensive meal at Chez Marcel, near the Bastille in Paris, to celebrate their first evening abroad, and then while the family slept in the back of the camper van, he would drive for a few hours down the Autoroute du Soleil until they were within spitting distance of Burgundy. They would wake up next morning under the limpid blue sky of middle France and send one of the girls on her bicycle to the nearest village to get some French bread – starting the holiday in fine style with the unique excellence of freshly baked baguette, unsalted butter and apricot jam, with the extra treat of pain au chocolat, croissants and some real coffee. He could almost smell it in his imagination.

Of course, it didn't happen at all like that. They had a simple but excellent pub lunch just outside Dover and were in fine bucolic holiday spirit during the quick trip on the hovercraft. Father Watson was champing at the bit trying to get past the gendarmes and the douaniers at the French customs.

'Bloody Froggies. What's all the hold-up about?' He gave a short sharp toot on the horn, which irritated the French official and stirred up some of the Anglo-French animosity that still lurked beneath the surface after countless centuries of strife between the two countries.

The French douanier noticed this bit of impertinence and resolved only to delay matters further. He motioned the car to stop beside him and put his official face through the window on the passenger's side.

'Bonjour Monsieur, bonjour Madame. Avez-vous quelque chose a declarer?'
'Non, rien.'
'Du whisky, peut-etre?'
'Seulement une bouteille.'
The Frenchman grunted disapprovingly and walked around the car to see if he could spot any defects, any breach of the regulations that he could utilise to admonish this impatient Anglais.
'Green card, Monsieur, s'il vous plait.'
Jeremy was like a racehorse waiting for the starting fence to rise.
The Frenchman beamed with pleasure as he examined the insurance card. Then his face became incredibly serious and a frown creased his forehead as he assumed the posture of pompous officialdom and pointed out with relish that the green card was not valid until the first of the month and that they would have to wait in the customs shed until midnight.
'If you will be so good, Monsieur, as to park your camper car over zere.'
Protests were furious but they fell on deaf ears. Offers to purchase another day's coverage met with the characteristic Gallic shrug indicating impossibility. Pleas that a day's holiday was wasted were met with an equally characteristic shrug of indifference.
The customs official was delighted with his triumph. Jennifer resigned herself to a few hours' rest in the drab surroundings of the Calais docks; Jeremy was chomping about with indignant rage trying to find the highest authority available who would hear his complaints. The two teenage daughters found the whole crisis hysterically amusing and giggled uncontrollably at sporadic intervals while they jumped up and down on the tummy of their younger brother, John, in an effort to get him to fart. They loved to see the carefully formed plans of the head of the family fall into total disarray.
As the evening shift of gendarmes and douaniers assumed their posts, it was decided to change the family tactic. An initial foray by Jennifer was met by the usual shrug of a civil servant who claimed to be hamstrung by the chains of officialdom. They left the motor caravan in the customs shed in the docks and spent an hour killing time in an unwelcoming Calais, and eventually fed at a friterie near the Gare Maritime. Jeremy thought miserably of Chez Marcel, the planned gourmet surprise in Paris that had been warmly recommended by

a business colleague. Ah well, c'est la vie. He started to drown his sorrows in some earthy French plonk.

After a few glasses of gros rouge the spirits of the adults were restored, but John became increasingly tired and truculent so they returned to the docks to put him to bed in the rear bunk over the engine. It occurred to Jeremy to try a completely new approach to engineer an escape. His eldest daughter was obviously receiving some admiring looks from the French youth that passed them in the street. She was dressed in some skin-tight trousers and a halter-neck top that revealed a few exciting inches around the navel to entice hungry male eyes.

'Sarah.'

'Uh, uh.'

'Look, your mother's going to put John to bed and I just want to have a look at the engine. Why don't you go and see the head honcho over there and explain the mistake and show him the green card.'

'If you like.'

Within minutes, a plump red-faced Frenchman was puffing along to the family camper van, chattering away to Sarah as if they were old friends.

'But, Monsieur, this is all one beeg mistake. It's entirely up to you. The card is valeed from midnight but if you wish, Monsieur, you may drive off anytime. It is entirely your risk, but Monsieur, we are all friends in this big Marché Commun and it is not necessary now to have a carte verte. It is, as we say, un raffinement.'

Everyone thanked him profusely and Sarah even blew him a kiss as he raised the horizontal pole and waved them through with a military-style salute borrowed from the French Foreign Legion.

Jeremy dared not risk any more offensive tactics for fear of being incarcerated in Calais for the entire summer, so he waved affably to the Frenchman and desperately tried to escape from the cobblestones and railway lines of the dockyard. Once out of the town, he erupted in a vituperative flow of anti-French invective, which if understood by the modern burghers of Calais could have put l'Entente Cordiale back several centuries.

Jennifer, in time-honoured wifely fashion, tried her best to mollify him. 'Relax, darling, we're on holiday. Think of it. Three glorious weeks away from the daily toil.'

She twisted herself out of the passenger seat and gave him a kiss on the neck and a friendly stroke on the head that completely dishevelled his carefully brushed hair. Now in his mid-forties, it took an increasing amount of time and skill to conceal his ever-widening bald patch with the remains of healthy hair.

'I wish you wouldn't do that, love.'

She stretched her arms back and laughed. Then in a schoolgirlish tune she started to chide him in song, 'Daddy's in a bad mood, Daddy's in a bad mood, tra-la-la-la-la-la-la.'

Soon the kids were joining in from the back half of the Volkswagen camper van and the combined chorus managed to get Jeremy smiling; it was the traditional way of the family to break the irritation that is so often the lot of the chef de famille.

He made a desperate effort to regain lost time but the road was empty of traffic, the wine was beginning to take effect, and he started to nod at the wheel. His eyelids became heavy and he could feel his head sagging. He started to peer into the distance and he kept having the unmistakable impression of little men in bowler hats, pinstriped trousers and rolled umbrellas leaping across the road ahead of him. He was a driver of long experience and rather than wait until he developed that feeling of total inconsequence about whether one slept or not, he decided that he would pull in for the night. The little brolly men were always a sure sign that he was pooped. He could, of course, have slapped his face a few times or ran around the van ten times to refresh himself. But no, these tactics were good for another ten kilometres; once the fatigue had set in it was safer to turn in for the night. That was one of the greatest advantages of these mobile campers. Like the proverbial snail, they carried a house on their back. He saw a track leading to some trees on the other side of the road. The area was fairly heavily forested and he imagined that the site he had chosen was probably one of the more romantic. He pictured to himself a background of pine forest providing its heavy scent and a view of many miles over the undulating farmland of northern France. He looked at the occupants of the van. All sound asleep. Thank God for that. He could park the vehicle, lift the elevating roof and hop into the bunk bed provided at the top. He was dead tired and couldn't have tolerated the usual gaggle of argumentative women trying to decide on the site for the night. They would be well pleased by his decision. He felt instinctively that this was one of the better stopping places.

As it turned out, there was little room for romance. The family was shaken awake by a severe jolt as a bulldozer removed the front bumper. The women screamed and Jeremy hastily donned his dressing-gown and emerged into the early dawn with his hair dishevelled and looking every inch an angry Englishman. He was met by a hail of Gallic abuse from a bulldozer driver dressed in the national workman's outfit of faded blue overalls and dark blue beret completed by a Gauloise Disque Bleu glued by dried mucus to his lower lip. The man seemed genuinely upset that the van was parked here and not the least concerned by the damage to the vehicle that Jeremy was inspecting like an insurance assessor. The Frenchman continued to gesticulate wildly, indicating the heap of damaged bricks and rubble behind the caravan that was apparently his job to move. Between violent bursts of emotion he would take a generous swig from a flask of cognac hanging from the canopy over his head. Occasionally he revved the engine of the monster Caterpillar to give his words more bite. He demonstrated the track clearly leading to a brick factory and the impossibility of access for a man with a bulldozer.

The chill of the near dawn was close to frost and with each venomous French phrase, the cigarette would glow as it bobbed up and down in time with his lips and puffs of vapour were emitted from the driver's throat. Together with the noise of the motor, the whole aspect held the combined terror of an encounter with a dragon.

Jeremy felt exceedingly ill at ease and was glad when his wife joined him. She had dressed hastily but he felt in need of an ally especially since her French, after two years at night school, was considerably better than his own.

'What the hell's this froggy fucker blathering about?' He said angrily in a tone of voice that the English reserve for people who are unable to converse in an acceptable language.

The Frenchman was now pointing wildly at the forest in the background and mumbling obscenities in an aggrieved tone. He took another swig from the cognac, allowing a compulsory pause during which Jennifer had time to translate.

'He merely says that he's got a job to do to clear this debris and that this is a bloody silly place to park a caravan when there's an entire forest behind you. And, I must say, I entirely agree with him. What on earth made you choose a rubbish tip? No wonder the man demolished the bumper. Probably thought it was an abandoned vehicle.' She stamped her feet angrily and climbed into the passenger seat, indicating that all discussion had ended.

Jeremy swore violently, bundled the bent bumper into the van and drove off in a display of displeasure and chagrin. He drove at a wild pace up the rough track and turned on to the main road like a competitor in the Monte Carlo rally. The atmosphere in the van was like ice. Jeremy was beside himself with rage and it often took ten miles of hair-raising driving to take the edge off it. The first incident was plainly bearing down upon them along the straight road in the shape of a small Citroën 2CV with lights flashing and horn honking. Jeremy retaliated and even accelerated as if he was about to take part in the cavalry charge at Agincourt.

'Out of the way. French bastard!' He kept his hand on the horn and blazed abuse at the opponent as the distances noticeably lessened. Everyone sat tense in their seats. Suddenly, there was a screeching of brakes and screaming of tyres and both drivers wrestling with uncontrolled skids finally arrived on the verge on the opposite side of the road.

After a huge exhalation of relief, Jeremy leapt out of the vehicle determined to bring this French road-hog to justice. He strode across the tarmac in his dressing gown and seeing that the lunatic driver was a woman did nothing to decrease his anger.

'Madam,' he bellowed like a schoolteacher refereeing a game of hockey. 'What in God's name do you think you are doing? Bloody women drivers! You could have had us all killed…!'

She was a small blonde girl slumped across the steering wheel, looking more dead than alive. She was in that extraordinary state of total immobility that seems to affect the fairer sex after any sudden emotion. It was only the indignant fist of Jeremy Watson banging on the roof of her beloved little car that stirred her Gallic emotions and she leapt out of the car like a tigress on heat.

'Espece d'abruti! Arretez d'esquinter ma voiture. Vous avez fait assez de conneries comme ca, idiot d'anglais!'

She tore at Jeremy and he, in turn, felt suddenly insecure as his dressing gown started to be pulled off him and he remembered that he was not wearing anything underneath.

The family were watching from the other side of the road in a state of detached but mounting horror at the sight of the 'old man' being torn apart by an angry French girl. Indeed it was only when the 'Mademoiselle' caught sight of the old man's old man hanging there in detached and wizened splendour that she desisted and recoiled in horror against the side of her Citroën.

She was almost speechless with fury.

'You dirty old English degoutant! Exhibitioniste! Cochon! Not only you go round wiz no cloze on but drive ze wrong side of ze road!'

Jeremy was hastily rearranging his dressing gown and clutching the torn part of the garment to restore a sense of decency. He had never been physically assaulted by a woman before. First she'd tried to assassinate him, then a full-frontal assault. And now she was trying to insult him… Oh my God! The horrible truth dawned upon him. Tenez la droite. After all these years of coming to France for a holiday, he had never before driven on the wrong side of the road.

He desperately tried to apologise but the French girl refused to be mollified.

'You wait here, Monsieur, je vais chercher les gendarmes.' She disappeared in a puff of smoke and the lusty roar of a lawnmower that only a French 2CV can emulate. Jeremy crossed the highway, clutching his tattered dressing gown with his head bowed in a pose of aching humility. He wife was nodding her head knowingly and the two teenagers were laughing riotously as if they had just seen a hilarious film sequence.

'She's going to get the bloody police.'

'What are we going to do?'

'Well, I'm not spending my hard-earned holiday in a bloody French jail, I can tell you that for free. It was bad enough last night in that customs shed. There is no habeas corpus here you know. It could be months before we are released.'

He started the engine and eased the van on to the road, this time making sure he was driving on the right side. They passed a milestone: Paris 108km. He would drive a few miles on this road and then take a side turning to the left and make a vast detour around Paris to avoid detection. The police would reckon that he was heading for Paris. In his mind's eye, he could see roadblocks being set up on the N1 to capture the fugitive.

Just a few miles more and then he'd turn off. She could not have reached a police station yet. He remembered the town he had passed through before stopping for the night was about ten kilometres before he turned off the main road. Actually, it was very like the town they were passing through now. Funny how all these French towns look alike.

He continued through the town. Paris 118km.

They both realised together. Oh Christ! They were going backwards. In his fury, he had forgotten that he had crossed the road when he parked for the night and had obviously hurtled out this morning not only on the wrong side of the road but also in the wrong direction.

He turned off on a side road and, like a gangster whose well-laid plans had misfired, he was desperately trying to work out police psychology. Finally he gave up and feeling more of a criminal with each passing minute as he glanced anxiously in the rear mirror, he decided to pull off into a small wood and to rethink tactics.

They decided to 'hole out' in the wood during the daylight hours and to creep out during darkness and make their way by a carefully chosen devious route round the eastern edges of Paris.

And that is how they came on the third day of the holiday to Fontainebleau forest. Two days of carefully planned sightseeing and gastronomic delights consigned to the waste bin but, nevertheless, Jeremy was undeterred and was already engrossed in the *Michelin Green Guide to Burgundy*.

Meanwhile, Jennifer had refused to be subdued and was busy at the stove filling the van with the glorious smell of frying bacon, singing merrily to all and sundry as she prodded the bacon and eggs to stop them sticking to the pan.

John was running around the van with his new red wellington boots trying to jump into all the puddles of water he could find. Jennifer glanced at the front of the vehicle and was not altogether unhappy to see Jeremy planning his voyage through France. He should have been a travel agent, she reflected. He would have been in his element planning exotic trips and gastronomic stopovers for his clientele.

The girls rapped on his side window and showed him some mushrooms. He wound it down and frowned at them as if he was going to have to bargain for a price.

'Look, Daddy, we've found hundreds for breakfast. Can you recognise the poisonous ones?'

'Huh! Haven't a clue. Your mother fancies herself as an amateur mycologist. I wouldn't touch them. Especially French ones. We'll all be poisoned in our beds.'

Sarah laughed. She loved teasing her father. She was paying back all those years of her childhood when he had teased her mercilessly.

'I can just see the headlines in *France Dimanche*. 'Hit and run caravan flasher found poisoned in forest'.'

The two girls giggled and Jeremy decided that a time came when the physical and basic part of manhood ultimately triumphed over the civilised and intellectual veneer. He threw his maps aside and, with a mighty yell, he leapt out of the car in hot pursuit of his daughters to demonstrate the age-old method of putting women in their place. It had become more difficult by the year but he was still a strong and fit man and he managed to catch Sarah after she had darted through the trees for several hundred yards.

He emerged from the undergrowth with her over his shoulder and her little miniskirt flapping like an ineffectual table napkin over her back, displaying a delightful little bottom shrouded in some pale blue panties. He was grinning from ear to ear like a hunter with a prize captive and all the time he was firmly, but not too painfully, whacking the backside of his struggling and kicking victim.

'Daddy, let me down immediately! John will get bad ideas.'

In fact, John was revelling in seeing his bossy elder sister reduced to size and Jeremy picked him up in the other arm so that he could join in the flagellation of Sarah's beknickered bottom.

Jennifer was laughing at the sight of her family in uproar and delighted to see her husband letting himself go; after all, that was what a holiday was supposed to be all about.

'Breakfast's ready. Come and get it!' She bashed on an empty saucepan like a cook at a ranch in the Wild West.

The family tucked into a good English breakfast with spirits much restored. Sarah kept making remarks about her father and the Keystone Cops but all the tension had eased. The holiday, it seemed, had begun, and the manhunt could be delegated to the past. No one, however, had dared mention the immediate future.

Sarah couldn't contain herself for much longer.

'Well, father, that was a great tour. Much more exciting than usual. I, for one, enjoyed the suspense of the cops and robbers chase.'

Hilary giggled.

Jennifer intervened and attempted to take the defence of her marital partner. 'Now, now, Sarah. I think your father has been through quite enough this last couple of days. We're here to give him his annual rest, you know.'

'But Mummy,' said Hilary. 'We all agreed – three days of Daddy's plans and then down to the sun.'

Jeremy decided to regain control and to try to re-establish his patriarchal status. 'The day when the teenagers take over the world hasn't arrived just yet and I'm still nominally, at least, in charge of this holiday.' He looked expectantly at his wife to check that he was allowed to proceed. 'It's still only ten past eight. We'll take the Autoroute du Soleil and head for Burgundy. With luck, we may get there for lunch. On the way, I promise only one stop – and that will be a surprise. After lunch we'll go along the Côte d'Or and one other stop, this time with refreshments.'

He laughed nervously and looked around for any signs of disapproval. The family were apprehensive. It was all starting to fit into a familiar pattern. Sarah was about to groan but thought better of it. 'We'll get south of Lyon and tomorrow, I promise you, we'll put the canoe into the water on the Ardèche. After our little excursion on the river, you can tell me where to go. I'll act merely as the driver.'

A sigh of relief. Jennifer conceded that it was a master stroke of diplomacy preserving family unity but still allowing the chef de famille to save face. One day as a culture vulture was about all she could take after all the incidents they'd packed into the past forty-eight hours.

Everyone agreed. Sarah made some silly remark to the effect that all the toll booths on the autoroute would probably be displaying 'Wanted. Dead or Alive' posters for father, but her mother silenced her in the final feminine way by firmly reminding her that she was becoming a bore.

John agreed. His little face and cheeky eyes looked seriously at Sarah. 'Sarah. You're becoming a bore. Mummy says.'

That set the final seal of approval and, with everyone laughing, the family Watson set off to see if they could make up for lost time and see La Belle France without further incident.

CHAPTER NINE
The Autoroute de Soleil, south of Paris

They followed the signs from Fontainebleau to the Autoroute du Soleil, the A6, and collected a ticket from the machine at the toll gate.

Jennifer studied the card and tried to work out the amount they would have to pay for the hundred kilometres or so along the new motorway that had been constructed eight years previously. She finally mentioned a figure to Jeremy, who merely responded with a disinterested shrug. He generally left the financial side of the holiday to his wife. Dealing with money matters every day made him want to forget them for a few weeks every summer, but he found that it was hard to rid himself completely of the habit of a lifetime.

'What's that in English?'

'About two pounds.'

'Two quid.'

Jennifer had hoped he would not enquire. She was keen to maintain his equable mood and knew that any suggestion of overcharging by foreigners would invariably undermine it.

'Two bloody quid! Christ! Two quid! Bloody extortion. We don't charge the Froggies for using our motorways. No charity with this lot. They use our roads, use our health service, and the British taxpayer just waves happily away. We come over here and have to pay through the nose for everything. Makes me bloody livid.'

Sarah chirped up from the back of the camper van. 'The way you go on, Father, I wonder we don't spend our holidays in Cornwall.'

'Your father comes to the continent for the perpetual sunshine, dear,' replied her mother.

Since the rain was thudding down on the roof with greater fury than ever and the grey sky showed no sign of it lifting, this remark caused Jeremy to grunt and drive on in ominous silence.

The beginning of August was always a bad time on French roads. The inhabitants of the large metropolis of Paris emptied like lemmings fleeing to the south for some sun. The autoroute was crammed with vehicles heading for the

Midi while the northbound lanes were virtually empty. The drive soon became a nightmare. The slow lane was cluttered with slow-moving old Citroën 2CVs and people with caravans travelling at about forty miles an hour. In contrast, the fast lane was like a speeded-up movie. Peugeots and Citroën DSs from Paris and mega-rich Mercedes and BMWs from Belgium, Holland and Germany were rocketing along in excess of one hundred miles an hour and there was hardly a gap in between them to overtake a caravan or a lorry. They would hurtle into the rear-view mirror with lights flashing and horns blaring. Whenever there was a hill, the situation would be compounded when a slow truck overtook a slower one and all the tail lights in front would flash on like a neon advertisement. Brakes would squeal and the cars would suddenly decelerate. This kind of driving on a wet and slippery road was bound to end in disaster for someone sooner or later.

The road was completely jammed with vehicles as far as the eye could see. Dead stop. Someone way up ahead had probably set out on his final holiday. Jeremy shuddered. He loathed the sight of blood and the scent of death.

The cars were completely stationary for about ten minutes. A police helicopter whirred overhead with a light flashing. They proceeded in a stop-go fashion for about half an hour and eventually came to a sign deposited on the central reservation. POLICE. ACCIDENT. The same helicopter flew overhead this time with two bodies strapped to its stretcher carriers. Jeremy shuddered. It could easily have been one of them. He loathed hospitals and doctors and the whole damned medical scene. He'd been in their clutches once before and had apparently been lucky to come through in one piece. Still, they always told you that. It was all part of the big medical hero image. Trying to live up to the lives of their TV lookalikes. Maybe he was being cynical. He watched the helicopter disappear into the grey sky. Poor sods. If the collision hadn't killed them, they'd probably be dead from exposure by the time they reached a hospital.

They moved forward slowly and the column still stayed in single file, the police out in force making sure they kept to a slow pace, whistling and waving in customary Gallic fashion. They soon saw the cause of the further delay. Obviously some motorists had their attention distracted and there was a further pile-up half a mile beyond, involving some five or six vehicles. The scene was one of dreadful carnage. Cars were mangled and glass shattered across the road.

A smear of blood covered the edge of the tarmac and two corpses were covered in sheets. Groups of people were being interviewed or comforted, some crying, some gesticulating. Blame was still being apportioned and the police were taking notes. A photographer was casually taking shots of the dead. An ambulance was setting off with its siren wailing and lights flashing. A Citroën Safari with a Red Cross flag fluttering from the radio aerial. The whole scene was a vile slaughter. A miniature episode that everyone had seen a thousand times on their television screens in their sitting rooms and read about in the daily newspapers. They were all hyper-immunised by the media.

They left the scene of the accident. Jennifer had refused to look and asked to be told when it was all over so she could open her eyes. The teenagers were gazing at it all like it was a movie. The repeated exposure to violent death on the small screen at home and the large screen in the cinema had numbed their senses. They weren't as delicate as their mother. Possibly evolution was preparing them for annihilation on a mammoth scale.

Jennifer could open her eyes now. Jeremy shuddered and felt as if he could retch. Was this a holiday? This blood; this carnage? Did all of this have to be part of the ethereal search for pleasure? He felt that he must get off this road as soon as possible.

They listened to the radio. They could still get one of the English programmes. Elton John was singing and vamping away on his piano. Jennifer looked at a map. The sooner they left this autoroute the better. It was getting to be a costly way of getting nowhere. He would turn off at the Sens exit. His secret schedule appeared to be going seriously wrong. Still it was only early in the day, twenty past nine.

After ten minutes they started moving slowly again. The speed picked up for a while and then they all came to another stop. People couldn't work out whether the inside or the outside lane was moving better. He plumped for the outside lane and nosed in front of a big Mercedes, who flashed his headlights angrily as if it made any difference. He was alongside a coach full of Germans probably heading for Spain.

The two columns fused into one and they passed the wreckage of two cars. The police had put a big white tarpaulin over them both and left them on the grass that divided the carriageways. How typically French. They almost seemed to glorify in the blood and horror of road accidents. The cars looked as if they were dead corpses waiting for some priest to come along and perform the last rites. No bodies, thank God. He was always very queasy when he saw mutilated corpses. He waited for the traffic to pick up speed again. Usually after the event the greyhounds went storming off again. They drove with restraint for ten minutes after the ugly spectacle of death, but it was soon forgotten and the modern madness behind the wheel returned. After all, it couldn't happen to them.

French had always referred to the Route Nationale 6 as the Road of Death, and obviously the Autoroute 6 that had replaced it was trying hard to vie for that gory title.

The two lanes formed again and the speed picked up. They still had twenty kilometres of autoroute before the exit for Sens. With each kilometre, the tension lessened and, as a family, they emerged from their reaction to the spectacle of horror. The death of other people only really worries us because we personalise with the ultimate truth of the event. We are not really sad. We dread that one day all the pain and suffering of a roadside end could well be the fate destined for one of us, but our sorrow passes too quickly for real grief. Only ten kilometres after these shocking sights, the Watsons were laughing at the sight immediately in front of them. A police recovery vehicle was towing one of the cars involved in the smash. Instead of being towed in English fashion facing forwards, this particular vehicle was being towed backwards with a sign on the front bumper that informed motorists that this was an accident car, and one rather sad-faced driver was sitting facing the oncoming drivers. It was all so Latin. The final humiliation of a road traffic accident, or 'Una disgrazia', as the Italians called it. This poor unfortunate man in his wrecked vehicle. The modern equivalent of the medieval pillory.

The Watsons laughed, but would they have laughed so freely if they had known that the poor man had lost his wife through the windscreen in the slaughter that they had all just witnessed? There was something about the haunting, disconsolate look of the man that froze their laughter and caused Jeremy to accelerate to overtake. But he never forgot that look. In the months to come it kept reappearing like a nightmare at unusual times and he only finally understood its significance a few months later when, at the very depth of his misery and his mourning, people laughed at him in that same heartless way.

Chapter Ten
Burgundy, France, early August 1968

After the horrors of the autoroute the N6 seemed more restful, but it still pre-served the motor racing atmosphere that is the essential ingredient of a French main road. Huge Citroën DS motor cars, the pride of French automotive en-gineering, appeared in the rear mirror at a frightening velocity with their over-sized bonnets looking like high-speed alligators about to open their jaws and devour anything that stood in their path. The middle lane had the nightmare quality of a medieval knightly jousting tournament. Who would finally give way as the combatants hurtle towards each other at breakneck speed? Jeremy usually found discretion to be the better part of valour when facing an oncom-ing Frenchman. Or woman. Again he shuddered at the memory of his previous encounter. So he tended to hug the inside lane and let the idiots fight it out among themselves.

They passed through Sens without a stop. The area around the Bishop's Palace and the cathedral were well-known as a tourist lure but he left it safely behind. The family were amazed. In times past, the women learned to dread the approach of a cathedral city. The camper van would be parked as near as possible to the main façade and the high-speed cultural circus would gradually gather momentum as they were shepherded around the nave and narthex, the crypt and cloister, the aisle and the altar. But Jeremy had gone through Sens like a dose of salts and was whistling nonchalantly to himself, unconcerned with the historic sights that were drifting by. In Joigny he made a brief detour through the old part of the town on the hill of St Jacques overlooking the river Yonne. They motored past some beautiful half-timbered houses dating back to the middle ages. The family were tense. This type of town was usually compulsory rampaging territory for Father clutching his *Michelin Green Guide*, but he merely muttered appreciative statements as he drove past and found his way back to the main road. Jennifer was worried by this abnormal behaviour. Something was definitely amiss. She sensed that her husband was hatching some mysterious strategy. They left the busy road soon after Joigny, following the valley of the Armançon, and took a small side turning off the main road in the town of Montbard and then another winding up a small hill.

He stopped briefly, consulted his Michelin map, No. 65, hummed a few bars from 'Johnny B Goode', then drove on for a further hundred yards before parking the camper van on the side of the road. He turned off the ignition and looked around at the amazed faces of his family. 'Boots and saddles, folks, let's wag it and shag it as they say in Oregon.'

'Really, Jeremy, what language in front of the children!'

'But there's nothing here except fields,' shouted Hilary in protest. 'I thought it was culture vulture time.'

'It is, but first a little walk. Better take the raincoats, the sky still looks angry.'

The general wail of protest was silenced by young John who took up his father's clarion call but rather confused the phrases. 'Troops and salads,' he shouted, and was then so delighted by the amusement he had caused that he repeated the phrase endlessly in a high-pitched excited voice.

They walked over a field of grass still damp from the morning rain. The sky was still overcast, still bearing the stamp of the Atlantic, but patches of blue were appearing to the south. The wind blew in gusts through the hedgerow as they walked in a huddled group, the two teenagers plotting conspiratorially in the rear, Jeremy breathing deep breaths of pure country air as he tried vainly to exorcise eleven months of polluted exhaust fumes from the depths of his alveoli, and Jennifer pointing out in vain the names of various wild flowers to John, who intermittently skipped ahead to urge them on, then lagged hopelessly behind.

They reached the crest of the hill and the mystery was unveiled. Nestling in the floor of the lovely valley, almost hidden amid ancient oak trees and pools of clear water, was the cluster of stone buildings that formed the Abbey of Fontenay.

'There she is,' Jeremy spoke in almost reverential tones as he surveyed the perfect harmony of the setting. 'The jewel of the Cistercian order.'

'And what a perfect way to approach it.' Jennifer picked up her youngest son and, using that device of doting wives, complimented her husband in baby talk. 'And what a clever daddy to read the map so well and give us such a nice surprise'.

'Oh, yukkety-yuk,' groaned Sarah, looking despairingly at her sister.

But Jeremy ignored the barracking and concentrated on the magnificent spectacle in front of them. As he grew older he found that life's beauties became infinitely more precious and he had to make a conscious effort to imprint the details on his brain, not so much as a sign of greater maturity but as a defence against the memory loss inherent in the ageing process. 'To think it was sold during the French Revolution and became a paper mill.'

He looked at his watch, picked up John and started to run down the hill, beckoning the family to follow. 'Come, let's hurry down, the guided tours are every half an hour and if we miss the next one we'll never get to the two-Michelin Star restaurant that I have specially chosen for lunch.'

They arrived breathless, with Jeremy in the lead in spite of the twin handicap of his age and the burden of John on his shoulders. He produced his wallet and indicated the need for five tickets with his fingers, but was surprised to see the monk shaking his head with profound disapproval and indicating by a gesture of his hand that they could not be admitted. Jeremy turned to follow the direction of his stare and gasped as he took in the sight of his eldest daughter. The heat generated by running had forced her to remove her Burberry raincoat and hang it over her arm as she stood nonchalantly at the edge of the crowd in a pair of vivid yellow hot pants that hugged her pelvis so tightly that every erotic crease was clearly outlined, and on top she wore a cheesecloth blouse that was so transparent that the mounds of her breast and her pert adolescent nipples were displayed for all to see. It was immediately apparent why the monk was indicating his displeasure and why the French males in the crowd had suddenly lost interest in twelfth-century ecclesiastical architecture.

'For God's sake, Sarah, put your raincoat back on,' spluttered Jeremy, genuinely shocked by his daughter's display of blatant sexuality. 'You'll get us deported from the country for public indecency. You ought to be ashamed of yourself.'

Sarah reluctantly draped the raincoat over her shoulders, much to the disappointment of the Frenchmen who once again redirected their attention to the buttresses and semi-circular bays of the façade, although their minds undoubtedly lingered on the much more pleasing semi-circular contours that they had briefly contemplated in such lascivious detail.

Sarah was pouting at her father's display of authority. 'For heaven's sake,

Daddy, we're not living in the Dark Ages. All that fuss about a woman's body. I'd no idea you were such a prude.'

Jeremy grunted and followed the crowd through the romanesque arch of the main doorway of La Porterie and into the porch of one of the most ancient Cistercian abbeys in France.

Lunch was as perfect, as Jeremy had promised. The venue was a delightful auberge in Rully on the Côte d'Or, which they entered through a flower-filled courtyard containing several quaint birdcages with noisy occupants, but happily they could not be heard from the terrace overlooking the river where they had a warm welcome from the maitre d' and were shown to a table in the shade of a trellis covered in vines. John had fallen asleep in his bunk at the rear of the van, so they left him sleeping peacefully, ensuring at least an attempt at a civilised meal. The parents ordered the specialities of the house, quenelles de brochet au coulis d'ecrevisses, and cotes d'agneau grillees aux herbes sauvages. The teenagers shared a steak frites.

In the land where worship of the culinary arts had almost replaced religion, any meal was a lengthy affair and even after two hours Jeremy showed no sign of impatience; they even have a saying in France, 'a man never grows old when at table'.

The remainder of the day passed uneventfully and they sped southward back on the less crowded Autoroute de Soleil, where they were delayed for a while in the notorious bouchons, the traffic jams of Lyons, and then picked up the autoroute following the Rhône on its way to the Mediterranean Sea. As they passed Valence they were cheered to see the sky change from the drab misery of northern Europe to the translucent pale blue of Provence.

The transformation always seemed to occur at the same latitude somewhere between Vienne and Valence. They crossed the Rhône near the massive construction works of the barrage of Donzère-Mondragon and climbed out of the Rhône valley towards the dry causses and the mountains of the Ardèche. The heavy scent of marjoram and thyme on the hot earth, the background clicking of the cigales, the dust and the benign caress of the late afternoon sun all served to remind them that they were in the South of France at last.

CHAPTER ELEVEN
Canoeing the gorge of the Ardèche river, South of France, August 1968

The following morning they rose early and had breakfast in a café perched high above the left bank of the Ardèche with a splendid view of the magnificent bridge that spanned the river just outside Vallon before it entered the famous Ardèche Gorge. Jeremy was fascinated to see a weather-beaten old peasant in blue overalls and a black beret attacking his traditional breakfast in a set routine; first a swallow of cognac, then some baguette dipped into a bowl of milky coffee and finally an entire raw onion and a whole garlic helped down by another generous draught of cognac.

Jeremy went off to the riverbank on the opposite side to prepare the canoe for launching, while Jennifer went into the small town and indulged in one of her favourite occupations, shopping for food. She arrived a full hour and a half later with her arms enfolding enormous loaves of French bread and dozens of parcels each with a hidden gastronomic delight.

Jeremy was spluttering with indignation at the time she had taken. 'Good God, woman, where on earth have you been? You've got enough food there to sustain us on an ocean voyage.'

Normally this kind of criticism would have been met with a firm counter-riposte, but Jennifer's mouth fell open in amazement and she giggled uncontrollably when she studied the apparition in front of her.

Her husband was kitted out in a bright yellow crash helmet that was several sizes too big for him. The small part of his face that was visible under this colossal piece of headgear was obscured by reams of adhesive tape designed to protect his spectacles from the buffeting of the waves. He had a huge life jacket on his chest covered with a fisherman's sweater, making him look barrel-chested like the Michelin man. Appearing under this inflated torso a pair of naked spindly legs crept down almost apologetically into some neoprene boots and his modesty was concealed by a ridiculous red plastic spray apron around his midriff.

'Dear Lord,' spluttered Jennifer. 'You look more like one of the Boston Bruins in a tutu than a serious river runner.'

'Thank you very much,' replied Jeremy in his best imitation of Tony Hancock. 'Now get your kit on and let's see what you look like.'

'Certainly not,' said Jennifer. 'I've no intention of making a buffoon of myself in public.'

'You remember what Mike Thomas told us. Crash helmets are meant to be de rigueur with these people. Remember him showing that film of the Austrian national champion drowning on the Lieser because he cracked his head open on an underwater rock? He had refused to wear a helmet.'

Jennifer had indeed remembered the sickening film and had been horrified that people even dared to pit themselves against the fury of an alpine torrent hurtling down the rapids of the narrow gorge of the Lieser near Spittal in Carinthia. Those images, particularly the one of the dead man being dragged up the steep rocks near the shore, had made her seriously question whether this type of action sport was for her. She had been reassured by the warm sun and the view from the bridge of the river drifting slowly past looking far from threatening. Besides, none of the other canoeists were wearing anything other than swimming trunks or bikinis.

'Suit yourself,' she shrugged. 'You can make a pantomime of yourself if you must but you'll have to accept me in my bikini. Otherwise I'll stay behind with the children.'

This was always her ultimate threat and Jeremy conceded defeat as usual while she went off like a mother hen to give last-minute advice to the children as well as a share of the food. She checked and double-checked that they knew the way to get to the rendezvous at Pont St Esprit, and the dozens of other things that mothers worry about.

'Don't worry, Mummy,' Sarah tried to reassure her. 'It's only two days and I am eighteen after all.'

'But you never know with these French, dear. They look at women quite differently around here. You can even feel it when you're walking in the streets. Make sure you stay at the registered campsite and double-lock the van at night. And do drive carefully – some of these local Ardèchois seem to drive like men possessed and as you saw on the way here the roads seem to have lots of hairpin bends.'

'Oh, go off,' said Hilary, getting as impatient as her sister. 'Don't fret so much. Anyway, the sooner you get Dad away from here in that outfit the less embarrassed I'll feel.'

'Don't worry, Mummy,' said little John, kissing her goodbye. Then, with a very serious expression for a seven-year-old said, 'I'll look after them.'

The launching itself provided an inauspicious start to the trip. Jeremy had loaded up the canoe with all the camping gear and food they needed for the two days ahead. By the time they were ready to put the boat in the water it was considerably heavier than he had intended and in spite of the steeply inclining slope of the riverbank they were unable to shift it.

'Come on, Jenny, put a bit of beef into it.'

'Oh, beef yourself,' she yelled back. 'Why don't you go down to the bottom end and pull while I push from the top?'

It was a good suggestion since it managed to get the boat moving, but it proved to be Jeremy's undoing. Once the heavy fibreglass hull had started to slide, it took control of the situation and carried all before it, including Jeremy, who was dunked unceremoniously in the river.

Onlookers who had gathered on the bridge in increasing numbers to ogle at Jeremy's extraordinary outfit were rewarded by this scene and cheered enthusiastically while the children shrieked with laughter. Jeremy floundered about like a walrus and meekly acknowledged the cheers with an awkward display of British embarrassment.

After much hegemony and discussion Jennifer and Jeremy managed to get into the canoe. They fastened their spray decks around the cockpits and with some trepidation pushed off gingerly into the middle of the river. They turned back to wave farewell to the children, but the boat rocked alarmingly and they realised that any contradiction of Newton's laws would land them both in the drink. The girls waved back at them and Sarah held John aloft so that he could see his parents disappear downriver, and he waved excitedly until they were out of sight.

The first few miles were disappointing. It was rather like the Serpentine in Hyde Park, except that it was moving faster. Canoes could be hired from a boatyard just below the bridge at Vallon and the first section was full of teenagers and families having fun in the hot summer sunshine. Laughter and the inevitable metallic music from cheap transistor radios formed a background against the occasional shriek of a young girl warding off or encouraging some sexual predators in rival canoes. Jeremy felt a twinge of disappointment; he had expected rugged grandeur and isolation – a chance to escape from the hordes of holidaymakers. Besides, he was getting increasingly tired of the odd looks he was receiving.

'Do you think it would be tempting providence to take all this clobber off?'

'Very daring,' mocked Jennifer softly. 'Unlike the bank manager to take risks.'

'Well, it's not exactly the roaring torrent we'd been led to expect by Mike Thomas.'

'He was talking about the Isère and some of the Alpine torrents where they hold whitewater slalom championships.'

'He said we'd be in for a few surprises. I definitely remember him saying that,' Jeremy mumbled.

'I've had more excitement on the Playland boating lake at Southport.'

The words were barely out of her mouth when they heard the unmistakable sound of water rushing over a shallow shingle bed. At first it was almost a hissing sound but as they rounded the corner the noise increased to a roar and the river seemed to drop away from them in a series of steps. Their hearts started racing and they were both a little frightened. Jeremy was desperately trying to remember all the rules of whitewater canoeing that Mike Thomas had taught them.

'Paddle to the right so that we can land to inspect it,' Jeremy yelled above the roar of the water.

He meant the right bank of the river, and started making deep strokes with his left paddle, but Jennifer had mistaken the order and was paddling furiously on the right, thus nullifying all his efforts. Soon they were caught in the drag of the rapid as the speed of the river increased to an exhilarating pace. 'Aim for the apex of the smooth V and keep paddling,' Jeremy yelled, desperately trying to remember his friend's advice.

They were hurtling down the centre of the river and soon the tongue gave way to a series of huge standing waves that caused the boat to buck violently and great waves of water to cascade over them. Cold spray lashed their faces as they both paddled furiously to try to keep the boat on an even keel but Jeremy's look of consternation turned to one of terror as he saw that they were heading directly for a huge rock that guarded the lip of an ugly looking fall. The river seemed to disappear from sight on either side of it.

'Paddle on the left, for Christ's sake,' he shouted, trying to make himself heard above the roar of the rushing water. Unwittingly they had committed a cardinal error. They had turned the boat sideways to the current and were moving at the same speed as the water, which was considerable, and now the river had taken control; they were at its mercy, tossed like a cork in the powerful current. The boat struck the huge rock with a sickening crack and tilted alarmingly, but they were just saved from capsize by the enormous weight of the water cascading down the side of rock spilling over the lip of the fall itself. The noise was deafening, and they were both terrified as the boat dropped vertically down the fall and buried itself momentarily into the huge stopper wave at the bottom. For a second the entire boat was submerged and the cold water took their breath away; then the buoyancy of the boat exerted itself and shot to the surface several feet beyond the bottom of the fall.

The transformation was unbelievable. Suddenly they were out of the nightmare of the swirling waters and glided into the cool, clear stillness of the pool below. The silence of the river after its sudden burst of energy was overwhelming and they shrieked with excitement and relief like a couple of delighted schoolchildren. They looked back at the series of ledges and the gigantic rock that had nearly upturned them. They had made it over that snarling tongue of white water.

The calm after the storm; the sudden release from all that pent-up terror. They laughed and whooped out of sheer pleasure, with Jeremy slapping the sides of the fibreglass hull like a horseman patting his horse after a difficult jump.

'We made it, we made it,' Jeremy shouted.

'Geez,' Jenny exhaled with relief. 'I was so damned scared, my heart felt like it was in my mouth. Now I'm a bit worried about these surprises that lie ahead. I don't think we can handle anything rougher than that.'

'Relax,' said Jeremy. 'We went down the V like a pair of champions.'

They let the canoe drift on its own and uncorked the bottle of red wine that was conveniently stored behind Jeremy's seat, passing it backwards and forwards for a few vigorous slurps; they both felt that they had deserved it.

The riverbanks had become steeper after the rapid and then they looked up at the sandstone cliffs above them on either side. They had entered the gorge of the Ardèche.

As they drifted slowly around the next bend they were confronted by a magnificent natural spectacle, the Pont d'Arc. Many millennia ago the river had come upon a solid wall of limestone and instead of taking the vast detour of the original course it had, over thousands of years, gradually eroded the rock until the river had burrowed a clear passage through it, leaving only a natural arch of white limestone that looked like a huge rainbow almost forty feet above the river. The Watsons drifted underneath, marvelling at this scenic wonder and the tenacity of the river that had chewed its way through this solid rock.

After the Pont d'Arc the river entered the long canyon of the Ardèche. They left the road and the tourists miles behind and they were utterly alone among the awesome scenery of the sandstone walls and rock formations rising several hundred feet above the level of the river.. The silence was broken only by the sounds of the river running over its shingle bed and the occasional plop of a fish jumping out of the water.

The noonday heat soon robbed them of the energy to paddle and they lay back in the canoe and let it drift. Jennifer removed her shirt and then her bra and applied some Piz Buin to the delicate skin that had remained shyly hidden from the sunlight. The smell of the oil always reminded her of holidays on the continent and the deep mahogany tan that she was determined to acquire.

An hour went by, maybe more, drifting along in this idyllic fashion, kissed only by the rays of the morning sun and the soft breeze. The canyon was broad and high at this point and they were in a world of perfect peace.

Jennifer let her hand dangle in the cool water beside the boat. 'I hope the kids are going to be all right.'

'Don't fret, love, you're like a mother hen. We've only been gone about two hours. Sarah's virtually a grown woman now.'

'That's exactly what worries me. She wears such provocative clothing. It's doesn't take much imagination to see every detail of her anatomy. The way those Frenchmen stare at her gives me the shivers.'

Jeremy laughed. 'If they could see you now they wouldn't even need to call on their imagination.'

Jennifer turned half round in the cockpit and grinned mischievously at him, and the sight of her lovely breasts sent a thrill searing through his body. The older she became, the more lovely she seemed to him. He stretched his arms out in a futile attempt to cup her breasts in his hands, but she turned again and picked up her paddle, flicking a spray of cold water over him to dampen his ardour.

'Come on, let's have some lunch before I start feeling randy.'

They paddled gently for a few hundred yards and then beached the canoe on a patch of white sand just beneath a small rapid.

Jennifer removed the wet spray apron and seeing the complete seclusion of the picnic spot she gently slipped her bikini bottoms down her legs and kicked the skimpy garment into the water. Naked, she stooped down and rinsed it in the water and laid it out to dry on the boat.

Jeremy started to feel his organ swell as he contemplated his wife's nude body; the soft curve of her buttocks always exerted a compulsive erotic attraction and as she bent over the canoe retrieving the food parcels he felt he was going to burst. The only thing that stopped him was her mocking giggle.

'Darling, you're surely not going to spend the entire holiday in that ridiculous outfit.'

'I'm not sure.' Jeremy looked around cautiously. 'One can never be too careful.'

Jennifer smiled as she lay out the groundsheet. 'I can never imagine how a nature girl like me ended up spliced to such an old worry-boots.'

'It's not just that.' He looked down apologetically, his feet shuffling nervously in the sand. 'It's seeing you like that. I'm afraid I've developed an erection.'

Jennifer burst into happy laughter at her husband's shyness. 'I've only seen the thing like that on about three thousand occasions.' She made a lunge under the spray cover, located it and gave it a powerful squeeze.

'Ouch, that hurt!' Jeremy cringed with pain. 'I felt your fingernails then; you could have drawn blood.'

'Get out of that awful clothing and come and have lunch. We'll deal with John Thomas afterwards.'

Jeremy regretted his impatience with his wife for spending so much time shopping in Vallon. She had bought small cartons of local delicacies that made a holiday in France the ultimate in gustatory delights. A long loaf of fresh crisp baguette, some saucisson d'Arles, pâté de chataigniers, some salade Piedmontaise, taboulé and a local goats' cheese called Picodon. All this was laid out like a feast on the groundsheet and after Jeremy had taken a photo of it, and another surreptitious one of his wife bending over naked beside it, they set upon the food with a vengeance. The physical exertion and excitement of the morning had made them ravenously hungry.

The warm red wine gurgling straight from the bottle and the crispy crunch of the fresh bread, the waves of garlic emanating from the saucisson and the smooth tang of the goats' cheese – they could only be in France.

After lunch they lay on the sand, soaking up the sun. Even with their eyelids closed they could see its redness and feel its heat. The canyon seemed to concentrate the sun's rays like an oven. The breeze had dropped and the only sound was the ripple of the river; even the birds seemed to have dozed off in the early afternoon heat.

'We need some oil otherwise we're going to fry in this heat. Where did you put it, Jen?'

'It's still in the canoe, I'm afraid. Just behind my seat. I'm too lazy to move. Be an angel and butter me.'

Jeremy walked to the canoe, now quite unconcerned by his nakedness since it seemed completely consistent with the peace and isolation of the beach they had found. He kneeled over his wife and poured the warm oil on her back and smoothed it over her shoulders, slowly caressing her body with tender strokes, massaging the oil ever downwards until he came to the soft mounds of her buttocks. This part of her body had always been the high point of eroticism for him and she knew this and would wriggle gently so that her bottom would undulate seductively under his gaze. His desire was mounting and his penis swelled aggressively. He parted the smooth mounds and poured oil down the cleft rubbing it slowly and gently like a painter, and Jennifer responded by arching her pelvis upwards, increasing his voyeuristic pleasure until it was almost unbearable.

He turned her over and massaged the oil into her chest, passing his hands over her breasts, kneading them gently but firmly, his palms gliding over the oil in decreasing circles coming slowly but firmly to the top and squeezing her erect nipples. He worked his way downwards over her navel and stroked his human canvas down to her thighs, and then worked inwards, making her purr with pleasure. Her neck and face were flushed as she mounted towards orgasm, and he finished her off by stroking her clitoris with the soft end of his shaft. Then, when her whole body was contracting uncontrollably, he thrust himself inside her. They slithered over each other with the film of suntan oil between them; it was intense, but almost too quick, as it often is when performed alfresco. Jennifer gazed up at the cliffs, her hands grasping the firm flesh of his buttocks as he thrilled her inside, moving like an athlete, until he was overcome by an immense grunt of final achievement and it was all over.

He lay on top of her like a wounded beast, his heart pounding violently as she held him close to her, and the musty scent of the bergamot oil mingling with the more earthy smell of sex as the sun beamed down on their naked love-locked bodies.

She loved to gaze up at the sky after he had consumed her and, almost more than the orgasm, she loved this feeling of tenderness afterwards as he lay there with all his masculinity spent and lifeless, his heart pounding against her breast. It was almost motherly afterwards, but it was more than that; it thrilled her to feel that after all these years she could still inspire this level of excitement in him. She would glow with happiness as she felt his heavy weight on top of her, listening to his heartbeat slowly returning to normal. God, how she loved him.

Jeremy was about to doze off on top of her when he heard a small rock fall high on the cliff on the far side of the river. His body twitched nervously.

'Did you hear that? Someone must be watching us.'

Jennifer giggled. 'There's a crowd of people up there on the edge of the canyon.' Jeremy stiffened with apprehension and withdrew himself from her in a state of panic.

'They've probably got cameras with telephoto lenses and already a dispatch rider is hurtling back to London with an unexposed film for the super-sleuths at Lloyds Bank head office.'

'Omigod,' Jeremy was genuinely concerned. 'You can never be too careful in the world of finance.'

'Oh, you bankers! Don't be such a cuckoo. They're at least half a mile away and five hundred feet up. It's one of the observation platforms by the roadside on the edge of the gorge. They're mere dots to us and there's no way they can see what we're wearing.'

'But we aren't wearing anything.'

She nudged him off her to get her breath back.

'Oh, screw them! They belong to another world. Let's go and have a swim.'

They ran through the silver sand, hand in hand like a couple of teenagers splashing into the water. The cool of the river gripped their bodies and they thrilled at the sensual pleasure of swimming naked. It was a feeling of purity and freedom uncluttered by the ridiculous trappings of modesty; they were naked as nature intended them to be. They shrieked and splashed each other, laughing like children; they had never felt so free.

They returned to the boat and packed up the scattered remains of their lunch. The sun was still burning out of the clear-blue sky as they cast off from the shore. They entered a new world, their own private paradise. It never occurred to them to put their clothes back on, but due to the heat of the sun they covered themselves with Factor 50 Piz Buin sun cream and wore wide-brimmed straw hats, but nothing else.

They paddled energetically downstream for a while to dry themselves, but the afternoon torpor, a combination of hot southern sun and rough red local wine, overwhelmed them. They lay back in the boat, gazing up at the rock formations as they unfolded above them. Jagged structures that had been carved out by the waters of the river when its surface was hundreds of feet above the present level. The Citadel. The Pulpit. The Cathedral. The various formations had names that compared them with the finest architectural creations of men, but the descriptions were totally inadequate. Nature had surpassed them in scale, beauty and artistic grandeur.

The river was less energetic here and they both fell asleep as the slow current guided the canoe downstream like a floating log. Occasionally it would bump lazily against a rock or one of the banks and brush through some overhanging branches.

They must have slept for ages. They probably passed a small sign on the bank saying Relais des Naturistes de la Gorge de l'Ardèche. They might not have seen it anyway. Jennifer never knew what exactly woke her up but she suddenly regained consciousness and shook the boat in amazement as she looked up at a naked man fishing from a rock in the middle of the river. An old-established nervous reaction made her clutch her breasts to hide them from view but the man was so casually naked himself that she felt even more ridiculous. He was puffing nonchalantly on a pipe and was brown all over his body. He wore a fisherman's hat at a rakish angle on the top of his head. His weathered penis hung down unconcernedly and was as brown as the rest of him. She stared at the dark shrivelled appendage; she hadn't seen a circumcised one before. She was instantly ashamed of herself. He removed the pipe from his mouth and smiled benignly and wished them, 'Bonjour Monsieur, Madame.'

The motion of the boat had woken Jeremy and they were both now looking around in amazement, but everywhere they looked people were naked. Small children splashing in the water, some teenagers playing a rough game with a ball in the shallows, and rows of people sunbathing on the banks of the river. All of them completely and unashamedly nude.

Jennifer suddenly saw the funny side of it; so that was what Mike Thomas had meant when he said they were in for a surprise, and all along she had been dreading some fearsome waterfall or a whirlpool that would drag them to the bottom of the river. She could still see the picture of his face chuckling away and as she turned around and saw her husband clutching his tool in embarrassment she started to laugh openly herself. The expression on Jeremy's face was a mixture of incredulity and horror as he sat up in the canoe and made a frenzied attempt to find his clothes. Oh my God, he was thinking, what if someone from the bank was to find me like this.

'Relax, darling, we're in a nudist camp. If you put on your clothes you'll stick out like a sore thumb.'

'What the hell are we going to do?' Jeremy spoke in a false tremolo, almost warbling with fear.

'Don't worry about it. They'll think we're one of them; after all, we're dressed for the part. Anyway, they must be used to canoeists passing through. They'll think we're a couple of harmless voyeurs who've come to join the fun.'

Their conversation was interrupted by a hearty woman who was halloing them in a northern English accent from one side of the canoe. They had drifted into shallow water and Jeremy turned in the direction of the voice to see a middle-aged woman standing stark-naked in only a foot or so of water. She had grabbed the prow of the canoe, so there was no escaping her, and Jeremy was desperately trying to look anywhere but at her vital parts. He had never seen a naked woman in the flesh before, apart from his wife, and he was relieved to find that the experience was not an erotic one. In fact, his John Thomas had almost shrivelled away in fright.

'You're from England, aren't you?' she said and, without waiting for a reply, continued, 'I thought so, and I recognised the flag on't back of t'boat.'

'Stern,' said Jeremy, correcting her for want of something better to do. He was already regretting purchasing the triangular British Canoe Union pennant that was fluttering proudly from its little stainless-steel flagpole.

The woman laughed rather too heartily for comfort. 'Oh, I see, nautical folks are you? Well, I'm a landlubber meself, as you can see.'

Jeremy was seeing all too clearly and, aware that he was beginning to stare at her breasts, he averted his gaze again, but everywhere he looked there was a medley of little black triangles and breasts and buttocks of all shapes and sizes. He had a morbid dread of getting an erection, an outward and visible sign that he was not a member of this fraternity, but luckily his appendage was as embarrassed as its owner.

'Are you both passing through or are you part of the club? By the way, my name's Rosie Winterbottom and I'm from Blackburn Sunseekers.'

'Not a very appropriate name,' said Jeremy cynically.

'Oh that,' she replied, still full of good humour. 'Everyone has a good laff about that.' And without further ado she turned her suntanned derriere and bent it provocatively for Jeremy to peruse if he so desired. 'Doesn't really live up to its label, does it? We'll 'ave to change our name by deed poll to the Sunnybums.'

Jennifer was warming to this woman and her disarming frankness about her body; it was something she rather admired. 'Can we introduce ourselves? I'm Jennifer Watson and my backseat paddler is Jeremy…'

'Smith,' Jeremy interrupted.

'What?'

'Jeremy Smith.'

Jennifer laughed. Her husband had obviously become so nervous and secretive that he might well have been working for the CIA rather than the dreary old Lloyds Bank.

'Not to worry.' Rosie continued. 'We have lots of unmarried here. In England it's a bit more respectable and our club's nearly all families but you know the Frenchies.' She gave one of those big wink expressions that signified surreptitious continental sex. 'I tell you what, why don't you camp the night here with us? There aren't many suitable places until you reach Pont St Esprit and it'll soon be getting dark. I doubt if you'll make it that far.'

'Very kind of you,' Jeremy said in a voice one assumes when refusing an invitation. 'But I think we'd better be getting along and...'

'But I'd love to,' cried Jennifer with enthusiasm, getting out of the canoe and dragging it and its reluctant occupant through the shallows to the sandy bank. Jeremy shrugged his shoulders. When his wife had made up her mind like this, resistance was useless.

'I think you ought to know, Rosie, that we were just paddling through and happened to be taking advantage of the seclusion and sunshine. We'd no idea that there was a place like this.'

'Didn't you see the notice?'

'No, we were both fast asleep – too much heat and too much wine at lunch.'

'Anyway, I guessed as much because of your tan. You can always tell a proper nudist. What about your friend? Are you sure he wants to stay?'

'Oh, don't worry about him – he's my husband, actually, he's just a bit embarrassed. It'll soon pass.'

Rosie cackled with laughter. 'That's a hoot, it's usually t'other way round. Normally the menfolk drag us along here and we're the ones that are embarrassed. Mind you, once the first few minutes are over it's rather pleasant and, of course, the kids love it.'

'Do you have any children?'

'Three. Two girls and a boy and they're expecting us at Pont St Esprit tomorrow.'

'Oh, you'll have to bring them along. They'll love it here.'

Her enthusiasm was so infectious and the place was so incredibly beautiful that Jennifer there and then gave up all thought of going further south and resolved to bring the children back here for the rest of the holiday.

After the first embarrassing half hour, Jeremy finally settled down and busied himself beaching the canoe and finding a place to pitch the tent. Old man Winterbottom came along to give a hand. He was not exactly the portrait of

Adonis in the nude as he stood surveying the tent with his eight-foot beer gut that he fondly referred to as his 'Lancashire 'otpot'. He was a jovial soul and eager to help, but Jeremy soon found he was more of a hindrance when it came to setting up a tent. He had a positive genius for putting in the pegs so that the tent was out of skew and Jeremy found himself constantly having to go round the other side to alter the pegs and realign the shape of the groundsheet. After the two men had completed several circuits, the tent ended up fully ninety degrees in a different direction to the one originally planned.

'Tha'll find that a good position for t'mornin' sun. Catch thee clean on the bonce if tha sleeps downhill. Or, of course, we could turn t'bugger round and have tha sleeping uphill.' He took off his cap and scratched his fat head. To Jeremy there was something incongruous about a naked man wearing a flat cloth cap, but evidently Alf Winterbottom did not think so.

'No, I think we'll leave her where she is,' said Jeremy, his banker's wit having already deduced that they could turn the sleeping bags around. 'Now if you'd like to crawl in the tent and hold up the pole I'll put the rest of the pegs in.'

'No, no, no. It'd be all ah could do to get meself and me belly in t'ole. Besides, ah gets very claustrophobic in them small tents. You hold t'pole and ah'll do the peggin'.'

This proved to be a disastrous mistake since Alf appeared to have no sense of symmetry, and the final result looked like a Bedouin encampment after a sandstorm.

Alf stood back a few paces to regard the construction, with its sagging ridge and double hump that gave it the profile of a dromedary. He removed his flat cap and scratched his navel. 'Ah think tha'll 'ave ter make do with that. Of course,' he looked anxiously around at the adjacent German tents that were models of efficiency and neatness, 'Bloody Jerries wouldn't think owt of it, but then,' he added, with a peculiarly northern British type of logic, 'they never won t'war, did they?'

Jeremy looked dubiously at the tent; there was no doubt that the mere sight of the edifice militated strongly against his banker's sense of neatness, but he was very tired and it was getting dark.

'Come,' said Alf, 'let's go and 'ave a wash and brush up and then we can see if t'wives 'ave got a spot of grub to eat.'

As it happened, the Germans never had a chance to look at the strange canvas structure since they were securely locked in their aluminium frame canvas chateaux that were almost as crisp and efficient as the homes they had left behind in Germany. Those who did see it regarded it as something of a curiosity.

Unfortunately a cow thought rather differently and regarded Jeremy's tent as an alien, and somewhat threatening, species and bit a large chunk out of the ridge of the tent, rendering the canvas shelter even more inadequate as a place to spend a comfortable night. Jeremy and Jennifer finally ended up in the top bunks of the Winterbottoms' caravan, sleeping against a background of old Alf's contented snores.

CHAPTER TWELVE
Ardèche, Rhône-Alpes, South of France, August

The next day, the Watsons paddled away downriver to Pont St Esprit, leaving the tent and their belongings in the care of the Winterbottoms. After several hours of lazy paddling down the Ardèche, and then the much larger river Rhône, they saw the old stone bridge arching across the river and when they were closer they saw the three happy faces of their children waving excitedly at them. Jennifer was delighted to see them again since she had been secretly worried at leaving them alone for even a night in a foreign country.

They had decided not to tell the children where they were going until they arrived back at the naturist campsite. They drove back along the edge of the gorge and followed some complicated map that Alf Winterbottom had drawn; the place was much less accessible from the road. When they finally caught sight of the first naked body, protests came from the most unexpected quarter, from Sarah, who only two days ago had been quite content to display her wares to a Cistercian monk.

'Oh, no!' she exclaimed. 'There's absolutely no way I'm going in there.'

But Jeremy had already gone into the little wooden entrance hut to pay the camping fees and book a pitch for the camper van. Sarah stared transfixed at the brown bottom of the naked youth who followed him inside.

'You must be out of your mind, mother. I've no intention of exposing myself to all and sundry. I mean, after all, that man with Daddy was quite young.'

'You were quite content to buy the smallest bikini that I've ever clapped eyes on to parade in front of the boys on the beaches of Provence.'

'But that's different, it covers up all the relevant bits.'

'Only just,' countered her mother.

'And anyway, it excites the boys' imagination more than if you were naked.'

'You'll see, darling, you won't find it at all embarrassing and no one will look at you in a funny way. Anyway, it's not about excitement and titillation; it's about being natural.'

'Oh no, not me, no way! You people can do what you like but I'm staying in my bikini.'

They parked the motor caravan alongside the sad remains of their tent and were welcomed by Rosie and Alf who were delighted to see them back.

It was a blazing hot day with a clear blue sky overhead and Jennifer and Jeremy were almost relieved to take their clothes off. The two younger children followed their example but nothing could persuade Sarah to part with her bikini, brief though it was. John had seen a sandpit and ran off with his bucket and spade and Hilary asked if she could go down to the river for a swim.

Sarah sat on the doorstep of the caravan reading a book to indicate to everyone her total disinterest in the whole business.

Rosie came over to the van clutching a box of Scrabble and invited them over for a game in the shade, under the awning of their caravan.

'I've never played Scrabble in the nude,' said Jeremy, doing his best to enter into the spirit of the thing. His wife admonished him with a rather shocked expression on her face. 'Really, Jeremy, what an extraordinary thing to say.'

'Sorry, dear, it's just that I rather wondered what the vicar would say.'

Jennifer explained that they occasionally played with the local priest and his wife.

'Oh, I don't think he'd mind,' said Rosie. 'We've got a priest in our club in Blackburn, 'aven't we, Alf? Holy Roller he is too.'

'Aye,' said Alf. 'It takes all sorts. We've even got a bone surgeon and a couple of lawyers. Right now, how many letters do we take, dear? I can never remember.'

'Seven it is and don't show them to anybody. Alf never remembers the rules of all these games. I say, would your eldest one like to join us or is she a bit upset?'

Jennifer looked anxiously back to the van, worried about the way Sarah was reacting. 'It's funny but I would have thought that she was the least self-conscious about her body of the whole family.'

'It's a difficult age, that, for the girls,' Rosie said. 'What would she be, about eighteen?'

'Just,' replied Jennifer. 'Hilary's three years younger, then little John's only six.'

'That's a big gap,' said Alf, rather tactlessly. 'Who's first to go?'

Rosie continued speaking, taking no notice of her husband. 'Funny that, though, because usually they get a bit shy around twelve or fourteen. Ours did, didn't they, Alf, even though they'd been doing it all their life. I tell you what, why don't I go and get our Lesley to introduce her to some of the youngsters. She's over there playing volleyball. You men take our turns while Jennifer and I make the introductions.'

When they had left the two teenage girls alone they returned to the Scrabble table but found that the men were drinking beer and discussing the state of the economy. Alf, it appeared, was in the cotton business and had had to diversify in order to escape the squeeze on the industry caused by the introduction of synthetic fibres. They all settled down to the game again and Jennifer was relieved to see the two girls walking down to the river.

Sarah could not help admiring Lesley's body; with her small firm breasts and slim athletic figure covered in a deep brown tan she looked the perfect nature girl. She was also relieved that Lesley had not tried to preach nudism to her or persuade her to undress.

'You probably think I'm a bit silly to keep my things on but I just feel more secure that way. I can't really explain it. Maybe I'll take the plunge later on.'

'Don't worry about it.'

'Anyway, I've seen a few girls walking around with their bikini bottoms on. Maybe I'll do that.'

'It's usually because they're having a period.'

'Oh, heavens,' Sarah's hand came up to her mouth and she looked horrified. 'You mean they…'

'Well of course, silly.' Lesley laughed. 'It's quite normal, it happens to all of us, doesn't it?'

'But you mean…'

'What?'

'You mean they'll all think I'm having a period.'

'Probably, but so what if they do?'

'Oh, golly, that's awful,' cried Sarah, at the same time unhooking her bra and in a lightning movement slipping off her panties. 'Wait for me here while I chuck these back in the van.'

When she ran back she was laughing happily. 'I feel better already, free as the wind. Let's go and have a swim.'

'All right, but after let's go and play volleyball. There are a couple of really dishy Swedish boys I'd like you to meet. They're great fun and I think one of them fancies me but the other one keeps hanging around just when things are warming up.'

An hour later Jeremy and Jennifer passed the volleyball court on the way to the supermarket to buy some food and wine for lunch.

They were delighted to see their eldest daughter joining in the fun with about thirty other teenagers.

'They all look so healthy and happy. Thank heavens Sarah has dropped her inhibitions at the same time as she dropped her panties. The look she gave me this morning made me feel quite degenerate.'

Jeremy grinned as he saw her leaping for the ball among all the brown adolescent flesh.

'Apart from looking like a human zebra with white stripes she could be one of them. If anyone at the bank last week had told me that I'd be capering around in the buff I'd have thought they were a little touched. Imagine what that truculent new ledger clerk would say if he could see me now.'

'Oh, you and your bank,' teased Jennifer. 'Sometimes I think that's all you care about.'

'That's not fair,' said Jeremy, suddenly serious. 'All I really care about in life is you and the kids.'

He hugged her close to him and cupped one hand over her breast and then withdrew, slightly embarrassed to have made such an intimate gesture stark naked in the middle of the campsite.

They could happily have stayed at the naturist resort on the banks of the Ardèche for the rest of the holiday. Hilary had fallen in with a group of friends and spent most of her time splashing around in the water or climbing the cliffs that rose steeply out of the river and jumping in from increasingly daring heights. Young John was content in his sandpit with a dozen other tiny rascals from all over continental Europe and Jeremy was basking in the sun and indulging himself in a little harmless voyeurism. He showed no inclination to embark on his usual cultural forays to look at castles or abbeys and was content to feast his eyes on the more natural architectural formations that surrounded him. Not even in his wildest fantasies did he imagine they came in so many different shapes and sizes.

Sarah had soon lost all her inhibitions about communal nudity and rapidly became the most eager naturist in the whole family, not only pressing her father to stay for the rest of the holiday but even trying to get him to promise to return the following year. Not a little of this enthusiasm was due to the fact that she had become moonstruck with one of the Swedes and was basking in the rapture of young tender love. She was so excited that she even confided in her mother and asked if the young man in question could come to stay with them later in the summer since he was planning to visit London after his stay in France.

Jennifer found herself again worrying about the sexuality of her daughter when she discovered that the young lovers had been kissing.

'But, darling,' she exclaimed, somewhat shocked. 'Surely you must be a little more careful when you're mixing with people who have no clothes on. I mean to say, it's not quite the same thing as a party at the tennis club.'

'Oh, Mother, don't be such a prude. I've seen his body and he's seen mine and we both like what we see.'

'Sarah, you don't mean that you've...'

'Of course not. Why do you older people always have to bring that into it?'

'But surely, dear, he must react in some way when you kiss. It's only normal, and...'

'Well, of course he does, but we only kiss in the evenings when we've got our clothes on. Really, Mummy, at times you don't seem to have the least idea what life's about.'

With that she stormed out of the caravan and went to rejoin Sven and the others, no doubt telling them of the impossibility of talking about intimate matters with the older generation.

Jennifer would have been content to remain at the naturist resort for the rest of the holiday. The children were blissfully happy, Jeremy was visibly relaxed and the very confinement imposed by the secluded spot with its limestone cliffs on one side and the cool flowing river on the other had banished all thoughts of wandering. Jennifer herself, who was something of a health fanatic, was feeling the benefits of the healing glow of the sun on her body and held wistful hopes that some of her inner ailments might be cured by her surprise conversion to the world of heliotherapy. Nevertheless, a nagging uncertainty disturbed her and she anxiously consulted her diary so that she could prepare

herself for the outward and visible appearance of an illness that had been trou-
bling her for months. When it came it could not have been in a more embarrassing place. Several days early and without the usual premonitory symptoms
she felt a damp trickle coursing down her leg while she was shopping in the
camp supermarket. The fact that she was entirely nude with a wire shopping
basket draped over her forearm made it seem even more bizarre. She dropped
everything and fled to the van leaving small pools of dark red menstrual blood
in her path.

She desperately ransacked the medicine chest in the van for a supply of
tampons but they proved inadequate for the task. She was flooding with blood
and large clots were appearing every time she changed the tampons. Feeling
weak she lay down in the bed and supplemented the sanitary pads she was
wearing with a large towel but even this was insufficient to contain the flow
and a dark red patch soaked through and appeared on the outside. She had
never bled like this since her miscarriage two years after Hilary had been born.

Jeremy arrived and promptly confused the issue by fainting; he never could
stomach the sight of blood. Luckily he had rapid powers of recovery and after a
few moments with his head between his knees he was able to fetch more towels
and generally tidy her up.

'My God, Jenny, what happened? Did you cut yourself, love?'

Even though she was feeling so weak, Jennifer managed a smile. 'No, you
cuckoo. Oh, what's the use? You bankers have no idea of bodily functions. To
think I was almost engaged to a doctor.'

'But you're bleeding like a stuck pig.' Then it dawned on him. 'Oh my lord,
it's not the… you know… the…'

Jenny nodded. 'A few days earlier than usual and completely painless. It
took me by surprise. Oh, Christ, I was so embarrassed. Jem, I can't face these
campers again after what happened in that supermarket. We'll simply have to
pack up and leave.'

Jeremy was not a man to argue with any of his wife's decisions. He saw to it
that she was comfortable, gathered up the children, left a garbled message of
farewell to the Winterbottoms and headed out of the campsite on the rutted
track up to the main road.

They found an amenable French doctor in the town of Orange who gave her a special injection and some haemostatic preparation together with a course of hormone tablets, Primolut N, that she was to take every two hours until the bleeding ceased. She was then instructed to continue with them three times a day and consult *un gynècologue* when she returned to England.

The drugs worked surprisingly quickly and in a few hours she was much better and rather regretting the absurd panic that she had generated. She glanced over towards her husband and it was obvious from his expression that he was happy to be sitting high up behind the wheel of the van again with the tyres humming away on the hot asphalt as they headed further south. Sarah, however, had red eyes from crying over her enforced separation from her beautiful blond Swede and the speed of their departure meant that she had not been able to give him her address in England to be able to contact her during his promised visit in the autumn.

Jennifer Watson had a positive fixation about good health and she could not abide the thought that the bodily machine that had served her so well was starting to misbehave.

Until the age of forty-two, she had been the picture of radiant good health. As the wife of a bank manager, she was sufficiently prosperous to look after herself well and had seemed to possess the gift of eternal youth. Her three children were all born without any difficulties after labours that she now looked back on with a certain pride. The midwife had told her that she was a natural child producer and had suggested that certain women like Jennifer should be reserved to bear children and society should pay them highly rather than squander medical effort on those who were less suited to the task. Far-out ideas for the time.

Ill health was almost unknown in her immediate family until her husband developed a duodenal ulcer that perforated, and this was attributed to work-related stress.

The children had the usual childhood illnesses, but none of them needed hospital admission until Sarah had fractured her leg after falling out of a tree. Jennifer herself was almost obscenely healthy and in her late thirties changed the diet to a vegetarian one for all members of the family except for her husband who insisted on bacon for his breakfast every morning and steak twice a week for supper. Jennifer and the children never touched meat in any form and at times she developed an almost messianic fervour in spreading the glad tidings of her conversion to vegetarianism.

At the local parish guild coffee mornings in Knutsford she would grow weary of the women who were forever moaning and groaning about their ills, ranging from premenstrual tension and its associated migraine and menstrual upsets to irritable bowel syndrome and cancer-phobia. To her the answers were absolutely clear; a faith in God, a stable marriage and the exclusion of meat from the diet. Even her husband's ulcer had been blamed on the fact that he had refused to adhere to the new discipline completely. All ill health, she maintained, including cancer, could be fought by a determined spirit and uncontaminated bowels. She regarded illness as a form of spiritual and mental weakness and her outspoken views were unpopular with some of the local women who were less fortunate than her in dealing with their ailments.

Her periods had always been as regular as clockwork and she had suffered minimal pain and discomfort. It came as something of a shock when she noticed about a year ago they were not only lasting a few days longer, for nine days instead of her usual five, but they were becoming heavier, alarmingly so at times. She started to pass large clots and these sometimes caused unpleasant cramps and on one occasion, she had almost fainted.

Since her opinions on the menstrual problems of others had been so forthright, she was unable to discuss her problem with any of her female friends and reluctantly consulted the local GP. Unfortunately, he was having one of his busy days and with a huge crowd outside in the waiting room, she realised that she was not going to get much of a consultation.

No sooner had she entered the room than old Dr Michaelson was going through his familiar social patter and had written her name on the top leaf of a prescription pad. He listened briefly to her story and flicked down her lower eyelid and asked her to put out her tongue. This was as far as his total health check-up extended without actually getting his arse off his chair and he had reached a diagnosis with no difficulty.

'Busy mother-housewife-cook syndrome, my dear. Many of the lasses get similar problems at your stage of life. Either hubby's a failure and you feel you should have married better or he's a success and he's never at home. Can't win either way.'

Dr Michaelson's philosophy of life was simple and unequivocal. He had already written a prescription for a tranquilliser and some iron tablets and tore it off the orange NHS prescription booklet with his customary flourish, which provided the only exercise in his working day.

Jennifer was a little puzzled that he had not examined her properly, but she was brought up with an unshakeable conviction that doctors knew what they were doing and thought little more of it. The tranquillisers tended to make her feel even more tired so she discarded them after a few weeks, but she continued with the iron tablets and felt that they were benefiting her. She borrowed a physiology textbook from the local library and discovered that the average menstrual loss was 50mg of iron per month and a normal diet including meat was only just sufficient to provide for this.

She could see that her loss exceeded this amount and her vegetarian diet was not adequate to provide all the factors needed to make up for it. She therefore did a complete U-turn in her dietary philosophy and declared that to be vegetarian was unnatural – that the human dental configuration proved that man was a carnivore – and forced the family to eat large amounts of liver, steak tartare and spinach.

She hoped that Mother Nature could persuade her periods to return to their normal pattern and that Father Time would eventually effect a cure. She resolved not to worry unduly about the problem. She did not even bother to mention it to her husband.

Jeremy was not the kind of man who concerned himself with a woman's 'underneaths'. His world was one of profit and loss clearly tabulated in neat columns of figures, and the vagaries of biology made him ill at ease. He was delighted, of course, when his wife dropped her absurd craze for vegetarian cooking and once more joined the real world of good living and good eating, not that they could afford to eat out very much nowadays. Their annual pilgrimage to France was their only excess.

After their hasty retreat from the Ardèche they spent three enjoyable days pottering around the Mediterranean coast. They passed through the Camargue with its wild white horses and gypsies and visited the medieval walled city of Aigues Mortes, where St Louis launched two of the Crusades. It was a flourishing port in the Middle Ages but the sea later receded, leaving it alone and isolated, its bastions and ramparts looming up out of the salt marshes. In Arles they explored the old Roman city and Jeremy went into a frenzy of ecstasy at the cloister of St Trophime with the exquisite romanesque carvings at the head of each column.

By now Jeremy was being accused of treachery by his two older children and he had to concede defeat and escort them to crowded beaches near Cavalaire.

After a few days he became restless and suggested a visit to the naturist *plage* at Ramatuelle, near St Tropez, which was only a few miles away, but was severely reprimanded by his wife for an unhealthy and lascivious tendency to voyeurism. He would have argued, but it was pointless and anyway he never won an argument with his wife. Instead he turned wearily to an article on gilt-edged securities in the overseas edition of the *Financial Times*.

By this time Jennifer's menstrual flow had ceased and her mistrust of all medication caused her to ignore the French doctor's advice to continue the tablets until she arrived home. Little did she realise that they had built up the lining of her womb to a considerable thickness and withdrawal of this hormonal support would result in catastrophic haemorrhage. Her innate sense of the theatrical ensured that it happened at a place even more bizarre than the previous time. They were being escorted around the beautiful Romanesque abbey of Le Thoronet, when the cramp started again in her belly and the telltale trickle of blood cascaded down her legs on to the grey flagstones of the chapel floor. She screamed with horror and felt sick and nauseous, her face drained of blood, becoming deathly pale as she fainted to the floor.

The ensuing scene was incredible to behold. People were jostling in the crowd to get a better view and the shrieking and arm-waving that the English associate with Gallic hysteria was made more impressive by the monks who were convinced that they were witness to a spiritual manifestation, a sign from the Almighty – possibly even the creation of a new saint.

Jennifer was eventually taken at breakneck speed in a Citroën DS ambulance to Draguignan hospital. She recalled the fluttering Red Cross flag on the radio aerial and the shrieking two-tone horn, but she passed into oblivion again and had no recollection of her arrival.

She awoke to find a blood transfusion running into her arm veins and later in the day, after four pints of blood, she was taken to an operating theatre for a curettage. The following day she was discharged to a worried husband with advice that she would probably need a major operation when she returned to the UK. Although she insisted that she was feeling fine, in fact the blood transfusion had made her feel superbly fit again but her husband would not countenance the thought of continuing with the holiday. She returned by plane with Sarah from Nice to Manchester Airport, with Jeremy grumbling somewhat unfairly about the astronomical cost she had caused him by her failure to tell him about her illness before they left home.

CHAPTER THIRTEEN
Knutsford, Cheshire, October

Jennifer waited for her September period before seeking medical advice, thinking, perhaps, that the curettage in France had cured her. But no, the next period had the same heavy flow with huge clots of dark blood lasting for more than two weeks. The severity of the bleeding had worried her and Jeremy was insisting that she make an appointment with a specialist in St John's Street, the Harley Street of Manchester. She was beginning to feel weak again and she looked pale. The insecurity of being ill in a strange land had pressed upon her the need for proper attention. She knew that if she procrastinated any longer she would have to suffer the ordeal of another catastrophic menstrual loss, feeling like a leaking bathroom tap pouring with blood and knowing surely that the body could not lose much more.

She phoned for an appointment with the local GP. Yes, Dr Michaelson was able to see her this afternoon. Would five o'clock be suitable? She was relieved. Usually you had to wait for about six weeks before the busy doctors could accommodate you. Even then it was a fight to get past the cool, composed nurse-receptionist, who generally tried any technique in the feminine tactics manual to reassure you that the real or imagined complaint was not worthy of the great doctor's time. With gynaecological disorders in particular she always carried with her the disarming knowledge that she had suffered from the same complaint for years yet she didn't go scurrying off to the doctor on the least excuse. She usually sealed the conversation by advising Sanatogen tonic for the truly feeble and Guinness and panadol elixir for those of tougher constitution. Jennifer was always left wondering whether the nurse really was a mine of pathology or a natural born liar. She certainly formed a protective barrier around the doctors and one had to be very ill indeed or give an extremely good imitation of it to get through to the medical inner sanctum.

Since Jennifer's complaint was a menstrual one, she thought she would have to battle hard to get past this piece of butchery, but to her surprise, the usual aggressive tone had disappeared and the nurse was all smiles and sweetness. At least that was how it appeared over the telephone.

'Of course, Dr Michaelson would be delighted to see you. How awful flooding like that on your holiday. You must be feeling terribly weak. Are you sure you wouldn't like a house call?'

A house call! Great godfathers. One had to be within spitting distance of the pearly gates to warrant a house call from the busy medical men.

'No, thank you all the same, but I think I'll be able to get around to the surgery.'

Good heavens. She had never been offered a house visit before. Not even when Jeremy had a perforated duodenal ulcer. She remembered that verbal tussle with the dragoness.

'Come, come, if he's that ill he'll have to go to hospital anyway. We can't operate in the home, you know. Modern medicine has travelled a long way since the horse and buggy days of the visiting doctor. There are tests and things to perform and these can't be done anywhere except in the surgery or the hospital. If he's as ill as you're trying to suggest you'd better take him straight to the hospital. If he's not that bad, pop him in the back of the car and bring him straight round. He won't be kept waiting.'

In fact, Jennifer reluctantly conceded that the old warhorse had been right. He had been seen immediately and there was the frightening sequence of clanging ambulance bells, long hospital corridors, stretchers being wheeled frantically by Greek porters, junior doctors requiring informed consent, explanations, waiting and then relief... 'He'll pull through. It was a bad one, though. Thank God you didn't delay in seeking medical advice. Another hour or so and he would have been gone. Those enzymes from the stomach eat up the insides and every hour counts. Your GP was quick off the mark. It makes a pleasant change.'

Yes, the warhorse had been right on that occasion and ever since then Jennifer had never argued with her, even if it meant bundling feverish kids into blankets and dragging them through the wintery snows. It was never that bad; at least they had a heated car.

All the same, she reflected, there was something distinctly odd about this new approach. Usually the practice was so busy that patients were kept at bay until the point of collapse.

She soon found out the reason for the change in pace. The village was swarming with gossip. Jennifer was feeling so weak and light-headed that she couldn't face the heavy manual task of shopping for the family by trudging around the enormous local supermarket. Instead she went to one of the few remaining old-fashioned merchants who still operated a delivery service. This allowed her time to go to Mrs Gaskell's Coffee House where she bumped into Mrs Cloughley and Dorothy Scott from the flower club.

'Haven't you heard? There's been such a scandal. Been in all the papers, it has. No one goes there any more. Oh! You can't trust them. Wonder whether any of them is qualified. Know what I mean?'

Jennifer didn't, and to try to sort out fact from fancy, she went up to the public library to read the back numbers of the daily papers. It was all there. The little village and its health centre had become famous during her absence.

There were several versions of the story, and the amount of scurrilousness and infamy that was alleged depended to a large extent on the quality of the newspaper that one was reading. As usual, *The Guardian* seemed to be the voice of moderation and had an interesting editorial on the points at issue. She felt comfortable with *The Guardian* and was sure that its version was the nearest to the truth. Unfortunately, it had, as usual, twice the number of printing errors as the gutter press, but there again, it probably had twice as many words on the subject. Swings and roundabouts. She settled herself in a corner chair to read all about it.

It appeared that the local health centre, consisting of four general practitioners, had taken on a junior as an assistant. The man had been absolutely charming and they were all impressed with how hard he had worked and how the patients, almost without exception, had spoken highly of him. They were so impressed with his general ability that they offered him a partnership and it was only after a further six months had elapsed that the horrible truth had dawned upon them. The man was not qualified. He had never been near a medical school in his life. The ultimate confidence trick had been perpetrated on this ultra-conservative village. It had taken a whole year before anyone discovered that the charming young doctor was in reality a laboratory technician.

Jennifer gathered up all her collection of daily papers from which she had pieced together the saga. To think that all of this had happened while they had been on holiday and not a ripple of it had reached them until this morning.

She chuckled quietly to herself. She found the whole thing rather amusing. She had always loathed the petite bourgeoisie of this little village and it gave her immense satisfaction to know that someone had taken them all for a ride. She glanced at her watch. She would quickly go home and cook an omelette and then collect John from kindergarten before her appointment at the scene of the crime.

The health centre, to all outward appearance, was unchanged, but inside it presented a very different picture. Instead of fighting for a chair and a copy of *Autocar* or *Cheshire Life* with a coughing, spluttering collection of the sick, it was possible to sit at leisure in the hushed atmosphere of the waiting room. There were only three other people there and they all looked knowingly at each other as if they were members of some secret society.

Dr Michaelson was delighted to see her, but Jennifer was shocked by the change in the man. His hair had visibly become greyer. He had aged ten years and the lines of strain were cast into prominence. He put his hand tenderly on hers as she sat beside his desk. His father had delivered her. He always told how it was one of his most difficult domiciliary deliveries. She had been a face presentation. Besides, they had been at school together and at one time they were almost on 'love among the haystacks' terms.

'Thanks, Jenny, for still coming.'

His eyes were watering slightly. He'd obviously been through an ordeal these past weeks and the desertion of so many of his patients had completely undermined him.

'Loyalty is a quality we don't often recognise until we confront the lack of it.'

She told him the problem of her menstrual flooding and the embarrassment it had caused her on her holiday. He examined her on the couch and performed a gentle internal examination, something he would scarcely have found time for in the hurly burly of the days before the scandal. She did her best to relax, although she hated these intrusions into her interior. With an old friend like Michaelson it would appear foolish to make a fuss. She reflected on how pleasant he was compared with the old battle-axe that he had stationed at his reception desk. The Ceres, the twin-headed hound guarding the entrance to the underworld. This image enabled her to relax her levators and allow Michaelson to fumble about sufficiently to arrive at a diagnosis. Finally, he mumbled, 'Fibroids, I thought so,' as if he had discovered hidden treasure deep inside her.

He removed his gloves and washed his hands in the running water of the corner wash basin as Jennifer put her panties back on, trying all the time to appear demure and casual. Michaelson looked pleased with himself. Gynaecology was not one of his strong points but this time he was sure his fingers had not betrayed him. He sat down and, with time on his hands and an empty waiting room, he drew a little diagram to show Jennifer the nature of her complaint.

'I tell you what, Jenny. I want you to have the best. This will almost certainly mean a hysterectomy and I'd like you to go down to London to see Angus Reith. He's just about the best there is. He's the senior consultant at my old medical school. Let me write him a letter and you can phone for an appointment.'

'Can't it be done in Manchester? I've known lots of women who had their wombs removed at the Manchester Royal Infirmary. Or even at the Altrincham General?'

'Oh, they can, of course. And normally that's where I'd send you, but you're a friend of the family and I think this is one occasion where we can pull out all the stops to work our way through the old boy network. My father used to teach Angus Reith at St Giles before he moved north, and I always send any special problems down to him. Anyway, your womb is a bit on the large side so I think you'd be better off under a really good man. Harley Street for you, Jennifer. You take my advice. He's reputed to be the best gynaecological surgeon in the country.'

Jennifer emerged from her consultation with a prescription for iron tablets and instructions to ring a certain number in London. She was also a little concerned about the fuss that Michaelson was making about a routine thing like a hysterectomy.

After she had left, Dr Michaelson smiled to himself and emitted a slight chuckle as he wrote the referral letter. He had rewarded her loyalty and confidence in him with his very best contact among the elite world of London specialists. He had also made it clear in the letter that she wasn't to be charged more than the usual consultation fee and although she was to be seen privately in his Harley Street consulting rooms she was to be operated on the NHS since they did not have private insurance. Little did he realise that he had made a fateful error and that Jennifer would have fared better if he had directed her to the local hospital. It was something he regretted until the end of his life.

PART THREE

THE OPERATION

A laparotomy is a surgical incision to open the abdominal cavity to perform an operation, and the first one in the world was performed on Christmas Day 1809.

That day saw the birth of operative abdominal surgery, which has saved countless lives, yet it did not take place in one of the great university teaching hospitals but in the front parlour of the house of an American country doctor in the small frontier town of Danville in Kentucky.

On the morning of Christmas Day 1809 the brave surgeon Ephraim Mc-Dowell performed the world's first elective laparotomy to remove a massive tumour from the equally brave patient, Jane Todd Crawford, who had to withstand the horrific pain of a large abdominal incision without the benefit of an anaesthetic; she merely recited some psalms. The doctor was brave because the abdominal cavity had never been deliberately opened with a surgical knife before and it was widely accepted that such an intervention would inevitably result in death from infection or blood loss.

Legend has it that the townsfolk of Danville had gathered in the square outside his house on the morning of the operation and were erecting a gallows, so that if the patient died at the hands of the 'dreadful doctor' he would be hanged in public.

Jane Todd Crawford lived with her family of five children in a small log cabin near Greensburg, some sixty miles from Danville. At the age of forty-four she was thought to be carrying her sixth child, and was causing concern with the local doctors and midwives because she was two months beyond her due date and she was afflicted with excruciating pains similar to those of labour.

The two attending physicians were in despair and had tried various potions and enemas used to induce labour and in desperation had even employed two midwives to jump up and down on her extremely distended abdomen. All this was to no avail and the poor woman had such a swollen abdomen that she could barely breathe, so they decided to summon the 'surgeon from Danville to assist with the delivery'.

Although the journey from Danville to Greensburg can nowadays be easily accomplished in an hour or so using modern highways, in 1809 it required a lengthy and difficult journey on horseback, crossing many mountain ridges and fording deep rivers. When McDowell set out on this arduous journey, the snow had already fallen deeply and there were added hazards from bands of skirmishing Seminoles and Cherokees, to say nothing of predatory wolf packs and bears. When he arrived he quickly appraised the situation and saw that the swollen abdomen did indeed have the appearance of a pregnancy, possibly a multiple one, with a size that was making it difficult for the poor woman to breathe.

Ephraim McDowell had always wanted to be a doctor, but there was no medical school in the United States at that time, so when he was twenty-two the family gathered sufficient money to send him to Edinburgh, where he spent two years studying anatomy under Alexander Monro and surgery under the tutelage of John Bell and John Hunter. For financial reasons he had to return home to Danville without earning a medical degree, but even with no letters after his name, the prestige of being educated at one of the world's most famous medical schools ensured that he rapidly built up an extensive surgical practice and he came to be regarded as the best doctor west of Philadelphia.

Without recourse to sophisticated imaging techniques it is often difficult clinically to distinguish a massive fibroid from a large ovarian tumour or, indeed, from a term pregnancy. Possibly because of his education in Edinburgh, McDowell performed a more thorough examination than had been performed by the local physicians and this included a vaginal examination where he found that the mass was inclined to one side and was mobile; his examining finger felt a normal-sized uterus and cervix that were pushed to the other side, all of which indicated that the mass was an 'enlarged ovarium'.

Clearly, he was very depressed by his findings and in an account given many years later to a medical student, Robert Thompson, he wrote, 'I told the lady that I could do her no good and candidly stated to her, her deplorable situation; informed her that John Bell, Hunter, Hay and A Wood, four of the first and most eminent surgeons in England and Scotland, had uniformly declared in their lectures that such was the danger of peritoneal inflammation that opening the abdomen to extract the tumour led to inevitable death.'

She was clearly devastated by this pronouncement, but told him that it was impossible to continue to live in her present situation since she was almost unable to breathe. He therefore continued, 'but, notwithstanding this, if she thought herself prepared to die, I would take the lump from her if she would come to Danville.' He ended this account by stating simply, 'she appeared willing to undergo an experiment'. This must surely be the first documented case in the world of informed consent.

Dr McDowell returned to Danville expecting to hear no more from her because the journey with the increasing snowfall that winter was long and difficult and dangerous by horseback, but she was a tough frontier woman and a few days later appeared on his doorstep. Unfortunately the arduous journey had caused considerable bruising over the lower abdomen, where she had rested the enormous tumour on the pommel of her saddle. He therefore determined to wait for a few days before deciding to perform the operation and, being a deeply religious man, he timed the procedure to occur on the morning of Christmas Day when many of the townsfolk were in church so that they could bring the efforts of their combined prayers on to his endeavour. He was joined by his nephew, Dr James McDowell, who had graduated a few months previously from the first medical school in America, in Philadelphia, to join the practice as a partner, and he did his best to dissuade his uncle from 'the experiment'. The kitchen table was dragged into the front room and Jane Todd Crawford was placed on her back on the table and tilted slightly to the right side. Ephraim McDowell then offered up a prayer saying, 'Direct me, oh God, in performing this operation, for I am but an instrument in thy hands, and am but thy servant, and if it is thy will, oh! spare this poor afflicted woman.'

He made a vertical incision nine inches in length from the sternum to the pubic bone and cut down with the scalpel until the tumour came into view, but it was so large that it was impossible to remove it entirely. He cut into it and removed 15lb (6.8kg) of a dirty gelatinous-looking substance and then extracted the lining of the cyst, which weighed 7.5lb (6.8kg). As soon as the external opening was made, the intestines spilled out on the table and, since the abdomen was completely filled by the tumour, they could not be easily be replaced during the operation, which was terminated in about twenty-five minutes.

During the whole of this ghastly painful procedure, Jane Todd Crawford remained motionless and merely recited the psalms in order to calm herself during her ordeal.

She stayed in McDowell's house and the bed in which she lay can still be seen because the entire house and gardens have been turned into a museum to commemorate this amazing feat of pioneering surgery.

Ephraim McDowell visited Mrs Crawford on a daily basis and on the fifth day he found her making her own bed and he reprimanded her severely. She continued to make an excellent recovery, and twenty-five days later she returned home in good health by the same route that she had come, which is now a long-distance footpath named the Jane Todd Crawford Trail.

The two of them never met again during their lives. Ephraim McDowell died at the age of fifty-nine of 'an acute attack of inflammation of the stomach', which was probably appendicitis and long before the time when a laparotomy could be performed to remove the infected organ. Jane Todd Crawford outlived him and died at the age of seventy-eight, and in McDowell's house there is a picture of her in her old age showing her displaying a locket with the picture of Abraham Lincoln, who was born in a log cabin at Sinking Spring Farm very close to where she grew up in Greensburg County, and to whom she was related as a cousin when he married one of her sisters, who thus became America's First Lady as Mary Todd Lincoln.

The often repeated story that the townsfolk had gathered in the square outside his house and erected a gallows is almost certainly anecdotal and untrue for several reasons. Firstly McDowell was considered the most famous, knowledgeable and skilful surgeon in that frontier area, which probably had few doctors, and he would have been treated with the greatest respect and unlikely to have been publicly hanged. Furthermore, his father was the county judge and his elder brother was the Sheriff of Danville, who was killed a few weeks later when he was involved, along with Davy Crockett and Daniel Boone, in a skirmish with some warriors of the Cherokee tribe at Licking river in Kentucky.

Unlike his modern counterparts, Ephraim McDowell did not immediately rush off to get this operation published and waited until he had performed two more successful operations on ovarian tumours in 1813 and 1816 before reporting the cases in a journal with a limited readership, *The Eclectic Repertory and Analytical Review of Philadelphia*. News of great surgical advances took a long time to percolate across the Atlantic and, even in America, McDowell's achievement was greeted with a certain amount of scepticism and even outright disbelief.

It was fourteen years later that the first ovariotomy was carried out in Europe by

John Lizars, a fellow student from Edinburgh, but the patient died and he then made three more successful attempts. It appears that the Edinburgh surgeon, JY Simpson, the inventor of the anaesthetic agent chloroform, which was used during Queen Victoria's eighth childbirth, was the first to introduce the word 'ovariotomy', a strange choice for the name of this operation in an age when most surgeons were reared in the classics and therefore etymologically correct.

The initial years of abdominal surgery were associated with an enormous mortality rate, mainly due to uncontrolled haemorrhage or peritonitis and sepsis, but the few women who survived spawned a new generation of pioneering surgeons who finally realised that opening the human abdomen with a surgical incision did not necessarily result in certain death.

The greatest of the ovariotomists in Europe was Charles Clay of Manchester. He studied at Manchester Royal Infirmary and, like Ephraim McDowell, received part of his medical education in Edinburgh. Like McDowell he also started in surgical practice in a small rural community, Ashton-under-Lyne, in the shadow of the Pennine Hills in Cheshire. After sixteen years he moved to the industrial city of Manchester where he established his surgical reputation. He was a member of the Reform Club and was a friend of my great-grandfather, William Sutton, who was a successful businessman in this thriving Victorian metropolis.

The first four of his ovariotomies survived, but with the fifth he was not so lucky; this turned out to be the first abdominal hysterectomy recorded, and it was a complete disaster. The operation was performed on November 17, 1843, in the first-floor room above his consulting rooms in Piccadilly, the large square in the centre of Manchester. As was usual in those days he was accompanied by several friends and medical students as spectators and since it was before the time of Pasteur or Lister nobody wore masks or surgical gloves, and the patient was given brandy and milk to alleviate the pain of the operation – this was a long time before anaesthesia was introduced by WRT Morton at the Massachusetts General Hospital in Boston in 1846.

Clay was certain that he was dealing with a massive ovarian cyst, so he made a long 60cm surgical incision from the xiphisternum to the pubis.

Unfortunately, once the peritoneum was entered the patient coughed and the massive tumour was extruded. Clay realised to his horror that it was a huge fibroid and, since the patient was now struggling and had to be forcibly restrained by the medical students, it was impossible to replace the hugely enlarged uterus back in the abdominal cavity, so he had no option but to proceed and perform a hysterectomy, leaving behind the cervix, the lower part of the womb. The patient died of a massive haemorrhage a few hours later.

The next year, Clay was more successful with a similar case but on this occasion he placed a ligature of Indian hemp around the supra-vaginal cervix to prevent haemorrhage from the uterine arteries. The patient lived for fifteen days, before she fell out of bed in a coma and never regained consciousness. Although this was tragic for the patient and her family it was also sad for Clay since she had survived the critical post-operative period and not succumbed to sepsis, which was the usual cause of death following a laparotomy.

From reading contemporary accounts of this woman's post-operative course it is difficult to determine the exact mode of death. She could have had a pulmonary embolus or she could have fallen out of bed in uraemic coma due to occlusion of both ureters by the ligature, but popular Mancunian folklore suggests that she was dropped on the floor by a couple of incompetent porters while the nurses changed her bed linen. If this is true then her death was entirely unrelated to the operation and Charles Clay could have claimed to have performed the first successful hysterectomy in the world.

In fact it was not for a further 20 years that he attempted another hysterectomy, and this time the patient survived. Interestingly he mentioned this during his important presentation to the Obstetrical Society of London in 1863 when he presented his experience of 395 ovariotomies with only twenty-five deaths. Almost as an aside he mentioned a 'successful case of the entire removal of the uterus and its appendages' which he performed on January 3, 1863. This was the first successful hysterectomy performed in Europe and it is important that it be emphasised because many reference books give priority to Eugène Koeberlé of Strasbourg who performed his operation on April 2, 1863, some three months after Charles Clay.

Nevertheless the first successful removal of a fibroid uterus was performed in the United States some ten years before this by Walter Burnham in Lowell, Massachusetts, in 1853. Although the patient survived, the diagnosis was wrong since Burnham thought he was dealing with a massive ovarian cyst. This time, the patient had the benefit of an anaesthetic in the form of chloroform, which caused the patient to vomit and extrude a huge fibroid, so he had no alternative but to remove the uterus. By an amazing coincidence, later in that same year of 1853, Gilman Kimball, in the same town, performed a hysterectomy with the correct diagnosis and the patient survived.

In those early years the mortality rate was horrific with only 30 per cent surviving the operation. Burnham performed fifteen hysterectomies during his thirteen-year surgical career but sadly only three patients survived, the rest dying from peritonitis, sepsis, haemorrhage and, somewhat surprisingly, exhaustion.

To put these events in a historical context it is noteworthy that both of these doctors served as brigade surgeons on the side of the Union in the American Civil War (1862-1870).

The initial mortality in these operations was extremely high since many of the early abdominal surgeons employed the long ligature hanging out of the lower part of the incision in order to allow the drainage of 'laudable pus' from the peritoneal cavity, in much the same way as when they were amputating limbs in battlefield surgery.

Appalling results were reported by Spencer Wells, a consultant at St Mary's Hospital and the Soho Hospital in London and a society dilettante who considered himself the greatest gynaecological surgeon in Europe at that time. He drove from hospital to hospital in London in his 'brougham and four silver grey horses' and, out of forty hysterectomies performed for fibroids, there were twenty-nine deaths – a mortality rate of seventy-three per cent.

Probably the greatest analytical surgeon in the speciality of gynaecology during the late nineteenth century was Thomas Keith, a wild-looking man born in the Manse of St Cyrus, near Montrose in the Scottish Borders. He was a lifelong sufferer from cysteine stones and required many operations, which probably accounted for his rather startling appearance. He performed his first ovariotomy in September 1862, but his initial mortality rate was high. This was around the time that Lister was advocating antiseptic surgery, although Keith found that the carbolic spray did not help to reduce his operative mortality. He therefore turned his attention to the method of wound closure, abandoning the long ligature and instead cauterised the cervical stump, which had usually been exteriorised by a metal clamp, and then dropped it into the peritoneal cavity, which he then drained with a rubber tube.

He was also a vigorous opponent of the technique of blood-letting, and out of 156 cases reported only six deaths (3.8 per cent mortality). His hysterectomy results were no less impressive and by the time he left Edinburgh for London he had recorded thirty-three cases with only three deaths.

Thomas Keith's example was taken up enthusiastically by contemporary surgeons and with advances in antiseptic practices in the form of hand washing, the wearing of gloves and face masks and the development of disinfected operating rooms, the mortality slowly fell to acceptable levels. These new techniques are reflected in the dramatic fall in mortality shown in the figures from the London teaching hospitals between 1896 and 1906 showing an impressive drop in mortality from twenty-two per cent to 3.5 per cent.

During the past hundred years the introduction of antibiotics, intravenous therapy, anticoagulation, safe anaesthesia and blood transfusion has reduced the mortality for both vaginal and abdominal hysterectomy to around 0.1 per cent. There has also been a concomitant reduction in morbidity, reflected by a shorter hospital stay and the use of the transverse incision, introduced by Johannes Pfannenstiel from Breslau in 1900, which gives a stronger and better cosmetic result. Nevertheless, it took many years for this incision, with its higher tensile strength making it less prone to wound dehiscence and incisional hernia, to gain universal acceptance.

It was often referred to as a 'bikini incision' and its cosmetic result was popular with patients, but for all its advantages it took a little longer than the disfiguring up-and-down midline incision and was also prone to allowing a collection of blood, with the resulting swelling called a haematoma; it required the insertion of a thin silicone tube attached to a suction drain to prevent this happening. Angus Reith and other surgeons of the Sir Lancelot Spratt generation loathed the added time it took and equally loathed the body consciousness of a generation of nubile young girls strutting around beaches in 'bits of string' but stopping just short of complete nudity.

Nature has provided another entry site for removal of the uterus without the need for an abdominal incision and that is by way of the vagina, which can be technically difficult unless there is some prolapse of the tissues allowing easier access. Unfortunately Jennifer Watson had a large uterus due to fibroids, which are benign tumours of the womb muscle that can grow to an enormous size, making it impossible to perform a vaginal hysterectomy.

As the day of her operation approached, Jennifer Watson became increasingly worried and with her inquisitive mind decided to look at some medical journals kept in the library of the University of Manchester, where she had attended as an undergraduate studying social sciences; happily, she had kept her library card up to date. There were several audits of mortality and morbidity following the different types of hysterectomy with large numbers of almost 2,000 cases, and the death rate appeared to be about one per cent, with an added 0.5 per cent if the womb was enlarged with fibroids, as it was in her case.

She knew many women among her friends who had undergone the operation unscathed, but she still had a nagging doubt and feared she might belong to that worrying statistic of the added 0.5 per cent.

CHAPTER FOURTEEN
The hospital switchboard, St Giles' Hospital, London, September 1968

The hospital switchboard was one of the busier exchanges in the west of London and employed about a dozen girls working hard at the holy board plugging and unplugging numerous sockets into tiny orifices. The annual telephone bill for the hospital amounted to some £500,000 and despite all sorts of warnings from the administration the charity of the National Health Service was often abused. Medical staff were meant to record any private phone calls and submit a monthly cheque to cover the cost of such calls. Most doctors resented this since they felt that if they were required to work untold hours and to live away from their homes they should have the right to ring their family or loved ones free of charge. Such niggling by the administration was thought to be bureaucratic and miserly. On the other hand it was well known that some of the junior staff coming from Australia or India were in the habit of indulging in lengthy chats with their relatives at home at the expense of the already overburdened British taxpayer. The hospital authorities had recently inserted a cunning device that only allowed the caller to dial a local call and this had tended to cause the antipodeans to fall back to letter writing.

During the evening the switchboard was less busy and from six o'clock to midnight was manned by a few disreputable-looking cronies of Mr Hare, the Night Beagle, who looked after the front desk. H-A would leave his post around midnight and entrust the front desk to one of the night porters and the switchboard was operated by the night telephonist, a curvaceous girl all the way from Liverpool called Marlene.

She had arrived in London, like so many girls from the provinces, with only a small suitcase, having left an anguished farewell letter to her parents. It was as if she was reliving the song 'She's Leaving Home', composed by John Lennon and Paul McCartney and sung by the Beatles, one of the bands that had catapulted her home city to fame as the world capital of popular music. Marlene, however, was not leaving to seek a liaison with a man from the motor trade as depicted in the song, but was hoping to find happiness with a Millwall supporter she had met in the pub after a match against her own team Everton at Goodison Park.

This affair had only lasted a few weeks but her pride kept her in the capital city, barely existing on some poorly paid jobs in bars and restaurants. She was delighted to accept the job of night switchboard operator at St Giles since the only alternative seemed to be the sex industry. Little did she know at the time of accepting the job that she was about to enter a sex industry of her own.

The number of telephone calls during the long hours of the night were few indeed and Marlene became bored, lonely and homesick, and sometimes she cried. She yearned after Penny Lane and the dirty ol' Mersey and she missed her dear fat old mum, but her pride would not let her contact her even though she had the national telephone network only an arm's length away.

It was Julian Rolleson who noticed her one night just as he was going to bed after a late call to admit someone with renal colic from A&E. She was drying the tears from her eyes and he brought her a cup of coffee from the vending machine in the entrance hall and sat down beside the switchboard as she told the long and complex story of her broken love life, the parental strife and the flight from home. She told of the misery and loneliness of this big city and how she found this job to be the loneliest of all. After H-A went home she had no company until eight the next morning, then the loneliness of an empty bedsit to pass away the day desperately trying to catch up on lost sleep.

Julian Rolleson had big brown eyes and they milked sympathy and confidence from women, and finally they loved him for those eyes and the fact that he listened carefully to anything they said, so they trusted him and usually did anything he asked. He also had the gift of making girls laugh, which took the tension out of the situation. If he had been an honourable man it would have been a delightful gift, but unfortunately he had a libido of almost Olympian proportions. He manipulated women for his own pleasure and had become such a successful rake that he would only buy a girl a drink if she agreed to go to bed with him. Amazingly they rarely refused and his sexual athleticism had reached a stage that some of the students started slipping an oestrogen tablet into his early morning tea to provide some nocturnal silence in the doctor's bedrooms during the difficult days before the final exams. They had to discontinue his medication when he started to mention one morning over breakfast that he was developing breasts. Surprisingly even 0.05mg of ethinyl oestradiol a day had not managed to curb his sexual lust.

Rolleson's ears drunk in Marlene's story and when she had finished and clearly felt great comfort in confiding in someone, he countered with a tale of his own. He explained to her that he had a rare medical ailment that would leave him with a permanent and painful erection if he could not be sexually satisfied every twenty-four hours. Priapism, it was called. He was sure she was a broadminded girl and would not be embarrassed by his being so frank. She blushed slightly. No one could call her a prude.

'Would you mind helping me since my regular girlfriend has walked out on me and I will be in agony by the time morning comes?'

'But I might have to answer the telephone. We can't do it on the floor. I mean, I'd love to help, but I can't leave the switch.'

'You're an angel, Marlene. You can just lean on the switchboard bench with your earphones on and I'll just come in behind you. It would help me terrifically much. You've no idea of the pain you're helping to relieve.'

She bent over as instructed, with her nose close to the sockets in the switchboard and the plug in her right hand ready to receive an incoming call, as he eased her skirt up and gently slid her panties over the pink flesh of her little Liverpudlian bottom. This was the finest sight of all. He parted her cheeks gently while she parted her legs so as to receive him, and as he slowly eased himself inside her the other end of her body received a call from a local GP who was trying to get a patient admitted. She connected him quickly with the resident medical officer and ignored the flashing lights because she was enjoying so much her mercy mission for the young doctor in distress. He also felt that he would sleep much more soundly after this nightcap.

Marlene had never had it this way before. Rolleson had never had it so good and between them both it became a regular feature in the telephone exchange during the wee small hours of the night.

Julian Rolleson would have made an outstanding racketeer but he could never keep a good thing to himself. He always had to expand his operations. He thanked Marlene profusely for her help with his illness, which was getting better by the night, but felt that some of the other doctors could be helped in a similar manner. No, they didn't all have the same condition, but all the same they suffered considerable strain during all the night duty they had to suffer and sometimes it was very hard to get back to sleep after an emergency call in the night. The nurses were getting very unsympathetic these days and she was the only person in the hospital at night who had a spark of decency and kindness. It was true that Marlene had a heart of gold and seen in this light she became a crusading angel providing succour for the overworked junior doctors.

It would usually go something like this: Tring... Tring, Tring... Tring... 'Dr Brackenbridge here. What time is it?'

'Doctor Brackenbridge. Maternity wants you for a forceps. If you need any help getting back to sleep afterwards you know where to find me.'

'Uh.' Awake now and brightening visibly. 'Oh, thanks a lot, Marlene. Good of you. I'll get that baby out as fast as I can.'

'No need to hurry, doc, I'll still be sitting here all night.'

Frank Brackenbridge would visualise exactly what she was sitting on and would greet the night with hitherto unknown enthusiasm. He would saunter along the corridor in his green operating theatre garb that most of the house-men slept in to prevent them having to keep changing their clothes in the middle of the night. Why put trousers and shirt on when one has to remove them three minutes later? He would whistle the theme tune of a popular hymn as he sauntered up to the labour ward in high spirits to be greeted by the High Priestess of all the Midwife Dragons, Sister Mallett.

'What you bleedin' whistlin' for?' she would say with a Cockney scowl. 'No bleedin' right to 'ave a smile on yer fizzog at this hour of the bleedin' night. Anyway the woman pushed it out with a wide episiotomy which I clobbered up meself.'

Normally Frank would have been furious at having been dragged out of his slumbers so unnecessarily and without even a shred of an apology from the old Chopper. Instead he beamed benignly, rubbed his hands together in happy anticipation and headed for the telephone exchange.

''Ello, Frank, mate. Fancy some coffee as well? Prefer it before or after, luv?'

Marlene had taken to coming to work without any panties under her dress so it was now only necessary to hitch it up, flash the old man and they were away down the expressway to funland. Coffee before or after? With milk or without? One sugar or two and then back to bed and it was just as Rolleson said – sleep did come more easily.

She would sometimes play games with them. When they knocked on the door she would put a blindfold on and ask them to remain silent. She would play blind man's buff and try to guess the owner by the size of his willy. Brackenbridge, of course, always gave himself away by clapping his hands together and rubbing his palms briskly at the sight of her bottom as if he was about to tuck into a good portion of plump chicken breasts.

She had been initiated sexually at a young age by some rather crude and conservative Scousers. It was the missionary position every time way back home in Liverpool or up against a wall and there was no question of any foreplay. She liked this rear-entry approach since she could feel them deep inside her as she leaned nonchalantly on the telephone desk. In addition some of them gave something extra by gently stroking her round the front and she would have a terrific orgasm accompanied by the flashing lights of incoming calls on the telephone switchboard.

Rolleson persuaded his 'chosen few on night duty' to pool their 'ash cash' as a gesture to the running expenses of Marlene. After taking a fairly large cut for himself for what he called 'administrative purposes', he presented her with a handsome cheque at the end of each month. Ash cash was the money that was paid by the mortician to the junior doctors if they were prepared to identify a deceased patient in the morgue and check there were no signs of life (an absence of circulating blood, a lack of a palpable pulse and evidence of retinal trucking due to blood clots static and separated in the retinal veins when viewed through an ophthalmoscope). Once they were satisfied that, to the best of their knowledge, death was due to natural causes and there was no suggestion of criminality or foul play, they would sign the death certificate and for twenty minutes' work were handed a cheque for £150 which they duly cashed in and handed over to Edison to give it to Marlene for services rendered.

At first she was inclined to refuse, since she was basically a girl of high ideals and good working-class principles and she could not countenance the thought that she was hiring out her body. Her mother had always told her that prostitution was the worst of all sins, although she had never really been able to explain quite why. Probably her father was given such short shrift at home that he regularly enlisted their services. Certainly the act of physical sex with Marlene's sixteen-stone mum would be formidable indeed. No, she couldn't bear the thought that she was being transformed into a whore. Besides, she enjoyed it and professionals were not meant to take any pleasure from the sexual act. At least that was what her mum had told her.

Julian Rolleson had been able to put her mind completely at rest. He had the gift of the glib tongue and was destined for a career in psychiatry unless some organised crime syndicate should enlist his services beforehand. He told her that the boys had been able to work far better since she had been helping them out. The patients received better treatment and the entire hospital was functioning at a higher level. She was to look upon the money as a gift. A small token of appreciation from some very grateful doctors. In addition, of course, by helping indirectly with the healing of the sick and suffering she was serving mankind in one of the higher callings.

Looked at this way she could cash her cheque with a clear conscience. Sometimes she wondered if she should get such pleasure from all this good work in alleviating the suffering of the patients. She was actually finding herself looking forward to her work in a manner to which she was quite unaccustomed.

The whole operation was highly organised. She worked for the healing of the sick some three weeks out of four. Rolleson procured a supply of oral contraceptives from the hospital pharmacy and since this tended to lessen her menstrual flow they felt that soon she might be able to increase the number of days on duty. Three weeks' holiday a year with a special bonus beforehand. Each night that Edison was on call she would report to his room for instructions just after the pub had closed. She soon learned that there were certain things that would turn him on in a big way. She had confided in him that she had spent a few months on the strip club circuit in Soho and that she had picked up a few tricks. He had bought a few appropriate records and she would strip slowly for him in a most tantalising way. This would send him delirious and he would then proceed to make love to her in more ways than she ever dreamed possible, usually accompanied by Alfred Brendel softly playing Mozart's 21st Piano Concerto, the theme tune of the film *Elvira Madigan*, Rolleson's favourite mating music. They would lie panting, wrapped around each other and when their respirations had settled to an acceptable level he would give her any particular instructions for the night ahead. He was beginning to love this damned girl and he had asked to be considered for a further six months on the junior staff at St Giles.

It's all ended with motives of the most worthy kind. To a sexual profligate like Julian Rolleson it was a matter of intense sadness to see that Nigel Lightfoot was still as pure as driven snow after six years at medical school and one year as house doctor at St Giles. It was hardly credible. Rolleson had taken him aside one day and given him a brief psychoanalytical assessment during a pub lunch at the Sun in Splendour. He had finally extracted a confession that the man occasionally masturbated although he was deeply ashamed of such self-abuse and Tony was under oath not to tell another living soul. Having established that the man's working parts were in order he concluded that he was just unbelievably shy. Here surely was a candidate for the therapeutic talent of Marlene the switchboard operator.

After their nightly erotic briefing session Julian told Marlene about his worry with regards to Nigel Lightfoot and enlisted her help. Here, at last, he said, was an opportunity for her to become a real therapist. Almost like a doctor. A specialist in the healing of the psychosexually ill. He had visions of having her on contract for a huge fee to the Masters and Johnson clinic in St Louis. Possibly he would set up one up on his own with Marlene as his trusted surrogate. At any rate Lightfoot was to be their first experimental patient, a sort of therapeutic pilot study – and then he had to explain to Marlene exactly what he meant by that, for she was not versed in the study of randomised controlled trials. Most of the lads had introduced themselves to Marlene after a night call to one of the wards. Rolleson had instructed them carefully after pocketing their latest envelope of ash cash. They were always woken up by the telephone operator and if they felt inclined they merely had to say, 'Can I come down for a coffee after I have finished?'

She would invariably reply in the affirmative unless someone else had got in first. But Lightfoot was a serious problem. He would accept the coffee invitation but when it came to knocking on the door he was overcome by an intense attack of shyness, embarrassment and inadequacy. Tony felt that Marlene had to be more proactive to fulfil her role as a therapist; more like a psychiatric social worker. For a mere telephone girl this was promotion indeed. A different approach was called for. Marlene was to pull out all the stops in organ playing parlance in order to sexually initiate this poor young man.

She called his room one evening just after he had gone to bed but before he had gone to sleep when, she thought, erotic fantasies would be at their most powerful.

Tring... Tring... Tring... Tring...

'Hello, Dr Lightfoot.'

'Uh.'

'Marlene here from the switchboard.' There followed a long pause, then she continued, 'I know I have no right to impose upon you but I've got a special problem that I would like to discuss with you. Would you have a minute? Would you mind popping down to the switchboard for a chat?'

Then it was, 'Coffee? Black or white? One sugar or two?'

'The problem?'

'Oh, yes. It's a little embarrassing but you're a doctor so I can confide in you as long as you promise not to tell a soul.'

'Of course.' He emitted a nervous cough. 'Hippocratic oath and all that.'

She had locked the door and pulled all the blinds down.

'It's just that... Nigel, you're the only one I know on the surgical side and I just had to ask you. I'm worried. I've heard about these melanoma things and that they can become a cancer, can't they?'

Lightfoot nodded. He liked this girl. She was so open and trusting. Girls generally made him uncomfortable which is why he had never accepted Edison's advice and also the reason why he intended to specialise in andrology, dealing only with men and their ailments.

He was usually terrified of the fairer sex but now she was needing his help.

She flushed slightly. 'I'm afraid it's in a rather an embarrassing place, but you're a doctor and you won't mind, will you?'

'N-not at all,' he stammered. 'We see these things every day. It doesn't do a thing to us.'

But it did.

She slowly pulled her dress up over her, first showing her thighs, then slowly revealing her little black triangle and inching up to expose her navel and then her breasts as her dress moved up over her head. She waited a second or two pretending to have difficulty getting the dress over her head. It gave him time to stare longingly at her naked beauty that started to make him react.

She threw the dress aside and stood there in all her naked splendour. Completely unembarrassed, she showed him a small mark on her left breast. His professional examining hand tried to finger it but she clasped the hand to her breast and moved in on him and felt the bulge in his groin pressing against her. It was working, psychological social worker, it was working.

She slipped off his pyjamas and felt his swelling. He was less embarrassed now. He had that male look of aggressiveness that stirred her up but he was still her pupil. She had to teach him.

The phone rang. Shit.

She let it ring twice while she massaged his erection. She couldn't lose her prey now.

'Nigel, I'm going to turn around and lean over the switchboard desk. I want you to watch my back carefully and as soon as you are ready, come in gently.'

She turned, completely naked, slowly moving her backside from side to side enticingly as she put the headphones and mouthpiece over her head.

'St Giles' Hospital. How can I help you?'

It was the bloody Catholic priest. Night Sister had called him to ring her back. He had to administer the last rites for one of his flock who was not expected to last the night.

'Hold on, please. I'll try to connect you'.

She dialled the night sister but she was thinking of Nigel. Slowly and erotically she moved her bottom round and round and he stood there mesmerised. He was pounding with lust and he started to approach her like an arrow homing in on an inviting target.

But Marlene was the tutor tonight. She wasn't going to let him remember his initiation as a bing-bang, thank you ma'am. Nowadays women wanted more than that. It was like some of the boys in Liverpool. They had to be shown the way.

Thinking only of her higher calling and, quite unaware that she had not yet connected Father McQueen to the night sister, she admonished Nigel into her telephone mouthpiece in a broad Liverpudlian dialect. 'Eh! Eh! Prickie. Where do you think you're going? Titties first, old son, titties first.'

CHAPTER FIFTEEN
Porter's lodge, St Giles' Hospital, London

'G'day, squire.'

The admiral looked up suspiciously from his desk at the hospital front entrance and gazed over his bifocals.

The high-pitched Australian whine continued. 'Where's the two-finger department, cobber? I'm the new gynae exchange registrar.'

The admiral blinked again and scrutinised the healthy apparition standing before him. He had been front door porter and head day beagle for the past forty-five years and had witnessed generations of newly arrived doctors taking up their first appointments at St Giles' Hospital. He remembered the old days when the young gentlemen invariably arrived in chauffeur-driven limousines. Those were the days when the young men training to be specialists were paid a token salary and it was essential to have private means to carry them through the lean years of their postgraduate training. He had witnessed the advent of the National Health Service and seen the profession dispersed through all the classes of society. He had grunted with growing disapproval at the number of 'doctors from foreign parts' that seemed to be gradually taking over the hospital service. Like many of his kind he had come from a solid working-class background and had served the establishment so loyally that he had taken on many of their attributes and prejudices. He was a right-wing conservative almost to the point of being fascist and, like so many of his kind, outrageously racist.

Yes, he thought he'd seen them all, but standing in front of him, with a grin from ear to ear, was something yet again. The admiral, normally never at a loss for a quick cockney quip, could only utter a grunt. Standing before the desk of the porter's lodge was a great bear of a man wearing an open-necked white shirt, white shorts stopping just below the knees and long cream-coloured tropical socks. Behind the grin was a freckled tan and on top of it all was an Australian bush hat. He looked as if he'd just jumped off Ayers Rock.

'Good ta meet cha,' he proffered a brawny hand over the desk. 'Ma name's Norm Garrett. Ah'm from daan unner, Sinney way. Ah'm on this new registrar exchange caper. Din they tell yer I wuz cummin'?'

The admiral muttered that no one ever told him anything these days and picked up the phone to bleep the senior registrar in obstetrics and gynaecology, Humphrey Hampson, who was in the operating theatre struggling to complete a difficult vaginal hysterectomy.

'Answer that b-bloody thing will you, S-s-sister,' yelled Mr Hampson from underneath his white surgeon's mask. His transistorised 'bleep', that irritating plastic electronic mother-in-law that was carried by all the medical staff, was nagging its metallic call from a stainless-steel shelf in the scrub room.

'Mr Hampson, it's the new registrar from Australia. He's down at the porter's lodge. Shall I bring him in?'

'Bring him in' was always said in the horsey voice of the senior theatre superintendent, Miss Fraser. She was one of the older administrative sisters, still reasonably attractive and well preserved but terribly spinsterish in her ways. She had greying hair and a frightfully, frightfully country house accent that revelled in organisation and committees but was totally useless when she was called upon to assist at operations.

She was full of good ideas but tended to concentrate on things that made a dramatic impact rather than on things that were really needed. The surgeons had repeatedly asked for items such as taps that did not splash water all over their genitalia when they were supposed to be washing their hands; for water that came hot when the hot tap was switched on. They even asked with a forlorn hopelessness for an air-conditioner to make the operating theatres a little more tolerable to work in. None of these 'cris de coeur' were answered but Miss Fraser always came up triumphantly with ideas of her own. Accordingly, the new Australian registrar was 'brought into theatre', metaphorically speaking, by wheeling in a stainless-steel trolley, on top of which stood a little speaker in a metal case. She flicked a switch and, in her best telephone operator accent, she announced dramatically, 'You can go ahead now, caller, you're through to Mr Hampson.'

She then retired one pace and smiled benignly at the little invention that had cost her many committees worth of pleading in the 'any other business' section when most of the tired committee members were aching to go home.

Humphrey swallowed heavily. He had enough on his mind as he tried to tie a bleeding vessel at the top of the vagina. He hated that bloody machine. It invariably seemed to bring out his stutter. He liked to make his telephone calls privately and most of the callers could be phoned back at a more convenient time.

Miss Fraser had refused to hear of his criticisms.

'Nonsense, Mr Hampson,' she had said. 'This is the second half of the twentieth century. We must utilise the fruits of modern technology to enhance the efficiency of our everyday lives.'

Humphrey had not bothered to argue partly because women like this intimidated him and partly because the portable telephone speaker had already been purchased. Miss Fraser had placed herself on red alert listening with her badger ears for the telltale bleep-bleep sound that could mean another excursion for her little device. Humphrey looked up shyly from his stool towards the electronic contraption as a strident Australian voice came from atop the stainless-steel trolley. It was evident that the 'strine' was totally unaware that the entire operating theatre full of doctors, medical students, technicians and nurses were his captive audience throughout the conversation.

'Hello, Hubert, me ol' cobber. I finally made it – only a fortnight late! But here I am, ready, willing and able. I don' like yer beer but I do like yer Pommie skirt.'

Humphrey was a little taken aback, not only by the brazen informality of the conversation for a first meeting, but also by the use of his nickname, which he liked to think was only known to a select few in the department. He was likened one day to the American Democratic vice-president who served under the swaggering lone-star presidency of LBJ – Lyndon Baines Johnson – mainly because he was rather thin on top for a man of his age and also there was some facial resemblance. The name had stuck but somehow when it was mentioned in public it made poor Humphrey blush. He tried his best to appear nonchalant and informal as he replied to the speaker.

'W-w-welcome aboard, old man,' he stuttered. And then in a suave man-of-the-world tone he added, 'I thought you had some p-p-pretty decent-looking girls back home, what?'

Suddenly he was embarrassed. He could feel the eyes of everyone in the theatre staring at him.

'Sure we do,' intoned the transistorised voice. 'But I didn't come all this way to poke Australian pussy. I came to screw some of yer Pommie Sheilas.'

One of the student nurses flickered an eyelash at her colleague and they could not manage to suppress a rather loud giggle. Humphrey was desperately trying to control his stutter so that he could formulate a sentence that would bring some order back into the conversation. His thoughts were interrupted by the continuing discourse of the Australian.

'I met Mike Marshall before I left Sinney. Had a few ice-cold tubes of Resch's. Sends his regards. He wised me up on the Sheila scene over here and told me you were the man to watch out fer. Said you were the dirtiest dick in town.'

Humphrey suddenly turned crimson and the entire theatre staff exploded into howls of laughter. The scrub nurse, who had a reputation for being a little on the coarse side, collapsed in shrieks of mirth and Joe Gibson rocked on his chair emitting great hoots and guffaws like a walrus in distress.

'S-s-s-simply not t-true,' spluttered Humphrey, trying desperately to defend himself. He was drowned by a cry of anguish from his amplifier.

'Hey, what's this?' he screamed. 'Some Pommie operator's trying to listen in on this call.'

Miss Fraser leapt to the rescue and spoke into the receiver in a tone of great authority. 'Roger Wilco,' she boomed in a manner reminiscent of her role in the wartime operations room under the cellars of Whitehall. 'You are speaking on a public address system. I repeat. A public address system. Roger Wilco. Over and out.'

'Damned lie,' swore Humphrey, trying his best to show that he was amused. 'That bloody man Marshall. Typical of his sense of humour to spread scurrilous lies all around the former colonies.'

Joe Gibson was still chuckling to himself.

Humphrey had finished the operation and Joe started to wake the patient and chart her IV fluids and post-operative orders for the recovery room staff. As he did this he was still grinning at the thought of Marshall imparting such gossip to the Australian. Poor old Humphrey was as pure as driven snow. In fact, some of the junior staff often wondered if he had ever had it at all. The whole field of sex seemed to embarrass him, which was odd for someone who spent all his working life up to his elbows in female naughty bits.

Norm Garrett looked in amazement at the telephone receiver and slammed it back on its rest. Roger Wilco, he thought. What kind of Pommie rubbish was that? Just like a bleedin' Spitfire pilot. He strode back to the admiral's desk with an accusing finger pointing angrily at the old man.

'You put me through to half the bleedin' hospital,' he said loudly. 'I got cut off. I'm no bloomin' wiser about where to go. What a bleedin' welcome. Not exactly the red carpet treatment.'

'Quite so, sir.' The admiral was adept at placating Mr Angry Man-in-the-Street. 'I think the best thing for you to do is to go to Blair-Bell Ward on the third floor. Ask for Sister Rheingeld and she'll introduce you to Lord Reith. Point of fact His Lordship's on the ward now teaching the students.'

The admiral wagged his head as he watched the jolly swagman mount the stairs. Cor blimey, they'll be sendin' some flippin' aborigines over 'ere next. Bush hat surrounded by corks on strings and all that. Looks like 'e stepped off one of them convict ships. His lordship'll have a pink fit when 'e claps eyes on 'im.

Norm walked along the corridor of the third floor blissfully unaware of the stares that he was receiving. It would have looked fine to be dressed in full tropical kit in a British hospital in Singapore, but in the centre of London it looked positively theatrical.

He located the nurses' station just inside the entrance to Blair-Bell Ward and found a staff nurse who was filling in some entries on the Kardex register of each of the patients.

'G'day, Nursey. Would that be His Lordship down there with all those short white coats?'

She nodded, doing her best to conceal her amazement at this healthy apparition in the doorway. 'He's teaching the students. He doesn't usually mind if you interrupt; in fact he's generally glad of any excuse to get away from them.'

'Okey dokey. Ah take it His Lordship's the one dressed to the nines and the ones with the coats stopping just north of the arsehole are the students.'

She nodded, losing interest now and, returning to her Kardex, replied in a rather haughty Surrey accent, 'I suppose that's one way of putting it, if you have to be so crude.'

Norm went down the ward to the huddle of people gathered around the X-ray viewer. The students were on one side doing their best to appear interested, but most of them would rather have been sunbathing in Hyde Park.

Reith was holding forth in his usual pompous manner and Sister Rheingeld was a respectable pace behind him, her face suffused with an expression of admiration that she reserved for her most revered consultant.

He had his thumbs tucked into the armholes of his waistcoat, accentuating his considerable paunch and displaying his ornate gold watch and chain fastened across his midriff. He looked like an old Victorian painting of Gladstone that used to hang over the fireplace in the homestead of Norm's grandparents in the Yarra valley. Norman was aware that he had arrived in a country where tradition stretched back over the centuries and in an unaccustomed display of reverence he dipped on one knee, bowed his head, doffed his bush hat and said, 'G'day, yer lordship. Good ta meet cha.'

The effect was shattering. Angus froze and the small muscles at the corner of his mouth started to twitch with anger; he seemed to bristle all over like a hedgehog in a hurry.

'The name is Reith, Mr Reith to you, sir, whoever you are interrupting my teaching session,' he snapped angrily, and then turned abruptly towards the door and walked out of the ward, leaving behind a bunch of students trying to suppress their sniggers, a panic-stricken ward sister and an equally flabbergasted Australian.

Sister Rheingeld's English was normally passably good but she was wide-eyed with disbelief that her champion had been so insulted that she started whispering hoarsely in broken English and, finally, as people do in time of stress, lapsed into pure German invective from her native town of Magdeburg.

'Gott in Himmel! What you do that for? You make him mad with anger if you say that word. It is, how you say, only a nickname.'

Norm was scarlet with anger and embarrassment and refused to share the joke. He left the room with a muffled oath about 'Pommie bastards' directed at the students and then turned and called Sister Rheingeld 'cunt features', before slamming the door and departing on a bender down the Kangaroo Alley section of Earl's Court that lasted several days.

He never really forgave St Giles for the welcome he received. No one took the piss out of Norm Garrett and certainly no one had ever mocked him in public to such a degree before. To some extent it was accidental but to Norm it was all part of some Pommie plot to insult the inhabitants of Cook's colony. He headed for France to see if the continentals were more agreeable and to savour the fleshpots of Europe.

Unfortunately, he forgot to take his driving licence and his hired car was stopped just outside Boulogne for trying to overtake a large Citroën DS on a double white line. The police had caught him by a scurrilous trick. They had stationed officers with high-powered binoculars several miles ahead at the crest of a hill and his progress had been followed carefully long after the felony had been committed. It came as a shock to Norm, as he was motoring along minding his own business, to be suddenly flagged down by armed policemen. His natural sporting instincts made him ignore the frenzied whistling flics and he pressed hard on the accelerator to try to escape but he was no match for the supercharged motorbikes of the French traffic police.

He was unaccustomed to the shrieking and arm-waving that accompanies a continental arrest and after a few pushes from the flic intended to enunciate his various crimes, he could take it no longer and landed the bewildered Frenchman a heavy right-handed hook into his ample midriff.

Unfortunately this secured him a rest in 'le clou' in Boulogne for several weeks as the consular staff in Paris tried to get him released through the usual diplomatic channels. Eventually he returned to St Giles, a jailbird of one month's standing, awkwardly explaining events to the bewildered Professor Bowen, the dean of St Giles.

Nothing daunted, he continued a life of unashamed profligacy in his off-duty hours and when called upon to attend the hospital he did so diligently but in a spirit that had already been soured. He criticised everybody and everything connected with the British health system and the British way of life, and it irritated him to find that his remarks met with so little opposition. The benign tolerance of the British and the total lack of response to his chides and sneers angered him still further and he became more drunken and more pugnacious by the week. He developed a venomous loathing for the place that affected his every action. Nothing done at St Giles was ever right in his judgment. The housemen in particular found him very hard to work with and they often found themselves in the impossible position of having to obey his instructions as their immediate senior but knowing full well that an eruption of the worst order might ensue when the consultants found the accepted rules and regulations abandoned.

This sorry state of affairs was a crucial factor in a tragic accident that occurred at the end of November. Medical mishaps are rarely due to a single cause and Norm Garrett formed only one link in a chain of events that were strung together in a macabre scenario. It was an even more bizarre twist of fate that sucked Jennifer Watson into this vortex of medical arrogance among the bickering factions of Reith's unit at St Giles' Hospital.

CHAPTER SIXTEEN
St Giles' Hospital, London, Late October

Towards the end of October the hospital started to rock with a most unsavoury scandal involving several of the housemen and the night telephonist. Predictably the central figure in the shadowy cast was Julian Rolleson, the sexual profligate of St Giles, who would have made an outstanding racketeer had he not chosen to dedicate himself to the healing arts. It appeared that the girl in question, a lively Liverpudlian lass called Marlene McCarthy, had distributed her sexual favours rather freely to some of the doctors on night call in exchange for the 'ash cash' that they received for signing the cremation forms. The whole affair had been discovered when the Roman Catholic chaplain had rung up to enquire about a terminal patient and had heard some rather lewd remarks on the line that had been inadvertently left open. The dean, as usual, had managed to suppress the scandal but was powerless to prevent the dismissal of the switchboard operator.

To make matters worse, the girl was now pregnant and had returned to London where the students had bungled an abortion attempt in Rolleson's room by failing to administer enough laughing gas. The fiasco had ended in an all-night party and when the police were eventually called they discovered a fully equipped theatre suite that had been purloined from the various operating theatres in the St Giles group of hospitals. The dean had entertained the Paddington Green police superintendent to an expensive lunch at the Royal Lancaster and had persuaded him of the wisdom of not pressing charges. Nevertheless the junior doctors were still left with the problem of the unwanted pregnancy, and the most natural person to approach was Patrick Stanley. Rolleson had arranged to meet the registrar in the 'Lust in the Dust', since he was on call for the labour ward and, of late, had taken to installing himself over there on an almost permanent basis.

Patrick took a generous swig of the ale that Rolleson had provided and settled back like an old-time squire to listen to a petition from one of his serfs.

'You've probably heard all the gory details, suitably embellished, no doubt.'

'Just let me get this straight. Was she the one with the very long dark hair and the freckles on her nose?'

Julian Rolleson nodded and Patrick continued wistfully. 'Christ, I wish you buggers had let the registrars in on the act. She had a lovely little smile, I remember her well.'

'It's a shame we didn't,' Julian admitted with a resigned sigh. 'We wouldn't be in the mess we're in now.'

Patrick was quick to see the inference and steered himself against the direction the conversation was being taken. 'Look, Julian, I'd love to be able to help you, you know that, but I can't just walk into theatre and terminate her pregnancy. Reith would have me hanging by my balls from the nearest tree. I can just see the bastard's face, he'd love any excuse to get rid of me.'

'Couldn't we get her admitted as an incomplete miscarriage and take her to theatre for an evacuation of the uterus? Nobody would notice the difference and she'd be discharged the following morning. If we did it on a Saturday evening she'd be home before Reith set foot in the place on Monday morning.'

Patrick pondered the problem. 'It's possible but there are so many things that could go wrong. If someone like Bodger admitted her he'd be sure to sniff a rat and he's desperately anti-abortion on religious grounds.'

Rolleson grunted with considerable malice. 'I hate to tell you this, but he could even be the father of the child. In fact the main reason the girl wants to get rid of it is the terror of producing a little brat with a Roman hooter and an oversized tool. He might be pious in his talk but he's as horny as a whorehouse cat underneath.'

'Well, holy cow,' whistled Patrick, 'my admiration for the lad goes up in leaps and bounds. 'Tis a pity he doesn't drink, though – I need some company over here of an evening. Anyway it's not just the doctors, some of the nurses over there are as pious as the Pope's big toe, and if someone like Sister Brewer was scrubbing she'd be quick to spot the difference. We'd have to dilate the cervix and puncture the amniotic sac. Anyone who worked in there regularly would be quick to see what we were up to.'

'But surely we could do it one night when someone like Sally Kirsten is on duty. She's such a bloody scrubber she'd surely turn a blind eye. Every time she sees an abortion she must think, "There but for the grace of God go I."'

Patrick laughed. 'You should know if anyone does. Rumour has it that you've got a *Good Sex Guide* out for everything in the hospital with a pair of knockers on it. Anyway, it's time you got off your backside and bought me another beer.'

As Julian struggled through the crowd to change the glasses, Patrick reflected wearily on his predicament. It was one of the crosses they had to bear as registrars in gynaecology.

He was an easygoing sort of fellow and scarcely a month went by when he wasn't approached by some colleague or acquaintance who knew of a woman who was in trouble. In fact he was virtually powerless to help despite the fact that he performed about a dozen terminations each week. He was merely the technician. The decision to terminate a pregnancy had to be taken by the consultants after a lengthy dialogue with the family doctor and the social worker. Once the patient was admitted to a National Health Service bed she belonged body and soul to the consultant she was under and it was out of the question for one of the junior staff to intervene.

Patrick remembered all too well the unpleasant altercation with Reith when he had accepted all the terminations at one clinic and even then he was acting as his deputy with full powers to arrive at his own clinical decision.

When Rolleson returned he knew that he had to give him some rather insensitive advice against the dictates of his friendly nature.

'Look, Julian, I'm afraid I'm going to have to be rather callous about this problem. I don't know how many people are involved in this business but from what I hear it's been a fair number. You'll simply have to get a contribution from each of them and get it done privately. These bastards tend to have a different set of moral standards when there's some filthy lucre involved.'

'It's not that easy, unfortunately.' Rolleson was playing with his beer mat and it was obvious that he was rather embarrassed. 'I'm afraid I've become rather attached to her and, well…'

Patrick was about to burst out laughing. It was difficult to believe that a sexual predator of Rolleson's reputation ever recognised such an emotion as love, but there was something about the expression in his deep brown eyes that made Patrick listen in silence.

'Well, we're going to get married when all this is over and I promised her that I would somehow work something out here at St Giles. It sounds silly, I suppose, but if we end up in some private nursing home I'll lose all my credibility with her.'

The bell had sounded for closing time and Patrick looked at his watch to see if Old Fred was abiding by the rules. Ten past eleven.

'Look, I tell you what I'll do. I know a cunning Irish ploy that would melt even the hardest of hearts. I'll ring a friend of mine, Oliver Wintrobe, who's in practice up in Holland Park and give him the relevant details. He's an old Giles man and a drinking crony of mine. Tell him I sent you and make sure he sends her to Hellman. Old Maurice will help anyone out even if the pregnancy is only a mere inconvenience, but for God's sake don't let him send her to Felicity or Reith; Felicity won't do them unless the girl's at death's door and Reith puts them through a trial that would put the Spanish Inquisition to shame. As soon as the OK is given I'll make sure she is looked after well and, if you wish, I'll personally do the honours.'

Rolleson mumbled his thanks and Patrick returned to the hospital, little realising that a seemingly routine request would precipitate the end of his career at St Giles.

Patrick retrieved his white coat from behind the door at the porter's lodge and ambled along the corridor to the television room to collect Bodger Brackenbridge. Bodger regarded alcohol as a vice and referred to the Sun in Splendour as a pagan temple.

'Come on, Bodger, hands off cocks, on with socks. It's time for a little action. Let's go and see who's for the midnight Caesar. Any idea of the state of play?'

Dr Brackenbridge eased himself reluctantly out of the comfortable armchair.

'Three down and one to go. At least that was the score when I was up there a couple of hours ago.' He was referring to the patients who had been induced during the morning for various obstetric problems. If they weren't close to delivery after this length of time in labour they usually had a Caesarean section in the interests of both the mother and the baby, although Bodger occasionally had the temerity to wonder if the main indication for the operation was to ensure that his registrar had an uninterrupted night's sleep.

Bodger Brackenbridge held an innate mistrust and suspicion of hospital doctors. He had been one of the brightest students of his year and had won the gold medal for medicine in the final exams. This was the usual prelude to a distinguished career on the academic medical unit, but Bodger had surprised them all when he had announced his intention of joining a general practice in the Quantock Hills of Somerset where he would not only look after the physical well-being of his patients but also cater for their souls as a lay preacher. Bodger had spent all his waking hours as a student either immersed in his books or leading various prayer meetings, and Julian Rolleson referred to him as the Captain of College Christianity. It appealed to Patrick's sense of profanity to think that under this religious cowl old Bodger had been getting his end away with Marlene – the night telephonist.

'It's been amazingly quiet this evening,' Bodger remarked as he followed Patrick along the corridor.

'For God's sake, man, never say that.' Patrick breathed beer and groaned at memories past of hectic nights dealing with never-ending emergencies. 'Never tempt fate, sunshine. Never tempt fate. The Good Lord is listening to our every word.'

Patrick looked up sheepishly to the ceiling. His image of the Almighty was essentially an impish rogue in black habit, with a long white beard, who inhabited the air space directly above Patrick wherever he happened to be at the time he thought of Him.

Bodger winced. He did not like the Lord to be talked about with such irreverence.

Their feet echoed down the long, empty corridors of the hospital as they clanked their way up to the labour ward. Most of the doctors were preparing for bed but obstetrics was one of the harsher disciplines when it came to the preservation of eight hours' undisturbed sleep.

'Women, you will have observed, usually obey the First Law of Maximum Cussedness and contrive to deliver their screaming little packages around three in the morning.' Patrick was expounding his philosophy of life in between breaths as they climbed the stairs. 'Another example of Sod's Law.'

'Why blame it all on God?' Bodger protested like a distressed theologian.

'Cross my arse and hope to die!' Patrick spluttered in mock Irish blarney. ''Twas nothing to do with Himself. 'Twas Sod I was talking about. One of the nine sons of Lug. Do you not know about our pagan Irish gods?'

Bodger grunted. He couldn't abide Patrick Stanley's total mockery of religion and, besides, he could never tell whether or not he was joking.

They climbed the last stairs to the labour ward on the fourth floor, puffing like two old men, as they collapsed in the easy chairs in Sister's office. They were greeted with genuine affection by the night staff. This late-evening visit broke the drudgery of night work for the nurses. It was an occasion when the girls could really mix with the resident doctors without the usual formality of the daytime rounds. One of the younger student nurses was dispatched to put the kettle on for coffee; the rest of them were draped around the room reading well-thumbed copies of *Hello* or *Cosmopolitan* and the occasional aficionados would be tackling some serious knitting or crochet work. Tonight the sister in charge was Lizzie Taylor and Patrick showed welcome relief when he saw her. She was relatively new in the department and was still something of an enigma. Patrick felt certain that, after their brief but exciting sexual encounter in the operating theatre a few weeks ago, he would have been able to lure her to his room in the residents' quarters, but each attempt had been met by a gentle but firm rebuff.

Even notorious ladies' man Julian Rolleson had received the brush-off. This was so unusual for him that he had loudly and widely proclaimed her frigidity and suggested that certain vital parts must be missing. Patrick knew from his last meeting with her that this was not true, but he tended to be very discreet in these matters and did not contest the point.

Tonight he decided he would give it another try since the censorship of his higher cortical centres had been more or less abolished by several pints of ale. He admired her delectable figure bursting to get out of the tight blue delivery suite pyjamas that had been specially designed to lift the health service into realms of high fashion and also to show the well-endowed girls off to their best advantage. Lizzie was at her braless best with her nipples clearly showing in outline at the front and all the rear buttons left undone except the bottom two to display an enticing suntanned back.

As she was pouring the coffee she had her little behind pouting at him and Patrick grinned lasciviously, puffing contentedly on his pipe, rubbing his hands together as if he was surveying a prime cut of roast beef. What more could a man want? With bluff Irish simplicity he told her that her backside looked splendid and, as if this were not sufficient, gently rubbed her bottom, finishing with a deft sweep of his practised fingers up the cleft just under her firm buttocks.

'Doctor!' she chirped indignantly, suddenly straightening up and spilling some coffee in the process. Then, although her eyes were twinkling, she admonished him in a firm Potteries accent. 'You ought to be ashamed of yourself. A middle-aged man like you.'

Patrick slumped back in his chair and grinned at her rebuke.

'I'm not middle-aged, woman. I'm just entering my prime.'

'Rubbish, man. Just look at you. You're going to fat.'

Patrick had always been rather body-conscious but, of late, he had been aware that the lack of exercise and the increased beer intake had started to catch up with him. He stood smartly to attention, pulling his abdominal muscles tight, inhaling deeply and pushing out his chest. He patted his belly affectionately.

'Look at that, Lizzie,' he said, showing his profile. 'A perfect specimen of masculinity.'

All the nurses made various noises of dissent and general ribaldry and to save further embarrassment Patrick felt that a display of authority was called for.

'Come on, Sister Taylor, let's go round and look at the customers while the coffee cools. How many have you got for me?'

The two of them went around all the patients in the first stage of labour while Bodger excused himself to attend to some routine ward work on the top floor – night sedations to prescribe, even though the patients were already asleep; blood tests for students to take in the morning; and a whole assortment of clerical irrelevance that occupied the life of the modern houseman.

Patrick proceeded from room to room with Sister Taylor, feeling the big bellies of the labouring women, giving them encouragement and writing orders for sedation or intravenous fluids if he felt they were needed. He entered each room with his mask on his face partly to look sterile but mainly to contain his beery breath. It was quite acceptable to have a few jars when on duty but it was considered poor form to breathe alcoholic fumes over the labouring patients.

At each bedside he would chat to them and sit on the bed for a few minutes and then write, 'Ceph. L.L F.H.H.R.' or some other abbreviated version of his clinical findings. After the third patient Lizzie Taylor stopped him in the corridor with a mischievous grin on her face.

'What the hell do all the hieroglyphics mean, doctor?'

Patrick was a little mystified but went on to explain, as if to a moron, that it meant it was a cephalic presentation, a longitudinal lie and the foetal heart was heard and regular. In fact it was the usual midwifery jargonese that Sister Taylor was surely familiar with.

'Bloody liar,' she teased. 'You never listened to any of those foetal hearts.'

'Quite right, Sister dear. In fact I'll let you into a little secret. It's a coded message that says Patrick Stanley was here so all is well.'

She laughed. Despite his outrageous pomposity she could not help liking him, but it was in her nature to try to cut him down to size.

'Oh, you're a clever bugger, aren't you?'

'There isn't much you don't notice, Lizzie. Now I'll tell you something about yourself. You've been married. It was a bad marriage and it ended in divorce or separation. Am I right?'

The effect of these words on the girl was like a karate chop. The smile instantly vanished from her face and was replaced by a look of surprise and worry.

'How did you know that? No one knows round here. Who told you?'

Patrick gave one of his knowing smirks. He so liked to be right in his judgments of other people.

'No one told me. I just know these things, that's all. That's why I'm such a great gynaecologist. I'm one of the world's great readers of the female mind.'

He walked back to the sister's office where the coffee was waiting. Lizzie followed him, just a little shaken by his perception. She had come to London to escape from the comments of family and friends about her failed marriage but she had no wish to be known as a separated woman. In a hospital like St Giles that seemed to be an open invitation to bed. Men had a nasty habit of assuming that girls who had been accustomed to regular sex needed it like they needed food. It was partly true but she did not like to be the willing victim of every male predator that stalked the hospital corridors, and there were plenty of them. She wished to remain a complete mystery and had managed to evade even the most direct enquiries until people had finally left her alone. The abruptness of Patrick's remark had caught her momentarily off-balance and her secret was suddenly out. She would have to speak to him later and ask him to keep his information strictly to himself.

They all settled down to coffee and the usual gossip that infiltrates hospitals at these sessions. They talked about the consultants and various titbits of scandal concerning most of them. Patrick had only been at St Giles for six months but he seemed to be a mine of information on the more salacious aspects of the staff social scene.

Lizzie tried to outdo him with lurid tales from the North Staffs Infirmary but somehow never quite succeeded, since Patrick had the Irish gift of storytelling and the added dimension of subtle exaggeration that could transform a mild event into an almost unbelievable tale. All these sagas involved Patrick somewhere along the line and were therefore told in the first person and although no one really believed him there was always just a tiny element of doubt.

One of his yarns was interrupted by the urgent clang of ambulance bells sounding in the street outside and the revolving blue light flashed its message into the night sky outside the window. Bodger leapt up enthusiastically and looked down into the street below as the ambulance drivers opened the rear doors and unloaded a stretcher. Patrick groaned at this intrusion and prayed to his pagan deities that the patient be destined for the intensive care neonatal unit that occupied most of the first floor. As one of the most famous units in the country it attracted many small parcels delivered in portable incubators from all over the Home Counties.

'I hope to hell that's an incubator they're delivering down there.'

Bodger strained over the window ledge to get a better view and almost lost his horn-rimmed spectacles from his Roman nose. The trouble with his particular shape of hooter was that once an object started on the downhill run the slope became progressively steeper and his goggles landed on his chin or, on occasions like this, could hurtle to the pavement six floors below. It only needed a little sweat to dislodge them from the bridge of his nose, and he always sweated when he was excited.

Although his clumsiness was almost legendary, he loved a bit of action and he felt his vocation was really being realised when he heard the shrill summons of the ambulance bells.

'Looks like an Indian lady. Must be for us. She's got a drip running. Must be serious.'

Sister Taylor sent one of the staff nurses down to the admission room and after finishing her coffee went down to help her.

Patrick nonchalantly picked up a spare copy of *She* to see if they had any good pieces of cheesecake with provocative tits. He soon found one and showed the semi-naked pin-up to Bodger.

'Look at that for a good pair of lungs. I should have become a nude photographer. We don't get jugs like that in the clinics at St Giles.'

Bodger was too impatient to focus his attention on the magazine and handed it back with only a desultory glance.

'Shouldn't we go down there and help out? She must be pretty ill if someone's put a drip up.'

Patrick yawned again, settled himself back into his seat, put his feet up on the table, and pulled up the collar of his white coat as if he was settling down to sleep.

'There are a number of rules you have to learn in obstetrics, Bodger, and this evening I'll be giving them to you one by one. Rule one is easy. Never go to the patient. Let them bring the patient to you. Lizzie Taylor will be back in a few minutes and if she's as good as I think she is, she'll already have the diagnosis and be telling us how to manage the case. Get the others to do the thinking; saves a lot of wear and tear on the cerebral cortex.' He puffed contentedly on his pipe.

Bodger could not listen to this any longer; he excused himself on some pretext and rushed down the stairs to the main hall. By this time the stretcher had been put on a trolley and wheeled into the lift and the patient had been installed in the prep room, just outside the delivery suite on the fourth floor.

The hall porter informed Bodger that he had missed the boat and since the lift doors had not been closed at the top floor, he would have to run back up the stairs.

Meanwhile, Lizzie Taylor had told Mr Stanley that she thought it was an abruptio-placentae and was telephoning the duty pathologist to come and collect blood for cross-matching. Patrick waited for her to finish and slowly ambled over to the prep room. They were unable to get much of a history since the patient only spoke Gujarati and the Indian nurse they had summoned to interpret could only speak Hindi. Anyway, the patient was writhing in pain and crying out, screaming and incoherent. Her eyes were rolling up in their sockets and sweat had formed on her forehead.

Patrick felt her abdomen. The uterus had contracted like a solid knot and the usual relaxation after each pain was missing. It felt as hard as wood. He listened for the foetal heart and was gratified to hear that it was still present although very fast, a sign that the baby was in jeopardy. The woman had a blood pressure way up in the sky, 240mm/130mmHg, and her pulse was racing. Her breathing was shallow and she was cold and clammy.

He washed his hands and put on some sterile rubber gloves to examine her pelvis to see how far labour had progressed. Sister Taylor poured some white antiseptic cream on his hands as he inserted them high inside the vagina. The cervix was still thick and uneffaced and was lying loose in front of the foetal head. With difficulty he could just get one fingertip into the cervical canal. He asked for a pair of Kocher's forceps and slid the toothed jaw along his finger, rupturing the membranes and releasing greenish liquor with flecks of blood in it.

As he did all this he was sitting casually on the examination bed, as if he was riding it side-saddle, while the nurses held the patient's legs apart. The collar of his white coat was still up, enhancing the image of the cool, casual character that he so liked to portray. It was so different to the appearance of Bodger after running up and down four flights of stairs. He looked like a wild man with his hair dishevelled, his glasses halfway down his nose and hopelessly out of breath.

'Rule two, Dr Brackenbridge. Never hurry. A huffing and puffing doctor is no good to man or beast. This girlie seems to have a concealed accidental haemorrhage, a placental abruption. Who the hell put this useless drip up and why didn't someone tell us she was coming?' He was bellowing at the room in general and no one in particular. He was angry at having to defer his bedtime on account of a patient from another hospital.

'The letter comes from Northfields Hospital in Harrow. Although it's on the opposite side of town it's part of the Charing Cross Group and she was heading for their obstetric unit at the West London but the ambulance men thought her condition was deteriorating so they pulled in here.'

'Sod them. Blood and glory boys. They just wanted to get back home earlier and create a bit of added drama in this neck of the woods. She could easily have made it down the motorway to Fulham. Bastards just wanted to ruin my beauty sleep.'

He took his gloves off.

'Get six pints of blood cross-matched and get another drip going with a blood-giving set. If you can combine it with a CVP line so much the better. These girls always lose more blood than it appears and the central venous pressure is the only accurate guide for replacement. If you don't know how, just wait for the anaesthetist but pour in a couple of litres of five per cent dextrose fast while we're waiting for the blood, and give her one-fifty milligrams of pethidine for the pain. Sister, I'll go and phone for the gas man and the paediatrician. We'll have to chop her as soon as possible before she runs into any blood clotting problems. Who's the consultant on tonight?'

'Miss Bundle, sir.'

'Oh Christ, just my Irish luck. I'll give Felicity a ring. Lizzie, get the theatre ready. Let's get this baby out as fast as we can.'

Patrick left the room for the sister's office and put through two calls. He asked the operator to get the obstetric anaesthetist to come to theatre as soon as possible then to tell the paediatric houseman to be ready to receive the baby in about half an hour. Then he asked the operator to get Miss Bundle at her home number. This was the worst part of the whole performance. Most of the consultants were perfectly content to let the registrars make the labour ward decisions since they were all highly experienced and they were actually the men or women on the spot. Reith didn't like to be disturbed at all unless it was for one of his private patients. The professor liked to be informed but always agreed with the decision. He usually supported it by some reference from an article in a learned journal and he would quote the authors and the year and month when it was written like a human Index Medicus. Even at three in the morning, he had a remarkable memory. Hellman always offered to come in and help since, as the most junior consultant, he could still clearly recall the days when he was in Patrick Stanley's position. Nostalgically, he missed the midnight action and would always reminisce with stories that could chill the blood of less hardy souls.

But Felicity Bundle was the worst. Like most fat females with missionary zeal, she found it almost impossible to delegate responsibilities and accept the decisions of another person.

She invariably disagreed with the management plan and recalled cases from her African days that were totally inapplicable to the setting of a London teaching hospital. Sometimes she truculently took an opposite view, leading some of the registrars to acquire the art of doublethink so they would deliberately suggest the wrong course of action and, when she disagreed, they would be sure that their patient would be treated correctly.

163

Patrick was half-tempted to ignore her altogether, but that could be asking for trouble in the event of a maternal death, and this particular patient stood about a twenty per cent chance of finishing her pregnancy in the mortuary. She had obviously developed extremely severe toxaemia and at Northfields they had recorded a very high blood pressure and her urine was solid with protein. That situation was dangerous enough since she ran the risk of having a series of eclamptic fits, any of which could be fatal, but now she had developed the more serious problem of a concealed accidental haemorrhage. The surface of the placenta had bled internally and stripped off half the afterbirth from the inside wall of the uterus. Not only was the baby in jeopardy from a sudden failure in the supply line but the mother had bled internally to the tune of several pints. Worse, that blood behind the placenta had formed a huge clot which had used up most of her reserve clotting factors, and if the situation was allowed to continue the blood would be unable to clot at delivery and the haemorrhage would be torrential and uncontrollable. Once this state of affairs became established, the mother was in real danger of losing her life and the modern approach was to prevent these complications by an urgent abdominal delivery if the patient was not advanced in labour.

Unfortunately this attitude was an innovation and far from widely accepted. Patrick knew that Felicity belonged to the old school that avoided Caesarean section at all cost, mainly because they used to operate as a last resort when the clotting problem was well advanced and the bleeding was then fearful to behold.

Patrick presented the case to her over the telephone and had to repeat several parts of it as the consultant surfaced from a deep sleep. She seemed to be reasonably malleable but when Patrick suggested a Caesarean section she suddenly woke up and dug her heels in. She recalled many cases in Africa that had been delivered vaginally and she rarely had any blood available. She carefully omitted to mention the others that had died because death in childbirth was still a pertinent hazard in Africa and received little more than a sympathetic shrug of the shoulders from the attendants or relatives.

Patrick knew full well that his plan of management was by far the safest and even carried the possibility of securing a live baby. He had either to ignore the consultant or threaten to refuse to deal with the case unless he was allowed to manage it his way, or trick her into agreeing to an operative delivery. The first two stratagems carried severe repercussions if anything went wrong and the third appealed to his Irish humour. He could always con an Englishman and English women were not much brighter.

'I don't think it's that straightforward. She's of Indian extraction and only 4ft 6in. The baby is a reasonable size and I'm afraid the pelvis isn't adequate for a vaginal delivery. We are committed to a Caesarean section for disproportion anyway.'

Felicity suddenly dried up. There was no answer to that and short of coming in to check his findings, which would have been insulting, she had to accept the fact and agree to a Caesarean section. She entreated him to be careful and to ring her back if he was worried. Patrick grinned and went into the surgeon's changing room and donned his green operating gown.

There were no porters at that hour of the night and he and Bodger carried the patient on a stretcher into the operating theatre while the nurses put on gowns and opened the sterile packs for an emergency Caesarean section. Once the patient was on the table, the two doctors went into the scrub room and started the almost religious ritual of ridding their hands and finger nails of any lurking pathogens with povidone iodine.

The anaesthetist arrived and Patrick's heart sank. He was under the impression that Joe Gibson was on call for obstetrics this evening, but instead Valerie Flipp arrived replete with handbag and gave one of her toothy smiles to everyone present.

Patrick greeted her with ill-concealed contempt and briefly told her the clinical problem and stressed the need for urgency since with every passing minute her condition was getting worse.

'All right, Mr Obstetrician, keep your hairpiece on. We'll do our very best. We can't do any more, can we?'

And as Patrick turned and muttered blasphemies into the sink, she continued to dither and fret, finding a place for her handbag, fiddling with syringes, ordering nurses to change this and get that.

'Now, my dear, how are you?'

The Indian girl was writhing with pain and becoming delirious. The narcotics had taken away any restraint and she started to tear at the drip sets and dislodged them both from her veins.

'Now, now, dearie. Does anyone speak her language? Can we find out if she's allergic to iodine or if she's on antidepressants or any other medications?'

'Holy Mother,' Patrick fumed. 'Is she allergic to iodine? What the fuck does that matter? If you don't stop dithering around she'll be answering that to the Indian version of St Peter.'

'No need to be vulgar, Mr Stanley. We do our humble best.'

She flashed him another of her toothy grins. Patrick put on his gown and gloves and tried to wait patiently in the corner. By convention, the obstetric surgeon kept well out of the anaesthetist's way since obstetric anaesthesia was a highly skilled and dangerous art due to the ever-present risk of inhaling stomach contents into the lungs. Patients were usually starved for about six hours before being given an anaesthetic, but in an obstetric emergency nature refused to tolerate such a delay, and in addition the stomach emptied less efficiently when a woman was in labour. If any of the acid was regurgitated into the lungs it meant almost certain death in a matter of minutes. The sudden state of collapse in childbirth is still known after the doctor who first described it – Mendelson's Syndrome.

Patrick cursed at his luck in getting this dithering female at a time like this. She was a poor soul whose marriage had crumbled, and after several years out of hospital practice she had returned to try to build a new life as an anaesthetist. She was good at the theory of anaesthesia but the practice was another matter and she only seemed able to cope with the most straightforward cases.

This struggling patient on the table presented a challenge even to the most skilful. The obstetric anaesthetist had to get her to sleep rapidly, slip an endotracheal tube into her larynx and inflate the cuff to prevent any possibility of regurgitating vomit.

Then they had to fix the IV drips and, in a case like this, insert a central venous pressure line to monitor the amount of fluid deficit and prevent any overload since they were replacing the blood loss very quickly, sometimes as much as six pints.

Patrick fumed into his mask. 'Silly bitch, pissing around. This sodding female is going to die on us the rate we're going. Where the hell is bloody Joe Gibson? I thought he was meant to be on call for obstetrics tonight.'

Valerie was losing her temper and kept stamping her feet as she failed time and time again to get the needle into a vein. She was barking orders to the nurses and was making little headway in gaining control of her screaming patient. Finally she appealed to Patrick hysterically.

'Can't you help? Can't you help?' Patrick rose and went over to the other side of the theatre, kicked open the door to the corridor and, keeping his gloved hands away from any contamination, instructed a nurse to get Joe Gibson on the phone and to hold the receiver close to his ear.

'Joe, wake up, you fart-faced fornicator. What the hell do you mean by sending this nincompoop over here when we've got a bad case. Seriously, Joe, it's like Paddy's market here. We've got an abruption going into shock and this virgin's tying her knickers in a twist. If you ever loved me, come and bale her out as fast as you can get your butt over here.'

He went back to the theatre and resumed his seat confident that help was on its way.

Joe Gibson was the ultimate failure. He was short and stocky with thick curly blond hair falling over his tanned healthy face. He seemed to live a life of almost perpetual pleasure, forever resigning from the hospital to help some friends run a water-ski school on the Costa Brava. He gave the impression of total nonchalance as he shambled into the operating theatre with a beery grin over his mask, which hung ineffectively under his nose like a horse's feeding bag. Joe spent most of his on-call hours in the pub when it was open or at the betting shop just around the corner when it was not. He was the eternal playboy. He drove a Porsche convertible fast and owned a powerful speedboat that he kept on the Mediterranean coast. He had been a middle-grade registrar in anaesthetics at St Giles for some years. Promotion was impossible since he was unable to pass the Fellowship exams and had almost set up a record for the number of failed attempts. It was one of the sights of summer to see Joe sitting on the roof of St Giles sunbathing with one arm around one of the nurses and the other one clutching a textbook of anaesthesia. He was always going to get it the next time, but study was difficult when his free hand was fondling the contents of a tiny bikini top.

But he was a great gas man, no doubt about that. Some of the others knew the dissociation curves for nitrous oxide and the effects of halothane on the lipoproteins of the cell membranes, but when you needed to get a problem case asleep you called for Joe Gibson. He entered the operating room as if he'd just been laying one of the nurses, which he had, but he immediately summed up the situation and in the coolest series of moves he had a needle in the vein, a tube down the girl's throat and had transformed the thrashing, shrieking Indian on the table into a quiet sleeping form that was ready for Stanley's knife.

Patrick gave a sigh of relief and started to clean the belly with some gauze swabs soaked in Hibitane.

'Sorry to call you off the roost like that, Joe.'

'That's OK,' he grinned. 'I'll ask Sister here to finish me off later.'

'Cheeky bugger.' Sister Taylor flashed her eyes half-angrily over the mask. 'You lot are all the same, always thinking of your oats.'

'What else is there to think about in a dump like this? The bloody administration should provide a nurse to service the doctors on call, like the geisha girls in Tokyo.'

'Isn't one enough for you? Breathing all those anaesthetic gases all day must be pickling your balls.'

Patrick suddenly became serious and ended this frivolous conversation.

'Are you ready to start, Sister? Suction ready? Tell someone to make sure the paediatrician gets here in time. Knife.'

And then he was off, the blade slashing through the skin, leaving a furrow with the glistening yellow layer of fat slowly reddening with blood from the cut vessels. Patrick did not bother to stop the bleeding because every second counted in a case like this. He incised deeper until the tough white layer of the rectus sheath was visible. The scalpel blade made a nick in it and the red meat of the muscle layer showed through. Deftly he used the blade to cut and turned the knife around in his palm like a sharp-shooter to push the layers back with the knife handle until the peritoneum was visible. He picked the glistening membranes up in some artery forceps and heard the soft hiss as the negative pressure inside the abdominal cavity sucked some air into the hole he had made. He cut down, making sure that he stopped just above the bladder.

Bodger took the Doyen retractor to keep the bladder out of the way and Patrick checked the rotation of the uterus and pushed a long, moist pack either side of it to keep the guts out of the way. He looked over his shoulder and was glad to see a dishevelled paediatrician busy arranging the equipment on the resuscitation trolley for the baby.

'Clip.'

He picked up the layers of peritoneum that slid over the lower part of the uterus off the back of the bladder.

'Scissors.'

He cut through the first layer of the uterus and extended the incision for several inches on either side of the mid-line.

'Sponge on a stick.'

He took some gauze, folded carefully on the end of a sponge holder from Sister Taylor, and carefully pushed the bladder down out of harm's way.

'Stay stitch on quarter length.'

This was a trick he had learnt from one of his first consultants. He placed a stitch through the uterine muscle in the middle, just beneath the line where he was going to make a big incision to deliver the baby. This would later on act as a marker so that he could always identify the thin lower segment of the uterus even if the bleeding was catastrophic.

'Clip that. Ready for the baby? Knife, please. Suction on.'

He deftly cut down through the uterus while Bodger held the nozzle of the sucker next to the knife to keep the cut area clear of blood. He stroked the scalpel blade down by a fraction of an inch each time until the scalp of the baby was just visible. Any further and he would damage the child. It would be nothing serious, admittedly, but it was bad form and had to be explained to the mother; it was also often the subject of jokes from the surgical registrars who regarded obstetricians as technically beneath contempt, with the baby bearing the birthmark of an incompetent surgeon.

As soon as he was through the uterine wall Patrick extended the muscle incision laterally on both sides with his fingers, then asked Bodger to take out the retractor and apply pressure over the top of the uterus while Patrick inserted his cupped right hand deep into the wound to guide the head out.

In this case, the baby was small and the protesting head of the newborn was suddenly thrust into the world of noise and sound and light from the peace and darkness of the liquor in the womb. Bodger thrust a suction catheter inside the mouth to clear the amniotic fluid from the throat and to stimulate the vital first gasp that would expand the lungs.

The baby was flat and blue due to the combined effects of the heavy sedation that had passed through the placenta from the mother and the foetal distress that had resulted from partial separation of the afterbirth from the uterine wall. Patrick clamped the cord and handed the blue limp form in a sterile drape to the paediatrician for resuscitation.

'Five units of syntocinon IV, please.'

Valerie was back in charge of the anaesthesia and she fussed around with her syringes and glass ampoules. Patrick fumed at the delay. Any competent anaesthetist would have been prepared with a loaded syringe of syntocinon which caused the womb to contract in order to expel the placenta and control the bleeding and was needed at all deliveries.

'Where the hell's Joe?'

'All right, all right. It's coming. No need for you all to act like an army of male chauvinists.'

'I didn't ask for a sermon on women's lib. It should have been ready long ago. Where's bloody Joe?'

Joe was lying prostrate out in the corridor with only his head leaning against the wall for support. This was unfortunate because Felicity Bundle had worried and fretted about the horrors and hazards of the case and decided to come and offer her advice and assistance. She all but tripped over the sleeping carcass on the floor, and peered over and prodded him with her ungainly foot.

'Who are you, sir?'

Joe never woke up from slumber easily and after a moderate intake of beer, the images and fantasies of that first half-hour of sleep often took on a highly realistic character. He gazed up at the hazy image of Felicity and had the uneasy feeling he was looking up out of a steaming cauldron at one of *Macbeth*'s witches.

'Go away, evil woman of the night; leave me to die.'

Miss Bundle took in air too quickly and made a strange noise like a pig at a trough, a sort of snore in reverse, inhaling instead of exhaling. She often did this when she was angry. She pushed her way into theatre still snorting.

'Sister? Mr Stanley? Are you all right, everybody? Is the patient still alive?'

'Everyone is fine, Miss Bundle, although we had a little trouble with the anaesthesia.'

'I'm not surprised,' she replied haughtily, 'with that derelict, Gibson, in a drunken coma out in the passage. He seems to be more anaesthetised than the patient.'

She turned to leave the room.

'I can see that I shall have to report this incident to Dr Squires in the morning. We can't have his junior staff passing out all over the hospital. Thank goodness you had Dr Flipp here to give a safe anaesthetic.'

Patrick was still laughing five minutes later, when the theatre was empty apart from himself writing up the operation notes and Lizzie Taylor cleaning the blood-soaked instrument. He went to her and fondled her shoulder lovingly. 'All that activity has made me very horny, Lizzie. Why don't you come and have a gentle Irish nightcap in my room during the meal break? I can recommend it as a way of losing weight.'

'Oh, go screw yourself. The whole lot of you ought to be castrated. If I was the matron here, I'd insist the entire male medical staff were marched off down to the knacker's yard.'

'I'll leave the door ajar and be lying there in the altogether waiting for you.'

'Sod off, you Irish leprechaun.'

'See you soon, Lizzie. I'll go and put on the soft music and slip into something sexy.'

Patrick returned to his room with a sense of delightful anticipation. He was sure that Lizzie would accept his invitation and he spent several minutes rearranging the lights and the furniture and selecting some suitable music to put on his cassette tape recorder.

It was important to create the right atmosphere since he was determined to make love to her in a more sophisticated manner than their previous bestial encounter on the operating theatre table. He opened a bottle of red wine that he had been given by one of the patients in gratitude for delivering her baby. Such gifts were rare in modern times although Patrick recalled the days soon after he qualified when patients were much more generous. It was a sign of the times. Either people were noticeably meaner or the doctors were regarded as mere functionaries, the white-coated cogs of the health service. He suspected the latter.

He waited for twenty minutes, looking greedily at the bottle of wine. He couldn't wait any longer so he uncorked it and poured himself a generous glass. The minutes slowly turned into an hour and, several glasses of wine later, Patrick debated whether to give her a ring on the labour ward but instead decided to get undressed and go to bed, leaving a note pinned on the outside of the door.

He nodded off but slept fitfully since his body was suffused with erotic expectations that he could not easily dispel. He kept waking up and looking at his alarm clock. The bedside light was kept on in case he had a visitor. The radiators made the room hot and sticky and finally he threw off the sheets and slept naked on top of the bed.

Next morning he awoke feeling demoralised and weary. He looked outside the door for his note and it did nothing to assist his recovery. Underneath his message she had written: 'Sorry I was so late. I had to take the late supper. Your hairy arse wasn't very tempting at 4am and anyway I'm surprised you think I'm that kind of girl. Letter follows.'

Patrick grunted. Hairy arse, indeed. He did not approve of the new veil of morality either and the letter that was waiting in his pigeon-hole in the doctors' common room was no better. It explained somewhat pedantically that she was not for the taking and that she was rather offended by his suggestion. She gave the impression of wounded innocence and proceeded to give him a lecture on how to treat young ladies that made Patrick cringe as he read it. To make things worse she seemed to be semi-literate and her spelling was appalling. The letter ended on a more optimistic note by suggesting that they meet at the Victoria Tavern in Stanhope Terrace at seven that evening.

Like a spurned lover Patrick initially decided to bury the whole affair in his memory, but as the day wore on he became more irrational and kept entertaining erotic fantasies about her. Twice during the afternoon operating list he had imagined himself fondling those soft, firm breasts again and he had been admonished by Reith with the usual sharp rap on the knuckles that brought him thundering back to reality. There was something about those breasts; a pair of pert adolescent mounds that seemed to have discovered the secret of perpetual youth, for their owner was well into her thirties. The more he thought about her breasts the more he decided that he would have to meet her after all, but this time he wouldn't rush into things.

One of the gruelling aftermaths of a weekend on call at St Giles was the fact that it was impossible to slip away early on the Monday afternoon since the professor held a meeting of his staff from six to seven on the first evening of the week. On this particular occasion they were gathered to review the pathology slides of the interesting cases that had been operated on during the previous month. It wasn't just a matter of looking at the pretty pictures projected on to the screen; one also had to endure the droning monotony of the professor of gynaecological pathology.

After more than seventy hours on call it was a dedicated man indeed who did not fall asleep at these sessions; an act that rarely went unnoticed in a gathering this small. Patrick had once been asked to leave by Reith for snoring loudly while the professor was discussing histological minutiae, but today his mind was more intent on the mammary glands of Sister Taylor than the adenoacanthoma that was projected on the screen. In fact, the more he thought about those delightful jugs the more he felt a spectacular erection developing beneath his pants. He slipped furtively out of the lecture theatre, left the hospital grounds, and took a shortcut through the back streets to the Victoria Tavern, a late-Victorian pub set in a quiet residential area among the green squares behind the Bayswater Road.

Lizzie was waiting for him at one of the outside tables and had bought him a beer, only half a pint, admittedly, but the thought had been there. He downed it in one gulp and then headed for the bar to get two more pints without bothering to ask her what she was drinking. He took a few generous gulps at his frothy pint of ale and brushed the foam from his lips before settling back on his seat. Lizzie was appraising him cynically, almost mockingly.

'Well, that was a profound display of peacock masculinity. Am I meant to be impressed by your capacity?'

'No, I was thirsty.' He was buggered if he was going to be interrogated by one of his own ward sisters. She was certainly attractive, though – more so out of the hospital uniform, with her black hair hanging down shoulder-length and eyes that could be beautiful if her face would let them relax more. The eyes were a soft brown that had humour in them but at times the face told of disillusion and fatigue. He surmised that most of her married life must have been an ordeal. He didn't really want to talk about her marriage unless she brought the subject up, but he was so desperately thinking of a different topic that he lapsed into stony silence, which she took to be a sulk. She was making little rivulets on the table with her index finger, linking small pools of spilled beer to each other. Her head was tilted slightly to one side, exposing her long neck and delicate shoulder bone.

'You're so angry with me, aren't you?'

'Not really. I'm afraid I'm a bit long in the tooth for girls who play hard to get.'

She laughed at his heavy-handed tactics.

'Oh come now, doctor, it makes it much more fun, doesn't it? More subtle. Otherwise it's just like going into a restaurant and ordering a meal.'

'I do wish you would stop calling me doctor – you know it annoys me. As a matter of fact I think you enjoy annoying people.'

'I suppose I do, really', she giggled. 'So I'm not forgiven?'

'I just don't appreciate sermons in the morning mail from people that I've been lying awake all night pining for. You sound so willing one moment then you act like a vestal virgin the next. We simple males are made of blunter emotions.'

It was all going rather badly, Patrick reflected. Any moment now one of them would walk out and he reluctantly decided that he would have to tread more gently.

She shrugged her shoulders. 'I'm sorry if that's the way you feel. I'm afraid I'm not the kind of woman that likes to be clubbed on the head and dragged to the nearest cave. I've had enough of that to last me a lifetime.'

Oh shit, Patrick thought, here we go. The anatomy of a marital breakdown never takes less than half an hour and he was hoping to get his oats before eight o'clock and then catch a tube home to avoid a marital breakdown of his own. The imagination plays cruel tricks on the mind of a man. He should not have been drooling over her breasts in such unsavoury fashion all day.

'Do you want to tell me all about it? I'm not quite as crude as you make me out to be and these big Irish ears were designed for listening.' He gave her one of his biggest smiles. She looked at him, this time more fondly, and she nodded her head in a gesture of resignation.

'I'm trying to forget it, love, that's why I came to this big lonely city.'

'There's no need to be lonely…'

'You're married,' she cut in. 'That only makes for more problems. Anyway, I did come to your room yesterday night but you were fast asleep.'

'Oh, no. You left a message on the door but if you'd come in you'd have found that I was awake most of the night.'

'Not when I came in; you were sleeping like a newborn babe and, besides, you were snoring.'

'Rubbish,' Patrick countered. 'I hardly ever snore except maybe when I'm deeply asleep and last night I was so keyed up that I hardly closed my eyes. That's why I'm so worn-out and irritable.'

She looked up at him again as if she was enjoying a good joke. Her eyes were twinkling merrily.

'If you were not so deeply asleep how do you think I managed to draw two butterflies on your bum?'

Patrick mouthed an Irish oath and let out an involuntary shriek of horror, leaping to his feet and clutching one buttock in each hand as if he had just sat on some drawing pins. This was too much for Lizzie, who collapsed into fits of laughter.

People at adjacent tables were looking at the scene in amazement, but with typical English reserve they soon turned back to their own business.

'Omigod,' yelled Patrick, 'what an unbelievable thing to do.'

Lizzie was still spluttering with laughter, cradling her head in her arms. Tears of mirth streamed from her eyes. She could hardly speak coherently.

'They're both in ballpoint. One's in blue and the other is in black and they've both got red wings.' Again she collapsed in peals of laughter at the recollection of her artistry.

'Christ on a bicycle,' Patrick was even more horrified as he tried to imagine the artwork. 'What if I'd taken a shower in the operating theatre changing rooms and Reith had seen them? He'd have thought I was a bloody fairy. A closet gay.'

Lizzie had to dry the tears from her eyes. She was still laughing at his face.

'I thought you'd have noticed them when you got up this morning.'

'I don't go inspecting my arse in the bloody mirror every morning,' Patrick bellowed indignantly.

Then another thought dawned on him, even more terrible since he was returning to his suburban home that evening. 'How the hell am I going to explain them to my wife?'

'Come on, love.' She placed her hand tenderly on his arm. 'Take me back to your room and I'll rub them off for you. If you're really nice I might let you paint something on mine.'

CHAPTER SEVENTEEN
St Giles' Hospital outpatient department, London

'What in heaven's name is going on down there, Sister? Are the students rioting for an extra ration of beer? It sounds like the storming of the Bastille. What's it all about?'

Reith was in an exceedingly irritable mood this afternoon. He detested outpatient clinics. Why had he taken up medicine in the first place? Because, he once told himself, he liked dealing with people. Well, he didn't any more. He'd had a bellyful of people over the years with their trivial problems and their smelly feet. To say nothing of their private parts. Some of them were like mobile compost heaps. In the old days, they used to take a bath before seeing their doctor. That kind of respect had all disappeared when the National Health Service came in. Now they seemed to deliberately go without one just to ginger up his afternoon. He couldn't abide the smells of the great unwashed of Paddington and Marylebone. He should have become a lawyer or, at least, something less seamy than a gynaecologist. He hadn't minded it so much as a young man but now he would far prefer to spend the afternoon on the golf course. It was a lovely day, too. His Scottish High Kirk conscience could not allow him to skip outpatients with the same carefree attitude as some of his colleagues. He had not missed once in all these years unless, of course, he was at a committee or a conference. He looked at the long stack of patients' folders and groaned audibly. The outpatient clinic sounded like a cattle market.

'What in God's name is going on down the corridor? The orthopaedic clinic sounds like a bear pit.'

Sister turned around. She hadn't bothered to answer him the first time.

'It's Mr Rundle, sir. He's dressed up like a working man with a flat cap and leading a deputation up to the hospital secretary to complain that the consultant's an hour-and-a-half late.'

'But he is the ruddy consultant, isn't he?' Reith shook his head in amazement. The antics of that chap Rundle never ceased to amaze the rest of the consultants. He often wondered what the general public thought of the profession when they saw the likes of Rundle playing silly buggers in a flat cloth cap. He was such an enormous chap that Reith was sure the patients would recognise him even if he turned up in a bearskin. Everything seemed to be falling apart. What in heaven's name would people think if Reith put on a bra and panties and sat out there rabble-rousing with the local washerwomen?

He sighed inwardly. What was becoming of the great place? The healing arts were indeed becoming a little bent.

'Let's see the first one, Sister.' He read the referral letter with disgust. It merely said: 'To the Consultant Gynaecologist. Re: Penelope Morton, age 48. Vaginal Discharge. For your expert opinion. Please advise and treat.'

'My God,' Angus groaned, passing the letter to the students at his side. No named referral, no attempt at treatment or even a diagnosis. Just shuffle her along to the nearest hospital outpatient department and that was their job done. These damned GPs would soon be suffering from the cumulative effects of writer's cramp and piles. No need to attend medical school just to direct someone to the nearest hospital. A policeman would do as well. Indeed old Mr Hare at the porter's lodge was a better diagnostician than a dozen of the local family doctors put together.

'Wheel her in, Sister,' Reith said wearily.

He sighed inwardly as he saw the woman, obviously one of the Notting Hill intelligentsia with obsessive psychoneurosis and inner suffering. She was the wife of a reader in sociology at the London School of Economics and she was devastated by a lifetime of socialism and honest-to-goodness idealism that had come to a focus on the delicate mucosa of her vagina. She had probably been beautiful once in a Virginia Woolf sort of way. She could still be called handsome since her underlying bone structure had not been eroded by the ill winds of Psyche. Her hair was prematurely grey and could have been dignified if turned to advantage, but it was heavily lacquered and heightened the anxiety that was drawn in lines across her pale face – lines of worry radiating from eyes that had cried too much. Furrows of hopelessness and fingers that fidgeted and plucked at a handkerchief that had been moist too often.

Reith asked all the usual questions but the patient sighed wearily. She handed him a piece of crumpled paper on which she had written the data that she thought might be relevant to her condition.

'Please, don't trot out all the usual questions about my periods and my bowels. I'm afraid I can't face going through it all over again.'

So saying, she folded both her arms on his desk and, laying her head in them, lolled from side to side to give the added impression of utter world-weariness.

Reith grunted in obvious distaste.

There was a certain code of ethics in the practice of medicine. A standard of behaviour to which both doctor and patient were expected to conform.

There were questions to be asked and answered. A history had to be taken in the proper manner. There were no shortcuts. To be merely handed a patient's ailments on a scrap of paper was tantamount to insurrection. It was the physician's final bow-out before the computers took over. Reluctantly, Reith unscrewed the paper and scrutinised the two sides of obsessive handwriting. This is what he read.

I am forty-eight years old and I am desperately concerned with the effect of my premenstrual tension on my life. The pattern is invariable. Exactly eleven days before the appearance of my menstrual flow I notice a change in the odour of my vaginal secretion. Two days later, with a sudden start, I feel as if I've just received a heavy blow to the head. I begin to experience fatigue, irritability, drowsiness and a degree of disorganisation. Fourteen hours' sleep each night fails to relieve the impression of utter weariness. My handwriting becomes irregular and jagged. Letters, even whole words, are skipped. When speaking I often have difficulty finding the right phrases. My movements are inaccurate and I often cut or burn myself in the kitchen. My appetite decreases, my bowel movements become less frequent, hard and difficult. My weight occasionally, but not regularly, increases slightly. The whole process culminates in a feeling of great distress, accompanied by insomnia and crying in the night immediately preceding the appearance of my menstrual flow. During all these days, the thought of sexual relations with my husband is abhorrent.

During menstruation the need for more sleep than usual remains felt but the other symptoms gradually disappear. Immediately after the end of my period my appetite increases markedly, my bowel motions return to normal, my need for sleep decreases to about six hours (as opposed to the usual nine hours). At this time I generally feel elated, look well and experience a strong sexual urge along with the ability to enjoy sex to the full.

This state of affairs lasts for three days, after which everything returns to the conditions I have described…

Reith folded the letter and passed it with ill-concealed contempt to one of the students for his perusal. The obsessive accuracy with which every trivial symptom was described had upset the consultant. Furthermore, the vaginal discharge that had been the presenting complaint in the letter from the general practitioner was hardly even mentioned.

He looked at her in amazement.

'What about your husband?' He hesitated, slightly embarrassed at his train of thoughts. 'He's not getting much of a look-in. I mean… Great Godfathers, three days a month… poor fellow.'

Reith's ideas on sexual counselling revolved around the male chauvinistic principles of how often one could get one's oats per week.

The woman shrugged the question away.

'My husband is a very good and sympathetic man. He doesn't often bother me.'

Angus could not bear this kind of ambulant psychosexual nightmare at the beginning of his clinic. He asked her to go with the sister into an adjoining room to get ready for a pelvic examination.

In order to expedite the proceedings, there were two examination rooms attached to each consulting room and the doctor could interview the next patient while the first one was getting undressed.

The second patient could not have been more different. She was a big West Indian woman who was suffering from the most dreaded complaint in her society; she was barren. Her husband had previously had children by other women back in St Lucia to prove his virility, so by inference it was undoubtedly her fault that the marriage was childless. She sat there with her big black face and serious eyes belying a great dignity as she tried to answer the questions put before her. She had a straw bag in her lap and her hands crossed around it. A frown of deep concentration creased her face.

How old was she when her periods started?

Were her periods regular?

Did she have any bleeding in between her periods?

Had she had any previous operations or illnesses?

Was there any TB or diabetes in her family?

'No, sir. Yes, sir. Thirteen, sir. No, sir. No, sir.'

'What did her husband do for a living?'

Angus looked up, sensing a hesitation in the reply. She leaned forward as if talking to the priest at confessional.

'Well, doc,' she said, her eyes looking very serious and confiding, 'Ah believe dat if a man treat you right, you got no business pryin' into his affairs.'

Angus shrugged. These extraordinary cultural differences no longer caused him any surprise. Imagine his wife not knowing what he did for a living – it was unthinkable. He plodded on with his line of questions like a well-trained interrogator. He liked to leave the more delicate ones to the end. He felt that usually he had established some kind of rapport with the patient by then.

'How many times a week do you have intercourse?'

She looked puzzled.

Angus flushed slightly and in that manner peculiar to the English language came out with some non-specific alternatives, none of which accurately described the act.

'You know, lie together, go to bed, make love?' And finally as if going too far, 'You know sex, sex?'

She wrinkled her brow into an expression of intense concentration. What a difficult question to answer. Finally she looked at Angus in a puzzled way and said, 'Well, doc, dat depends wedder he come home for lunch or not.'

The outpatient session ground on through the autumn afternoon. Angus tried to teach the two students who were seated respectfully beside him in their short white coats; pockets bulging with newly acquired stethoscopes and patella hammers.

The woman with the vaginal discharge had the most normal vagina; there was not a hint of vaginal discharge. Angus reassured her that all was well.

'Perfectly healthy down there. Not a hint of cancer or anything nasty.'

'But all that discharge, doctor; what can I do about it?'

'Nonsense, girl. That's perfectly normal. Every woman has that. It acts as a natural lubrication. Without it you'd squeak when you walked.' It was a joke in poor taste but it was the best he could do in the circumstances. He gave her some pessaries of lactic acid and explained how to insert them. In fact live yoghurt would have done as well. Or nothing at all. He wrote the findings on her case notes.

At the end he summarised succinctly. 'It is not a pessary she needs in her vagina.' She needed a little more comfort from her husband who was paying too much attention to looking after the needs of humanity and saving the planet but directing rather too little on the inhabitants of his own little nest. He knew this and she knew this, but Reith dismissed her with a prescription for some pyridoxine because he had neither the time nor the inclination in a busy health service clinic to delve further into his patient's personal problems. Even with the best will in the world he couldn't alter her social circumstances and it was this that was causing her premenstrual syndrome.

The old West Indian was given a thorough pelvic examination and put down on the waiting list to come in for a dilatation and curettage before her next period so that they could find out if she was ovulating. She was given a card with her name and number printed out by the computer that had processed her when she registered: 54826, Pentecost Smith, TC1 8/8/69 D&C Blair Bell, Cons. Mr Reith.

She was no longer just a name. She had a number. She had become part of the Great Health Scheme. On her behalf, and at her request, with absolutely no payment involved it would delve into her pelvis to try to find out why she had remained childless.

There followed a series of cases that Reith told the students were a handful of crap. Most were patients with abnormal or irregular vaginal bleeding mainly caused by the amateur attempts of the local GPs to pry into the secrets of endocrinology. Angus deplored the activity of the big drug companies in encouraging general practitioners to dabble in a subject that was in reality highly complicated. Reith regarded this as poaching on consultant territory. The sex steroids were for the specialist and he detested family doctors interfering with problems they little understood.

Angus passed most of these cases on to Patrick Stanley who was already seeing three times as many patients at a hectic pace. Angus decided to impart some of his knowledge to the fledgling doctors at his side. He turned on his swivel chair and peered over his half-moon bifocals at the dishevelled duo that were attending the gynaecology clinic that afternoon. He took off his glasses, rubbed his tired eyes and gazed wistfully at the fading afternoon sun before launching into a long monologue about iatrogenic disease and abnormal uterine bleeding.

He leaned back, assuming his most pompous posture, with his hands clasped over his ample midriff with the thumb of his left hand hitched reassuringly over the gold chain that secured his old-fashioned gold watch to his waistcoat. He embarked on a learned discourse about the harm that doctors could do to their patients often with the best of motives.

'Cartridge? Have you any idea of the incidence of iatrogenic diseases?'

'Partridge, sir,' the student corrected politely. Reith took not a blind bit of notice, nor was he interested in a reply.

'Well, Cartwright, it is in the order of twenty to thirty per cent of the cases we see here in outpatients. The more advanced the pharmacology, the more sinister the side-effects. I've seen a woman die from aplastic anaemia due to one course of chloramphenicol. There's a young lad in our neighbourhood who is totally deaf because his mother received large doses of streptomycin when she was pregnant. Neither of these antibiotics should be prescribed when safer alternatives exist. Even aspirin is not without hazard. I recall Mr Forth presenting a case at one of the Grand Rounds last year of a young labourer who required a twenty-pint blood transfusion because of gastric haemorrhage caused by the ingestion of only two aspirin tablets. No drug is entirely free from hazard. We would do well to remember the words of wisdom of that great healer, Sir William Osler, when he reminded his young doctors of their duties to their patients: 'Primum non nocere. First do no harm.'

Reith looked around. He liked to hear himself speak. Perhaps he would be awarded a knighthood for his great teaching. Sir Angus Reith. It rolled well off the tongue.

Sister was looking slightly agitated. She dreaded these long teaching episodes when there was still a crowd of patients to be seen. Reith had seemingly forgotten about a frail lady in her early fifties whose condition had started this bout of pedagogy.

'Before we embark on a discussion of abnormal bleeding from the genital tract perhaps you would be so kind as to tell me the difference between "epi" and "poly", Carson.'

'Partridge, sir.' He looked blankly at his feet.

Reith turned to the student's partner.

'And what about your learned friend? You, sir. You look as if struck dumb by some celestial manifestation. Are you not both from the Oxford and Cambridge intake? I thought knowledge of the classics was a prerequisite for entry to such hallowed halls of learning.'

Miles Jamieson tried hard to stifle a yawn. He found troglodytes like Reith totally boorish. Coming from an aristocratic lineage that had carried him through Eton and Magdalene College, Cambridge, he sensed in Reith the peevish attitude of the poor grammar school boy who had made it. Pure trog. He disdained even to answer. He looked vacantly out of the window. It had been a mistake to come to this tedious session on such a fine day. He would be rowing on the Thames from Putney to Mortlake with the Hospital Eight if he had not listened to the absurd dictates of Partridge's conscience.

'Well, you won't find the answer written in the sky, laddie. Epi means on or upon, and epimenorrhoea denotes one period following on from another. This is an older usage and many people, particularly the Americans, prefer the prefix poly, which means many.'

He looked pleased with himself and went on for twenty minutes explaining the significance of a confusing set of conditions from menorrhagia and metrostaxis to metropathia haemorrhagica. Finally he turned from the blank faces of the students to the bewildered patient who might have been listening to an address in Swahili for all she could understand.

'I've been telling these young doctors about your condition. It's all part of the "change" and should get better on its own. No need for tablets or anything. If you're still having trouble in six months, come back to see us. Give her an appointment for six months, Sister. If she's better, she won't turn up. These people never do anything for themselves.'

'Wot 'bout me palpitations?' the old woman mumbled.

'You'll have to go somewhere else about that. I only deal with the region just below the belt. Good day, madam. And now, Sister, the rest of the patients can be seen by Dr Stanley while these two young gentlemen and I partake of a cup of tea to fortify us for termination time.'

Marlene waited outside Reith's consulting room with growing apprehension. She had already been kept waiting for three hours and the nervousness and nail biting had grown steadily worse. She knew that he saw the abortion requests last and had managed to identify one of them, a girl about her own age who worked as a sales girl at Woolworths and had been rogered at a local party by some character who had failed to leave his visiting card. She had been in to see Reith and had left after only three minutes, sobbing into her handkerchief and running headlong down the passage crying and wailing like a banshee.

This sight had done nothing to assuage the mounting doubts that arose within poor Julian's room the previous week when he had tried to induce an abortion. She thought she was being sent to see Hellman whom she remembered from her switchboard work as a mild-mannered man. She wasn't at all prepared for the prospect of seeing Reith, whose attitude to abortion was well known. Julian had been to see Oliver Wintrobe, as Patrick Stanley had suggested, and had tried to persuade him to send Marlene to see Hellman, who virtually believed in abortion on demand, like many of the younger generation of gynaecologists.

Unfortunately Dr Wintrobe had been insulted by a remark made by Hellman on the standard of care given to one of his maternity cases and refused to refer any more patients to him. Instead he wrote a letter to Reith and promised Julian that the consultant would be bound to be sympathetic when he heard the story. Even Julian's monumental confidence had been eroded when he realised she would have to see Reith, but he had assured her that no one would dare to turn her down after hearing the tale that Patrick had concocted. She just had to remember her lines and keep to the story and, above all, not allow herself to be stamped on by the old bastard.

'Miss McCarthy? This way, please.'

Reith was addressing the students and took no notice of her entry. The sister indicated that she was to sit down in the chair beside the desk. Reith was pouring scorn on the modern epidemic of promiscuity and wanton irresponsibility, which he regarded as the major social evil of modern times. The boys looked uneasily at the floor. Neither of them looked virgin material and their obvious discomfort was not lost on the gynaecologist. Their behaviour was their own business and besides he was a great supporter of the double standard. He almost expected medical students to lead a virile and active sexual life, yet he insisted that the young girls be paragons of virtue. It was this absurd doctrine of the dark ages that had driven his own daughter away from home.

He turned in his chair and appraised his next victim. Marlene was terrified. Her hands were clammy with sweat and her heart was beating so loudly and rapidly that she felt the whole room must be able to hear it. Reith stared hard at her and she was unable to meet those cold, penetrating eyes. She lowered her gaze and looked nervously at her handbag, which she clutched on her lap. She opened it and handed him the letter she had been given by Dr Wintrobe.

Silence. The wall clock ticked noisily. The students cringed with embarrassment and their hearts went out in sympathy to this delicate flower that was about to be trampled on so mercilessly.

Reith read the letter and grunted in obvious distaste at the contents. He folded it up and put it down slowly and placed a paperweight on top of it. He took a deep breath, folded his arms and, like an inquisitor who was about to destroy his captive, he stared hard at the girl as she squirmed in her seat.

'So.'

Silence. Uncomfortable silence.

'Well, young lady, you'd better start explaining in your own words exactly why you have come to see us.'

Marlene was so nervous she wasn't sure if she could find her voice. It came, but only hesitatingly, with a faint stammer spoiling her Liverpool accent.

'I'm expecting, sir. I'm pregnant.'

Reith relaxed immediately. He turned to the students with an exaggerated grin on his known ritual; he should have been on the stage. He held out a congratulating hand that she, poor dumb, distracted wretch, clenched in sick charade.

'Allow me to say how absolutely delighted I am to hear the news. Another lovely bouncing baby is going to enter the world.' He turned again to the students; Jamieson looked as if he was going to throw up. 'Gentlemen, this is indeed a cause for joy. We have had several wretched women in here this afternoon who are utterly barren and would give anything to trade places with this lucky girl.'

This was too much for Marlene. The floodgates opened and she burst into tears, weeping openly into her handkerchief at the hopelessness of her predicament.

Himmler would have loved Reith. The man would have gone far in the SS. The twin lightning-streak motif and the jackboots. His expression suddenly changed. The act was over. His face clouded with anger and his grey eyes looked like steel. He thumped on the desk and shouted at the weeping girl.

'You filthy little trollop. You waggled your little backside around the beaches of Spain luring all the local louts like a common whore. Then as soon as you slip up you come back to the National Health Service so that we can clear up the mess free of charge. That's what you want, isn't it? An abortion. That's it. That's why you've come here. You want to get rid of it. Suddenly a bit of Spaniard isn't any fun any more.'

'Yes, please,' she sobbed. 'An abortion, please.'

His tone changed again. Contempt.

'Just like that. Just like a chip shop.' He mimicked her pathetic voice. 'An abortion, please, and six penn'th of chips and go easy on the vinegar.'

Then he straightened in his chair and looked despicably at her as if she was trash. 'Get in there with Sister and get your things off quickly. That's one thing you're good at. Let's see if you're really pregnant and what those tablets have done to you.'

She left the room still crying. She was absolutely terrified and Sister tried to mother her and comfort her. She had much the same views on abortion as Reith but she dreaded these scenes and, above all, she couldn't bear to see the girls crying like this.

Reith turned on the students again. For some reason he felt he could always count on their loyal support, probably because they never voiced any kind of protest against his weekly tyranny. He brandished the referral letter at them.

'Bloody fantastic. Incredible. I've never heard of such wanton criminality. A Spanish medical student gets the little madam pregnant and then stuffs her full of methotrexate. What's methotrexate? Jamieson, what is methotrexate?'

'Uh. Must be a drug of some kind, sir. To cause abortion, I suppose.'

Reith sighed hopelessly.

'Jamieson, you don't seem to know anything. You are intending to go into a medical career aren't you, laddie? Partwright, what is methotrexate?'

'Partridge, sir. It's an anti-cancer drug, I think. They use it for malignant moles.'

'That's right; it's a folic acid antagonist. It works on the principle that, since folic acid is necessary for DNA synthesis, it is used more avidly by the fast-growing cells like cancer cells than by normal body cells. What are the fastest-growing body cells, Jamieson? The ones needing the most folic acid?'

'Uh. Must be blood cells, I suppose.'

'Almost right. Near enough for a Cambridge intellectual anyway. Bone marrow. The elements that go to form the white cells and the platelets. That's the most serious side-effect. Bone marrow aplasia. And of course, gentlemen, as you well know, the foetus requires large amounts of folic acid for the rapid growth of its body tissues. So if you hit a woman hard with an anti-cancer drug you should kill the foetus or cause it to be malformed and it will presumably abort or be stillborn.'

Jamieson was fascinated. Bloody clever, he thought, Christ, these Latins were smart bastards. He'd never have thought of that.

'So you'll have to do an abortion or she might produce a damaged infant?'

Reith swung around, white with anger.

'I'll do no such thing. The little hussy can live with the nightmare she brought upon herself. I refuse to be blackmailed by a Spanish gangster. I'll tell you one thing, laddie, I'll have his balls off when I get hold of his name. I'll make damned sure his dean gets to know about this. A character like that should never be allowed to enter our noble calling.'

He left the room and Partridge and Jamieson looked at each other in amazement.

There was a whole common room full of junior doctors and students waiting to hear about Reith's latest outrage in outpatients, and this particular episode would provide a sensation.

Reith gave Marlene the most callous and brutal internal examination. She winced with the pain, the roughness and the indignity. He took off his gloves and washed his hands then turned around while he dried them with a towel and watched her embarrassed efforts to dress herself in front of his penetrating gaze.

'Well, you're certainly pregnant. About ten weeks and if your story is correct you took those tablets at the worst possible time. Your baby will almost certainly be deformed in some way but quite plainly it is not going to result in an abortion.'

She looked horrified. She was so immersed in her lie that the reality and finality of what he was saying struck deep at her. She went suddenly pale and felt defenceless in her slip. She looked at Sister for some support, some indignant outrage, but the face was passive. The sympathy had gone. It could have been chiselled in stone.

'You're not...' She stopped and formed her words slowly. The tears were gone. She was more sure of herself. Reality returned.

'You're not going to help me, then.'

He shrugged his shoulders non-committally as if he was discussing a business deal with all the cards stacked on his side.

'Why should I? It's your little mess. Why don't you go back to your little Spanish boy and get him to marry you? Then you could ask some nice Spanish doctors to help you out.'

'I can't do that. They're all Catholics over there.'

'And so, I imagine, are you,' he screamed. 'You filthy little hussy. An Irish Catholic from Liverpool. Am I right?'

'Me dad's a Catholic. So what's that to me?'

'It's everything to you. What would your father say if he saw you now? Would he be proud of you?'

She was dressed now. The tears gone. Her Irish temper was roused. Her brown eyes flashed with anger and her small body trembled with tension. She screamed back at him.

'He's just like you. A pig. A pompous stuffy pig.' She spat on the floor. She yelled hysterically at him. 'You should both get together in a muddy shitty pig sty. PIG!'

She ran for the door but he caught her by the arm. He used his full parental type of authority. The last time someone had answered him back like this was his daughter Louisa and the painful memory came back, viciously slapping him in the face.

'You come back here next week, young lady, and bring the name and address of that Spanish boy and we'll talk about this further.'

She wrenched herself free and angrily pushed him away.

'Piss off. Pig. Piss bloody off.'

She ran out, slamming the door and tearing down the passage to the street outside where a nervous Rolleson was waiting for her. She threw her arms around his neck and burst into floods of tears as she tried to recount her nightmare encounter with one of the bastions of the medical establishment.

Julian Rolleson spent a gruelling hour-and-a-half trying to placate Marlene. She had been terribly upset by her encounter with Reith and, naturally, she was putting the blame on the characters that had got her into this fix in the first place. It took three vodka, Bacardi and gins with a dash of coke, to give it taste, before she stopped sobbing. Then a promise that all would be all right and a final promise that once it was all sorted out, the two of them would get married. Eventually Julian slipped two Mogadon tablets into an egg flip and tucked her in for the night in his bed.

She went out like a light, but he was left with the increasingly urgent problem of how to get rid of Brackenbridge's baby. He was obsessed with the fact that the poor girl would deliver another hopeless bumbling Bodger into the world, complete with Roman nose and horn-rimmed glasses and, since one was enough for any cosmic system, he reasoned that he had to find a means out of this mess. If he could be sure it was his own he would probably throw in the chips, say 'Sod it' and marry the girl.

She had already made him experience the emotion of love, and then, as he tucked her sleeping body into bed and saw the tear stains still on her lovely face, he felt intense pangs of guilt. Why had he not kept her for himself? Why on earth had he tried to operate a stud farm like Playboy Mansion, London? Now he was regretting it. He was developing a conscience but maybe it was a shade too late.

He looked worriedly at his watch and went out into the London streets. He needed the mass presence of the city at night. The traffic, the lights, the noise. All the faceless shape of a big metropolis. He walked down the Edgware Road. The crowd stimulated him. He had to concentrate on the solution to the problem. The abortion capital of Europe and what an arch cock-up they had made of it so far.

And they were supposed to be on the inside. He was disgusted with himself. He retraced his steps back to the hospital. He had to contact Patrick Stanley again. Even if it meant a private job, Patrick would know where to send them. They would just have to pool the ash cash for the rest of the year to pay for it.

He rang the internal phone in the television room. Stanley generally goggled at the box at this hour of the night unless he was actually working on the labour ward. It acted as a sobering-up period between his two big bouts in the pub, one just before supper and the other just before closing at eleven.

The telephone was answered by Patrick Stanley himself. His strong Dublin accent was easily recognisable from that of the other doctors.

'Who d'you want?'

'Is Mr Stanley there, please?'

'Who wants him?'

Rolleson was puzzled. There was no mistaking the voice; he identified himself.

'He's not here.'

'C'mon, you bloody Irish gremlin. I can almost smell you down the phone wires. What's the game?' Pause. 'The plan misfired.'

'I know, the students told me all about it.'

'D'you mind if I come over to talk to you?'

There was a silence at the other end. Patrick had no wish to get further involved. He had lent them a fantastic fabrication that had once helped him out when he had got a girl into trouble in his student days. He knew that he could never say no to a woman and that was one of the reasons why they were twisting his arm to help them out.

'Meet me over in the Lust at nine o'clock and try to get a small table so that we can talk. You'd better line up a couple of pints – they'll both be for me. If you want one, you'd better make it three. Talking is thirsty work.' He returned to the television. It was of no real interest but he was a compulsive viewer. It was the only way of communicating with the outside world when incarcerated in this living hell of a place.

After a while, he switched off. The choice was insufferable. Malcolm Muggeridge on one channel and Hughie Green on the other. Both of them gave him neurodermatitis so he ambled up to the labour ward to monitor the action and see if the night staff held out any promise. Then he crossed over the road to the pub. Julian Rolleson was seated behind a row of full beer mugs as if he was out to get mightily smashed.

Patrick downed a pint in about forty-five seconds, then smacked his lips and gave the matter in hand some serious reflection. They both agreed that Reith was a callous bastard and that it had been a tactical error to send Marlene to one of his Gestapo sessions. Having seen one consultant in the hospital, you belonged to him body and soul, as of right, unless he chose to refer you to someone else. The medical meritocracy could not countenance the concept of the common herd chopping and changing in midstream. It would end up like a cattle market.

'We'll see if we can call his bluff at coffee tomorrow. We have an antenatal clinic in the morning and he likes to hold court over coffee with the houseboys and the two students. I know for a fact that the college is circulating all consultants with a form to get the views of the profession on the workings of the Abortion Act. Hellman and Felicity have both had a questionnaire and I've just seen one in Reith's pigeonhole. He always opens his mail at the coffee break and loves to talk about college politics so that he can impress us all as to how important he is. I want you to make sure that those two students, Jamieson and Partridge, come to the clinic in the morning. It will mean changing with two on obstetrics but Reith wouldn't know the difference. I'll tee them up and make sure they trot out the right type of answers. Especially that bloody Old Etonian. He thinks he's too damned good for this planet. Then you'd better get hold of Brackenbridge. He's a bit ambivalent on abortions for religious reasons. Furthermore the boss scares the shit out of him and he always says yes to anything he's asked. If Reith asked him to jump over a cliff, the dumb bugger would do it. He'd probably bodge the attempt by landing on a convenient ledge but, still, he would do it.'

He paused for liquid refreshment and then wiped the froth from his lips with the back of his hand and returned to his subterfuge.

'He's a real arse-licker. Probably got a pure growth of *Strep. faecalis* on his tongue. You tell him that as soon as I start talking about rubella and get Reith to agree on those grounds, he's got to mention this particular case. It's got to come from him, not from me. Reith knows I can't stand him and if I said anything he'd deliberately take the opposite view. He's like that. Pig-headed Scot. And if the Bodger doesn't come in right on cue, you tell him I'm going to drop him into the shit right up to his eyeballs. Make sure you tell him that I know about his involvement in this. You got all that? Right. Now I suppose I have to buy the next round. What d'you want? A pint?'

Hitherto Reith had never seriously questioned his own attitude on the abortion issue, but as he drove home that night a sense of distinct uneasiness descended upon him.

It was not merely the behaviour of the girl that had reminded him so painfully of his own Louisa as she packed her bags and left, eighteen long months ago. He realised that his attitudes had become more entrenched since the liberalisation of the Abortion Law that had divided his once happy family so savagely. His reactionary stance was by no means unique. Many of the most celebrated academic names in the speciality were vigorously opposed to the changes in the law and in doing a few terminations each month he counted himself a liberal. He realised that this was only relative. Relative to those who did none at all.

But this girl this afternoon seemed so recalcitrant. He had never been insulted like that in his own clinic. And yet he had turned her down knowing full well the horrors that would surround the birth of a malformed baby. The emotion surrounding the thalidomide babies would ensure a hostile press if the facts ever became known. It was the utter scurrilousness of it all. He had a distinct feeling he was being blackmailed by some faceless Spaniard who had performed an act of therapeutic malevolence that was quite monstrous. Why should he, a respectable London consultant, be forced into a corner by such salacious behaviour? He was sure he was right. The girl must return to Spain. Quite rightly, the ball should be put back into their court.

The last case of the afternoon had had all the qualities of a Whitehall farce. He had been visibly upset by the Liverpudlian girl and wished to conclude the outpatient session as rapidly as possible. He had groaned inwardly when he saw an Indian patient who couldn't speak a word of English. He had refused to allow the husband to act as interpreter and instead they had found a young Indian student nurse to translate.

Reith had been in a hurry and had become impatient at the dialogue between the two Indian women prattling away endlessly like a couple of myna birds, which was difficult because the patient spoke Urdu and the interpreter came from Bombay and only spoke Gujarati. He was only trying to ascertain simple facts such as the number of children she had had, and even this had caused an almost interminable exchange, leading to him losing his temper and sending her to the examination room without giving an adequate history.

He had asked her quite clearly if she was sure she wanted the operation, and since she had three children in the UK and another three in India he suggested that sterilisation would be a prerequisite of the abortion. She kept grinning and saying yes, and he assumed she understood what he said. He raised no objection and arranged details for her admission. He was tired and eager to go home. He felt that he had adjudicated fairly over the abortion requests and had accepted one out of three, which was his usual batting average.

He was incredulous when an irate Indian had beaten his way past Sister and started banging on the desk like a barrack room lawyer. The man was in a state of great wrath and demanded angrily to know what right they had to execute his son. Thus far he had been plagued by daughters and he was sure that the present issue would be the long-awaited son. He was going to write to his MP, and involve the Race Relations Board, civil rights groups and even take the case to Amnesty International.

Angus was absolutely flabbergasted. The GP's letter had quite plainly recommended termination on social grounds and he had been particularly sympathetic in view of he fact that she was an immigrant and already had a large family. The whole thing was a ghastly mistake. The woman had said yes at all the wrong times mainly because it was the only English word she knew, and Indians tend to shake their heads vertically when they mean no, which is quite different to the accepted convention in the western world. In fact the family had intended to come to the antenatal booking clinic but the local GP had got the message wrong. The mistake was easily corrected and apologies were proffered all round, but Angus disappeared in a huff of anger and impatience.

He stopped at a little-known pub on the way home where he wouldn't be recognised and downed two double Highland malt whiskies. He was just praying that his welcome at home would be of the more pleasant kind and that he would be allowed to relax and forget the ordeals of the afternoon. He couldn't face another round of marital strife. The battles had been increasing lately and this evening he was ill-prepared for another skirmish. The thought of this took him to the bar and he ordered another double. It was gone nine o'clock when he drove his car up the gravelled drive, realising now that marital disharmony was inevitable but at least he was prepared for it. His breath reeked of peppermint.

CHAPTER EIGHTEEN
The underground passage to the operating theatre, St Giles' Hospital, London

All this stress. It was taking hours, even days or weeks off his preordained span. Ever since his elder brother had died, Angus had become obsessed with his temporal existence. George had died at fifty-eight and he was only a dermatologist – no bloody stress in diseases of the skin.

Said the doctor as he took his fees, 'There is no cure for this disease. Come and see me again in a month.'

He strode along the underground passage that went beneath the main road. The traffic shook constantly overhead. The basement was crammed with dozens of pipes in different colours with valves and engineering messages. 'Danger, 10,000 volts. Keep clear. Fire sprinklers. Keep clear. In case of fire, these doors will shut automatically. During fire alarm stand well clear.' What doors? He couldn't see any doors. Just a tell-tale puddle of water on the floor where British engineering efficiency had failed to make a watertight pipe.

This was Hades, the underground abode of the hospital electricians and Sam Charters, the Prince of Darkness, and his infamous venereology clinic.

He pounded down the passage at a fast walk, his steel-tipped heels clattering in the basement and echoing from the concrete walls.

Bloody Hampson. Why couldn't he tell me the problem himself? He detested the idea of being ordered to perform a task by a mere switchboard operator. Besides, he liked to have a little time to think about the problem. Get his mind in order.

He wasn't some kind of instant Action Man. Sister Brewer had insisted on buying that ridiculous portable telephone. Surely this was just the occasion for it. He'd bring that up with her at the next Theatre Users' Committee, which he chaired every other month when he was in control of the situation. Silly old cow. What the hell could it be? Hampson was an experienced man. He had never called him before during an operation. He recalled the last time he had heard Humphrey stammer over the phone. It was about a year ago – maybe more. He had informed him blandly that a woman was about to die and he thought he'd better let him know in case there were any repercussions. No, he didn't require any assistance but he merely wished to inform the boss. Angus grinned. In fact the woman had not died and the following day Humphrey, having created such a drama, was basking in the role of saviour of womankind. Despite his stammer and rather ridiculous appearance, he was an extremely competent man and Angus had great faith in him, and was pushing hard to get him a good consultant post. He was certainly first-class consultant material.

So what the hell was all this about?

More disturbing thoughts were suddenly shattered by a deafening blast on a horn close behind him. Angus almost jumped out of his skin and flattened himself against a wall as an orange electric tractor hummed past, pulling some stainless-steel containers with the lunch for the patients in the New Wing. This blast on the horn had added another twenty beats per minute to his tachycardia. A big black man was driving the vehicle and he brushed past Angus, narrowly missing him. His mate was a more cheerful West Indian who was standing precariously on the bumper of the last truck wearing a beanie hat. He waved at Angus as if he was trying to promote tourism in the Caribbean. 'Hi der, man. How is you today?'

Angus gave a stiff British nod, feeling again that his consultant status was yet again being eroded. Would Sir Hector have stood aside for an electric delivery vehicle driven by a couple of black characters in white jumpsuits with Rastafarian hairstyles? He would not. Certainly not. But then – in those days they didn't have a working-class substrata of immigrants that had left the former colonies that made up the vast British Empire to seek a better life in the United Kingdom. The working man in those days was born within the sound of Bow Bells. At times Angus felt like a professional version of Alf Garnett. Maybe he was just born into the wrong age.

He arrived at the door of the operating theatre and marked time on the tacky mat that was designed to remove germs from the feet, but which in reality probably provided a breeding ground for pathogens on its sticky surface. He refused to get into operating pyjamas if it was such an emergency. Yet his antiseptic Listerian training could not dispense with years of tradition in a matter of seconds. He grabbed one of the gowns that were usually intended for the theatre porters transferring the patients from the wards and hurriedly put it on over his best Savile Row suit. Then he grasped a pair of overshoes made of thick white calico and tied them around his shins. No mask, no hat. He saw the answer in a strange contraption of head and face gear that had been introduced by the hospital authorities to cover up the long locks of hair and fuzzy beards that were so prevalent among the orthopaedic surgeons and the new generation of junior doctors, students and technical staff.

He wrapped the flowing headdress around his bald pate and smooth-shaven face and stomped along to the gynaecology theatre in his clumsy footwear, looking like a cross between the Sheik of Araby and an aspiring cosmonaut, and peered through the theatre doors at a scene of incomparable chaos.

The anaesthetist was lying prostrate on the floor with the rubber mask intended for the patient over his nose and mouth. Like a sympathetic trade unionist, Humphrey Hampson had fainted on the far side of the table and was lying with rubber gloves crossed over his chest, and white wellington boots with toes pointed ceilingwards, like the effigy on the tomb of a medieval crusading knight of the Order of Saint John of Jerusalem. Sister Brewer was shrieking hysterically and, holding her arms above her head, kept informing everyone that she was sterile. The poor anaesthetised patient completed the sorry scene by lying unconcernedly naked with a huge stainless-steel laparoscope protruding from her navel as if she had been struck by the Sword of Damocles. Nurses large and small were trying in vain to revive the fallen duo with little success.

Angus took in the chaotic scene and grunted to denote his disapproval. He reached for the fire bucket in the theatre corridor and poured half the water over the still figures of Hampson and the anaesthetist to try to wake them up. The rest of the cold water he threw over Sister Brewer to silence her unnerving shrieks. With a deft flourish, he removed the laparoscope from the woman's belly, put it in his red fire bucket, and shuffled out of the room without a murmur, leaving the half-drowned attendants to sort out the confusion when they woke up.

This story and its obvious embellishments as they drifted around the medical common rooms of the London and provincial hospitals contributed greatly to building an image of Reith as a quick, cool-thinking individual who could deal with almost any situation. In a sense it proved to be his undoing because he lived beyond the projected image. His behaviour at times seemed to be that of a man seeking to do something outrageous, yet at the same time he was contained by an old-fashioned conservatism that isolated him from the rest of his staff.

In fact, this episode ended in tragedy. The anaesthetist in question, Michael Silver, was one of the senior registrars who was extremely bright academically but whose social life was a complete disaster. Many of the surgeons had remarked on his instability and his vagueness, not realising that he was leaning increasingly heavily on drugs. He had experimented with many of the injectable anaesthetic drugs such as fentanyl, but had once been caught administering a large dose of morphine into his own ante-cubital vein just after he had put the patient to sleep in the anaesthetic room. The nurse who had watched him had not taken the matter further because she realised that his career would lie in shreds around him if she reported her finding to the authorities. Instead she had played the Good Samaritan and had virtually blackmailed him into stopping the narcotic injections with the threat of disclosure. For a while he had improved, but slowly had lapsed into a different form of mental oblivions. He had started to sniff the anaesthetic gases.

Many of the surgeons were aware that during the operations he kept removing the rubber mask from the patient and taking a few deep breaths. He always maintained that he was testing the apparatus to make sure that it was functioning. Besides, they were so wrapped up in the intense concentration required during a surgical operation that they rarely paid much attention to the anaesthetist at the top of the table. Most anaesthetists were fairly strange anyway. They had an even higher suicide rate than the psychiatrists and Michael Silver was known to be one of the odder ones. His incessant fiddling with the knobs on the anaesthetic machines and his puffing away at the mask were rather taken for granted.

On this occasion, however, he had suddenly keeled over and collapsed with an ominous thud on the floor, still holding the rubber mask over his face. Hampson had already plunged the pointed trochar of the laparoscope into the abdomen of the patient, which was distended horribly by three litres of carbon dioxide to push the guts out of the way of the vicious instrument. Having virtually stabbed the girl through the navel he let out a satisfying puff of CO_2 and introduced the long telescope. At this stage he was mortified to see his colleague crash to the ground and felt a reeling sensation of panic. In a flash, his days in His Majesty's armed forces came rushing back. He had been a compulsive fainter. During the long hours standing at attention on the parade ground in the sticky heat of Cyprus, he would battle with his cardiovascular system to stave off a syncopal attack. The moment one of the platoon fell to the ground with the crashing of an untended rifle, Humphrey would feel himself going. He was eventually discharged on medical grounds because of his falling sickness. Here it was happening again. His head started to spin and the ground came rushing up to meet him.

Reith's dowsing revived the flustered Hampson, but Michael Silver lay still as death. He never recovered consciousness and died the following week in the intensive care unit, having lapsed into hepatic coma. The post-mortem revealed massive centri-lobular necrosis of the liver due to constant abuse of hard alcohol, halothane, nitrous oxide and other noxious vapours as well as a plethora of recreational drugs that were increasingly being used by young people at parties.

Chapter Nineteen
The antenatal clinic, St Giles' Hospital, London

Most of the doctors loathed the antenatal clinics except Brackenbridge, of course, and everyone had by now surmised that the boy was not normal. It was not the nature of the work, it was the sheer volume. If one could sit down and have a five-minute chat with each patient in a leisurely manner it would be a pleasant enough way of spending a morning, but it was like a factory, a huge assembly line of bloated women lying on their backs like upturned beetles in a long row of cubicles. There were about ninety patients to be seen, fifteen of whom were on their first visit so they had to have the whole works; a complete physical examination. Reith took one side with one of the housemen, and Stanley and the other houseman looked after the other. So far, so good, but that was where the equality stopped. Reith habitually arrived forty minutes late and conducted the clinic in the grand manner, interviewing the ladies at his desk and then seeing them in the cubicles in much the same way as he did in Harley Street. He was accompanied by two or three students, so with his attendant retinue, he presented an impressive sight despite the squalor of his surroundings. He refused to tolerate any interruption and a sister hovered around him like a queen bee attending to his every whim and foible. He would only see the important people and the wives or daughters of professional colleagues.

On a busy morning he would see about ten or twelve of the patients and would leave at about half-past eleven for Harley Street to overhaul the sexual apparatus of the rich.

For Stanley, the clinic was a nightmare. He had about three minutes, on average, for each patient and those having the booking visit required a full physical, a vaginal examination, a cervical smear and a letter to be written to the family doctor or local clinic. He had to deal with most of the problem cases, look at the x-rays and monitor the special risk cases with ultrasound cephalometry and oestriol results. In addition the housemen came to him with their problems and he had suddenly to switch his mind to an entirely different case, run off to the other side to examine a new patient and dispense advice that allowed little room for error. On top of this, his pager seemed to shriek incessantly as he had also to deal with all the problems and queries on any of the patients belonging nominally to Reith or Felicity Bundle on the gynaecology or obstetric wards. The constant stress was ulcerogenic and conducted on the sunny side; for the clinic had all the class distinction inherent in a bullfight arena. Hospital architects rarely considered the working conditions in the structures they erected and one side of the clinic was always delightfully cool, while the other was like a solarium with the sun burning through the frosted glass in summer and a bank of radiators giving out waves of heat in winter. The architects, with their usual occupational cunning, had made it impossible to open any windows any more than six inches because of the well-known propensity of hospital inmates to leap out of the building and commit hari-kari on the concrete below. Since the antenatal clinic was in the basement, the rationale behind this strategy was tenuous in the extreme, but nevertheless it was impossible to open any of the windows to get some fresh air.

Reith, of course, worked on the shady side while poor Stanley, whose pace of work was giving off about three times the number of kilocalories, had to labour in the fiery furnace.

It was difficult to remain cheerful under these conditions but a surly attitude from him could cause immense resentment; he was a play actor too, and he wore a plastic smile as he trotted out the same remarks, the same questions and the same pleasantries. Sometimes his mind would wander since so much of the antenatal examination was pure routine.

On this particular morning, he was thinking of the forthcoming coffee time and his attention was not on the generous breast he was palpating; in his haste he asked a question that was more pertinent to the examination of a pregnant abdomen.

'Does it move well?' he asked with a feigned air of great concern as his hands fondled the breast tissue in search of any potentially cancerous areas. This was the question he routinely asked when he was feeling the foetal parts but somehow his timing had gone out of sync. The patient looked a little puzzled.

'Wot! Me titties? Lorks, no – only when I wiggle 'em to turn me hubbie on!'

Patrick blushed furiously and tried to extricate himself from this embarrassing situation. He was greatly relieved when he had finished with that patient and, seeing that it was half-past ten, was able to make for the doctors' coffee room.

Reith was holding court as usual. He was sitting behind his desk opening his mail with a long Andalusian-style letter opener and discoursing on each item that he read as if the whole intimate circle required 'The Thoughts of Consultant Reith' to guide them through the day.

The two students were lounging in the corner with Jamieson looking more bored than usual. Bodger Brackenbridge was endeavouring to pour the master's coffee but was visibly rattled over something and was being admonished for his clumsy efforts.

'Put some of it in the cup, laddie, I'm not a pussycat, y'know. Come in, Stanley. Have some coffee. You're working too hard, laddie. Only one sugar for me and I'll have a clean saucer if you please.'

He was waving a travel brochure around like a claymore. 'Where shall I take my good lady this summer? The walking holiday in the Cairngorms was a bit of a failure. Two weeks of dismal Scottish mist and I began to feel like the Ghost of Ben MacDhui meself. Didn't improve the temper of the good lady either. This year it has to be guaranteed sunshine. Where do you recommend, Jamieson, you're supposed to be widely travelled. What about the Bahamas?'

'Boring,' said Jamieson, emitting a huge yawn as if to emphasise the point. 'Full of nouveaux riche. I suggest somewhere like Cozumel, if they haven't wrecked it by now. Take her turtle riding.'

Reith blinked. He'd never even heard of the place but he didn't like to admit ignorance. Anyway, he couldn't imagine Helena riding on a turtle, she might scratch her precious skin. He looked it up in the index but Lords Bros didn't appear to have it in their repertoire. To avoid further embarrassment he changed the subject by opening some more mail. It was a brown envelope bearing the familiar insignia of the Royal College of Obstetricians and Gynaecologists. He opened it and read the contents, frowning as he went.

Patrick Stanley helped himself to a cup of coffee and settled nonchalantly in the furthest corner.

'What a load of nonsense,' breathed Reith. 'Even the college has taken to conducting Gallup polls. I can't think what's got hold of everybody. They want us all to fill in a questionnaire on our attitudes to abortion. Very well. You lads can help me with this. They even suggest it here. "Please discuss your replies with your juniors before returning the questionnaire to the college." They can't trust us old fogeys to be honest any more. We'll soon see about that.'

He took out his Parker 61 and set about the questionnaire as if it was his final examination paper. After he had completed the introduction he started firing the questions at his audience.

'How many do we do here each week? About three or four I'd say.'

'One,' Patrick said tersely.

'Come, come. I see a good half-dozen in that godforsaken clinic.'

'You only allow three to be seen and we average only one a week on your operating list.' Then he added as an afterthought, 'I do a list of about nine or ten day cases on Wednesday for Mr Hellman.'

Stanley's tone was so firm that it brooked no argument. Then as if to atone for his corrective manner, he suggested that Reith might do some elsewhere and that Stanley could only speak for the health service patients.

If looks could kill, Reith would have stabbed his registrar many times in the next few seconds. Reith detested the members of his speciality who had made small fortunes by doing abortions on a massive scale in the licenced clinics around London. In fact, he did perform a few privately himself but they were very few and he didn't like the snide tone that Stanley had just used. He did not at this moment, however, intend to make an issue of it. He just glowered at his registrar as Patrick nonchalantly sipped his coffee, realising that he had gone too far again and hoped that the floor would conveniently open up so that he could make a hasty exit.

Reith looked back at the form and continued to go through various questions with the others. Stanley remained tactfully silent. They were dealing with the various methods used for mid-trimester abortions and the replies were fairly standardised.

Finally in the summing up Reith was expected to indicate by a tick whether he considered himself for or against the Abortion Act, and if he ticked 'for' he had to say whether he was liberal in his interpretation of the clauses of the Act or if he tended to be rather conservative.

Reith looked at his small captive audience, beamed winsomely and made a tick with his pen. 'I think I would judge myself as a liberal in these matters.'

He then folded the paper away and looked at the surprised expression on the faces of his juniors. He was playing to the stalls. He crossed his hands in front of him, took a slow and deliberate sip of the awful tasting mixture of chicory and coffee that the NHS provided and asked Brackenbridge for his judgment.

Bodger was visibly shaking. He glanced sideways at Stanley but there was no getting away. It was Stanley on one side or Reith on the other and at this moment in time Stanley held a much more powerful weapon over him. He looked at the floor but it seemed to rush up to meet him. He gripped his saucer and with a slight accentuation of his usual stammer he mumbled something.

'Don't mumble, laddie, if ye've an opinion to give, let's all be hearing it. It's not the Spanish Inquisition. Ye're in a democracy, laddie, for better or for worse. I'm not allowed to eat you.'

'I'd, well...' He bumbled to a halt and then, as if he was hurling the greatest insult in his life, he blurted out, 'I'd hardly call you a liberal, sir.' He took a deep breath and stared intently at his shoes.

Stanley tried to suppress a smile.

Reith put on a pained expression and feigned surprise.

'Oh. And what would your opinion of me be, Dr Brackenbridge?'

'I'd... I'd say you were just the opposite.'

Had he gone too far? He was desperately wishing he had never become involved in all this.

Suddenly he was rescued by Jamieson, who had stopped being bored.

'What about that poor kid yesterday who had a deformed foetus because of taking methotrexate? Surely she didn't know the effect it would cause. She must have taken them in good faith from her boyfriend expecting that they were abortifacient tablets.'

Reith gripped his letter opener and felt his anger mounting. He was suddenly being put in the witness box by his juniors.

'Did you hear of that piece of moral turpitude, Mr Stanley? This dismal little creature had cast her net out for a Latin lover and got herself pregnant by a Spanish medical student. They can't have heard of Hippocrates over there. The wretched lout gave her a course of methotrexate to deform the foetus so that we'd be morally bound to grant an abortion. Have ye ever heard the likes of that? Moral and professional blackmail. What do you think, Brackenbridge, or whatever your name is?'

'It is, sir.'

'It is what, laddie?'

'It is Brackenbridge.'

'Well, I know that. That's what I called you, didn't I? Don't hedge, laddie. Stop dodging the issue.'

Brackenbridge took a munch at his sandwich and chewed thoughtfully, wrinkling his forehead like a theologian who was trying to answer a difficult technical point on the remission of sins. 'Morally wrong. Yes, I'd agree with that. Yes, I think he has committed a wrongdoing in wilfully giving her those tablets. But are we not equally morally wrong in allowing a pregnancy to continue when we know it has a high risk of producing a deformed offspring? Wilfully allowing a damaged human being to be born?'

'I didn't ask for a sermon, laddie. I suppose you think that murdering the poor devil is more socially acceptable.'

Bodger looked down again. He had never really sorted out his views on this issue. Basically he felt it was murder and loathed each procedure to the extent that he had asked to be excused performing them on grounds of conscience.

Stanley saw his hesitation and couldn't prevent himself from joining the discussion.

'Plainly, if you really considered it as murder, you'd never ever do them in either the public or private sector. Do those bits of tissue we suck out through the curette really have a soul? Personally, I don't think so otherwise I would never wilfully destroy it. It has never existed. It is merely redundant unwanted tissue as far as the mother and society is concerned and if we know it's deformed it's even more disposable than normal. The use of the word murder is purely emotive. No one ever knew it, or named it, or loved it, and we cannot grieve for it and we should never involve emotional terms when we remove it from the womb. It is deliberate evasion of the issue. If gynaecologists really thought of it as murder, why do they perform more murder in private practice, than in the National Health Service? Is murder less a crime if the customer can afford it?'

Reith suddenly went crimson and started clenching his paper knife as if he was about to convulse. This was exactly the way his daughter used to speak.

It triggered a spot in his brain that sent him into a ferocious rage. He struggled hard to control it. His breathing became laboured and the silence, the apprehension and the oppressiveness in the room was apparent to everyone. The words when they came were almost whispered, but the silence was still enough to pick up the sound of a dropped pin.

'Get back to your work. All of you. Except you, Mr Stanley. I'd like a few words with you.' Patrick's heart started beating faster. It was like being at school with the headmaster. He realised he had gone too far but it was a subject that concerned him deeply. He had rejected the Catholic faith over it and could not help getting heated.

The others downed the last disgusting dregs of hospital coffee and departed for the antenatal clinic. After the door had closed the silence was heavier than ever and to Stanley it seemed to last and last.

Reith did not look at him. He turned that infernal letter opener over and over again. Stanley was not a Brackenbridge, however. He wasn't going to cower before the High Priest. He looked wistfully out of the window and wished the old bastard would get it over with. He looked over to where Angus was going through the agonies of preparing a speech. Their eyes met and all the animosity of the consultant came down on his registrar.

'I'm going to be frank with you, Stanley. You're new with us here. New to teaching hospitals. We're by no means satisfied with you. All my colleagues in the department are sick of your high-flown attitude to everything. Come down to earth, laddie. A little respect for your elders; it would do no harm. I would never have dared to speak to my consultant in such tones. I'm aware that times have changed but we still hold the reins of power. One word from me and I can kill your career. I can crush you like a baby bird. Time you thought of these things. Where do you go from here without our recommendation?'

Stanley was not going to be subdued by such nonsense. He knew for a fact that his standard of work could not be criticised. He knew that Felicity Bundle, for all her difficulties and tantrums, thought the world of him. He got on well with Hellman and did a morning list of terminations for him and helped with a research project on what the media had scathingly called 'lunchtime abortions'.

So what were his alternatives? To recant. Yes, sir. Very sorry, sir. Or he could call the old bastard's bluff. Being Irish, he chose the latter course.

'Look,' he said, in the most patronising tone he could muster. 'We're all trying to help you. This case will be the end of you. Look what the *News of the World* did to that female gynaecologist in Doncaster for refusing to abort that thirteen-year-old who had been raped by some soldiers. The public exposure ruined her. And that's nothing compared with this. Come on, be reasonable. They will crucify you – the whole bloody media will tear you apart.'

He stood up and came near the desk. Reith looked up – cornered but not beaten, like an animal wounded by a surprise attack – terrified that his aggressor might strike again. This was not at all the reaction he had expected. Generally, his power and authority could cower the most hardened spirits into submission.

But he was still in command. He could rely on professional secrecy when it came to the crunch. In sneering tones he looked up at Stanley.

'And who'll tell them?'

'I'll bloody tell them. That's who'll tell them. Believe me, I'll bloody well tell them.'

And he turned arrogantly and marched out of the room. Reith suddenly lost his temper and angrily stabbed the letter opener into the woodwork on the top of the desk. Then he felt cold and empty and almost frightened. He stared vacantly as it quivered back and forth. Even as the oscillation ceased he continued to stare like a blind man trying to extract some order from all this confusion.

He wearily took off his white coat and hung it up on the peg at the back of the door. He put on his jacket and walked out of the room. He told Sister that he was leaving for a meeting and Mr Stanley and the others would have to finish the antenatal clinic.

He went out of the main gate of the hospital and walked down the road for a quarter of a mile to a row of telephone booths outside Marylebone Station. The first three had been damaged by vandals and were either without flex or the whole receiver had been torn from the wall.. He looked at them with disgust and entered the only booth that was still working.

From memory he dialled a number. A Mayfair number. He was doing this more frequently lately. It seemed one way of coping with the mounting stresses of his life. He waited for the ringing tone to answer and while he waited he looked guiltily around in case someone from the hospital should recognise him. At least none of the telephone operators could listen in on his conversation. He felt the mounting tension he always felt on these occasions. His puritan background basically disapproved but it had become almost a necessity to preserve his sanity. He started to worry that she was away and, just as he was about to give up, the phone was answered.

Yes, she could see him in about an hour. He was immensely relieved and as he walked out into the busy sunlit street, he felt almost better already. He hailed a taxi and ordered the driver to take him to Shepherd's Market in the heart of Mayfair.

In acting out this sequence, Angus was resorting to a device used throughout time by middle-aged men in difficulties. He was relying on another woman to offer him help and comfort and, to ensure that he received this and none of the complications of a deeper relationship, he was willing to pay dearly for it. The expense never worried him. He almost saw his excursions to Mayfair as a therapeutic exercise that was saving him from tranquillisers, or the Highland malt that was the traditional passport to oblivion for so many of his Scottish countrymen.

Like so many successful, men, Angus Reith had blasted and bulldozed his way to a position of power and was suddenly intensely aware of the loneliness and hostility that surrounded him. A large part of this was due to his own intransigent attitude and stubbornness and somehow the abortion issue had crystallised them into a man fighting a rearguard action, leaving a heap of debris in its wake.

The first casualty had been his own daughter, who had walked out of his life and never again communicated with him. He had no idea of her whereabouts, although he had a shrewd suspicion that she still kept in touch with her mother, but between the two of them there existed a conspiracy of silence that excluded him.

Helena had never forgiven his attitude to Louisa's abortion and had returned to modelling much against his will and had launched herself into a series of affairs with showbusiness personalities that she scarcely bothered to disguise. His pride and possessiveness had gradually been eroded and the pedestal upon which he had put his wife had also crumbled away with it.

The marriage had degenerated into a series of marital skirmishes that rose bitterly between long episodes of silence and tension. Nevertheless, he could not bring himself to either apologise to Louisa or even to speak to Hellman, whom he felt was the malevolent hand behind this tragedy.

Now the issue had come once again to the fore, and his junior staff and even the students had risen against him. It was only natural that he should head again for the house and the person that had led him sympathetically through his previous crises.

Behind every successful man is a Helga or a Monique. For Angus, it was Mandy, a whore with a heart of gold or sufficient acting ability to make men think she had, and enough class, cunning and good taste to give her clients exactly what they required. She was expensive and her telephone number was passed on only by word of mouth and introduction among the best gentlemen's clubs in London. She had no need to advertise and her dedication to her calling assured that she could rent an expensive suite in Mayfair, drive a Lancia Flavia and join the jet set twice a year; in winter skiing in Gstaad or in summer sipping passion fruit cocktails in Martinique. She was a professional who enjoyed life to the full, but that enjoyment needed an endless supply of money, and to ensure that she got it, she went about her job as a call-girl with selfless determination to provide her clients with everything they required. Since they were mainly middle-aged men with money, their main need was a sympathetic ear embellished with sexual overtones that made the high price seem worthwhile.

He rang the bell at the entrance hall and awaited permission to ascend. His heart started to beat faster with excitement and guilt, like a schoolboy breaking bounds for the first time. An electronic voice summoned him from behind a copper radio speaker on the wall. The tone was metallic but the Cockney accent reassured him.

'That you, ducks?'

He smiled and introduced himself to the wire grille of the speaker as if addressing the Delphic Oracle. A buzzer sounded and the door opened automatically. He went in and climbed the stairs, one at a time, leaving the tuneless piped music and plastic flowers of the entrance hall behind him.

She was waiting for him on the landing. She wore a long black see-through negligee that revealed a slip of bra and even briefer panties, all in black. She was tall and blonde and tended to over-accentuate her make-up. She had to, she was thirty-five, going on forty, and the ranks of the profession were forever filling with younger flesh like a bottomless jar. She smiled at him and took his hand.

After all, they were old friends. He had trod these steps many times before.

Angus sank into a cosy armchair while she poured him a stiff whisky and made pleasant conversation. He started to relax. There was something about her and these surroundings that dissolved away his troubles; they melted away in her sympathy and comfort.

She handed him his drink and poured herself a gin and tonic, then nestled warmly against his knees, in front of the gas log fire. He stroked her hair and then all the problems came tumbling out; his troubles at work, his troubles at home. This business about the abortion girl. He became incensed against the Abortion Act, the girl and particularly his registrar, Patrick Stanley. She listened sympathetically. She was a good listener; she had to be. Many of her middle-aged clients paid more for her ear and it was less demanding than her pussy.

She knew the needs and wants of all her regular visitors. Some just wanted her to listen to their problems, some had slightly more bizarre tastes and these required a complex ritual of play-acting that she had learnt over the years. It was worth it to her. These men were intensely loyal. She was like a second wife to them and, moreover, a wife who indulged their fantasy life and never let it appear ridiculous.

Reith was relatively simple. He liked to get his current bone of contention off his chest over a drink of Scotch and then, when this had purged him mentally, he required a sexual catharsis. She was able to sense the precise moment. He did not like to make suggestions, for he was still intensely shy after all these years, but he expected the programme to flow with all the order and exactness of a difficult operation.

After a time she rose and stood on the carpet in front of him and carefully and tantalisingly undid the bow that held her lace negligee. She removed it, slowly revealing her brown suntanned body still secure in her underwear. She looked him straight in the eye and his eyes were always averted at this stage. The piety of his Scottish upbringing came out with all the guilt and repression of the Presbyterian kirk. He knew he should not be watching a woman undress like this but the thrill of his wrongdoing was exhilarating. Furthermore, as a consultant gynaecologist, he was supposed to be impervious to the pleasures of the female flesh. That may be true in the aseptic surrounding of the hospital, but once outside he was as intense a voyeur as any man. His eyes kept darting back furtively like a ferret, as she unhooked her bra and slowly eased the straps over her shoulders and dropped the garment on the nearest chair. She started to fondle her breasts in an act of intense erotic narcissism, displaying the pink nipples between her groping fingers.

Slowly her hands descended like eddying currents over the rest of her body and started to slide down to her panties and ease them slowly from her hips. Reith's eyes kept stealing surreptitious glimpses and the sweat on his brow and the beat of his heart were increasing with the suspense. She displayed the merest glimpse of her little black triangle and then drew her panties on again. Although the finale was never in doubt, Reith was going berserk. She turned slowly to show her back to him and with deliberate fingers she revealed the cheeks of her bottom inch by inch, bending over as the panties descended to the floor. She leaned over and grabbed the armrests of the chair to support her as she gyrated her buttocks slowly in front of his eyes and slid her legs further apart, opening everything in front of him. Just as he was about to burst, she stood up and turned around to face him, looking stern and beautifully naked. The pleasant smile had vanished and her face assumed the sadistic stare of the disciplinarian. She took out a huge black leather belt and fastened it intricately around her middle.

He stood up, trembling slightly, and allowed her to undress him. He stood straight, staring to the front only, smelling the proximity of her nude body. She removed all his clothing and folded each item neatly on the chair, for he was a man of strict habits since boyhood. He lay submissively on the bed, face down with a towel underneath him.

She went to the cupboard and selected a gruesome bullwhip with nine tails of knotted leather. She cracked the whip for effect and noticed the muscles tense in a mixture of fear and sexual anticipation. She brought the whip down hard on him, causing a shriek of pain to sear through his body.

She did this three times, making sure that she made a sharp crack of noise and taking care not to break the skin with the marks of the lash.

Three was enough. He was sobbing pathetically, a sign that he had suffered enough but was still excited. She put the whip away and settled astride him with her moist vagina resting on the nape of his neck. She parted the cheeks of his bottom and stroked her finger in smaller and smaller circles towards the edge of his anus.

She could feel his excitement mounting beneath her and when his breathing was reaching fever pitch, she pushed her finger deep inside his rectum, at the same time sitting hard on his neck, forcing his head to suffocate in the pillow.

He gasped in pain and ejaculated on to the towel beneath him, then fell into a relaxed heap, breathing deeply and sobbing like a miserable wounded turtle.

After a few minutes, she went to the washbasin to wash her hands and slowly put her clothes back on.

He joined her and obsessively washed the semen from the towel despite her assurance that it was going to the laundry. He was deeply ashamed of himself and insisted on cleaning up his mess. He was even afraid to look up at her as he dressed but she kissed him sympathetically on the cheek as he was adjusting his tie.

'It was all right, wasn't it? Please don't look so sad.'

He managed a smile. Her sympathy could always dissolve his shame. He reached for his wallet and took out £100 in ten-pound notes. He thanked her and took his leave by the door.

'I'm sorry I'm so disgusting. If you don't want me to come again, I'd rather you said. I don't want you to feel that you have to put up with people like me.'

She adjusted his lapels and straightened his tie, giving him an affectionate kiss on the lips. 'Believe me, Angus, most of my older customers prefer something a little unusual, that's why they come here. As for me, I honestly prefer it than having a big lump of a Yorkshire pudding on top of me thrashing around with a pecker that refuses to come. Believe me, luv, some of 'em are as romantic as steamrollers. I actually look forward to your visits.'

Angus grinned sheepishly and squeezed her hands. She kissed him again and giggled happily before leading him out on to the landing.

'And Angus…' She hesitated. 'If I were you, luv, I'd swallow my pride on this occasion and let her have the abortion. The way things are at the moment it would be for the best. Any other way and I see nothing but problems.'

Angus looked at her and then gazed thoughtfully down the carpeted stairway.

'Yes,' he said. 'I think you're probably right.' He seemed weary but then he looked back at her and grinned. 'In fact, I'm damned sure you're right.'

He waved her farewell and with sprightly steps two at a time descended to the main hallway, letting himself out through the heavy oak door on to the Mayfair street. He breathed in deeply and suddenly felt surer of himself. He would ring his secretary from his club and get Stanley to abort the little trollop that had caused him so much irritation. Stanley could suck it out himself. He'd enjoy doing that; the insolent fellow would probably end up as an abortionist anyway. Certainly if Angus Reith had anything to do with it.

He inhaled the smell and the throb of the busy city. He looked at his watch and, frowning slightly, set off at a brisk pace for a luncheon date with some colleagues and friends in the exclusive gentlemen's club atmosphere of the Naval and Military Club – the In and Out – in Piccadilly. He had arranged to have lunch with four of his best friends – a plastic surgeon who worked at East Grinstead, a lawyer from the city who was Louisa's godfather, and two backbenchers from the House of Commons who were friends from his university days at St Andrews.

He handed his coat and scarf to the cloakroom attendant and went down to the hall to put a call through to his Harley Street secretary telling her to telephone Mr Stanley and instruct him to arrange for the Irish girl to be admitted for termination of pregnancy. There was no need for further identification. He had forgotten her name, but Mr Stanley would know the one he meant.

He clasped his hands together, cracking the joints of his knuckles. He was feeling good again as he joined his circle of distinguished friends for a dry sherry before lunch.

Chapter Twenty
Stoke Poges churchyard, Buckinghamshire, autumn

Three days later Michael Silver was buried at Stoke Poges in Buckinghamshire. The old grey stone church with its connections to Thomas Gray's *Elegy Written in a Country Churchyard* was as pleasant a place to be buried as one could wish for, not that the surroundings mattered much to the dead. Silver had lived in the village as a child and his family had a small burial plot near the old yew tree by the lychgate.

It was a cold misty October day and the dank smell of the rotting autumn leaves seemed to penetrate to the marrow. Patrick shuddered as the coffin was lowered into the hole in the ground and Silver's weeping mother threw a handful of damp soil on to her son's earthly remains. The priest mumbled some fitting prayers like an automaton and then the party shuffled out of the churchyard to the waiting cars. It was all so unreal. The fog seemed to envelop them in its grey wet blanket and seal them off from the rest of the world. The only sounds that could be heard were the scuffling of the dead leaves underfoot and the jerking sobs of the womenfolk.

There were half a dozen of the junior doctors from St Giles who had come to pay their respects to their former colleague. Most of them took their leave of the family outside the church gate muttering embarrassed and inadequate condolences and excusing themselves on the pretext of having to return to some essential commitment at St Giles. Patrick Stanley had come with Joe Gibson who as one of the anaesthetic registrars was probably more affected by his death than any of the other doctors present at the funeral. The feeling of gloom and unreality was so complete that the two of them decided to take a walk among the huge old beech trees of Dorneywood and while away the time until the pubs opened for lunch.

They walked for several minutes before either of them spoke. The dead oak and beech leaves came halfway up their shins in places. Patrick pulled his duffle coat hood over his head to protect him from the cold and looked more like a mystic druid than an aspiring gynaecological surgeon.

It was Joe Gibson who broke the silence. 'My God, that was horrible. I've never been to a burial before. It's bad enough when the bloody priest presses the electric button in the middle of a prayer and the casket whirrs electronically away on a moving belt and disappears through the curtains to the fire beyond, but that cold damp hole in the ground… Oh, Jesus, I thought I was going to throw up when I thought of old Michael down there.'

'Old Michael… I like that,' Patrick grunted. 'The poor sod was only thirty-four.'

'I still can't believe it. We all knew he was a bit weird and into all sorts of experimental drugs but no one had a clue he was that far gone. He was artistic, far too artistic for a doctor. Used to write beautiful poetry. Once I went along to a poetry reading with him in some way-out place in Islington; he was very well received. They were a weird lot, mind you, most of them as high as kites on acid and I remember a really freaky soul in the kitchen making psilocybin omelettes for everybody.'

Patrick turned to his friend and hunched up his shoulders, making his duffle coat hood tilt forward, looking very serious and sounding very Irish. ''Tis my belief, Joseph, that that bastard Reith drowned the lad. If poor old Hubert had been breathing in, instead of out, when the water hit him, we would have a very serious staff shortage at St Giles at the moment.'

'Poor old Humphrey; he's taken it all very badly. He was as white as a sheet at the graveside. I thought for one horrible moment that he was going to faint again and fall in the hole. Poor fellow seems to feel responsible for the whole thing.'

''Twas murder,' said Patrick gravely.

Joe Gibson stopped walking and looked at Patrick in amazement.

''Twas murder of the first degree.'

Joe looked sceptically at his friend, almost willing him to continue, but Patrick remained silent, merely shuffling his boots through the dense pile of dead leaves that covered the floor of the forest.

'You've no proof to support such wild statements.'

Patrick shrugged. 'I only know what I've been told. A week or so back we had a few jars in the Lust in the Dust after the gynae path meeting. Old Humphrey was reasonably well-oiled and told me a yarn in confidence.'

'In confidence.'

'Well, more or less, so I suppose I can tell it to you "in confidence".'

215

'Go on.'

'Well, about ten years ago Reith had a very dishy private patient who made her living by nude modelling.'

Joe chuckled. 'I can't see old Reith with his Victorian ideals taking too well to that.'

'On the contrary. Apparently she was all innocence and sweetness. Husband had walked out on her and she was supporting two small kids. Anyway, it was pure *Health and Efficiency* stuff, good wholesome frolicking and prancing about in the buff with a table tennis bat in her hands.'

'Placed discreetly to cover up her beaver.'

'She didn't have one. This was in the old days when no one dared show a full-frontal with pubic hair. She'd had them all removed by electrolysis to save the darkroom technicians the trouble of fading out the little black triangle, which in those days was not that easy.'

'You should recommend that line of work to that piece you singed a few months ago.'

Patrick looked crossly at his friend, then picked up a pile of dead leaves and deposited them on his head. 'Listen, you fucker, d'you want to hear this story or not?'

Joe was still reeling from the ferocity of the attack.

'What d'you do that for, you bloody leprechaun? All over my best bloody suit.' He picked the dead oak and beech leaves out of his hair.

'Well, anyway.' Patrick cleared his throat.

'This bird had a lump on one of her tits and Reith admitted her for a biopsy and frozen section.'

'Reith?'

'Yes. In those days he still did the odd radical mastectomy – refused to confine his surgical skills to the pelvis. The older generation of gynaecologists used to do the breast surgery and still do in continental Europe. Old Ivor Jenkins had come out of the Second World War and found that the ranks of pathologists had been thinned out of all proportion to their role in the conflict. Apparently, they were veritable cannon fodder, for some reason. So without really wanting it he became professor of pathology at St Giles and turned his head to operating the frozen section machine.'

'Christ, what a shambles.'

'Right. Apparently it was an absolute disaster. They'd all be up in theatre waiting for an answer over the telephone with the patient prepped and ready on the table. All they'd get would be a collection of Welsh mumblings and bumblings and the silly old sod would invariably sit on the fence. On this occasion, apparently, he was vacillating as usual and finally said that he couldn't be sure that the tumour was entirely benign. So old Reith went ahead and chopped the tit off.'

'A radical mastectomy? Lymph nodes as well?'

'Yep. The whole works and with it, of course, the poor girl's livelihood.'

'And it was malignant?'

'Not at all. The paraffin section came back a few days later and it was completely benign; not a hint of malignancy anywhere.'

'Jesus Christ.' Joe shook his head in disbelief.

'The worst thing about this particular episode was that Reith stormed down to the path department basement just after the paraffin section report came through and found old Jenkins virtually comatose beside a couple of empty whisky bottles.'

'Did he report the incident to the Consultant Staff Council?'

'He threatened to but he realised that old Jenkins would be finished. He couldn't even get a job in general practice. Who the hell would appoint a failed pathologist, and an alcoholic at that?'

'So what did he do?'

'He enlisted the help of Jenkins' wife and made it clear to him that if he had any evidence that he had touched a drop of booze over the following two years he would bring the whole matter to the attention of the General Medical Council.'

'And?'

'The result was that Jenkins went on the wagon and was saved from an early death from cirrhosis. Praise all round for the great saviour Reith and a noose-hold around the neck of the pathology department every time His Lordship gets into trouble.'

'And one titless model.'

'Yeah and how we often forget that one titless model.'

217

They walked on in silence for a few minutes as Joe tried to make some sense out of it. He tossed the arguments backwards and forwards and then stopped and looked at his friend in exasperated disbelief.'

'Oh come on, you bloody Irish gremlin, the post-mortem clearly showed advanced cirrhosis of the liver.'

'Post-mortems can be fiddled. It's well known Reith is in cahoots with Prof Jenkins. I'll bet a pound to a penny it was death by drowning.'

Joe could not believe his ears, but as he looked into his friend's face he had never seen such hatred. 'You don't really believe that, Patrick?'

'I know I hate the bastard's guts, that's for sure. He's the kind that would do away with his grandmother if he had to. Christ, he was upset when I asked to go to the funeral today. Accused me of deliberately trying to stab him in the back. 'No loyalty to your consultant, Mr Stanley.' Patrick imitated Reith's lowland Scottish accent. 'That's what the bastard said.'

Joe grunted. 'Not a single consultant there today, you notice. None of the senior anaesthetists, even. I'd have thought old Harry Squires would have tried to come. After all, Michael worked for him for four years.'

'He was an embarrassment to them. Once that happens they're glad to be rid of you. If I'd known I would have to work for a malevolent sod like Reith, I'd never have come to this godforsaken place.'

They walked on in silence again. Joe Gibson was a little disconcerted by Patrick's conversation. He seemed to be more prepossessed with his own problems than with any feeling of remorse for the deceased. The deceased. My God, that word stank of the grave. Joe could not help feeling that one day someone would be walking away from his funeral muttering impersonally about 'the deceased'.

'It doesn't seem to have bothered you very much, Patrick.'

'What?'

'The funeral.'

'Och, I've been to dozens of them. Coming from a good Catholic family I've that many relations that there's always someone to be buried. Mind you, we're not so morbid about it where I come from. Usually we find someone who plays the fiddle and the uncles bring in some of the best potteen. More like a party, really.'

Joe shuddered and was beginning to wish he had come on his own, but

Patrick again interrupted his morbid thoughts with further irrelevance.

'Who would have believed that a German Jew sat under these trees and wrote some of the finest descriptive music ever composed.'

'Wagner?'

'Oh, Mother of Mary.' Patrick cast his eyes upwards. 'You English are a terrible bunch of philistines when it comes to the arts. Felix Mendelssohn, of course. Don't tell me you've never heard of him, although sometimes I think your idea of culture is the members' bar at Lords.' He glanced at his watch. 'Talking of bars, Joseph. I've an awful thirst on me. Let's go and have a liquid lunch at the nearest pub then I'd best be heading back to the mill. Reith has a big outpatient clinic this afternoon and the old bastard will cuss me from here to the middle of next week if I'm not there to give him a hand.'

CHAPTER TWENTY-ONE
St Giles' Hospital, London, October

'Oh, Christ, I'm going to be late again.' Patrick went pelting up the stairs at Earl's Court underground station, his heart pounding alarmingly. 'Hell's teeth, I'm unfit.'

He ran down the tunnels and cursed the length of the interchange between the deeply tunnelled Piccadilly Line and the Circle Line, which was only just beneath street level.

He just made it to the platform when the underground train arrived and he was thankful that there was no further delay. He simply couldn't afford to risk the wrath of 'His Lordship' again.

Patrick had many failings in life, but one that doggedly clung to him was a total inability to get out of bed on time in the morning. He had tried all sorts of ruses to help himself in this dilemma, but to no avail. When the alarm went off, he would always snatch another five minutes and, invariably, he ended up in a frenzy of shaving, tooth brushing and leaping around in the disordered chaos of being late for work. He swallowed a glass of cold milk as an inadequate breakfast, ran as fast as he could for quarter of a mile to South Ealing Piccadilly Line station and emerged from the underground station at Marylebone in a sweat, with that wild-eyed dishevelled look of the truly disorganised man.

No, this particular early bird never caught his worm. Once at work, he would sit in a corner of the doctors' dining room and, much to the chagrin of the waitresses who were trying to clear away the remains of breakfast, he would take a mug of tea and peruse the morning papers, and then he'd have a crap, wash and brush his hair in the on-call rooms and be more or less ready for work by about ten o'clock.

That was the way things went three days a week when the registrars were expected to be in by nine o'clock at the latest. He was on call two to three nights in the week and the only compensation there was that he could lie in and didn't have to suffer the ordeal of commuting to work. That left Thursday, the main operating day, and today, Wednesday, when Lord bloody Reith, like the out-of-date tyrant that he was, insisted that his grand round started promptly at the unearthly hour of eight o'clock and woe betide anyone who was late for it. And Patrick was going to be late again – the third time in the six months he had been at St Giles.

He had tried everything to rouse himself for the Wednesday round. To be in by eight meant leaving from his local tube station at South Ealing by seven at the latest. The vagaries of the underground seemed to be increasing of late and it was not uncommon to be greeted by a blackboard announcing, 'London Transport regrets that owing to staffing difficulties, etc… there would be unforeseen delays during the rush hours.' Unfortunately this had been his excuse on the two previous occasions when he was late and it had been met with precious little sympathy from the consultant. He was merely told to set his alarm clock earlier and that if he could not afford an alarm clock he was to see Reith's secretary who would purchase one for him and deduct the cost in instalments from Patrick's salary – the indignity. A monstrous suggestion drawn up only to embarrass him in front of the students and nurses.

In fact, he had two alarm clocks and he was still unable to get out of his pit. He tried to set them at ten-minute intervals but that invariably went wrong. He would even deliberately advance the clocks so that he might deceive himself into believing he was late. Unfortunately, even in the grey hours before dawn, he was still too intelligent for that and grinned out of his stupor with a 'Ha! Ha! You can't fool me' expression, and fell asleep again. His wife used to push and pull him until he had to get up. She used to run a bath for him until she found him fast asleep in the lukewarm water and forever after lived in terror that her beloved would expire by early morning drowning. Now that she had left for her parents' house in Sussex on an almost permanent basis he was unable to call upon her willing services. They had been even more willing before the kids were born. They were twice a night people in those days, and the daybreak razzmatazz always ensured that he was physically joggled into wakefulness. Now that she had left him alone in London, yet another means of waking up was removed from him.

In the Army, a hulk of a sergeant major would bash on the end of each bed with his swagger stick, bellowing about the bunkhouse like a mad bull. 'Come on, yer lousy bleedin' lot. Hands off cocks, on with socks. Git out of yer wanking chariots!' He'd even tried that. He invariably woke up with a thumping erection and since there was no wife to demolish it these days, he would bash his bish until he'd have to leap out of bed to the wash basin with warm semen dribbling between his fingers. That, he concluded, was no way for an aspiring professional man to greet the working day, and although he was a great proponent of the masturbating arts, he always behaved like a lapsed Catholic and ended up in an apologetic guilt-ridden discourse with himself and the Almighty while shaving in the mirror. No, he muttered, to his reflected image, there has to be a better way – but, so far, it had eluded him.

Only two more stops before Marylebone. He glanced at his watch. He might just scrape into the hospital before His Lordship. He rocked backwards and forward, his toe and heel supporting himself in the crush of bodies, clinging to one of the hanging straps. With his thoughts still on masturbation, he grinned to himself at some of the memories of his Army days. He recalled a particular instance, when he was serving as company medical officer stationed up at Catterick camp in North Yorkshire. He had come in (late as usual) to the morning sick parade and his heart had fallen when he saw that the room was crammed to capacity. The orderly had called for the first patient, whereupon half the room had risen to their feet. It appeared that they all belonged to C bunkhouse and one of them appeared to be the spokesman for the rest. He explained that they had come on behalf of Corporal Tasher, who apparently indulged in such an excess of self-abuse that none of the men had managed to get a full night's sleep for the past four months. Tasher apparently pulled his wire to such a degree that the others did indeed look a tired and haggardly lot and they were all requesting sleeping tablets. Tasher himself, however, beamed radiantly and looked like a living advertisement for health foods. Patrick had caused something of a regimental sensation by tackling the problem in a somewhat unorthodox fashion for the Royal Army Medical Corps.

Instead of prescribing pills or inserting bromide in his tea, Patrick had instructed Tasher to collect a pair of boxing gloves from the quartermaster's stores. The men in the billet made sure that these were tied on every night and everyone slept happily ever after.

Patrick was chuckling to himself at the recollection of these events until he noticed the uncomfortable stare of a fellow passenger peering over the morning edition of the *Times* looking at him as though he was a man possessed. He was also aware that this was his stop and he hurtled out of the train and raced along the street to St Giles like a thief on the run.

He leapt across the main driveway of the hospital just in front of a large black Bentley limousine and was frozen to a halt by an angry honking on the horn. He spun round as the driver's side window whirred electrically down, to be met by a look of withering condescension from his consultant, Angus Reith himself.

'I trust you're not rushing like a mad thing on my behalf, Mr Stanley.'

'Oh, no, sir,' Patrick lied unsuccessfully.

Reith unhurriedly took off his leather driving gloves and extinguished an expensive-looking cigar into the stainless-steel ashtray and glanced with ill-disguised contempt at Patrick Stanley who was desperately trying to regain his breath and composure and making wild attempts to bring some order into his mop of unruly Irish hair.

'Tell Hampson that I'll be ten minutes late this morning. I have to see Lady Duckworth in the private wing. Tell him to start seeing the minors.' He eased the limousine forwards and disappeared in a puff of exhaust and affluence down the ramp leading to the consultants' underground car park.

Patrick ambled along the corridor to Blair-Bell ward, slowly regaining his breath and his composure, and as he came into hearing distance of Sister's office, he imitated Reith's characteristic walk. He grinned. He was a master at imitating the way people walked. He entered the ward and his grin broke into resounding laughter as he saw the whole cortege breathless and at at- tention, with Sister holding the consultant's white coat at arm's length, like a gentleman's valet. He stepped up to her and made to get into the coat, but she whacked him on the shoulder in abject dismissal. The joke had gone well and everyone relaxed again and started to chatter.

Humphrey Hampson looked at his watch – five past eight.

'I thought I was going to have to m-m-make an excuse for you again, old s-s-son.'

'Just been to see a patient in the wing,' mocked Patrick in Reith's pompous London-Scottish twang and then returning to his own voice. 'I was just about demolished by the old bugger. He said to start the round without him but I wouldn't bother, we only have to see them all again when the master of cere- monies finally arrives. He's gone off to see Lady D. I helped him take her box out last Tuesday.'

Lady Duckworth was the wife of the esteemed professor of medicine at St Giles, who had retired many years ago to farm in Dorset. His name still lived on at the hospital, whispered and remembered with great reverence, and his ghost still walked the corridors. He had been the president of the Royal College of Physicians and had been responsible for establishing a professorial chair at the hospital. Since the fame of such departments shone many years after their brightest suns were eclipsed, it was the medical unit that set the academic reputation of the hospital, although in truth, it had lapsed into mediocrity after the passing of Duckworth and his elite colleagues.

Nevertheless it was to St Giles that he had returned when Lady D had noticed some staining of her noble knickers, many years after the change of life. Post-menopausal bleeding is always a potentially serious symptom and since she also mentioned that she wet herself when she teed off at the local golf course, it was decided to send her up to Reith at St Giles for an opinion, since he was not only a gynaecologist of renown, but also a passable golfer and would be sympathetic to a lady with a damp drive.

Angus had diagnosed a moderate degree of prolapse with some excoriation of the cervix that had probably given rise to the bleeding. He had treated her like royalty, admitting her to the most comfortable room in the private wing, and grabbed hold of Stanley, his registrar, with whose assistance he had done a vaginal hysterectomy with more than his customary care. He had visited her twice daily and given her more attention that any of his other patients. Such was the courtesy shown to one's hospital colleagues, especially one so influential in the medical establishment as Lord Duckworth. He may now be a Dorset farmer in his retiring years but he still had hot lines to the corridors of power and therein lay the elusive knighthood that Angus Reith so relentlessly pursued.

After ten minutes of mindless chatter in which the junior staff tried to sort out any problems or questions that the consultant was likely to ask, the great man arrived on the scene. The same charade was enacted, only this time it was for real. Reith, after removing his own jacket, eased himself into the starchy, spotless white coat proffered to him by the equally starchy sister. Most consultants went round in their Savile Row suits but Mr Reith preferred the more dashing appearance of the white coat. Mind you, he always wore a waistcoat and his gold watch and chain underneath.

He nodded to the assembled crowd of students, nurses and junior doctors and apologised in a most affable manner to Sister for keeping her waiting and mumbled something about Lady D. Sister enquired about her health out of politeness, and some reverence for her husband who had terrified her so much when she herself was a junior nurse. Lord Duckworth, before he entered the pages of *Burke's Peerage*, was something of a rake among the junior doctors and was known by the nurses as 'God's Gift', presumably to women, and as 'Golden Balls' presumably by those who had been lucky enough to have seen him in action.

Angus glanced through the glass partition that separated Sister's office from the rest of the ward. He saw the long line of beds with all the patients firmly tucked in. He nodded approvingly. That's how he liked them, firmly held down by the sheets; they were less truculent that way.

'Well, gentlemen,' he said. 'Let us care for the needs of the sick, the halt, the maimed and the blind.'

This remark, which was trotted out unchanged almost every week of the year, was met by polite and restrained laughter, and the retinue followed their chief in strict pecking order like a white-coated posse of stuffed dummies.

The first five beds were occupied by the new patients who had been admitted the previous day and who were scheduled for operations on Thursday, the day Mr Reith had his all day list in the operating theatre.

The crowd gathered around the first patient and the screens were drawn around to ensure privacy – that is if one considered it privacy to show one's intimate parts to a crowd of twenty or so people.

The consultant stood to the right of the patient near the head of the bed, with Sister Rheingeld on the other side. The houseman was a few respectful feet away from the consultant, and the registrar and senior registrar lounged on the bed table across the foot of the bed as if it were a bar. This annoyed Reith, but he was aware that Mr Stanley seemed to require some support before the noon hour. That was one of the troubles with employing ex-Army doctors. Charters, the consultant venereologist, was much the same. The students were arranged behind in a semi-circle with the student responsible for presenting the patient's case history well to the fore.

The student nurses were ranged well to the rear, it being tacitly assumed that learned medical discourse was beyond their limited understanding and that they were only there for the atmosphere and essentially to provide some decoration, since most of them were very attractive.

The first patient for the collective appraisal was deaf. Dr Brackenbridge, the houseman, told the assembled cortege that this patient was a spinster and had never had intercourse in her whole life. She had presented at the outpatient clinic with irregular bleeding after the menopause, which she had felt was a curse from God for entertaining impure thoughts in her younger days. Reith looked impatiently at Brackenbridge. The fellow always had to bring God into the saga at some stage of the proceedings. He had never come across a houseman quite like him. Besides it was embarrassing to come out with such intimate details about a frail old lady who had her crochet work on her knee and was looking quite bewildered by this large crowd in front of her. Reith cut him short and started teaching the students about post-menopausal bleeding and its special significance as a sign of possible cancer. He was careful to refrain from using the feared word itself and disguised it with medical euphemisms such as new growth or neoplasia. He needn't have bothered, since the dear old lady was totally deaf and, like most deaf patients, she had left her hearing aid at home, having rationalised that such devices would be unnecessary among the amenities of a modern hospital.

The consultant was interested in Brackenbridge's reference to impure thoughts in her younger days, since her cervix had looked slightly suspicious of an early cancer when he had looked at it the previous week in the outpatients' department. Carcinoma of the cervix was virtually unheard of in women of virgin status. His academic interest prompted him to ask her rather a personal question. He leaned close to her ear and spoke with precise diction.

'Have you ever had intercourse?'

She looked at him with a startled expression, cupping her ear as if to clarify the question.

He tried again, this time a little louder. 'Have you ever had intercourse?'

'Once,' she replied firmly. 'During the Great War. Never again.'

She started to laugh and the students and nurses politely joined her, more to ease their embarrassment than for the value of the humour.

'Broke me leg,' she continued, much to everyone's amazement. 'Had to go to hospital and get patched up.'

Some of the students were looking incredulous and she added for explanation. 'Never ridden a horse since. Once was enough.' She joined in the laughter that crossed all the faces at the obvious misunderstanding. Even Reith was amused, although it had upset his teaching session.

The round continued like a royal progress. The next three beds were all occupied by patients who were in for infertility investigations, one of them being Pentecost Smith, who was looking large and dignified in a white linen nightdress provided by the hospital. She had her arms folded across her ample breasts and answered all Reith's questions with great sincerity, like a devoted slave in a Hollywood epic about the Old South.

'Lordy, Mr Reith, suh, ah only hope you is goin' to get me with child,' she exclaimed, and there was an uncomfortable hush as several innuendoes flowed over the consultant. Happily he took them for their intended sincerity and gave her an affectionate squeeze on the arm and a reassuring smile to put her at ease.

At times, he could be utterly charming, and even Jennifer Watson in the next bed, who entertained a healthy suspicion about hospitals, was surprised to see how, when he wanted, he could exude confidence and sheer charisma. This was only with the elderly and the pure in thought. To the others, and the area abounded with them, he could be unbelievably rude. He taught the students at length on Jennifer's condition and since the fibroid could be felt abdominally, all the sixteen students, with hands of differing temperature, kneaded and pummelled her belly as if they were making bread. Reith then launched into a diatribe about uterine fibromyomata and all the disasters and problems that could accompany them if they were not removed. She listened in a detached sort of way, uncomfortably aware that it was her pathology that he was discussing with such abandon. Reith sensed her anxiety and patted her shoulder in a reassuring way, telling her that none of these complications would happen to her and that a hysterectomy was a simple procedure performed many times each week in the hospital. Several patients on the other side of the ward were recovering from the surgical assault of the previous week and apart from the occasional wince when they moved, they looked a reasonable advertisement for the ordeal. Nevertheless, she had a nagging doubt that all would not be well. The same kind of feeling before a big jet takes off when you wish you had decided to travel by sea.

Another person in the room who entertained similar terrors, but for different reasons, was Marlene. All the insults of the outpatients' department were returning and as the assembly of students and doctors approached, she was bitterly regretting her temper tantrum and particularly calling Reith a pig. She knew that he would soon exact his revenge and in her flimsy nightdress in front of this impressive assembly, she presented easy prey. But Reith had no intention of wasting further emotion on her. He pretended not to recognise her and when Bodger started to present the case history, he cut him short.

'Ah, yes, I remember the sordid details. I don't think we need waste our precious time on this kind of nonsense. Put her first on the list, to be done before I arrive to start the majors. Mr Stanley, I think you had better return after the round and spell out, in words of one syllable, the basic principles of birth control.'

With that, he moved on to see the post-operative cases and the others that were on medical treatment. Patrick shook his head almost in pity. Christ, that man was a bastard.

Reith's grand ward round was an integral part of the hospital ritual. The appearance of this middle-aged, portly, pompous consultant every Wednesday, surrounded by a retinue of white-coated attendants and students, was part of the British hospital tradition. To the elderly patients it was a source of comfort in a world that seemed, increasingly, to be ruled by youth. To most of the other patients it was a charade. Few of them had been seen by Reith in the outpatient or casualty departments and even fewer had been operated on by him, although his name hung so possessively over their beds. Nevertheless, they were his hospital property and it was condescending that once a week he should nod patronisingly at them and try to pick faults with the work of the junior staff. In truth the nurses all seemed so busy and the doctors' visits on the ward were so infrequent that most of the bedside manner, and nearly all the words of wisdom and encouragement, emanated from the friendly chit-chat of the ward maids. Mrs Mop had superseded Hippocrates and Florence Nightingale, for better or for worse.

These more perceptive patients were right; the round was a charade. It was all part of the expensive state-subsidised melodrama that gave the consultants, in particular, and the medical staff, in general, a deeply cherished belief in their own importance. Few positive decisions were made and the round had all the ingredients and uselessness of a ceremonial visit by a member of the Royal family.

After the round, 'His Lordship' would whisk off to the lecture theatre in the medical school to teach the students for an hour, while Patrick and the houseman were left to heal any wounds caused by the brusque manner of the consultant and to organise the order for the operating list on the following day. The simplest way was for the two of them to repeat the round in a business-like manner with Patrick issuing instructions, and Bodger and a senior staff nurse copying them down diligently in their diaries and notebooks. Sister would have no part in this, and, feeling that her part in the weekly play-acting had finished, retired to coffee, biscuits and a recent issue of the *Stern*.

For Patrick this was a hectic time, since he was meant to start a follow-up clinic for cancer patients at half-past nine and then perform a series of outpatient terminations; lunchtime abortions, as they had been christened by the press. This was part of a clinical research project under the auspices of Maurice Hellman, who took all the credit but did little of the work. Hellman was only young as consultants went, but he was fast learning the pattern of coercing the junior rats to foot the treadmill the hardest. The project was designed to quell the critics of abortion law reform who claimed that the permissive young dolly birds were using the hospital beds and operating theatres to the exclusion of the old biddies who had to wait for months to get their prolapsed wombs hitched up. Accordingly, those girls with early pregnancies for termination could be dealt with in the outpatient operating theatre without being formally admitted and were therefore no inconvenience to any one except Patrick. They were escorted into the theatre by a social worker who chatted to them casually as if they were in a coffee bar while Patrick emptied the contents of their uterus with a plastic collapsible suction tube. Afterwards they were offered lunch, much to the chagrin of the anti-abortion lobby, which considered this an abuse of taxpayers' money. They were allowed home an hour or so later so that they could rejoin the social whirl, go to another party that evening and, as likely as not, get laid again and apply for another menstrual extraction the following month.

This morning Patrick was relieved to find that Norm Garrett was spare since his gonococcal cultures had been contaminated by an over-growth of *Proteus vulgaris* and his somewhat dubious research had to be temporarily abandoned until he could produce another pure line of cell cultures. Patrick merely dictated the order of the operating list since he knew Reith's preferences, and spent a few minutes placating Marlene and reassuring some of the other patients who had been ruffled by Reith's dour Scottish remarks.

He then left in the direction of the outpatients' department leaving Norman and Bodger Brackenbridge to finish the business round. From the outset Norman was in a grisly mood. He held grimly on to the remnants of a foul hangover caused by imbibing a vast number of tubes of Resch's and Foster's beer the previous evening up at the North Middlesex hospital, one of the main frontier outposts of Australian doctors in Britain. It was so Australianised, in fact, that Melbourne beer was served on draught in the doctors' common room. At least there he felt at home, and the transition to St Giles, with all its pomp and ceremony and the tiresome company of pukka poms like Brackenbridge, was too much for a system already poisoned by aldehydes and other noxious breakdown products of ethyl alcohol.

'Awright,' he said, suppressing a belch. 'Who's first?'

'Mrs Whatsername.' Bodger consulted his notebook but it was not recorded. The staff nurse didn't know her name either, and they couldn't ask the patient because she was deaf and would think they were making further enquiries on equestrian matters.

'The old duck with PMB. She'll need a chest x-ray and ECG, and don't forget to tell the anaesthetist she's on anti-hypertensive drugs. What's this one for?'

Jennifer Watson rather resented this cattle market approach, but chose to remain silent.

Bodger consulted his little notebook. 'Total hysterectomy for menorrhagia.'

'What's her haemoglobin?'

He flicked her lower eyelid down to see the colour as if he was assessing the health of a slave before an auction.

'It's 12 grams. Her GP had her on a course of iron. We'll cross-match her for two pints.'

'Stick yer tongue out, love. Let's see yer fingernails. Aw, c'mon, she's all right.

You're only going to chop her box out. In Australia we wouldn't get blood up for her. The red stuff's expensive, you know. You bleedin' poms use far too much of it. Just get her group and tell them to save the serum. You don't need blood for a hysterectomy unless the patient's already anaemic.'

Bodger looked nonplussed; the awful predicament of a junior faced with conflicting orders.

'But Mr Reith insists on blood being in the operating theatre for all majors and all terminations.'

'Mr Reith, my dear fellow,' Norman mimicked, in a poor imitation of a Scottish accent, 'is fifty years behind the times. No blood for this girl. Who's next?'

For the second time Jennifer began to feel slightly ill at ease, but soon dismissed these fears as natural apprehension before a big operation. No matter how they all minimised it, the whole thing was rather frightening and, for a woman, it really did seem like a big procedure. It held an emotional content far beyond the visible scar. It was the final seal on her reproductive abilities; not that she wanted more children, but it was pleasant to know that the capacity was still there. And the monthly curse, although so often a nuisance, was always deep down a reassuring sign that you were still a mature woman in the prime of life. Somehow the memory of the first thrill and mystery of it all, in the early teens, never really disappeared, and now it was all to be finished by the incisive thrust of a surgical knife.

Her thoughts were interrupted by the ward maid who was dusting the cupboard beside her bed. Somehow she sensed Jennifer's inner worries and endeavoured to cheer her up in the down-to-earth manner of the cockney.

'Not to worry yerself, ducks. They like to put the wind up you the day before. Makes you feel more grateful to them when they pull yer through. Most of 'em pull through. We don't seem to lose many.'

CHAPTER TWENTY-TWO
Gynaecology operating theatre, St Giles' Hospital, London

Thursday was Reith's operating day and the organisation bore many of the stigmata of a primitive ritual designed to placate some ferocious tribal chief. The great man would arrive in the operating theatre on the dot of nine o'clock and expected his first patient to be on the table, towelled, catheterised, painted and prepared but not anaesthetised in case he was unaccountably delayed by central London traffic congestion. For many of the patients this was a terrifying experience. Lying naked on a cold corrugated rubber mattress under the glare of a huge overhead spotlight while masked and gowned attendants splashed iodine on the body and gradually covered their nudity with sterile green towels. Stories of the horrors of medieval surgery without anaesthesia came flooding into their pre-medicated minds and they would beg old Harry Squires to put them to sleep. He would pat them amiably on the head and return his attentions to the morning crossword puzzle until he heard Reith's heavy footsteps coming down the corridor, whereupon he would slap a rubber mask over their face, ask them to count to ten backwards and send them off to the land of nod for an hour or so.

Between eight and nine in the morning there was an hour of shame where all the patients who had angered or irritated the consultant were operated on by the junior doctors. Most of these were terminations of pregnancies for one reason or another and they were performed by Patrick Stanley while Joe Gibson administered the noxious vapours at the top end. A constant stream of casual conversation flowed backward and forwards between them. 'Suck-it-and-see time again, Paddy.'

'TOP. *Top of the Pops* again, folks, with yours truly, Patrick Stanley, on the suction curette and the man with the mostest, Joe Gibson on the halothane bagpipes.'

They would both chuckle lasciviously not only because it made the task at hand less depressing but because it arraigned the piety of Sister Brewer and Bodger Brackenbridge.

'Who's the first little victim for Murder Incorporated this morning, Paddy?'

'A little floosie that used to work on the switchboard here. She insulted the old bastard by calling him a pig. I wish I'd been there; I'd have given anything to have seen his face. Strict orders from Harley Strasse to get her pregnancy into the bucket before His Lordship arrives on the scene.'

So it went on. Joe would put the girls to sleep and the technicians would sling their legs up in the stirrups and Patrick would set about aborting their offspring. Brackenbridge usually excused himself from these sessions on the grounds of religious objection but this morning the horny old bigot couldn't resist another gander at Marlene in the altogether, so he shuffled around the room mumbling irrelevancies and feeling as hopelessly out of place as a monk at an orgy.

Patrick made no effort to spare anyone's feelings. He did not particularly enjoy the job at hand but he clearly realised that it had to be done. Parliament had seen fit to pass an Abortion Act and it was the job of the gynaecologists to see that it was done safely and with a minimum of fuss. In the early months the tissue was virtually unrecognisable, just blood and liquor and pieces of placenta. After twelve weeks it became considerably more gruesome when bits of legs and intestines and skull from the tiny creature were clearly distinguishable and had to be extracted piecemeal with the sponge forceps. It was only with these mid-trimester abortions that the operator was aware of the destruction he was causing.

Every child a wanted child. That was Patrick's belief and despite the occasional cri de coeur from his buried Catholic conscience he would rather deal with the problem this way than revert to treating the horrors inflicted by the backstreet abortionists. He didn't usually think of the moral arguments any more but the presence of the unhappy Bodger brought them back fleetingly. Patrick normally regarded abortion merely as a technical exercise. He inserted the Karman catheter through the cervix then pressed the button of the electric suction pump, easing the catheter in and out of the uterus until a grating feeling like cutting an unripe pear told him that it was empty. There was a fierce sucking noise as the blood and tissue was forced down a wide plastic tube into the glass chamber of the suction machine.

He was a technically superb surgeon and for Marlene the procedure was over in minutes. She hadn't felt a thing and her blood loss was minimal. She had been in good hands top and bottom.

'Another future pope in the bucket, Paddy.'

Bodger felt as if he was going to vomit and hurriedly left the room, deeply ashamed of the scene he had witnessed. Joe Gibson and Patrick continued to act out their comedie noire, delighted that they had scored a direct hit on the hapless Brackenbridge.

'You know what they say on those Underground posters, Joe?'

'Yeah, we've heard it all before. It's quicker by Tube. Next patient please, Sister.'

Proctalgia fugax. Reith was suddenly seized by an incredible muscle spasm in his rectum; his entire pelvic floor muscles had contracted in spasm, causing unbelievable agony. He let out a gasp of pain and threw down the scrubbing brush in the stainless-steel sink and grasped his agonised fundamental orifice with a semi-sterilised hand.

Sweat appeared on his brow and his whole frame was gripped with pain. He steadied himself on the sink, his face contorted with the distress that was searing through his body.

Patrick, who was scrubbing up next to him, looked concernedly at his chief.

'You all right, sir?' fearing that the old fellow was having his anticipated coronary.

'Proctalgia fugax.'

He nodded in sympathy. He had suffered the odd bout of it himself. An occupational hazard among doctors caused by sudden ischaemia of the levator ani muscles. The attack came on without warning and built up quickly to an agonising pain right inside the anus. Usually the attack subsided in about thirty seconds but was occasionally followed by a second and rarely a third episode. Attacks would come every six weeks or so in various degrees of severity, but why it should be common among the medical profession had never been satisfactorily explained. Proctalgia fugax is said to be associated with excessive frequency of sexual intercourse. Possibly therein lay the relation with the healing arts. Reith had no doubt that the seat of his affliction originated in his salacious activities in Mayfair.

The attack subsided but left the surgeon shaken and subdued. He recommended the ritual scrubbing of his hand with a new nail brush but somehow the enthusiasm had left him. He was expecting another lancinating attack up his backside.

Reith loved his operating session. It was the high point of his week. The time when he could purge his body and mind of all the accumulated tension and frustration. He could shout and shriek and know that his orders would be obeyed instantly without question. It was all part of the melodrama dictated by the open belly and the blood running freely. Your life in their hands. Here he was King Omnipotent for one glorious morning of each week.

He dressed for the day. Special Dutch-style clogs with his name carefully written over the top. A light-green operating suit that he had purchased on a Stateside trip to Boston when he had visited the Massachusetts General Hospital put him in a class above all the others in the hospital. His outfit was tailor-made while the other surgeons looked like a collection of circus clowns in the extra-large, extra-short uniforms supplied by the National Health Service. Reith made no concession to the new disposable age. He refused to wear paper hats and masks and insisted that Sister Brewer kept a supply of the old-fashioned cloth caps and linen masks especially for him. He had to look the part to placate his rampant ego. But obstetrics and gynaecology was a messy business full of blood, amniotic fluid and slippery babies, so to distinguish him from the general surgeons and the orthopaedic people he wore a large brownish red apron that gave him the appearance of a Smithfield butcher from years ago, though no one would have been disrespectful enough to suggest this. With his half-moon gold-framed glasses he had all the authority of the Victorian era and his entrance into the operating theatre was always met by a hushed silence from the theatre staff. His wrath was truly dreadful and all the girls were secretly terrified of him. Some of the more saucy ones permitted themselves a repressed giggle when they saw the great man clutching his bum, but when they saw that he was in awful pain their pretty eyes registered genuine concern.

'You better do the first case, Stanley. These bloody attacks leave me quite shaken. Like a coronary thrombosis emanating in the rectum.'

Patrick nodded sympathetically.

'I've had a few myself.'

'They get worse as you get older,' Reith muttered miserably.

'I had a friend who worked up at Edgware General,' Patrick told him. 'He had an attack that lasted the whole day. Just about crucified him.'

'Jesus God.'

This information brought on a second attack of proctalgia fugax and Stanley felt he had better keep silent in his sympathy. This time Reith tried not to drop the nail brush but he let out a groan of anguish, arched his back and looked up at the ceiling, his face contorted with distress. He had never had an attack in the operating theatre before and he resented his levator ani preventing him from enjoying his cutting. The attack subsided after about thirty seconds but beads of sweat had appeared on his brow and his apprehension showed in the scared grey-blue eyes above the mask.

'Who's first on the list?'

'That hysterectomy with the menorrhagia and twelve-week fibroids.'

'Did I see her yesterday?'

'Third bed on the right. The one from the North. She's a semi-private, isn't she?'

'Oh, I remember now. The one old Michaelson sent me. He sent her to my rooms in Harley Street. I can't abide that kind of thing. Poor as a church mouse. Couldn't possibly afford the operation fees so he sends her through the old boy network. Michaelson was at medical school with me. One of the dimmer lights, I seem to recall, which is why he ended up in general practice, of course. Should have had the sense to send people like her to the normal clinic. I see all new patients there anyway and it saves all this embarrassment about fees. She seems rather anxious about it.'

Patrick nodded. 'She's rather an intelligent girl who has never been ill before in her life and I think she's been caught a bit off-balance by all the drama involved in being referred to Harley Street.'

'Of course she is. Wouldn't you be? The silly old buffer sends her all the way to London for a routine hysterectomy that could easily have been done locally. Enough to scare the pants off anyone. It's only a wee fibroid. As if we haven't got enough work on our hands as it is. Well, laddie, you're always clamouring for more operating so this should be a nice easy start for you.'

It was true. Patrick had felt very seriously deprived of operating experience in the months that he had worked with Reith. Previously, he had served as a junior registrar in Chichester and had been taught carefully by the young consultants there. He had gradually been allowed to do all the major operations except for radical cancer procedures and even those he became increasingly involved in. He was a naturally gifted surgeon with a delicate touch and a fine way of handling the instruments, and he had been offended by Reith's refusal to let him do anything but the most minor procedures like sterilisations, abortions and cone biopsies of the cervix. He had tried to reason with the consultant but had been rebuffed in no uncertain terms.

'Laddie,' he had said, 'You come to the capital city to learn things my way. Forget everything you have learnt before out in the backwoods and, first of all, learn to assist properly. When you're a competent assistant, I'll show you how to operate. And you'll operate my way. After two years you'll be one of the best.'

The pomposity and arrogance was so typical of Reith, and Stanley bitterly resented having to accept a servile role again after all his successful operating in Chichester. For the past six months he had been rapped on the knuckles by the great man for not pulling hard enough on a retractor or cutting the ends of a knot too long or too short. He had been vilified and insulted and all the time had done his best to keep his quick Irish temper under control but, in spite of all his efforts, he had clashed more and more with Reith as the year had progressed.

Now he was being offered the chance to operate again and instead of leaping at it with enthusiasm he found that he was nervously apprehensive. Reith had drained all his confidence away and he was out of practice. As he dried his hands on a sterile towel and slipped into the green gown one of the nurses offered to him and opened with the servility of a well-trained valet, he was desperately trying to think of an excuse. He was sure that Reith would never normally have let him operate on one of his semi-private patients. They were usually regarded as sacred property, for his knife only. Now he felt trapped like a rat in a cage. He moved over to the side of the patient and waited for the nurses to empty her bladder with a catheter and paint the inside of the vagina with povidone-iodine solution to rid it of some of its bacterial flora, and a solution of Bonney's blue dye to aid the surgeon in recognising the vaginal walls when removing the uterus from above.

He took a sterile kidney dish from the scrub nurse and glanced at Harry Squires to see if the patient was asleep. Harry was about halfway through his crossword by now and the endotracheal tube in the patient's throat told Patrick that she was unconscious.

The stainless-steel dish was full of gauze swabs, sponge holders and small gallipots that held three different types of antiseptic solution. Reith was very old-fashioned and meticulous in his ritual cleansing of the skin over his operating field; chlorhexidine, cetrimide, then alcoholic tincture of iodine: it would take a brave bug indeed to trespass over these traditional guardians against sepsis, and Reith took great pride in his low incidence of post-operative sepsis. In fact it was no lower than that of his present-day colleagues but Reith compared it somewhat unfairly with the times of his youth, before the antibiotic era.

Patrick dipped the gauze swabs into the antiseptic solutions and painted the still body with all the flourish of a modern artist. His chief liked to sterilise a wide area of skin and insisted on thorough cleansing from the nipple line to mid-thigh level. This gave Patrick time to peruse the body that he was so carefully defending from pathogens. A good pair of breasts for a woman of forty-plus. Patrick approved of the still form on the table. Something that doctors are not supposed to do. He flicked antiseptic over each breast with his gauze swab and then descended down the front to the area of the navel where he proceeded to dig voraciously as if the umbilicus was the devilish seat of uncleanliness. She had a good figure. He continued to discard the gauze swabs into a stainless-steel receiver at his feet and pick up new swabs from the kidney dish, all in one movement. He worked his way down the body, the lower abdomen joined to the shaved pubic area showing some faint stretch marks, evidence of her child-bearing years. She was neither thin nor fat but her pale soft skin was that of a woman who had looked after herself, who had taken pride in her body.

He handed the dish to a waiting nurse and reached out for the green sterile towels. He took one last look at the naked defenceless body, so like a corpse apart from the rhythmic regulated breathing accompanied by the wheeze and puff of the anaesthetist's respirator. He could never view a feminine body with complete dispassion and over the years he had formed a dubious but harmless pastime of rating the body on a scale from nought to ten. Despite her middle age Jennifer scored seven, which was well above average, for Patrick had never yet awarded his top marks to an anaesthetised torso. It meant, however, that he would fall headlong into his first confrontation with Reith because he was towelling her for a bikini-line incision, a special favour for those who requested it, and for those who came in the top five marks on the Stanley Scale.

The lower transverse incision was first described by Johannes Pfannenstiel in 1920 and has many advantages for gynaecological operations: it gives adequate exposure of the organs beneath, and is popular with patients since it runs crosswise just north of the pubic hair line and can be hidden by most bikinis. Not only does it follow Lange's lines, the natural skin creases across the body, thus allowing it to heal better and leave the minimum of scar tissue, but it is almost impossible for it to burst open during the post-operative period and spew guts all over the belly of the horrified patient. Wound dehiscence, although rare, is almost uniquely a complication of vertical scars.

Like all arguments in medical science, incisions have strong antagonists and protagonists and the actual method of attacking the insides of a patient often sparks feelings of high passion among surgeons. The disadvantages of the Pfannenstiel incision are the increased likelihood of bleeding and subsequent haematoma formation in the layers beneath the fat, making it almost obligatory to insert a small polythene tube as a vacuum drain. In addition it takes several minutes longer to perform and it was this more than anything else that earned it the arch disapproval of Angus Reith who regarded surgery as a form of competition. Almost a sport. A kind of manual obstacle race and dexterity test performed against the clock. The best man was naturally the fastest operator, although he had to work within the limits of safety to secure a live patient at the end of the game. To assure the sport Olympic status one would have to extend the rules somewhat to detract points for the number of extra days a patient spent in the hospital, since the minutes saved in theatre could add days to her stay on the ward and weeks to her recovery in a convalescent home. This aspect did not concern Reith; he merely wished to demonstrate his speed to the hushed admiring audience in the operating theatre and his operations were always punctuated by anxious glances at the electric clock on the wall of the operating theatre just behind old Harry's head.

As Patrick draped the towels over the patient he could hear the consultant trying to teach a gaggle of students about fibroids of the uterus with particular reference to the patient on the table. He had already press-ganged an unwilling volunteer to act as second assistant. Patrick was hoping that he would soon become so immersed in his self-appointed surgical teaching legend that he would forget his proctalgia fugax. Unfortunately this was not to be. He did not elbow Patrick out of the way in his customary manner but humbly took a stance on the assistant's side.

He washed his gloves in some sterile water to remove the chalky powder and smiled benignly at Sister Brewer over his half-moon glasses. The steely grey eyes sent a shudder down her spine and the smile did nothing to dispel the terror that descended on her during his operating sessions. None of the other surgeons bothered her or berated her the way he did and she was becoming increasingly convinced that these mornings with Reith would induce in her a state of premature menopause. Nervously she returned his smile but he was already exchanging pleasantries with Harry Squires and her smile faded behind the mask to her habitual expression of tension.

Reith's gaze descended to the arrangement of the green towelling and his benign smile gave way to a loud Scottish oath of great antiquity, happily muffled by the gauze surgical mask over his mouth. He took a deep breath and moderated his tone to one of ill-concealed contempt.

'This is not Beverly Hills, laddie. We're not running a plastic surgery clinic. Change those towel clips. When you're with me we do things my way. A straight up and downer so that we don't have to be here all day.'

'She particularly asked for a Pfannenstiel, sir,' Patrick lied.

'I don't give a tinker's fart what she wants. If she travels two hundred miles to be under my care she has things done my way. Now let's get on with it. Give the lad a knife, Sister. Everything all right your end, Harry?'

Harry grunted as he concentrated on the crossword. 'A range of Scottish hills beginning with C. Seven letters.'

'Come on, laddie. Don't be so finicky. Slash her open. I like a no-nonsense incision so we can see what we're about. Cheviot Hills.'

'No... Er... No, I don't think so. Four down couldn't possibly begin with V.' Patrick couldn't resist an inspiration.

'Campsie. They're a range of hills somewhere near Glasgow.'

'You concentrate on the matter at hand, Mr Stanley, and leave the senior staff to sort out the crossword. A good surgeon can't afford to let his attention wander. Anyway, they're not hills, they're fells. And they are nearer Loch Lomond than Glasgow. What does four down sound like, Harry?'

'I think it's land lubber.'

'I've got it. Cuillin Hills. They're on the Isle of Skye.'

'That's it, Angus.' Harry shrieked with excitement. 'It must be that because the last letter has to be N.'

Angus beamed happily; he so liked to be right. His bad mood was clearing rapidly and he began to regret the decision to allow his junior to take over the operation. He leaned towards the gaping wound, hollering out advice like a frenzied supporter at a football match.

'Come on, Stanley, lad, we haven't got time to go clipping off all the bleeders. Just bash on and get the peritoneum opened. Leave the abdominal wall to look after itself. Anyway, you always find they've stopped by the time you come out.'

A knot was tightening in Patrick's stomach. He was becoming increasingly resentful of these intrusions. Either the bastard lets me operate and leaves me alone or he takes over himself, he thought.

He hated the critical scrutiny of his every move. Besides he was a delicate, careful surgeon who had been taught to secure every bleeding artery as the operation progressed. He had always been contemptuous of Reith's slash and thrust tactics in constant battle against the clock. His Irish temper was starting to boil but he was desperately trying to control it more for the sake of the patient than for his fear of his consultant.

'Where is that damned student? Come on in, laddie. You're not just a spectator. No good standing there with your hands held in front of you like an out-of-work druid. We need you to pull on this retractor. Haven't I seen you before?'

Andrew Jennings grunted something noncommittal and managed to return Reith's penetrating gaze. After his last performance with the consultant gynaecologist, he was terrified to do anything to sully the operating field and had approached the inner sanctum of surgeons with his sterile gloved hands held out in front of him like a sleepwalker. He had an uneasy feeling that Reith had recognised him, although only an inch of face was visible between the top of the mask and the bottom of the cap. Nevertheless it was the same inch that he had exposed on the previous occasion when he had been accused of swinging on the operating theatre light.

'Now, Mr Student, cast your eyes down into the female pelvis to see a sight that the pornographers and decadents are happily denied. What do you see, laddie?'

Andrew was nonplussed. He could see lots of things but he could not divine the answer the consultant expected him to give. Rather than make a fool of himself, he chose to retreat into a cavern of silence.

'The uterus, boy, the womb. Hysteros. The Grecian seat of the soul. The hidden secret of feminine mystique is revealed to you from within and all you do is rock back and forth on your heels.'

In truth, Andrew was pumping his calf muscles in order to prevent himself from fainting, more from fear of Reith's inquisition than the sight of spilled human blood.

'What in heaven's name are you doing, Stanley? You're surely not going to take her oophers out. Stop blithering about, boy, we'll be here all day. Just chop out and close up. A quick twenty-minute job. How old is she, Brackenbridge?'

Bodger shuffled forward. His job on these occasions was to peep discreetly over the master's shoulder and answer any and every question about the patient. Her age, her haemoglobin, her last menstrual period, the details of all her previous pregnancies, the drugs and medicaments she used over the past two years, how many times a week she had intercourse and whether she enjoyed it or not. He had to station himself just within earshot of the muffled queries emanating from beneath Reith's mask but just outside the range of a quick about-turn that would unsterilise or contaminate him. He had to act as an expensively trained gun dog fetching and carrying x-rays and bottles of blood in between answering a battery of questions and at all times hold himself in readiness for the need of a third assistant. Slave, courtier and clerk of works rolled into one.

'Brackenbridge.'

'Here, sir.'

'How old is this old buzzard?'

'Forty-six, sir.'

'There you are, Stanley, another ten years of life in those old ovaries. Leave the blighters alone and put a long straight on the round ligament and broad ligament together. Here, let me show you. Long straights, Sister. And another. Now give the boy some scissors and let's get on with it.'

Patrick could have argued but he was resigned by now to the feeling of total persecution. Although the risk of ovarian cancer was small, the disease usually presented at a very late stage and was invariably fatal. His approach was to

remove the ovaries and prevent an early menopause by giving replacement oestrogen and testosterone implants for ten years or even more. In America they
were giving them for life and there were ominous mumblings that by cutting
down on the incidence of arteriosclerosis, hypertension and ischaemic heart
disease, all of which could be prevented by oestrogens, there would develop a
nation where the women would have twice the life expectancy of men. Alexis de
Tocqueville's prophecy of the ultimate matriarchal society would be complete.

Patrick merely shrugged away his thoughts and inserted a needle and catgut
on either side of the pedicel that was held between the clamp, and as soon as he
had tied the first part of the knot he asked his overbearing assistant to gradually
release the pressure on the clamp and then catch the pedicel again between the
claws of the instrument.

'Ease and squeeze, sir.'

'What for?'

'So I can put another tie around the ovarian vessels.'

Reith grunted with disapproval but nevertheless did as he was told.

'A surgeon should have complete faith in his knots. Only one on the ovarian,
two on the uterine. Any more is a waste of catgut but… please yourself.'

Although Patrick had gained a small victory he had an uneasy foreboding
that Reith would win the next round of the fray.

The operation continued to progress in this uneasy truce. The bladder edge
was picked up and the pelvic peritoneum incised just above it and the bladder
pushed down out of harm's way. Reith insisted that this be done by a gauze
swab wound over the index finger for more delicate separation of the tissue
layers. Patrick felt that a gauze swab in a holder was perfectly adequate.

Reith won.

Patrick insisted on dissecting the peritoneum off the back of the uterus with
a pair of curved scissors. Reith scoffed at this and claimed never to have seen
anyone do such a senseless thing. Patrick carried on regardless. Patrick won.

The uterus was now held to the vagina by the cervix and a thin parcel of tissue
that contained the main artery and vein to the organ. Just a centimetre lateral to
the uterine vessels lay the ureter carrying urine from the kidney to the bladder,
and as it burrows under the uterine artery it is extremely vulnerable to serious
damage by the gynaecologist's scalpel. Patrick carefully pushed the bladder and

cervical fascia away trying to get the ureter out of the dangerous area.

The size of the uterine vessels varies according to the state of activity of the uterus. In pregnancy they are vast but in the menopausal woman they are tiny. In a uterus with a large fibroid they are moderately enlarged and can bleed fearsomely if they are not adequately tied. Reith was reared as a surgeon before the days of blood transfusion and though he cared little about the small bleeders under the skin he showed the large arteries of the body a healthy respect. Stanley belonged to a new generation who were satisfied by a double tie with catgut and a scientific belief that a ligated artery was soon filled with blood clots and an improperly ligated one would make its presence known before the surgeon closed the peritoneum. Over this seemingly trivial point the two generations collided, the two temperaments clashed like a lion and a unicorn.

Patrick applied a single claw-toothed pair of Kocher's forceps over the uterine artery and vein as they wound their way up the side of the uterus.

Reith insisted he applied another.

Patrick refused. He would continue the operation in the manner to which he was accustomed.

Reith bristled with anger. His breathing became laboured beneath his mask.

The uterine vessels were cut over the single clamp and another clamp was placed alongside the cervix to enclose the vessels of the cardinal ligaments. The vaginal wall was opened just beneath the bladder and the reassuring blue of the painted vaginal walls showed him that he was well clear of the cervix. He carefully cut an ellipse around the vagina marking the edges and the angles with clamps, two long straights for front and back and two Allis clamps for the angles. The utero-sacral ligaments were secured to the vaginal angles in two choleycystectomy clamps and the uterus was cut from its attachments until it was free. It was pulled out of the abdominal wound by the surgeon and passed together with an assortment of clamps to the cupped hands of Sister Brewer like the heart of an Aztec maiden taken during a ritual sacrifice. It was borne away solemnly to the sluice on a stainless-steel dish by one of the junior nurses.

A generous teacher would have congratulated Stanley on a delicate piece of dissection but Reith was bristling for revenge. He was determined to teach this young puppy a lesson.

'Too much bloody ironmongery in the pelvis. Looks like the steelworks of

Port Talbot down there. I've never seen so many damned clamps. Sister must have used about three hysterectomy sets.'

Sister was about to leap to the defence of Mr Stanley but the warmongering look in Reith's eyes stopped her in her tracks. The vaginal vault was closed. The angles secured. The utero-sacrals ligated on either side. The only clamps remaining were the solitary pair of Kocher's clamps, one on each uterine artery.

This was when the arrogant bastard would learn to respect the experience of older and wiser men. Reith seized his opportunity.

'What would happen, young man, if your single clamp were to slip before you secure your knot?'

Patrick was enjoying himself. He had gone his own way in defiance of the old sod and so far the operation had gone well. One more clamp and tie and they were home.

'Happen, sir?' He almost mimicked Reith's accent.

'I always apply them so that they are never under any tension when they are released. Anyway, such a thing has never happened to me before.'

Reith stared at him straight in the eyes and, with a voice of sadistic menace, he slowly released the clamp before Patrick had a chance to tie it.

'Well, it has now, sunshine. It has now.'

The whole orderly scene was suddenly thrown into confusion. Patrick looked with horror at the huge spurting artery and the pelvis filling up with bright red blood. Sister Brewer shrieked for the suction machine to be turned on.

Reith grinned malevolently at the chaos he had caused. Patrick grabbed a large laparotomy pack to try to compress the artery and clear the blood from the field of vision. There was so much blood in the pelvis that he could no longer identify the spurting artery.

'Sucker, Sister, quick.'

'Suction,' she shrieked at one of the other nurses.

'It's not working, Sister. The machine isn't working.'

The machine was wheeled forward and the main switch turned on but the familiar whirring sound was absent. The nurses fiddled with the knobs and yelled for a theatre technician.

'Plug it in, for God's sake.'

'It is plugged in but it won't switch on.'

'Then get another one, and hurry up.'

'Send down to casualty for another suction machine.'

'Get more big packs, Sister.'

Reith was chuckling mirthlessly at the panic he had generated. He was enjoying the sight of his registrar squirming with terror.

'You'll have to ligate the internal iliacs, laddie, and I'll bet a pound to a penny that ye'll have no idea where to find them in a pool of blood.'

Patrick's expression showed his resignation and Reith, with consummate ease, put his hand down the side wall of the pelvis and with a knowledge of anatomy born of thousands of operations he compressed the iliac artery that fed into the uterine artery.

'Find the internal ring of the inguinal canal and follow it directly down over the brim of the pelvis until you come to the bifurcation of the iliac vessels. Take the lower road and feel for the pulsation and press it against the bony wall of the pelvis.'

Reith's expression was one of sheer pleasure and triumph as he assumed command of the situation. He could have asked Stanley to pick up the end of the uterine artery in another clamp and tie it off, but having demonstrated his ability to act as a heroic life-saver he had to pursue the act to its conclusion.

'Come on, laddie, let's show you a bit of real surgery and it may save a life one of these days if you ever encounter uncontrollable bleeding at a Wertheim's or a Caesarean hysterectomy. Aneurysm needle threaded with 2-0 catgut, Sister.'

Patrick was submissive now, ashamed of his earlier state of panic but still ruffled by the wanton act of malice caused by his consultant.

'Watch this, laddie. Burrow the end of the curved aneurysm needle just underneath the internal iliac artery and come up just this side of the vein, like so...'

His action, instead of being accompanied by a cessation of blood, provoked a sudden flood from the region near the tip of the needle. This time the blood was a darker red; venous blood. He had torn a hole in the external iliac vein, the huge thin-walled vessel bringing blood back from the leg.

Reith's confidence turned suddenly to dismay as he realised he now had two bleeding areas to control and they were still without a suction machine to keep the operation area free of blood.

Harry had abandoned the crossword and was checking the pulse and blood

246

pressure of the patient who, by now, had lost more than four pints of blood. He increased the speed of the drip that was running into a vein on the back of the hand by an infant's scalp vein needle. He looked anxiously at the surgeons. Reith sensed his concern and nodded.

'She needs blood, Harry. I think we'd better cross-match four more pints. Sister, get the vascular clamps sterilised, it's going to be difficult to patch up this vein without them. Mr Stanley, you will have the rare honour of seeing me do some vascular surgery. In the old days we used to have to patch a lot of veins during the big cancer operations, didn't we, Harry? Of course, nowadays you fellows just shine some x-rays at the patient and you lack the operative experience of our generation. Even muff up a straightforward hysterectomy. Mr Student, I want you to press on the vein just distal to the tear with a pair of sponge-holding forceps. Give the boy a sponge on a stick, Sister. Dr Brackenbridge... where is Dr Brackenbridge?'

He half turned around, narrowly missing Bodger, who was getting increasingly alarmed by the situation. 'Brackenbridge, get the blood from the fridge and ask the for another two pints on emergency cross-match and another two on full cross match for afterwards.'

Bodger's mouth fell open and he remained motionless. The full horror was dawning on him and it was evident that it was going to be himself, the innocent party, who would bear the full brunt of Reith's anger.

'Go on, man. Don't just stand there with your mouth gaping like a goldfish.'

Bodger dearly wanted to disappear through a hole in the floor but he realised that he had no alternative but to tell the truth.

'There isn't any, sir. We just grouped her and asked the lab to hold the serum.'

Reith suddenly went pale and then he started shrieking with anger. His words became an almost incoherent babble of sound as he berated the houseman.

'For God's sake, what is the matter with you all? No blood, no sucker. No damned nothing. Blood is always cross-matched for my operations. It's a rule of the house. I'll have your guts for garters over this one, Brackenbridge. Get on the phone to the blood bank and get two pints of O-negative blood from the flying squad reserve and ask for four more pints on emergency cross-match. This old bird is going to need every drop by the time we've patched up Mr Stanley's mess.'

The theatre was full of tension now. Reith had played God once too often and even now was trying to pass the blame on to his registrar. Stanley was too dumbstruck even to react; his intuition told him clearly how this drama was likely to finish.

The nurses were silent. A hushed audience watching some kind of primeval sacrificial rite. The greater the tension, the more Reith played to the gallery. He was supremely confident now of his famous ability to save the day.

With Andrew Jennings damming back the venous flow from the right leg, he ligated the internal iliac artery and then mopped out the pelvis using several large laparotomy packs, each one handed by a chain of instruments and hands to a nurse in the corner who weighed it and calculated the blood loss mopped up on the linen cloths. He managed to locate the uterine artery stumps with considerable skill and found it to be still pumping blood but at reduced pressure. Obviously it was receiving blood from a collateral supply. He double-tied the stump with strong catgut.

No longer was he the assistant. He was the master surgeon with total control communicated through every movement of his fingers. He only had to stitch the delicate walls of the iliac vein by obstructing the flow in a J-shaped vascular clamp and patching the wall with an intricate stitch as the instrument was slowly withdrawn.

With the ties on the uterine vessels the field was now clear of blood and his mood of confidence returned. He felt able to indulge in his usual repartee with his old friend Harry Squires.

'Splendid anaesthetic, Harry. An almost bloodless operating field.'

The usual reply was not forthcoming. Angus looked up at his old colleague and the worried frown spoke for itself.

The circulation had stopped. Jennifer Watson was dead.

CHAPTER TWENTY-THREE
Gynaecology operating theatre two, St Giles' Hospital, London

Immediately after the circulation had stopped, they made frantic efforts to get the heart going again but Harry Squires was altogether too old for such eventualities as this. A more competent anaesthetist would have had the patient hooked up to an ECG oscilloscope and would have dealt more rapidly and effectively with the shock using plasma expanders before the emergency O-negative blood arrived. He would also have double-checked that blood was available before the procedure started and would certainly have sent for it when the patient showed signs of losing an excessive amount of blood.

Harry was only good for routine work. Any grave emergency left him impotently puffing at his rubber bag and issuing inconsequential orders to no one in particular. He should have been put out to pasture years ago. Had it not been for his association with Reith, he would have been doing the rounds as a private dental anaesthetist on a few mornings each week, while his wife shopped at Harrods for a few groceries, before returning to their retirement cottage in the country.

Reith was more dramatic. As always with him, the answer lay in the knife. With a savage thrust he ripped open the chest wall just beneath the left breast and with the brute strength of his hands he cracked open two of her ribs. He insinuated a hand in the opening he had just made in the rib cage and started to pump the ventricles by squeezing them in the palm of his hand.

Unfortunately this normally efficient pump had failed because of a loss of circulating blood volume. It simply did not have the venous return to maintain an adequate output and Reith's efforts, although commendable in certain types of cardiac arrest, were a poor substitute in this instance.

Nevertheless, it did get some haemoglobin coursing around the system to supply the vital brain centres with much-needed oxygen.

Five minutes of this futility elapsed but there was still no blood and the patient was obviously beyond resuscitation.

Patrick Stanley pulled off his gloves and, without even a murmur to Reith, left the room. He was badly shaken and looked as white as a ghost. He went into the sluice and puked continuously until he was retching painfully and bringing up thick green bile tinged with blood. He knew that he was too upset to continue so he telephoned Humphrey Hampson, explaining tactfully the situation, and asked if he could come up to help. Then he dressed, left the building hurriedly and crossed several of the drab slum streets in Paddington until he found a working men's pub where he would not be recognised. He ordered a triple Irish whiskey and a pint of Dublin stout and, like so many of his fellow countrymen in times of stress, he resorted to the distillates and ferments of malt and hops to induce a state of total oblivion and mental paralysis.

Reith looked like a wild man, uncomprehending, almost unbelieving, but frightened by the situation that had so rapidly broken free from his control. He was still castigating his junior staff for their failure to cross-match blood, and the events that had led up to the catastrophic haemorrhage had been eradicated from his memory.

Luckily, one of the theatre staff nurses had reacted to the news of the cardiac arrest in the prescribed manner and had picked up the nearest phone, giving the cardiac arrest alarm to the operator. A piercing electronic shriek went out on all channels of the switchboard to the bleeps carried by the cardiac arrest team and as each member pressed the emergency button on the tiny transistor radio, the telephone operator's voice informed them of the location of the disaster.

'Cardiac arrest. Gynae. Theatre two.'

Within minutes six breathless doctors and two technicians arrived pushing the resuscitation trolley, equipped with oscilloscopes, defibrillators and a whole range of life-saving drugs and infusions. They quickly took in the scene and unpacked the equipment as each one set about his allotted task. The patient's legs and arms were connected to an electrocardiograph oscilloscope, while one of the anaesthetic registrars busied himself with a quick dissection of the subclavian vein in the neck to give rapid access to the circulation and to measure the central venous pressure; the other dissected out the saphenous vein just above the ankle and inserted a long catheter, injecting a heavy dose of sodium bicarbonate to counteract acidity caused by circulatory arrest, and in the subclavian vein they poured a litre of plasma to increase the circulating blood volume.

Although the boys were quick, vital minutes had been wasted in this exercise. Harry Squires should have had an effective drip running in the patient's arm, which would have given them rapid access to the venous system. They communicated their views on his inefficiency and since he resented being pushed aside so unceremoniously by these arrogant youngsters, he shuffled out of the room, pushing the auxiliary anaesthetic machine in front of him like a barrow boy at Smith Street market. After a long life attending to all sorts of operations, death was no stranger to him and he was unable to divine the reason for all this anguish.

As if nothing remarkable had happened, he phoned the women's surgical ward and ordered them to pre-medicate the next case and send her up to theatre in twenty minutes' time after he had finished his coffee break.

Back in the operating theatre the scene was pandemonium with everyone barking orders and nurses scurrying around breaking ampoules of intravenous drugs and drawing them up in disposable plastic syringes. At this stage, Jennifer desperately needed blood and her life was hanging by a very slender thread. Technically she was dead. Her heart had stopped pumping and her lungs had stopped breathing. All her vital activities were being maintained artificially.

The atmosphere suddenly changed as one of the hospital's most eminent specialists arrived on the scene – the consultant cardiologist at St Giles, Vanessa Erickson, a stunning blonde in her late thirties. She was one of those fantastic women who had defied the male-dominated medical establishment and had risen to the top of the profession through sheer brilliance and personality. She was not only visually beautiful; she lived her whole life at a frenetic pace. She was a champion fencer and had represented the UK at the Commonwealth Games when she was at university. Now she divided her sporting life between extreme skiing in winter and kite-surfing in summer and more recently a bizarre addiction to bungee-jumping, usually in exotic places around the world.

She was a terrifyingly fast driver and in her meadowlark-yellow Porsche convertible she always seemed to have a brace of eligible studs fawning after her. They could never dominate her. She had ruled marriage out of her life on the grounds that it was incompatible with her career, and had then proceeded to shock the medical hierarchy by selecting a man to father her child. Like a farmer choosing a prize bullock at an agricultural show, she had singled out a brilliant professor of moral science at Oxford on the grounds that he possessed the genetic material she required for her offspring. Her sexuality was obvious but like many of Scandinavian descent she was able to keep it under control and indulge it only at those special times when she felt like it.

Right now she was in charge of the cardiac resuscitation unit and her voice, as she surveyed the disaster area, carried the conviction of someone born to command.

'For Christ's sake. What a bloody cock-up. She looks as white as a ghost. Why the hell hasn't she had any blood?'

Angus grunted. The shambles surrounding his normally orderly session made him uncomfortable enough but the starchy presence and biting tongue of Vanessa Erickson made him fume inwardly with impotent rage.

Her senior registrar, James Deakin, briefly filled her in on the events leading up to the cardiac standstill and assured her that the houseman had gone to fetch some O-negative blood.

She glanced at the ECG trace on the oscilloscope and swore softly to herself.

'We've got to get some oxygen to that ventricular muscle or she'll be as dead as a dodo – if she isn't already. Get another bag of plasma and hook it up to an IV, James, and give it to Mr Reith. It doesn't matter if it isn't sterile. She's got more to worry about right now than a few bugs.'

Angus was handed a plastic giving set with a sharp needle on the end. He was still pumping wearily with his right hand and his hesitation belied his lack of comprehension.

Vanessa chimed in again, a note of impatience in her voice.

'Shove it in the aorta or the common iliac artery, Angus, and once you're in give the aorta a strong but brief squeeze.'

Angus was now completely amazed. Access to the circulation was invariably by way of the venous system, which carries blood back to the heart. He had never heard of anyone using an intra-arterial infusion to resuscitate a patient.

'What the dickens is the point of that, madam? She needs more venous return, surely. I can't see the point of shoving fluids in backwards.'

Vanessa gave one of her knowing smirks. She always reckoned that gynaecologists had brains that were so small that they were unable to think beyond the narrow confines of the female pelvis.

'Angiographic studies have shown that rapid intra-arterial perfusion results in retrograde filling of the coronary arteries. Her myocardium must be grossly

ischaemic by now and the cells there need the little bit of oxygenated blood
that remains in her circulation. She's living on borrowed time anyway but it's
all we can do until the red stuff arrives.'

Angus muttered beneath his mask. He could not abide this woman and her
smart-arse methods at the best of times, and he certainly did not approve of
her marching into his theatre and barking out orders to everyone, himself included. She hadn't even bothered to don the sterile operating theatre clothing.

Instinctively, Dr Erickson reached into the pockets of her white coat for her
cigarettes. Apparently, she only stopped smoking when she was eating, sleeping
or making love. Realising that she would not be allowed to profane the sterility
of the operating suite with cigarette smoke she returned the pack to her pocket
and glanced back at the monitor to see if her manoeuvre was having any effects.
Nothing. The trace on the monitor was as flat as death itself.

'It looks hopeless,' she sighed. 'She should have had blood ages ago. That silly
old buffer hadn't even managed to get a proper drip going. You might as well
give up.'

There is a moment in the modern way of dying when the medical attendants
cannot believe or accept their failure. Death in the shape of a medieval tarot
card had confronted them again but even now they were reluctant to let go.
Reith was still squeezing the heart chambers of a corpse but at least he felt he
was still trying to save his patient's life. It required a positive action to stop this
seemingly futile intervention. Jennifer could still be said to be alive while he
was pumping the heart, but the moment he removed his hand from inside the
chest she was dead.

Actual death is one step removed from the time of death itself.

The decision to stop resuscitating was easy but the reality was more difficult.
The judge is spared the sight of death, but not the executioner.

As Reith hesitated, the silence was interrupted by Bodger Brackenbridge
charging through the doors like a scrum forward, clutching four bottles of cold
red blood to his chest. They were seized from him before he had time to drop
them and poured by pressure infusion pumps into the body that needed the
life-giving fluid so desperately.

After two pints the ECG showed some intrinsic cardiac activity on the oscilloscope. Not much, but enough to give them some hope. The cardiologist ordered

some intra-cardiac adrenalin which Reith pushed into the cardiac chambers as he paused to give back some much-needed strength to his own fingers that had been squeezing the heart continuously for more than half an hour.

Vanessa Erickson stared intently at the monitor, watching the effect of the drug on the cardiac tracing.

'Give her another shot of adrenalin. This time give it through one of the cut-downs. Ten ml of one in ten thousand.'

All eyes were on the monitor now. The atmosphere in the theatre was tense but expectant. This was the most crucial stage. If the heart was capable of respond-ing to the adrenalin with any kind of electrical activity the cardiologists could probably convert it to an effective rhythm by the use of modern technology, but if it was totally unresponsive it meant the heart muscle was dead, and if there was no pump there was no circulation. The sine qua non of the life equation.

Vanessa was still barking out orders.

'She'll need some more calcium chloride. Give her fifteen ml of one per cent and another bottle of bicarbonate. Is someone writing all of this down? Gibson, keep a chart of how many milli-equivalents of electrolytes she's had and how much fluid we've pushed in.'

'She's fibrillating, Dr Erickson. Look, she's fibrillating.'

One of the medical registrars was the first to recognise the bizarre pattern on the electrocardiograph of ventricular fibrillation. Reith could feel the worm-like activity of the muscle of the ventricles. A shimmering useless response as far as pumping blood was concerned but at least an electrical response. It showed that the muscle cells were not completely dead.

The consultant cardiologist was now obviously excited and took over the therapeutic activity like an army field commander.

'OK, stand by to shock her. I'm going to try to defibrillate her, Angus, I want you to remove your hand sharpish when I give the word. Meanwhile, I want you to keep pumping as hard as you possibly can.'

She turned to the audience of medical people milling around the table.

'No one to touch any metal near here,' she bellowed. 'We don't want another death on our hands. One corpse in the working day is quite enough for me, thank you. Electrode jelly on the chest, please, Sister. Plenty of it, dear, you don't have to pay for it out of your own pocket. Stand clear of the table, everyone.'

She depressed the trigger of the big plate electrode and Jennifer's body jolted and twitched with the shock of 440 volts of direct current.

All eyes were again on the television screen to see if the defibrillation had worked. At first it was a fluorescent splatter of activity from the disturbance of the electric shock but then the bright green dot started to trace out the familiar patter of the QRS and T waves of the normal cardiac complex.

Everyone breathed a sigh of relief and Bodger started to clap like an appreciative spectator at a wrestling match until he was silenced by a venomous look from Reith. The tension in the room seemed to lessen, but Vanessa nodded her head from side to side as if she was not entirely satisfied with the result. She was a born perfectionist and could not readily tolerate any deviation from the normal cardiac trace.

'That's something, I suppose,' she grunted. 'She's dropping beats, though. Look, James, that's Wenckebach's phenomenon. She may come out of it in a few minutes if it's only due to anoxia.'

They watched the tracing for a few more minutes and then took a hot-wire recording on a strip of graph paper to study it more carefully. Vanessa always phrased her words in accordance with the traditions of the male society who had elected to join.

'Oh, shit. She's gone into complete heart-block. That means we'll have to pace her, James. The long period of anoxia must have damaged the sino-atrial node.'

The senior registrar looked again.

'That doesn't augur well for the brain and the kidneys.'

Vanessa shrugged. She wasn't a woman given to such emotions and only concerned herself with the organ of her speciality, the heart. The professor of internal medicine would have to look after the rest. Now that the heart was functioning again she wanted to get out of the operating theatre. Like most physicians, she found the surgical atmosphere oppressive.

'Angus, would you be so good as to sew up your handiwork on the chest and abdomen so that we can take her down to the intensive care unit. My staff and I feel rather out of place among all this blood and gore.'

She turned to her senior registrar.

'James, I want her on an intermittent positive pressure respirator and get her arterial blood gases done as soon as possible. It might be worth giving her twenty ml of twenty per cent mannitol since she's almost certain to have some cerebral oedema. The kidneys are bound to be knocked off but the medical people can deal with that problem later. Once the venous pressure has been stabilised, be careful not to overload the circulation.'

She addressed the consultant gynaecologist again. 'Frankly, Angus, I wouldn't hold out much hope for her. The resuscitation measures were far too slow to get off the ground. In a central London teaching hospital we ought to be able to do better than this.'

She turned smartly and left the theatre, as Angus squirmed with indignation. Nobody spoke to him like that. Much less a woman. He stitched the layers of flesh together again, scarcely able to contain his temper. Finally he threw his operating gloves on the floor, breaking the silence with a series of terse threats about the repercussions that were bound to follow. Everyone was to blame but the great man himself. Like every driver after a road traffic accident he was blind to his own faults, he could only blame the others. In particular Stanley for failing to operate in the manner that he dictated, for failing to double-clamp the uterine artery and for being so truculent and insubordinate to his seniors. Brackenbridge for the unbelievable omission of failing to have a supply of cross-matched blood available. The nursing and technical staff for failing to check on the suction machine, and the axe even fell on his lifelong friend Harry Squires for his bumbling incompetence in the treatment of hypovolaemic shock. He was surrounded by fools and imbeciles and everyone within earshot was included.

Angus Reith was beside himself with rage as he changed from his theatre clothes to his Savile Row suit. In thirty-five years of operating he had never lost a gynaecological patient on the operating table unless she was suffering from an advanced malignant condition. Some of these patients had required radical procedures in which virtually all the contents of the pelvis had to be removed.

During the intricate dissection of the cancerous lymph nodes on the pelvic side walls it was difficult not to tear one the of the large veins or arteries and, in a woman usually old and already frail from cancer, the bleeding could be cata-strophic. One could always justify such deaths as part and parcel of the heroic process of trying to save someone who, left to one of the crueller processes of Mother Nature, would be dead in a few months anyway. But this woman today, she was in the prime of life and her pathology was entirely benign. This was a terrible disaster and unless he covered his tracks very carefully the shit would hit the fan, soiling his hard-earned reputation as a meticulous and brilliant surgeon beyond redemption.

He took Jennifer's hospital notes over to his office in Harley Street and slowly and deliberately wrote his own account of the operation. He made no mention of his deliberate removal of the clamp nor the lack of cross-matched blood. The account was designed as a piece of testimony that may have to be given in court and he was careful not to lay the blame at anyone's feet since he himself was ultimately responsible for all the patients under his care. He knew that there might well be an inquest in a case of this nature and he also knew that well-kept notes were the doctor's best defence in a court of law.

His next task was to inform the coroner. This was potentially the most difficult stage and the outcome depended very much on who was dealing with hospital deaths at the moment and also, to some extent, on how busy they were. One thing was certain, if he had detailed one of his juniors to speak to the coroner, a post-mortem at the hands of one of the Home Office pathologists would have been mandatory. There was just a chance that a man of his reputation in the medical establishment, speaking personally and politely to the coroner, might be able to secure a post-mortem in the hospital pathology department. He would then be able to have a word with Professor Jenkins before the findings were presented to the coroner.

As luck would have it, he was put through to a man named McLaren whom he had met at the annual dinner of the Apothecaries Guild some weeks back and as they chattered away they had both become immersed in Scottish Highland folklore. Normally Reith made a point of being rude to non-clinical colleagues but on this particular occasion the Scottish bond had secured ten minutes of Angus Reith at his most convivial. It was about to pay dividends.

McLaren was delighted to speak to Reith again and was rather moved by the humility with which the great man described the desperate and difficult surgery that had been fraught with so many dangers. His knowledge of gynaecology was scant in the extreme and he was not aware of the intricacies of the operative procedures on the female pelvis. His own dissections of cadavers were made easier by the lack of bright red blood that tended to obscure the view of the operative field. He was also aware that he was speaking to one of the top men in the speciality and it seemed impudent on his part to create any difficulties. When Angus suggested that this was a matter that could be dealt with in the pathology department of a famous teaching hospital, it would have been impertinent to the point of bad manners to disagree. Indeed he was only too relieved to get off the subject of materia medica and chat about the old clans of Ross and Cromarty. After some ten minutes of this trivia Reith returned the receiver to its rest and breathed an audible sigh of relief.

At the other end of the line McLaren was rather perplexed. It was most unusual, unheard of in fact, to report a case to the coroner unless a death had taken place. He had an uneasy feeling that something was amiss. He was uncomfortably aware that he was appointed by the public to ensure that the medical profession was beyond reproach. He made a note to inspect all the death certificates from the North West Metropolitan region over the next few days and if necessary he would have to intervene, even at the expense of hurting the feelings of his Scottish colleague.

The next move for Reith was to ring the sister on his female surgical ward and to leave specific instructions on how to handle the husband. She had already heard of the tragedy by the bush telegraph that exists in every hospital and her Teutonic upbringing ensured that she would not react with the type of melodrama that would have nauseated the consultant. She was told to inform the husband that a disaster had occurred and that his wife had nearly died during the operation. She was to give no reasons but to escort the husband to the waiting room and provide him with a cup of tea. On no account was he to be interviewed by Stanley or Brackenbridge and when he was so installed and aware of the extent of the disaster, she was to call Reith, who would be waiting in his Harley Street rooms. Sister Rheingeld, despite her usual overbearing manner, was utterly loyal to him and could be relied upon to carry out every instruction faithfully.

He wondered if he should feel any obligation to inform Dr Michaelson, the local GP who had sent her so far from home to meet her fate. Reith quite absurdly blamed him for the whole episode and with ill-concealed disgust asked his secretary to get him on the line. Michaelson behaved in the characteristic style of the country GP, full of emotion and sorrow, and told Reith all sorts of intimate background about the family that he could well have done without.

He did, however, promise to break the news to the grandparents who were looking after the children. He added somewhat unnecessarily that at least he was relieved to have sent her to one of the best hospitals in the land. It was only then that Reith realised the enormity of the damage they he had wrought and how the woman would probably still be alive if she had been operated on in some local hospital or indeed if she had avoided doctors altogether.

He quickly dismissed such thoughts from his mind and tried to rationalise the events in much the same manner as his father would have done. Fate was in divine hands and if God had willed that she should die then there was precious little a mere mortal could do about it. Anyway he was used to the spectre of untimely death in a lifetime of clinical medicine and hid behind the physician's smokescreen of callous indifference. He looked for the first time at the admission notes made by Brackenbridge.

She was only forty-six, a year older than his own wife. How would he react to the information that Helena had been killed in an accident? The face of the deceased merged in his mind with that of his wife and he found that the image was disturbing. He tried to brush away the thought and looked back at the hospital notes. Three children and one miscarriage. Two girls, eighteen and sixteen, and then a long gap after the miscarriage and finally a small son of six.

'Where's my mummy? Granny, when is mummy coming back from hospital? I'm missing her.'

He could see a small child, miserable, unable to understand. He could see a grandmother with tears in her eyes, trying hopelessly to explain, to make death sound understandable to a child.

'Mummy's gone for a long sleep, dear. She's gone away from us.'

A wave of nausea overtook the consultant. He started to shake violently and became covered in cold, damp perspiration. With little warning, he vomited hideously all over the mahogany desk, and then his head collapsed into the mess he had made while his body shook with misery and anguish.

Because of his action, a little child would never remember the love, the comfort, the softness of a mother.

'I want her. I want to see her.'

'Mummy won't be back, dear. She's gone for a long sleep. She won't ever wake up again.'

PART FOUR

THE COVER-UP

D eath on the table.
Death before complete recovery from anaesthesia.
Death within twenty-four hours of an operation.
Death due to unnatural causes or where there is a high index of suspicion of unnatural or criminal circumstances.

Death suggesting an element of negligence or lack of proper medical care. And so on.

All these, and many more, must be reported by the doctor in charge of the patient to the Officer of the Coroner for him or her to decide the correct course of action to be taken.

This was to protect the public from any conspiracy by the profession.

'All professions are a conspiracy against the laity.'
George Bernard Shaw

CHAPTER TWENTY-FOUR
Humphrey Hampson's house in Chelsea, London

'Where the bloody hell have you been?'

Humphrey Hampson stared angrily at the wretched apparition that leaned drunkenly against the wall outside the front door of his smart residence in Chelsea. Patrick Stanley looked terrible as he slouched into the room and collapsed into the only armchair. He hadn't shaved for two weeks and the dirty shirt and duffle coat that he was wearing had all the authenticity and stench of a genuine derelict from the Salvation Army hostel in Tower Hamlets. His eyes were haggard and bloodshot and sunken deep into their sockets. His face told, with bruises and old blood, the story of several scraps. Hampson changed gear from anger to surprise and finally to sympathy for his friend.

'Jesus Christ, when you bloody Micks go on a bender you don't believe in half-measures. You realise that you've been missing for two bloody weeks. Even your wife's been worried about you although she mentioned that it's happened once or twice before.'

'Two weeks. I'd lost track. I didn't think it had been that long. I had a lot of thinking to do.' He was talking slowly like a patient recovering from amnesia.

'Where the hell have you been?'

'Dunno. I meant to go to every bloody bar in the East End but I don't think I made it. I've been in brothels and doss houses and I think I spent a night or two in jail.'

'What do you mean, you think you spent a night or two in jail?'

'I dunno. I tell you, I had a lot of thinking to do.'

'Jesus, you look awful. Why don't you take a bath while I get you something to eat? If the patients saw you like that they'd run a mile. We've had enough trouble with morale since the accident. Several of them have signed their own discharge or refused to have any surgery done.'

Patrick was staring vacantly into outer space with the worried look of a lunatic that sent a slight chill flitting down Humphrey's spine. He briefly considered calling for psychiatric help and admitting Patrick for the night. The poor fellow already seemed to have acquired a police record and it seemed too much to give him a psychiatric one as well. Humphrey tried to keep the conversation going.

'We decided to put you on sick leave for a while and I've been taking your calls. I didn't mind for a few days but I had no idea that you'd be away for this long. Reith didn't seem too worried, he thought you'd been under rather a lot of strain lately and that had probably contributed to the accident.'

'The bastard.'

Patrick turned slowly to face Humphrey and it was apparent that he was not really drunk but his eyes were burning with hatred. He spoke very slowly.

'I'm going to fix that arrogant bastard. I've thought it over carefully during the last few days. I'm going to take legal proceedings against him. I've decided to file a charge of manslaughter.'

He looked at Hampson like a child seeking parental approval.

'By removing that clamp he deliberately killed that woman. He might just as well have pointed a loaded revolver at her head.'

There was a long silence. Humphrey looked down at his feet. He remembered that Patrick had disappeared while the patient was still on the operating table.

'Patrick, you don't seem to realise. She's not dead. She's up in the intensive care unit. She's unconscious but very much alive and there's still some hope that she might come round.'

Patrick looked at him and stared hard, his eyes registering frank disbelief. Suddenly it was all too much and he slumped forward off the chair and fell unconscious in a heap in front of the gas fire.

He slept for thirty-four hours.

When he woke up he was surprised to find himself in a strange bedroom between newly laundered sheets and even more surprised to find that he had been bathed and shaved without apparently waking from his slumber. He looked out of the window on to a suburban street and wondered vaguely where he was and whether it was morning or evening. He had been through similar sensations during the past fortnight but usually he was in some filthy establishment or out of doors in his damp and dirty duffle coat. Now at least he was clean and to some extent refreshed by a long sleep. He grabbed a dressing gown that hung behind the door and ventured forth to explore his new surroundings.

Downstairs he followed the appetising smell of frying bacon and deduced that it must be morning and, seeing Hampson dressed in casual wear, he further deduced that it must be the weekend. Humphrey greeted him warmly and like the efficient bachelor that he had become over the years, he soon rustled up some bacon and eggs and strong black coffee.

Over breakfast, Humphrey recounted the events of the past fortnight and Patrick listened with growing amazement at the web of lies that had been so intricately spun.

A few days after he had left, it had become apparent that Jennifer Watson was going to survive the acute episode but her future prognosis was in doubt. In order to 'clear the air', as Reith had put it, and to exorcise any lurking suspicions that an operative error had occurred, the consultant had called a meeting of all of those involved in the case. Professor Jenkins had shown them the uterus which he removed from a large formalin jar and had placed unceremoniously on an old baking tin lid. He demonstrated the carcinoma that had started at the inside of the cervical canal and had spread out into the tissues adjacent to the uterus to involve the lymph nodes on the pelvic side wall. He then spent some time showing them the microscope slides projected on the wall of the pathology museum by an old-fashioned epidiascope that had been part of St Giles as long as anyone could remember. The microscopy showed an extremely aggressive adeno-squamous tumour that had arisen from the endometrium but because of its position just inside the neck of the womb it had behaved clinically in the more sinister fashion of a cervical carcinoma by spreading directly outwards and rapidly involving the lymphatic nodes and distant spread.

Reith had then taken over and pointed out to the non-gynaecologists in the audience that this was an unusual type of tumour and often caught people unawares because the outer part of the cervix that was visible on vaginal examination appeared healthy and even the smear that he had taken in this case was negative for malignant cells. Furthermore, the only symptom was heavy vaginal bleeding and on clinical examination the uterus was bulky from the tumour, but this was indistinguishable, even by his own expert hands, from the much more common condition of fibroids.

Consequently they were not prepared at operation for the vigorous bleeding they encountered when they found that the growth had eroded into some of the large veins of the pelvis. Nevertheless, he castigated the junior staff for not having blood readily available, which was one of his standing orders, and he blamed the theatre nurses and technicians for not checking that the suction apparatus was in working order before the start of any major operation. He left little room for doubt that he had saved the day and that it was only as a result of his skilled surgical presence that the woman was still with us.

'But there was no cancer at all,' Patrick interrupted. 'I saw her box with my own eyes. It was a perfectly normal bunch of fibroids. We sent that uterus down to the path lab. It must be lying down there somewhere.'

'Well, I'm sorry, old son, but the one we were shown was clearly marked with the patient's name and number. The one you're talking about has probably been sold to one of the local Indian restaurants and passed off as chicken liver curry.'

'It's not fucking funny, Humphrey,' exploded Patrick. 'Can't you see that the bastards are trying to cover it all up? Those two old buggers are in cahoots over this. There was no suggestion of cancer. What about Sister Brewer? She was there. She'll tell you that he removed that clamp like a cold-blooded murderer.'

'There's no point being so dramatic, Patrick, it isn't going to achieve anything. I spoke to Sister Brewer afterwards but she's been almost hysterical the past two weeks. She's absolutely terrified of Reith anyway and he's been cursing at her incessantly about the failure of the suction machine. Apparently she used to take five milligrams of valium before scrubbing for Reith and she feels responsible for the whole thing. You know what women drivers are like after a road accident, they seem to invent a whole new version of what actually happened.'

Patrick was beginning to feel the supports for his charge slowly slipping away beneath his feet. He suddenly remembered the student.

'What about that fellow from Cambridge who was first assistant? What the hell was his name…? Jennings, that's right, Jennings. He's a fairly bright character, he'd be able to testify in court about what actually happened.'

Humphrey shook his head.

'I'm afraid not, Patrick. I asked him to tell me what happened but he was holding the handle of a bladder retractor and he couldn't even see into the pelvis. Anyway, he's new to gynaecology and he admitted that he hadn't the faintest idea what was going on. He seems to have some kind of persecution complex and he's convinced that disaster has stalked him ever since he entered the medical school. Apparently, Reith threw him out of the operating theatre soon after he arrived for adjusting the light with his sterile gloves. He was just swaying on the end of his retractor and praying like grim death that he wasn't going to be held responsible for this disaster. Anyway, do you want me to tell you about the meeting or not?'

Patrick nodded and Humphrey continued to describe the atmosphere in the basement room of the pathology department. The professor of internal medicine had taken the floor. He was a relatively young man by professorial standards and although he was receding a little at the front of his scalp he made up for the deficit by long, flowing blond locks that swept down to his shoulders and were tied in a ponytail at the back. This effect, and the enormous bow ties he chose to wear, gave an overwhelming impression of trendy intelligence. He loathed gynaecology not only because it was such an intellectual abyss but because he found the whole subject rather distasteful.

He soon switched the attention of the audience from the 'underneaths' to the enormously more fascinating organs that were being supported artificially by modern technology. He presented a patient whose lungs were being ventilated by a servo-triggered respirator, whose heart was being stimulated by an artificial pacemaker and whose kidneys had ceased to function completely and therefore all the products of nitrogenous excretion had to be filtered out of her body by artificial haemodialysis. He was less enthusiastic when he came to her cerebral function and suggested that the period of anoxia must have been of sufficient length to have inflicted considerable damage to her brain since she was still deeply unconscious after ten days, which was a poor prognostic sign. He regretted it deeply, as if he were personally responsible, that they had not yet invented an artificial brain, since they would then have an almost wholly artificial creature and he hinted, somewhat unnecessarily, that they would then be able to banish religion as superstitious nonsense. They had started to debate the Dawson-oriented ideas of the professor of medicine when Reith brought the house to order and insisted that some kind of future plans had to be made for the welfare of his patient. The meeting then erupted into a squabble about medical ethics between the realists and the sentimentalists.

'Who was the leading realist?'

'The professor of internal medicine. He felt the prognosis was hopeless and that they were merely keeping a vegetable alive, and a costly one at that, so he rather callously suggested that someone should pull the electric plugs out of their sockets.'

'Someone?'

'Exactly. Someone, but not him.'

He became rather queasy when old Goldberg, the radiotherapist, challenged him to go right on up there and switch the machines off. He tried to excuse himself on the grounds that she wasn't his patient.'

'Old Goldberg deals with cancer every day. He probably knows more about the vagaries of death than any of us do. Do you know he once told me straight out that he's dying of leukaemia. Just like that; as cold as ice. He looks so bloody pale that I believed him.'

'Oh, I'm not so sure,' Humphrey said. 'I've been around this place longer than you and he's been telling everyone that for years. He's almost proud of it. He blames it on the radiation that he so selflessly administers. He's another one with a persecution complex. First of all he escaped from Hitler and ever since he's been trying to get away from the gamma rays provided free of charge by the National Health Service. Either that or he wants to become a modern medical martyr like Madame Curie. Anyway, his leukaemia never seems to get any worse. But, regardless of that, he really put the cat among the pigeons by suggesting that in the circumstances the carcinoma could not have been adequately eradicated by surgery because they had not dissected out and removed all the lymph nodes and that if they were really concerned about the survival of the patient she ought to be exposed to a full course of megavoltage radiotherapy.'

'Christ, he didn't,' interjected Patrick. 'What happened?'

'Well, Prof Jenkins bloody nearly passed out and even Reith almost fell off his chair.'

'Oh, fuck me for a fart-horse.'

'What a horrible expression.'

'Oh, come on, Humphrey, stop playing silly buggers. This is beginning to sound like the players' scene in Hamlet. You know bloody well that this is a cover-up. Why should you go round questioning Sister Brewer and Andrew Jennings like a Scotland Yard detective if you didn't harbour suspicions of malpractice? I insist you support me in reporting Reith to the correct authorities. I see no reason why he should get away with this.'

There followed an ominous silence made all the more irritating by Humphrey picking intently at a hair protruding from the end of his nose, a distressing habit that he resorted to in times of stress. He was carefully considering his words and when he spoke he had a genuine expression of sadness.

'I'm sorry, old friend, but I'm afraid I can't do that. I've been thinking about it and I realise that I'm taking the coward's way out but I've simply got too much to lose. I'm on the brink of being appointed a consultant myself and I know that if I play my cards correctly I have a chance of getting the next post at St Giles when they create a new one in the next year or so. In addition Reith is wanting to hand over his private obstetric practice to a younger man and he's no longer on speaking terms with Hellman because of that abortion on his daughter. He's approached me...'

'In the last few days?'

'Yes, in the last few days.'

'He's bought you out. The bastard knew that you'd be the only one in a responsible position to smell a rat. The bastard's tried to buy you out.'

Humphrey looked uncomfortable again but he knew he had to speak everything that was in his mind even though it might hurt.

'I'm afraid that you've hit on the one word that matters. Responsible. We wouldn't have a leg to stand on in a court of law. I've read the operation notes written in meticulous detail describing all the difficulties encountered with the cancerous growth and how the complete removal required a difficult dissection around the external iliac vein, resulting in profuse haemorrhage and...'

'But he's never written an operation note in years. He always leaves that to the junior staff.'

'I know that, but the lawyers and particularly the judge and jury don't know that. They have to go by the facts presented to them and it'll be his word against yours. That's where we get back to the word responsible. You've been blind drunk for two weeks and he's had you followed by a private detective agency. Apart from the fact that you picked a fight with one of their men, the events that they have chronicled would make very squalid reading in a court of law. Besides, he has also been informed that you spent two nights in Stepney police station.'

Patrick had listened to the last part of this oration with open-mouthed astonishment. Not that the facts presented caused him any surprise but because he had felt a peculiar itch around his jock area and on examining the region through the fly of his borrowed pyjamas he had found the whole area devoid of pubic hair. He had often wondered about Humphrey living alone and, at times, he had entertained a flitting suspicion about the man having homosexual tendencies. Now, as he contemplated his period of unconsciousness, he entertained a genuine terror about the personage who had abluted him so conscientiously. He suddenly changed the subject and his Irish accent became almost demonic with panic.

'Humphrey, who the hell bathed me and put me to bed?'

Hampson was relieved that the spirit of Reith's inquisitor had temporarily left Patrick.

'Well, I knew you had a little something going with Sister Taylor on the labour ward so I asked her if she'd mind helping out. I couldn't possibly have taken you upstairs to the bathroom on my own and I'd sooner not undress you and bathe you.'

Humphrey smiled benevolently but soon sensed the expression of genuine amazement on the Irishman's face. 'Nothing amiss, I hope?'

By now Patrick had explored his nether regions more carefully. A blue silk ribbon had been lovingly tied in a bow around his balls.

'On no,' said Patrick uneasily. 'Nothing at all.'

Chapter Twenty-five
Humphrey Hampson's house in Chelsea, London

Since Humphrey Hampson had adopted the role of Patrick's saviour he continued to be responsible for him over the next few days. He telephoned Patrick's wife on several occasions but she showed no inclination to help. Indeed the last time he called her she involved him in a long and bitter harangue, in which she ordered him to inform her husband that she was seeking a divorce on grounds of incompatibility, was leaving with all her belongings and going to stay with her parents in Sussex, having put their South Ealing house up for sale. She did not wish to have Patrick staying at their home ever again.

Humphrey was never at ease when he was involved in emotional issues and he began to stammer badly, which only served to confuse the issue. Mrs Stanley eventually lost her temper with him and became extremely abusive before slamming down the telephone. At the other end of the line Humphrey was left looking very hurt and perplexed, staring like a scolded child at the silent receiver in his hand.

To make matters worse, Reith had accused Humphrey openly of harbouring a fugitive and had hinted darkly that his loyalty to his consultant must be held in question by his recent behaviour. This was rather ominous in terms of their recent conversation about his career prospects, and Humphrey arrived home feeling that his Good Samaritan act was causing him a great deal of trouble. Patrick had installed himself in Humphrey's house as if he had no intention of leaving.

'I've cooked an Irish stew the like of which you're never likely to taste again.' He was dressed in a dark striped chef's apron that Humphrey had acquired from Heal's. He was obviously in high good humour and Humphrey noticed an almost empty bottle of Irish whiskey beside the cooking range. Patrick was becoming an expensive guest. 'When the English cook this traditional Irish dish it's usually an abomination. I like to compare it to a beef bourguignon cooked slowly to perfection in Irish whiskey instead of red wine.'

Humphrey looked horrified. 'S-s-s-s-surely to G-g-g-god you haven't put that entire b-b-bottle of whiskey in the stew.'

271

'Indeed I have, Humphrey, and it'll be a piece of haute cuisine the like of which you'll never forget as long as you live. I have to admit,' Patrick added shyly, 'that a little slipped down the throat of the cook.'

Humphrey took off his coat and went to the toilet. Like many a man who was accustomed to living on his own he left the door wide open and sang softly to himself while he was emptying his bladder. At the end of the performance he emitted a long, low resonant fart, grunted with pleasure and entered the living room still doing up his flies.

'Quite a performance! I wonder what you do for an encore?'

Humphrey spun around in surprise and was horrified to see the pert form of Lizzie Taylor in a trouser suit curled up on his sofa. Humphrey was crimson with embarrassment and his stutter became so uncontrollable that he was unable to get out an adequate sentence.

'S-s-s-s-s-s-s-ist T-t-t-t-.' He almost choked with his efforts and Lizzie giggled sympathetically at his distress.

'Don't worry, Humphrey. I've heard much worse lavatorial music at much closer quarters. I was only joking. Can I get you a drink?'

'Thanks, Lizzie. S-s-s-scotch.'

'There only seems to be Irish at the moment. Anyway, I can't taste the difference. If you keep him here much longer he'll start painting the walls green.'

Humphrey cringed almost visibly. The walls of his flat were an artistic delight, covered in soft nineteenth-century English watercolours and Ackermann prints of the Cambridge colleges all framed and lit with the very best of taste. He looked back at his attractive guest.

'Thanks for the other night, Lizzie. I couldn't possibly have managed him on my own.'

She handed him the drink and he relaxed in his favourite armchair in front of the gas fire. It was strange to hear the chatter of other voices in his usually silent house.

'I wouldn't say it was a pleasure but I've seen worse than that in casualty; tramps that haven't had a bath in years.'

Humphrey giggled at this description of his colleague. He tinkled the ice in his drink against the crystal glass of the tumbler as he remembered their combined efforts to rescue Patrick from oblivion.

'Anyway,' she continued, 'it helps to see someone at their worst before…' She hesitated and looked Humphrey in the eyes. 'I might as well tell you; he's asked me to go and live with him.'

Humphrey was relieved that he was going to get rid of his lodger so easily, but he was surprised to feel a slight pang of disappointment, almost jealousy. He was rather fond of this girl but his starchy English gentleman exterior would never allow such emotions to show.

'I'm glad for you. He desperately needs someone at a time like this.'

'There's just one thing…'

'Yes?' Humphrey turned his sympathetic gaze towards her. He would have made a lovely father.

'I'd just hate to think I was taking him away from someone else. I've been through a similar kind of hoop myself.'

Humphrey placed his hand on her arm, comforting her. 'I wouldn't worry about that, Lizzie. From the sound of her voice on the telephone, I think she'd be only too delighted to be rid of him. I gather the marriage has been on the rocks for quite some time.'

They were interrupted by Patrick banging on the casserole, which was his way of summoning them to the table. He looked at them anxiously as they sampled the first mouthful of his creation. Lizzie went through all the motions like a gourmet on the silver screen but Humphrey started coughing and spluttering and grabbed for a glass of water.

'C-c-c-christ!' He swallowed the contents of the glass in one gulp and held it out for a refill. 'I say, old m-m-man, this is pure alcohol. A chap could easily get drunk on food like this.'

'Good Irish cooking, Humphrey, just like my old mother used to make, although in her case the spirits were illicitly distilled and a good deal stronger. In this godforsaken country something like ninety per cent of every mouthful of my Irish stew goes in tax to the government.'

'Well, I like it,' said Lizzie. 'I've never met a man who could cook before.'

'Call this c-c-c-cooking?' spluttered Humphrey. P-p-p-pickling would be a better word. Actually it's not half bad once you realise you're eating firewater.'

There was a long silence as everyone ate the stew, a sign of great satisfaction to every innovative chef. It was finally broken by Patrick himself.

'Well, Humphrey, what news from Murder Incorporated?' This was Patrick's new way of referring to Angus Reith.

'He grows from strength to strength with every passing day, although Prof Porter is getting very agitated about the amount of time and money that this is costing his unit.'

'Surely that's what they pay him for?' Lizzie interrupted, angry that the human issues should be overshadowed by financial ones.

'He sees all this in terms of cost-effectiveness and health economics.'

'And what does he think of me?' Patrick was beaming radiantly and in his semi-drunken state he assumed they were talking about Reith.

Humphrey paused; there was an awkward silence as he knitted his brows into a frown, unsure whether to be truthful or tactful.

'He refuses to allow you to work on his unit ever again.'

'Three cheers for that.'

'But the hospital authorities are starting to baulk at your absence. If it continues they want some form of medical certificate. Hellman has agreed to have you as his registrar but he wants you to start tomorrow.'

'Good old Maurice, ever the liberal lifesaver. I don't suppose that endeared him to Murder Inc.'

Humphrey frowned again; once again he was the victim of divided loyalties. 'I wish you'd stop calling him that. Anyway, Maurice has severed his connection with Reith ever since he did that abortion on his daughter. I think he has, at last, realised that he can sink no lower in his opinion.'

'Except possibly to pick an innocent Irishman off the floor.'

'He's only trying to help.'

'I know, I know.' Patrick had obviously been drinking all afternoon. 'I've nothing against old Maurice except when he gets his premenstrual tension and then takes three days off with dysmenorrhoea, leaving his registrar to do all the clinics.'

Humphrey laughed and Patrick explained to Lizzie about Hellman's monthly attack of migraine. Then he changed the subject and announced bluntly that he had asked Lizzie to live with him.

'So I heard,' said Humphrey, 'but what about the house? Your wife told me on the phone that she had put it up for sale.'

'I soon sorted that out,' Patrick replied aggressively. 'I took the axe out of the woodshed and chopped the For Sale sign down.'

'Isn't that ill-ill-illegal, old man?' bleated Humphrey. 'After all, the sign belongs to the estate agent.'

'Illegal to plant that monstrosity on my property.' Patrick took another healthy swig of his whiskey. 'I carried the sign on its pole round to the estate agent's office and dumped it on the head man's desk. I told him to shove the thing right up his arse or I'd set the IRA on to him.'

CHAPTER TWENTY-SIX
The office of the professor of medicine

It was decided to hold a clinical decision meeting to determine a policy of clinical management for Jennifer Watson, and the best place to hold it was in the office of the medical unit where the professor of medicine reigned supreme and did not have to share office space with other consultants.

Among those present were the professor of medicine and his registrar, Reith and Humphrey Hampson, Sol Klenerman, the consultant neurologist, and the renal surgeon, Philip Spence. It was a small gathering and one that could be expected to reach sensible decisions in a short period of time. The 'sensible decision' the professor was referring to was the final extinction of this patient who was involving his staff in a great deal of time-consuming and, in his view, useless work.

The professor's registrar began by giving a short progress report on the patient they were discussing. He was an intense-looking young man with horn-rimmed glasses. He coughed nervously before starting.

'Her initial progress was good. We managed to wean her off the respirator after two days and apart from a small patch of left lower lobe pneumonia which is responding to antibiotics and physiotherapy we are not really worried about her chest. As far as the heart is concerned she initially required pacing but she eventually returned to sinus rhythm so we were able to remove the internal pacemaker. Since then we have not had to use the external pacemaker and that too has been removed as has the cardiac monitor. Her ECG has settled to a normal rhythm and shows only very mild ischaemic changes. Her heart seems to have recovered completely and Vanessa, of course, is delighted.'

There was a polite outburst of laughing. Everyone in the room was delighted not to have any further involvement with the man-eating consultant cardiologist.

'I still think she should have come.' It was Reith.

'She sent her apologies and felt that her continued presence on this case was no longer necessary.'

Reith grunted and the registrar continued.

'At the moment the patient is devoid of all cardiorespiratory technical aids but shows little sign of cerebral recovery and is in complete renal failure.'

There was an uncomfortable silence as he finished, and at this point the professor took over the meeting.

'So there we are, gentlemen. We appear to have reached a point beyond which science can be of no further assistance. Unless, of course, we put her in the transplant programme, which to my mind, would be unthinkable and indeed, even unethical.'

Reith interrupted him somewhat aggressively.

'And why, Professor, would that be unthinkable?'

The professor sighed. He had been expecting difficulties from Reith.

'Listen, Angus, I have about twenty patients waiting in the renal unit on the transplant list, most of them young and healthy. You know how desperately short of cadaver kidneys we are and it simply isn't fair to them.'

'All right,' Reith replied, 'I concede that point but just how sure are we that her brain will never recover? After all, she managed to breathe spontaneously after a few days – how can we be so sure that she will not slowly recover at least some cerebral function?'

Klenerman, the neurologist, chipped in at this point. He was a crisp Jew, almost totally devoid of emotion, who spoke with an unmistakable middle-European accent. In his speciality the skill lay in diagnosis, not in therapy, since most neurological diseases were incurable. Apart from the occasional benign cerebral tumour, he hardly ever had a grateful patient and his face, looking as if it was chiselled in stone, belied the misery of his subject.

'It's inconceivable that she will make any kind of useful recovery after this prolonged period of unconsciousness. She is almost completely devoid of re-flexes and has no deep pain sensation at all. She is what the lay people call a cabbage, and is likely to remain so.'

Reith was on the defensive again. 'Surely she has a cough reflex?'

'She has, and that's about all she has. In a sense it's a shame that she does, since she would die quite quickly from aspiration of mucus, saving us a great deal of time and effort.'

Reith hated this cold, unemotional sod almost more than anyone else on the staff. He desperately tried to control his rising temper.

'What about the EEG?'

Klenerman hesitated and then shrugged. 'So what about the whole subject of electro-encephalography? It's an artificial way of measuring something that we know very little about.'

'And it shows?'

'Minimal activity.'

'But not an entirely flat trace?'

Klenerman hesitated again, knowing that he was on difficult ground. 'Not entirely flat but so what? I still think we're wasting our time. The woman is to all intents and purposes decerebrate and likely to remain so.'

'Gentlemen,' Reith rose slowly to his feet. 'As long as she displays patterns of brain activity there is still an element of hope. From the evidence presented at this meeting I see no reason to withdraw our services. May I remind you, gentlemen, that as long as she is in this hospital, she remains nominally my patient and I refuse to countenance any sacrifice of life on the grounds of economics.'

He turned to Philip Spence. 'A word with you, Philip, if I may? Could you come along to my office in five minutes?'

Spence nodded, albeit reluctantly, in the affirmative, and there was an audible sigh of resignation from Klenerman and the professor of medicine as Angus Reith turned abruptly and left the room.

Five minutes later, the renal surgeon was in Reith's office.

'It's madness, Angus, and you know it. The whole Senior Staff Council will think we've taken leave of our senses.'

'Philip, I'm appealing to you as a friend of long standing. We trained here together and we have a lot more in common than those cold-blooded academics in that meeting. All I'm asking...'

'For Christ's sake, Angus, they know exactly why you asked me to come up here. I had to scale a wall of disapproval to get out of that room.'

'Exactly, and that's why I asked you in front of them so that they know exactly where the request is coming from.'

'But Angus, these cadaver kidneys are damned hard to come by and we've got dozens of young kids on the waiting list. It simply wouldn't be ethical to put this girl of yours ahead of them.'

Angus Reith looked very solemn as he stared across the large mahogany desk.

'I would never in a million years ask you to do that, Philip. All I want is that you bear her in mind. If you ever find a kidney of her type that's going begging just remember she's lying there.'

Philip Spence shook his head. 'I can't see why you're pushing for this. I mean, we're both surgeons, and there can't be a surgeon in this world that doesn't carry some mistake on his conscience. I know I do but we just have to accept it as the luck of the draw. We do our best but we're bound to lose out occasionally.'

'I know that, Philip, I know that.'

'Then for God's sake why not leave her to die in peace?'

Reith leaned forward and transfixed him with his most penetrating stare.

'Because I'm convinced that once we can get her kidneys working we can get her out of the clutches of that medical unit and that damned professor of internal medicine. Once I have her on my ward under the care of Sister Rheingeld she'll damned soon regain consciousness. Remember what Sir Arthur used to tell us when we were surgical dressers looking after his post-ops? "Breathes good, pees good, is good." She'll come right in the end, you mark my words. All I'm asking from you is to sort out the middle bit of the equation – get her to pee good again.'

Philip Spence rose wearily to his feet in readiness to leave the room, but then he turned and placed his hands firmly on the mahogany desk. He was a formidable character in his own right but this discussion had all the characteristics of a collision with a steamroller.

'I'll do it under these conditions as long as no one else is available and furthermore I am quite unashamedly going to use her for an experiment. We've been developing a new technique and so far the animal work has gone well but we haven't had the nerve to try it on a human. In her particular case, I don't consider that to be unethical, do you?'

Reith held up his hands and bowed his head, silently agreeing to the bargain while Philip Spence continued.

'For the life of me, Angus, I cannot see why you cannot let her go and rest in peace. This ongoing misery must be a nightmare for the family.' He turned abruptly and left the room.

CHAPTER TWENTY-SEVEN
Renal transplant unit, St Giles' Hospital, London

Jennifer waited patiently unmoving, unthinking, uncaring in her bed in the renal unit until at last a pair of kidneys arrived of the correct tissue type. The only living recipients for this particular tissue type were ill or unavailable so Jennifer's unconscious form was wheeled yet again to the operating theatre.

Amazingly her body tolerated the kidney transplant well and she only had two minor rejection episodes, both of which were controlled by immunosuppressants and corticosteroids. She was free of all her electrodes, transistors, catheters and cannulas. She no longer needed to be monitored for blood urea or uric acid, serum potassium, sodium, chloride and bicarbonate. She could now be transferred to the normal female ward where she was put in a side room and turned every two hours to prevent bedsores and looked after with affection. Every now and then, Sister Rheingeld was sure that she noticed a flicker of recognition in her eyes or some new facial activity, and they all swore that she was improving.

'Getting better,' the nurses told each other. 'She has such a determination to live. It's the will to live that counts.'

Jeremy and the two older girls came to see her, frequently at first, then less so. They brought her flowers and told her stories of their home and university and of the growth and development of John, the little one, who had been told she was dead so never came with them on these visits. She never responded to their presence, and finally only Jeremy came down on her birthday, and each time after he left her bedside he wept at the sheer futility of it all.

It is unlikely that he could ever have forgiven the doctors at St Giles for what they did to his wife if he had known the truth. The conspiracy of silence had prevailed and he remained convinced that the accident had occurred because of a heroic surgical attack to prevent the spread of cancer. Somewhat irrationally, he blamed the French doctor in Draguignan for failing to detect the cancer at an earlier stage.

EPILOGUE

It is almost ten years since the events described here took place. Jennifer Watson is still alive, but unfortunately far from well. She remains deeply unconscious and oblivious to the world around her. Over the years it had become obvious that the cancer had been eradicated completely since Jennifer showed no sign of recurrence. At times, Jeremy found himself wishing that the malignant process would return and take his wife silently away. He rebuked himself for such vile thoughts but deep down, he found that he wanted to forget her. In his mind, she had died together with all the happy memories of family life.

Since she had left home his existence had been one of almost perpetual gloom. If she had died he might have recovered from the grief and adjusted to a new life but these visits to London, seeing her alive but unconscious, only served to perpetuate the misery. Sometimes he had the unworthy, but understandable, thought that he could never forgive St Giles for keeping her alive.

She is still there in that corner bed at St Giles. The nurses still look after her with devotion and Sister continues to imagine signs of improvement. She has been through several attacks of pneumonia but with modern antibiotics, and her will to live, she has always pulled through. Last winter she was so bad that she had another cardiac arrest. The bells started ringing and the arrest team went through their well-rehearsed ritual and resuscitated her again. They were much quicker this time and she probably sustained only a little additional brain damage. Sister is sure she would have thanked them, if only she could speak.

Even Reith, in an ongoing act of penitence, includes her in his weekly ward round. Every week he encourages the nurses and they encourage him. They are all sure she is getting better.

Each Christmas, she is given presents by the nurses and by the hospital Father Christmas who visits all the wards with his little elves. At Easter, a chocolate egg is mashed up and put into her naso-gastric tube to remind her that Christ has risen.

Paralysed, unconscious, turned every two hours, doubly incontinent, but slowly getting better.

Lightning Source UK Ltd.
Milton Keynes UK
UKHW022211281120
374276UK00008B/232